Praise for Lorelei James's
Rough Riders series

"...[P]roves once again why James is one of the best in the business."
~ *RT Book Reviews on* Cowboy Casanova

"...a thrill to read for anyone looking for not just steamy sex scenes (of which there are plenty) but a story that has true meaning. I'm giving this book five flying stars, two thumbs up, a high five and any other accolades that can be bestowed upon the author. Take it from me: Lorelei James deserves a lot of praise for this latest masterpiece..."
~ *Night Owl Reviews on* Gone Country

"...more than a story about two single parents finding love. *Gone Country* is the story of people finding their way in this big world, learning to deal with everything life throws at them and then being lucky enough to find that one person that makes them feel like no one else can. It's truly a masterpiece..."
~ *Guilty Pleasures Book Reviews*

"The main reasons I keep coming back to read Lorelei James are her smokin' hot, larger-than-life, sexier-than-anything heroes, the heroines who pull those heroes into line, the erotic lovin' between said characters, and the sense of family in every book. It's a rare author who can combine those, plus other, elements into a scintillating, edgy, romantic, and *real* read..."
~ *The Good, The Bad, and The Unread on* Gone Country

Look for these titles by
Lorelei James

Now Available:

Dirty Deeds
Running With the Devil
Wicked Garden
Babe in the Woods
Ballroom Blitz

Wild West Boys
Mistress Christmas
Miss Firecracker

Print Anthologies
Three's Company
Wild Ride
Wild West Boys
Two to Tango

Rough Riders
Long Hard Ride
Rode Hard, Put Up Wet
Cowgirl Up and Ride
Tied Up, Tied Down
Rough, Raw and Ready
Branded As Trouble
Strong, Silent Type
Shoulda Been A Cowboy
All Jacked Up
Raising Kane
Cowgirls Don't Cry
Slow Ride
Chasin' Eight
Cowboy Casanova
Kissin' Tell
Gone Country
Redneck Romeo

Gone Country

Lorelei James

SAMHAIN
PUBLISHING

Samhain Publishing, Ltd.
11821 Mason Montgomery Road, 4B
Cincinnati, OH 45249
www.samhainpublishing.com

Gone Country
Copyright © 2013 by LJLA, LLC
Print ISBN: 978-1-61921-500-9
Digital ISBN: 978-1-61921-529-0

Editing by Lindsey Faber
Cover by Scott Carpenter

First Samhain Publishing, Ltd. electronic publication: December 2012
First Samhain Publishing, Ltd. print publication: November 2013

Dedication

To all the women like me, who have great daddies for their daughters...

Chapter One

August...

"Sierra Daniels. Please stand."

She stood. So did Gavin.

"Would you like to say anything before we discuss your case?"

Gavin glanced at the members of teen court and then at the magistrate. "Permission to speak on Sierra's behalf, Your Honor?"

The magistrate's hard gaze zoomed to him. "And you are?"

"Gavin Daniels, Your Honor. Sierra's father."

"Permission granted. What's on your mind, Mr. Daniels?"

"I understand that a community service sentence is often handed down in a case like this. I agree that it would be a good lesson for my daughter. But I respectfully request you consider an alternative."

"And why is that, Mr. Daniels?"

"Because we will be moving out of state next week." Gavin shot Sierra a harsh look when she opened her mouth.

"Next week?" the magistrate asked skeptically.

"Yes, Your Honor. The day of my daughter's arrest last month I was meeting with Judge O'Connor and he granted me sole custody of Sierra at her mother's request. Since I'm no longer legally bound to live in Arizona, we'll be moving closer to family."

A pause. "Where will that be?"

"Sundance, Wyoming."

From the corner of his eye he saw Sierra gaping at him, but Gavin kept his attention on the magistrate.

"In light of this being your first offense, your guilty plea and the security guard recovering the stolen item, I will dismiss the charge— provided you have no contact with the store and you have no subsequent incidents in the next six months. Then this infraction will be expunged from your juvenile record."

The magistrate looked at Sierra. "And to be honest...your father forcing you to move to Wyoming is punishment enough."

"I hate you and I'm never ever *ever* going to forgive you for this! Why are you ruining my life?"

Choking silence filled the air.

"You done?" he asked coolly.

"Will you change your mind about making me move to Bumfuck, Wyoming?"

"Not on your life, sweetheart."

"Don't call me that!" She stomped off.

He listened to her footsteps fading on the tiled floor, counting out the seconds.

Wait for it... Wait for it...

Slam.

Yep. There it was. God knows her tantrum wouldn't be complete without a house-shaking door slam.

Gavin loaded his lowball glass with ice, then filled it with Crown XR. He knocked back half the whiskey in one swallow.

Damn kid was driving him to drink—something even her psychotic mother hadn't been able to do. Wasn't the first time Sierra had professed her hatred for him—nor would it be the last.

His announcement in teen court today had come as quite a shock to her. But her arrest had been the last straw, especially after his ex-wife had called shoplifting "a teenage rite of passage" and excused Sierra's bad behavior.

Problem was, bad behavior had been the norm for Sierra since the beginning of her freshman year. She broke curfew without explanation or apology. She lied about her plans. Her grades had slipped. She'd become surly and defiant with an air of entitlement—much like her mother.

Sharing joint custody with his ex-wife meant his attempts at keeping their daughter on the right path were largely ignored whenever Sierra stayed at Mommy Dearest's house. So Gavin considered it a sign, an omen, hell, a blessing, when Ellen suddenly announced she was moving to Paris with her boyfriend *du jour.*

After years of custody battles, she signed over full custody of her only child for one year. Evidently Ellen didn't want parental responsibilities spoiling a good time in gay *Paree.*

His self-centered ex hadn't considered how her actions would affect Sierra. Once again he'd been left holding the bag, standing helplessly outside her bedroom door, listening to his daughter cry.

That's when he'd known they both needed a drastic change.

He'd called Rielle, he'd called Charlie and Vi, and he'd called a moving van.

By this time next week they'd be living in Sundance.

If they didn't kill each other on the eighteen-hour drive to Wyoming first.

Chapter Two

"I can't believe the man is kicking you out of your own bedroom. What an asshole."

Rielle ignored Rory's comment and lugged the box of yarn downstairs into the last bedroom on the main level.

Rory followed her. "Mom. Seriously, you don't have to stay here. My cabin will be empty next week when I'm back at college in Laramie."

"I appreciate the offer, but this is fine. And it's not like Gavin is throwing me out—" her eyes narrowed on her daughter, "—which he has every right to do because he owns this house."

Rory plopped on the bed. "I know that. But you have to admit you never thought he'd move here permanently and take over ownership."

Rielle moved a stack of bedding off the dresser. "It's my own fault since I've been dragging my feet on getting West Construction to start on my building plans."

"I still say it's lucky that you've stayed on as caretaker and he shouldn't expect you to just move everything at a moment's notice."

"He's lucky? I'll remind you that *I'm* lucky and I wouldn't even be living here if it wasn't for Gavin saving me from financial ruin."

"Financial ruin," Rory scoffed. "He only bought the land and buildings to one-up the McKays—which is ironic since he *is* a McKay."

"Gavin's last name is Daniels."

Rory waved off her comment. "Semantics. If it looks like a McKay, acts like a McKay...then it is a McKay."

Pointless to argue with her headstrong daughter when it came to her opinions on the McKay family—opinions that she herself often shared.

"When do they get here?" Rory asked.

"They left Scottsdale today, but Gavin said they're taking a couple extra days to play tourist. Sierra starts school in a week, so I'm assuming they'll be somewhat settled in by then."

"Have you ever met the precocious and precious only child Sierra?"

Rielle used a decorative pillow to whap Rory's arm. "Watch it, Aurora Rose Wetzler. Lots of folks around here said the same thing about you when you were sixteen."

"Huh-uh, mamacita, that argument ain't gonna fly. You rode herd on me from the time I was a little tyke. I never had the chance to get into trouble."

"And look where me cracking the whip got you—a graduate assistantship at UWYO as you're working on your Master's." Rielle stood in front of Rory and tucked a strand of her wild blonde hair behind her ear, like she'd done a hundred times. She still experienced that same overwhelming burst of love as she had the first time she'd cradled the squalling baby in her arms twenty-four years ago. "I'm so damn proud of you, Rory."

"I know you are, Mom." Rory hugged her. "But stop this mushy stuff or we'll both start crying. There'll be plenty of tears when I leave."

"Don't remind me." She clutched her a little tighter. At six foot one, Rory towered over her by eight inches—making her daughter a supersized version of her instead of a mini-me. Rory's green eyes—identical to her own—contained a devilish twinkle. "What?"

"Let's get this shit done because I have a surprise for you later. And no groaning 'cause it's gonna be awesomely fun."

"I'm almost afraid to ask."

They cleared out both the bigger bedrooms upstairs. Rielle opted to leave the existing furniture in the great room downstairs. If Gavin wanted to replace it with his furniture, fine, but somehow she doubted his home furnishings from Arizona would mesh with the western décor.

She propped her shoulder against the doorjamb, letting her gaze wander. She'd spent months decorating this main room, scouring auctions, secondhand stores and yard sales for funky western pieces. Using a little imagination and a lot of elbow grease, she'd repurposed everything—from rusty tractor parts and old wooden household implements to rodeo memorabilia.

The room reflected her personality and life philosophy: quirky, bohemian, old items interspersed with new. Some pieces were high-end, some were low-rent. Vibrant colors and random fabric patterns and textures. Organic mixed with luxurious. Her heart told her to clear this space because everything in it was personal, but her practical side warned that Gavin might see an empty room as a hostile move.

But dammit, she did feel like her house was being invaded.

Rory poked her head out the swinging door separating the kitchen from the great room. "Your martini is ready."

Entering the kitchen reinforced Rielle's melancholy mood; the house teemed with life with Rory in residence. Music drifted from her iPod speakers and she danced around the island, singing to country tunes.

Plates of appetizers were arranged across the eat-in service bar.

Rory shook the cocktail shaker vigorously and filled martini glasses with pale yellow liquid.

Rielle squinted at the three glasses. "You expecting someone else?"

"Yep. And there she is, right on time."

"Who?"

The door swung open and Ainsley Hamilton meandered in. She ditched her high heels first thing. "I hope you made those drinks strong, Rory, because I've had a bitch of a day." Ainsley grinned at Rielle. "Heya, neighbor. You ready for this?"

"Ready for what?"

Rory mimed zipping her lips. Then she said brightly, "Belly up to the bar, ladies, and sample my latest concoction. A lemon-drop martini with an Asian twist."

"Sounds heavenly," Ainsley said. "What's the twist?"

"Candied ginger and lemongrass."

Rielle slid onto the barstool. Even if the cocktail tasted like crap, she'd get an A for presentation. Sugar-rimmed glasses, a slice of lemon, pieces of lemongrass twined around a cocktail pick weighted at the bottom with a chunk of amber-colored candied ginger.

Ainsley raised her glass. "To the support of good friends."

They clinked glasses and knocked back a swallow.

"Wow, Rory, this has got to be your best drink ever," Rielle said, sucking down another taste.

"Thank you, but I can't take full credit. I tweaked the recipe from a guy who bartends at the hipster joint in Laramie."

"It's fantastic. Damn potent, so I'll only have one." Ainsley tipped back another swallow. "Unless you're driving us into town?"

Rielle frowned. "Who's going into town?"

"We all are. See, Rory and I got to chatting...about our discussion at your fortieth birthday party last week."

"I cannot be held responsible for anything I said since you all got me drunk." Her head had pounded so horrifically the next morning she'd literally taken a dirt nap in her garden.

"This spilled out when you were sober, darlin'," Ainsley reminded her.

"You sound more like Ben every day with *darlin'* this and *darlin'* that," Rielle retorted.

"I'll take that as a compliment." She preened. "But it is what my loving—but clueless—husband said that caused your distress, so I feel the need to fix it."

Rielle drained her drink, hating the reminder of Ben's comment when he'd jokingly guessed her age as fifty, not forty. "You're not responsible for the dumb shit Ben says any more than you are

13

responsible for the dumb shit *all* men say."

Rory refilled Rielle's glass and sent Ainsley an insolent look. "I knew you'd take the wrong tack." She set her elbows on the counter. "Mom. You're not old. And we're gonna deal with your claim that you look like a crone, because it's a seriously fucked-up self-image."

Her cheeks heated, but her tongue sharpened. "So where is your other cohort in crime, Doc Monroe? Has she set up an appointment with a plastic surgeon as her part of this embarrassing intervention?"

"Joely planned to be here but she had to deliver a baby." Ainsley got right in Rielle's face. "Dial down the animosity, sister, and listen up."

"You still wearing your large-and-in-charge big-girl panties, Miz Bank Prez?"

"At least until I get home and Bennett makes me strip them off." She grinned cheekily. "And here's the mushy, gushy stuff that makes you squirm...unless you've been knocking back tequila shooters. You've become one of my best friends since I moved in with Ben. You're a wonderful person, funny, sweet, thoughtful and you work harder than anyone I know. You're beautiful inside and out. I see it. Rory sees it. It's a pity you don't. We thought maybe if we helped you change your outer appearance, then you'd see it as well as feel it."

Rielle remained quiet and traced the sugared rim of her martini glass. Upbeat Ainsley didn't pull any punches—and to think that was why she hadn't initially liked the woman. They'd started out on the wrong foot when Ainsley had been sneaking around with Ben McKay. But after Ainsley stood up for Ben and bitch-slapped her for the shitty way she'd treated him, Rielle realized she'd wronged them both.

It'd taken a couple months for Rielle to swallow her pride and apologize. Luckily Ben and Ainsley were ready to let bygones be bygones. Now she and Ainsley were tight—much tighter than Rielle had ever been with Ben.

"Mom? Are you crying?" Rory asked with an edge of fear.

"No." She raised her head. "Just feeling idiotic for opening my mouth. It sucks dealing with this stupid female pride and age thing."

"But see, you don't have to deal with it alone." Ainsley snagged a section of Rielle's baby-fine long blond hair. "Rory. How long has your mom worn her hair this way?"

"As long as I can remember."

"That's because it's an easy style," Rielle protested.

"No, it's a *dated* style," Ainsley corrected.

"Well, forgive me but I don't have time to fuss with a fancy hairdo when I spend my days digging in the dirt or sweating in the kitchen."

"Which is exactly why you need a smart cut. Not every style is high-maintenance." Ainsley held onto Rielle's chin, turning her face to the left and right. "You have amazing bone structure. You hide it instead of highlight it. We need to fix that."

"And how would *we* do that?"

Rory grinned. "By placing yourself in Nikki's hands tonight."

"Nikki?" Rielle knew her eyes grew comically wide. "Isn't that your friend who sported a purple and lime green Mohawk in tenth grade?"

"She's toned down the shock factor. We've already discussed this and she's come up with a cool cut for you. She swears this style is easy to manage and it'll take ten years off your face."

"But I don't think your face is the issue. It's all this hippie hair." Ainsley knocked back her drink. "So let's whisk you off to the beauty shop and transform you from a hippie-chick into a hip-chick."

"I don't know if this is such a good idea..."

"Here's where I'm playing hardball." Rory loomed over her. "You've always told me change is inevitable. Have you been putting expectations on me that you aren't willing to apply to yourself?"

"No! I have been making changes in my life." Most were forced, not that she'd admit that.

"Then it shouldn't be such an ordeal to add this change to the list."

"But—"

"You know what?" Ainsley interrupted. "I think your mom is afraid to look hot and have men notice her. Once she's no longer hidden behind all this scarecrow hair, she'll hook herself a man. Just you watch."

"Scarecrow hair?" Rielle repeated. "Really, Ainsley?"

Ainsley's eyes didn't contain a bit of malice, just concern. "You need to do this. For you. We'll be right there, every snip of the way."

Maybe the drinks bolstered her courage. Heaven knew if the decision was left up to her, she'd never do it. She slid off the barstool. "Fine. But if I end up looking like Carrot Top, there's gonna be hell to pay."

Ainsley draped her arm around Rielle's shoulder. "Darlin', the truth is, even that might be an improvement."

Chapter Three

Late Saturday afternoon Gavin pulled into the parking area of the former Sage Creek Bed and Breakfast.

The five-thousand-square-foot, two-story structure had large windows stretching along the main and upper floors. This time of day the sun reflected off the sections of glass in tones of amber and rosy-gold. The siding had been crafted out of rough-hewn lumber and applied vertically, horizontally, crossways, creating the impression of depth. A copper-colored tin roof covered a wide-planked porch that spanned the entire length of the front side. The porch supports were notched logs, worn into a smooth vanilla-hued patina in some places and left rough with chunks of bark in others. The concrete work at the base of the house was covered by round, grayish river rock, so the foundation appeared built from cobbled stone. The steps continued the western theme, constructed from old railroad ties, the centers shored up with marbled-looking concrete. Even the split-rail fence separating the parking lot from the porch resembled an old-fashioned hitching post. The overall impression of the place was rustic with western flair. Charming. Welcoming. Homey.

Homey. As Gavin listened to the engine cool, he had to remind himself this was his home. He'd owned it for almost two years, but he'd never cooked a meal in the kitchen. Never washed a load of clothes in the laundry room. Never flopped on the couch and watched a Cardinals football game. He'd always treated this place like a hotel.

No more.

He glanced at his daughter, gauging her reaction to their new home. "So, Sierra, what do you think?"

She peered over the top of her pink sunglasses. "It's bigger than I thought. Rustic, but it works in this setting with the different types of trees as a backdrop. It looks more like an upscale hunting lodge than a single family dwelling."

The kid knew the lingo after being around the real estate business her whole life.

"Holy crap. Who is that?"

"Where?"

Sierra pointed. "There. By the fence."

Gavin saw a shapely, jean-clad ass bent over a wheelbarrow. The woman stood and turned to grab the wheelbarrow's handles, giving him a front-and-center view of her low-cut tank top. The full swells of her cleavage bounced nicely as she started downhill. Her face was hidden beneath the bill of a brown and gold University of Wyoming ball cap.

"You don't know her?" Sierra asked. "Is she seasonal help or something?"

"Maybe." Where was Rielle? She always met him on the porch with her pack of dogs.

They climbed out of the Lexus. Gavin continued to stare from behind his sunglasses at the woman heading toward them, showing a lot of sun-kissed skin. When she removed her cap, revealing artfully tousled short blond hair, and smiled at him, Gavin's jaw nearly hit the dirt. "Rielle?"

"You were expecting someone else?" She stepped closer, slipping off her glove before offering her hand. "You must be Sierra. I'm Rielle Wetzler. Your dad has talked about you nonstop."

"Most of it bad, I'm sure." Sierra smirked and Gavin held his breath, waiting for the snarky sixteen-year-old to emerge. "I'll admit Dad said nothing to me about you."

Gavin was tempted to correct his daughter, but Rielle had already engaged his sometimes-prickly child in conversation.

Sierra started sharing her favorite parts of their tourist excursions. Rather than stand and gawk at this sexier version of Rielle, he returned to his car and began unloading luggage and tried to figure out how they were going to make this situation work.

The circumstances were unconventional, but his buyout offer hadn't exactly been normal either. After they'd hashed out an agreement, he'd asked her to stay on the premises as a caretaker, although she refused payment for the position. His property manager called her every other month to check in. Gavin and Rielle were friendly, but he didn't know her. He hadn't seen Rielle beyond her role as his personal chef, maid and property custodian. And because of that line—she'd essentially worked for him—he'd never noticed such a hot woman existed beneath the tie-dyed clothes and Marcia Brady hair.

You're a superficial asshole.

Maybe, but it didn't change the facts. Gavin hauled luggage to the porch, his depraved brain compiling a list of Rielle's overlooked attributes. When he turned around Rielle and Sierra were staring at him. "What?"

"Dad. I said I'd help you like three times. Didn't you hear me?"

"No, sweetheart, I didn't. Thinking about too many things, I guess." R-rated things about the scantily clad and surprisingly hot

Rielle that he couldn't share with his daughter. "Let's leave this stuff here and do a quick tour." He faced Rielle. "Is that okay?"

She shrugged. "It's your house."

He detected tension in that answer and knew they needed to discuss specific living arrangements tonight.

"Besides, I'll be in the garden until dark."

"We'll catch up with you later. Charlie and Vi invited us over for dinner."

"The food oughta be good since Vi's a great cook." She grabbed three balls of dirt from the wheelbarrow and set them on the railing. "Take her some of these golden beets. They're her favorite."

"Sure. Thanks."

"Plastic bags are under the sink. See you." Rielle lifted the wheelbarrow handles and Gavin had the urge to offer his help. But by the looks of the toned muscles in her arms, shoulders, back, ass, thighs and calves, she didn't need help. He glanced at Sierra after Rielle disappeared around the side of the house. She wore an odd look. Shit. Had she caught him checking Rielle out? "What?"

"This will be weird, having someone else live with us."

"I know. But we'll figure out a way to make it work." He set his hand on her shoulder. "Let's check out our new digs."

"Dad. No one says *digs*. You are such a dork."

"I didn't think anyone said dork anymore either," he teased.

After Sierra's initial outburst about their sudden departure from Arizona, she'd come to a grudging acceptance that something had to change. He suspected she was secretly relieved for the chance to start fresh and she had acted enthusiastic when she'd told her mother about the move. Gavin didn't kid himself it was genuine, but rather a way for Sierra to show her mother she'd be too busy with her new adventure to miss her, but he hoped in time she would embrace this new life in Wyoming.

"This place has a lot of personality," Sierra commented on the great room. "Is the furniture and stuff in here ours?"

"No, it's Rielle's."

"Where is our furniture?"

Hell if I know. "Why?"

Sierra whirled around. "I hope it ended up lost or in the Dumpster."

His gaze sharpened. "Why would you say that?"

"Because it was ugly and boring. Like you walked into a discount furniture store, saw a perfectly put together living room set, and said, *I'll take that crap.*"

That's exactly what he'd done. "And that's bad...how?"

She pointed to a chair comprised of half cowhide, half distressed leather with braided piping on the front and animal hooves as the feet. "This is a seriously awesome piece. It says a lot about Rielle. She's picked pieces that are unique, yet funky. I'll bet she even made some of them." Then Sierra poked him in the chest. "You could learn a lot from her."

"Meaning what?"

"Meaning...we're starting over, right? We need to shitcan that ugly furniture we've had forever. What bad taste demon possessed you to buy it in the first place?"

Gavin suppressed a grin. It boded well Sierra had bounced back to her annoyingly sweet and pushy self after clearing out of Arizona. "Because I spent damn near six months searching for furniture with your mother right after we got married. I hated everything she picked. So after the divorce, when I moved into the condo, I chose big, comfy pieces, without damn flowers or checks or stripes. Plus, the furniture had to be stain resistant, because you, dear daughter, have a tendency to spill ice cream, cereal and pizza." He kissed her forehead.

Sierra twined her arms around him and sighed. "Dad. I'm not six anymore."

"Sometimes I wish you were."

"I know. But promise you'll let me help when we pick out new stuff for our place, okay?"

He hugged her tightly. This was the daughter he'd missed in the last year when the teenager from hell had inhabited her body. "Okay."

She squirmed away. "Show me the rest."

The main floor was comprised of the enormous kitchen, the dining room and the great room. Down the hallway were a bathroom and two bedrooms, both with en-suite bathrooms. Gavin noticed Rielle had relocated to the biggest room in the far corner. He fought a pang of guilt for kicking her out of the master suite.

This is your house. Remember that.

A wide staircase opened onto the landing of the second floor. Another comfortable lounging area stretched out in front of the windows. Gavin turned down the left hallway and walked past the bedroom he intended to use as an office. He opened the door to the master suite and glanced up at the skylights spilling sunbeams across the plush carpet. The angle of the roof provided architectural interest. On the far side was a set of French doors that led to a private balcony. He poked his head into the bathroom, happy for the oversized shower, but ambivalent about the garden tub.

"This is a lot bigger than your bedroom in Arizona." She hip-checked him. "You could sneak someone in here. Have wild parties and I'd never know."

He snorted. "Like that'll happen."

"It should. I wouldn't mind if you...ah, got involved with someone."

Gavin gaped at his daughter. Since when did she care about that? And what the hell was her vague reference to *someone*? Then she flitted off, down the other hallway.

The last bedroom and Sierra's room were opposite each other on the other end of the hallway. She squealed upon seeing her stuff. "I love it! This is exactly where I would've put everything. So can we hang my TV and set up my computer right now?"

He checked his watch. "We have to be at Charlie and Vi's pretty quick so the TV will have to wait until I find my tools. But let's hook up your computer."

That task finished, they hauled everything from the car. He showed Sierra the small servants' staircase connecting the second floor directly through the kitchen. Sierra tried the handle on another door. "Where does this go?"

"Basement."

"There's a whole other level?"

"Yes, but it's unfinished and Rielle uses it for storage."

"What are *we* gonna use it for?"

His immediate thought was to ask Rielle's permission and he had to remind himself for the tenth time that he owned this place. "Maybe that's where our old furniture is."

"I hope there's another wood burning stove down there, so we can just chop it up and torch it."

Gavin laughed. "Come on. Let's package up the beets and head to the McKays."

Sierra didn't speak as they started up the driveway to Charlie and Vi McKay's place.

"Sweetheart? You all right?"

"Yeah. This might sound random, but what am I supposed to call them? I mean, they are my grandparents. When they visited us I didn't think too much about it because I wasn't sure I'd ever get to know them. But now? We're living up the road from them. I bet we'll see them all the time."

Another issue he should address. Did he remind Charlie and Vi that he preferred they didn't drop by unannounced? Or would he come across like a jerk?

"Is this weird for you?" Sierra prompted.

"Unbelievably. Just when I think I've wrapped my head around it...I realize I don't have a clue how to deal with any of this *we're your family* stuff. And then they're all cowboys. I am so far from a cowboy..."

"So Mr. I've-always-got-the-right-answer-and-I-can-lecture-you-for-hours-on-it...doesn't have the right one this time?" She snickered.

"Wow. That might be a first, Dad."

"Smart aleck. I trust you'll be on your best behavior?"

"I polished my halo before we left."

He smiled. "Come on. I'm starved." He glanced at the bag of beets in the backseat. Maybe if he "remembered" them after the meal, Vi wouldn't insist on cooking them *for* the meal. God. He hated beets.

"Quit stalling, Dad, here they come."

He plastered on a smile.

Charlie and Vi met them on the porch. Vi hugged them while Charlie offered his hand.

Then they stared at each other.

But it lasted about a minute. Awkwardness vanished as Sierra jabbered enough for both of them.

Chapter Four

Rielle had just popped the top on a bottle of Moose Drool beer when Gavin wandered into the kitchen.

Speaking of drool. Man, oh, man. The last year had been very good to him. He'd always been attractive in the charming and confident manner of a businessman. But since she'd last seen him, he'd slimmed down and toned up to the point he was almost...buff.

She'd chalked up his previous physique—or lack thereof—to sitting behind a desk all day. But his appearance had undergone a serious change in the last year. He'd chopped off his wavy dark brown hair in favor of a modified buzz cut. Now his blue eyes, framed with ridiculously long black eyelashes, were his most striking feature. He sported a neatly trimmed goatee which accentuated his leaner cheeks and the strong line of his jaw, both more prominent with his overall body weight loss. The man still didn't smile as much as he should, so her heart skipped a beat when he leveled a smile at her.

"Don't suppose you've got an extra one of those for me?"

"Extra what?" Why was Gavin staring at her mouth? Why did she have the urge to lick her lips?

"An extra beer."

"Oh. Yeah. Sure." *Get it together, Ree.* She reached into the bottom shelf of the refrigerator. When she turned around, Gavin was right behind her—checking out her butt.

He blushed and stepped back. "Sorry. I don't expect you to wait on me, Rielle."

She handed him the beer and the opener. "Maybe we oughta talk about our expectations."

Gavin nodded.

"It's a beautiful night. Let's sit outside."

He motioned for her to lead the way.

She flipped on the lights lining the walkway and lit the kerosene lamp on the table between the glider swing and her favorite rocking chair. She curled up in the rocker, setting it in motion as Gavin settled on the swing. The kerosene flame flickered in the breeze behind the glass chimney, throwing a golden glow against the house. Neither she nor Gavin said anything for a few moments. Normally silence didn't bother her, but tonight it did. "Sierra get settled in all right?"

"It helped having her stuff already here. I have to admit I'm happy each bedroom has its own bathroom. The girl is spoiled. She's never had to share a bathroom with anyone."

"Rory and I shared a bathroom until I built Sage Creek. Even then, she came into my bathroom to get ready in the morning. Come to think of it, she still does that."

"It sucks that Sierra isn't willing to share any hair care tips with me."

Rielle laughed. "Was it her idea or yours to get the buzz cut?"

Gavin buffed the top of his head with his palm. "Mine. I started to see some gray and I'm not ready to invest in Grecian Formula for Men, so I bought a pair of clippers and hacked it off. I save myself fifty bucks a month at the barber."

"Well, it looks good. Really good." Feeling stupid for tossing out a compliment, she angled her head away from his prying eyes.

"Thanks. I have to admit I didn't recognize you with your short hair."

"I've heard that a lot in the past few days." Rielle felt his eyes on her, measuring her, but she couldn't meet his gaze.

"So it's a recent change?"

"Last week."

"You look great, Rielle."

"Thanks."

More silence.

Rielle peered up at him, only to see him staring at her. "Gavin. Can I be completely honest?"

"By all means."

"How is this situation going to work?"

He stretched his arm across the back of the glider. "I have no idea. I understand I sprang this on you. But as long as we're being honest, I've owned this house and the land for almost two years. And yet, you still haven't made any plans to build your own place. Why?"

"Because I never believed you'd really move here."

He frowned.

"You've visited exactly four times and not at all in the last year. You've never brought your daughter. So I figured if you planned to relocate to Sundance, it'd be after Sierra went to college." She pointed her beer bottle at him. "And you are wrong. I *have* been in contact with Chet and Remy West about my building plans. I just wasn't expecting to have to get started on the damn thing this fall."

"So you're fine and dandy with us taking up residence here?"

"Yes. No." She exhaled a sigh. "Look, I know you own the house. But it's been my *home* for six years, not just a bed and breakfast. I know every square inch of this place because I spent a decade designing it."

Gavin's face was unreadable, but not formidable so she continued.

"It would've been better if you had thrown me out after you took ownership. But you didn't. I stayed on as if nothing had changed. Now I can't help the resentment that you two are invading my house and encroaching on my space. It's wrong; I know that. But as long as we're being honest I might as well lay it all on the line."

The only sounds between them were the squeak of the glider and the creak of the rocking chair.

Finally, Gavin sighed. "This is so fucked up."

"Agreed. That's just the personal side. We haven't even talked about the fact I run all of my businesses out of here."

"Businesses...plural?"

Maybe his shock about her owning multiple businesses pissed her off a little. "Yes. *Businesses.* In addition to selling organic produce, I sell honey. I handspin various fiber into yarn. I'm at the end of my growing season so I can't abandon my plants—that means using water from your well since I haven't drilled for one on my property yet. So regardless of what you decide for our personal living arrangements, on the business side, I'll have to be here every day. I've made commitments, Gavin, and my word has always been the only thing I've ever had of any worth."

He stopped the glider and rested his forearms on his thighs. "I understand that, believe me. And despite your erroneous accusation, the living arrangement situation isn't solely my decision. So tell me what else you're committed to in your businesses."

"The small bakery here closed three years ago. I stepped up to fill the need for fresh baked goods because I installed industrial ovens when I built this place. Three days a week I bake dinner rolls for Fields, the upscale organic restaurant in Sundance. I provide stone-ground wheat and rye bread to several other restaurants and grocery stores in the area. I can't just stop because then they'll assume they can't depend on me, and they'll quit buying all the other food stuff I supply, which is a lot and my main source of income." Rielle inhaled slowly, trying hard not to show the panic she felt.

"I don't know how you formed a negative impression of me, but I don't plan to throw you out on your ass."

"Don't you see that's almost worse?" She leapt to her feet and paced, words spilling out unchecked. "You came here with Sierra to be a family. I get that. I'm not your family and yet, under our current agreement, I'll be living in your house as if I am. You'll want to hang out, just the two of you. Fix meals together, watch TV, help with her homework, play games, invite your McKay relatives over. How can I live here without feeling like an interloper...in what's always been my home? On the other hand, how can I live here and not get to watch what I want on my TV, and sit on my furniture in my living room? I'm just supposed to...what? Lock myself in my room?

"Not to mention I've always treated you like a guest at the B&B or my boss. I'm not in either of those servant or employee roles now. I don't know how I'm supposed to act around you. Or Sierra. Will she treat me like the hired help? Will you?"

Strong hands circled her biceps, stopping her pacing.

Gavin loomed over her. "Dammit, Rielle, take a breath."

She froze. He had big hands. Warm. Not girly soft like she'd imagined, but a little rough.

"For Christsake. Please quit looking at me like I'm going to hit you." He gentled his hold and his thumbs swept the inside of her arms, but he didn't release her.

The crazy thing? She didn't want him to. How long had this man owned such a powerful presence? And why hadn't she noticed?

But she was aware of Gavin's intense gaze on her mouth. She self-consciously licked her lips. His avid eyes tracked the movement of her tongue.

That deliberate focus caused a falling sensation in her belly that she hadn't felt in a long time. Maybe ever.

"Ree?" he said a bit hoarsely.

"Sorry. This panic has been building since you called with the news you were moving here."

"It wasn't my intention to put you on notice. I'm not the enemy."

"I know."

"Good." He dropped his hands. "I'll need something stronger than beer if we're continuing this conversation."

"Me too. And since I'm not waiting on you..." She cocked her head. "Need me to show you where the liquor cabinet is in *your* house?"

"No, smartass. And here I always thought you were so sweet."

"I am." She batted her eyelashes and he laughed. "You pegged me as a non-confrontational, go with the flow, peace, love and good vibes type, didn't you?"

"Maybe. You itching to prove me wrong?"

"More than I already have?"

"Ouch. Point taken. But then again, we don't really know each other, do we?"

"No." *But I'd really like to change that.*

"I'm curious. You saw yourself in the servant and employee role. What role did you assign me?"

"Stick-up-his-ass, my-way-or-the-highway ruthless business tycoon."

25

Gavin grinned. "Not far off the mark. But I am looking forward to showing you a different side of me, and seeing that different side of you."

She was too. Way more than she wanted to admit to him and maybe to herself.

Rielle Wetzler was a dichotomy.

On one hand, given the serious financial bind she'd wound up in a few years back, Gavin assumed she had no head for business and flitted through life like a paisley butterfly.

But hearing her talk about her businesses showed him not only was she on top of her game, she wasn't a pushover. In fact, she'd thought through the repercussions of this living situation on a much deeper level than he had.

He hadn't lost track of their conversation until he'd put his hands on her. Then like the village idiot, all he could do was stare into her pale green eyes and imagine taking a big bite of her full bottom lip.

And it didn't help matters when Gavin realized her pretty blush and bright eyes meant that she felt the surprising zing of attraction too.

He grabbed the bottle of Crown XR from his room and returned to the kitchen. He doubted Rielle drank whiskey on the rocks or even neat. He stirred Coca-Cola into her glass, topped his off with water and headed to the porch.

Rielle had moved to the glider.

He'd barely sat down beside her before she launched into questions. "What prompted the sudden move to Crook County, Wyoming?"

"How much do you know from the McKays?"

"Nothing beyond Sierra had some issues and you pulled up stakes, hoping to straighten her out."

Gavin gave her the rundown of Sierra's troubles. "Did you ever deal with anything like that with Rory?"

She shook her head. "It strikes me as odd that the kids who have the most are usually the ones with sticky fingers. Rory kept a low profile throughout school and stayed out of trouble. It was hard enough for her being the granddaughter of hippies who were rumored to grow pot and live in a commune."

Rielle had mentioned those things before, as had the McKays. "Any truth to the rumors?"

"About the commune? Yeah." She turned sideways and set her feet on the seat, near his thigh. "My folks let anyone down on their luck crash here. One time, I counted thirty people living in that rundown shack they called a house. Used to be a thick grove of scrub cedar trees blocking the shack from the road, thank God." She took a drink—almost angrily. "It was cathartic to watch West Construction level that damn building with a bulldozer."

"I'll bet. Does this house sit where that one did?"

"Close. Rory and I lived there with my parents until she turned three. I'd busted my ass making a cabin at the back of the property inhabitable, so we'd both be somewhat free of their influence. I let Rory have it after I built the B&B. She still stays there when she comes home. She's an adult and she deserves her own space."

Gavin knew she'd only touched on her struggle to raise a kid on her own, when she was just a kid herself. "How'd you support yourself as a young mother?"

"When Rory started school I worked cleaning motel rooms so I was done by the time school let out. We'd always grown our own food, so I just continued doing what I was taught. But I seemed to have extra so that same year I started selling the leftover produce to locals. The business grew so by the sixth year I didn't have to work at the motel. During that time I'd gone from cleaning rooms to running the front desk to working in the sales and catering office. And I realized the perfect job for me would be running my own B&B."

"And you made that a reality."

"Yes, I did. The one smart thing my parents did was buy this land. They paid cash for it thirty-odd years ago and no one ever questioned how or where they'd gotten the money, so neither did I." Her bare feet had inched over until her toes rested on the outside of his thigh. She nudged him. "Hey, how'd did I end up a topic of conversation? We're supposed to be talking about this screwed-up living arrangement."

Gavin curled his fingers around her ankle to stop her from kicking him. Or maybe to keep her from leaping up as she was prone to do. Or most likely, he just wanted an excuse to touch her. "We're getting to know each other, which I believe is standard procedure before a man and woman move in together."

"Gee, Gavin, you're making it sound so romantic," she said.

That brought up another point. "So we get all these living together specifics ironed out between us. Will it bother you if people in the community think we really are living together as a romantic couple?"

"I could give two shits what people think. I've dealt with labels my whole life living in Sundance and I'm still here, still doing my own thing. So maybe you oughta worry what people will think about you, the rich-tycoon-cum-secret-McKay-lovechild and your impressionable teenaged daughter, being shacked up with someone like me."

Gavin laughed. Rielle was really trying to rile him and it wasn't working—well, not in the way she'd intended. This sexy opinionated woman riled him up in ways he'd forgotten he could be riled. "Like you, I could give a shit what folks say about me."

"Really? And what about Sierra? Do you care what kids at school might say to her?"

"Sierra might've made some bad judgment calls recently, but she has a lot of me in her and she calls it like she sees it."

She toasted him. "I wish Rory had been more like that at Sierra's age. Heck, I wish *I'd* been more like that."

"You ready to hammer out specifics on divvying up shared living spaces?" he asked her.

"Hit me with your best idea, tycoon."

Tycoon. Sassy little thing. "Here's what I think will work. Since your bedroom is on the main floor, the great room is your space. We'll stay out of it unless you've granted us permission."

Rielle said, "That sounds fair."

"The upper living space is ours. We'll use the existing furniture until we buy new."

"The movers stashed your pieces in the basement."

"According to Sierra, that stuff can go to a good home or to Goodwill. We've decided to get new furnishings that fit with the house."

"Oh."

"We'll have to share the kitchen in the morning. As far as food, we'll label everything in the fridge and freezer. Assign us cupboards to store canned and dry goods. That'll keep our food separate. Same goes for clearing out a spot for our small appliances and dishes—"

"Unless you hate the dishes I bought for the B&B, you're welcome to use them, since I have place settings for twenty. Same for the silverware, cups and glasses."

"I don't much care about dishes and stuff, so that'll work."

"Good. When it comes to my baking pans, mixers, knives, pots and pans...those will be off limits. Since there are two dishwashers, we'll each have one." She leaned forward. "Our policy should be clean as you go because there's nothing I hate worse than coming into a kitchen piled with dirty dishes."

"I'll pass that along to my little mess maker," he murmured. "Which goes to say we're responsible for cleaning our respective areas in the rest of the house too?"

"Yep. The kitchen appliances are typical, no huge explanation is needed on how to run them—even for a teenager and a longtime bachelor."

"Funny."

"The washer and dryer are in the basement utility room and I don't have a specific wash day, so I'll work around your schedule since there are two of you and one of me." She paused. "Sierra does her own laundry?"

He nodded.

"I eat supper very early or very late so I'll be gone by the time you're ready to fix the evening meal." He must've frowned because she said, "What?"

"I don't know. We'll be in the same area around the same time. I just wondered if you'd be interested in sharing a meal with us sometimes."

Her lips curled up in a sneaky smile. "I'll have to check my schedule and get back to you."

Gavin was so charmed by this woman. Part prickly, part funny—totally sexy. "You do that." Her toes spread out like a cat's claws and she made a soft purr when his fingers brushed her instep. "How's tomorrow night look?"

"Like leftovers." She propped her chin on her knee. "What's on your menu?"

"Pasta. I say that with vagueness until we've checked out what the local grocery store carries."

"I love any type of pasta. I'll contribute a salad and bread."

"See how easy that was? This living together stuff will be a breeze for us."

Rielle laughed. "You say that now. How about if we revisit this conversation in a week and see what's changed?"

"Does that mean you're putting cocktails on the terrace with me on your schedule for next Saturday night?" he asked lightly.

"Sure. It's not like I'll have a date or anything."

"I find it hard to believe that men aren't lined up to take you out." His gaze roved over her face. "Especially if they saw you like this."

"Like what?" she asked softly.

"With the firelight from the lamp glowing on your face."

"How often do those smooth words slide off your tongue?"

"Never." He blinked. What the hell was going on with him?

"Oh. Well, thanks then." She pushed upright and scrambled back.

Gavin drained his whiskey and followed her into the kitchen. "I'm glad we got this somewhat resolved, Rielle. But the booze and the drive have made me a little..." *Loopy? Foolish? Melancholy? Hopeful?*

"Has made you what, Gavin?"

"Ramble more than usual." He smiled at her. "Good night."

Chapter Five

Sierra could not believe her dad was making her ride the bus home from school.

The school bus.

Who gets stuck riding the bus? Especially in high school?

Losers, probably.

Great way to start her school year.

Hoisting her backpack higher, she walked to the semi-circle where the buses were belching diesel. She started with the last one, searching for number one eleven. Some kid hung out the window of one thirteen and yelled out, "I love you, Sierra!"

She ignored the jerk, who was no doubt being sarcastic since she was the new girl, and kept her head down.

At least she hadn't been a total pariah, but being fresh meat in the small high school had made her a novelty. She'd met so many people she couldn't keep them all straight. But she knew the novelty would wear off, probably within a week.

A shadow fell in step with her and she glanced over at the freckled redheaded cowgirl.

Marin Godfrey had taken it upon herself to befriend Sierra first thing in homeroom yesterday. They had two classes together and lunch, so Sierra hadn't had to sit by herself.

"Hey, Arizona. You took off fast after the last bell rang."

"I didn't want to miss my bus since I didn't ride it yesterday."

"Your bus is always in the middle. I'm jealous. All the good people ride on your bus. That's the one everyone wants to be on."

Sierra wondered what *good people* meant.

Marin smiled. "You'll see. Perverts ride on my bus. Always trying to cop a feel. And the grade school boys are the worst."

"So the school secretary wasn't bullshitting my dad? Everyone in high school really rides the bus home every day?"

"Not everyone, not every day. Like the jocks have practice after school. But everyone else? Pretty much."

Bizarre. Didn't any of these people have cars? In Arizona everyone she knew had a car and no one rode the bus. She didn't think her school district even *had* buses. "What if there's a drama club meeting or something?"

"If there's an activity or a club meeting, it's held after supper, not after school, if it can be helped."

"Why?"

"The school is big on parental involvement and that means scheduling stuff when adults are done with work. Most the kids who ride the bus have chores to do after school anyway."

Chores. Such a foreign concept to her. After school let out in Arizona, she'd flopped on her bed and napped or watched TV until her dad got home from work.

"That's why there's no morning bus service," Marin continued. "Gotta get them early chores done. So what're you doing when you get home?"

"I'm sure my dad will grill me on how my second day of school went. If I made new friends. What I had for lunch. If I have homework."

"That's better than cleaning the chicken coop." Marin pointed to the open door. "This one is yours. You've got my number. Call me later if you want." She raced off.

Sierra reached the top step on the bus and the driver stopped her. "You're Sierra?"

"How did you know?"

The older lady laughed. "Darlin', I know every kid on this bus and have for years, most their parents too. So it's nice to see a new face."

"Oh. Which stop am I supposed to get off at?"

"Third to last stop." Then the driver's eyes were on the mirror, watching someone behind her. "Jimmy Dale, don't you be messing with Liesl on the ride home, you hear me? Or I'll make you sit up front."

"Yes, Mrs. Craftsman."

Sierra walked down the aisle. Little kids sat up front. A guy wearing a gray hoodie had claimed the last seat on the right. His athletic shoes hung off the end of the seat and he radiated a "back off" vibe. She chose a spot four seats up on the left.

Two girls from her history and math classes nodded at her as they passed by, sliding into the seat opposite the hoodie wearer. A junior high couple sat two seats ahead and immediately started making out. Four guys she recognized from the lunchroom pushed and shoved each other, tossing out, "Hey, baby, we love you," all the way to the back of the bus.

At least the spot next to her had stayed empty.

When the bus pulled out, she slipped in her earbuds and cranked her iPod, the universal leave-me-alone sign, focusing her attention out the window.

Maybe that wasn't an obvious signal in Wyoming; she felt a tap on her shoulder.

She ignored it.

Less than thirty seconds later, a more insistent tap was followed by a loud, "Hey! I'm talkin' to you."

Sierra met the blue eyes of the dark-haired boy, about twelve, draped over the edge of the seat in front of her. He motioned for her to take out her earbuds. "What? Am I in your seat or something?"

"Nope. Man, you're hot. Like really hot."

Awesome that the elementary set thought she was dateable. But if this kid tried to cop a feel like Marin had warned, she'd deck him.

"Bet you can't guess who I am?"

Her mind supplied *a pain in the butt,* but she said, "I have no idea."

"Guess."

She shook her head.

"Come on," he cajoled. "Just one time."

"Look, kid, I—"

"One guess," he repeated stubbornly.

"Leave her alone, Ky," came from the back of the bus.

Who had warned this kid off? She slowly turned.

The hoodie guy had removed his hood and was staring straight at her.

Oh hello, gorgeous. The guy was hot...beyond words actually, with long brown hair that nearly brushed his wide shoulders and dark scruff on his cheeks. He certainly didn't look like he belonged in high school.

"Shut it, Boone. I wasn't talkin' to you," the kid in front of her retorted.

Boone? Now that was a western name.

The kid tapped her shoulder again and she forced herself to quit gawking at the beautiful Boone. "What?"

"*Now* do you know who I am?"

"Not a clue, little dude."

He scowled. "I'm not *that* little."

"Quit bein' a pain in the ass, cuz. She don't wanna play your game."

Next thing she knew, hot Boone from the back of the bus plopped in the seat across from her and smiled.

Oh. My. God. He had a killer smile. Pure bad boy. With dimples.

"Hey. I'm Boone West. Who're you?"

Sierra blinked.

"See? She don't wanna talk to you neither," the kid in front of her sneered.

That's when she realized she hadn't answered. "I'm Sierra."

"Sierra...?"

"Daniels."

"But she's really a McKay," the kid crowed.

"What?" echoed from about twenty people on the bus.

Great. Were they looking at her with scorn? Or envy?

"It's what I was tryin' to tell you. You're my cousin." He grinned. "I'm Kyler McKay. You can call me Ky. There are lots of our cousins on this bus."

Wait. Boone had called Ky cuz. So did that mean... *God no. Please don't let me be related to him.* She glanced at Boone.

He was looking at her curiously. "You're a McKay? I thought you said your last name was Daniels?"

"It is. It's a weird story. My dad found out a few years ago that Charlie and Vi McKay are his birth parents."

"Ah. The long lost McKay son. I've heard about him."

"You have?"

"Yep. Sundance is a small town, becomes even smaller with the West and McKay family connections." His stunning topaz eyes roamed over her face. "But no one told me about you."

Sierra blushed crimson.

"Well, *I* knew you were gonna be on the bus. My mama told me to keep an eye out for you so you didn't get off at the wrong stop," Kyler said.

"Mine did too." Another boy the same age as Ky scooted next to him and leaned over the seat.

"And who are you?" Sierra asked.

"Anton McKay." He jerked his thumb over his shoulder. "Our cousin Hayden is up there with the little cousins."

"How many McKays are there?"

Kyler tapped his fingers. "On the bus? Me, Anton, Hayden, Eliza, Liesl, Peyton, Shannie, Gib, Braxton, Miles. So ten."

"Holy shit."

Boone laughed. "There are at least that many McKay kids that don't go to school yet."

Sierra blurted, "So am I related to you?"

He shook his head. "I'm related to two branches of the McKay family tree because these guys' grandmas were Wests. But you and me? Not even distant kin."

Thank God.

When Boone flashed her that mega-watt smile she about died. Had she really said that out loud?

"So what year are you?" he asked.

"Sophomore. You?"

"Senior. I didn't see you around today."

"That's probably because you were in the principal's office," Ky said with a snicker.

"Don't make me pound on you, boy. You remember the last time you mouthed off to me."

Ky scowled at him. "Didn't hurt *that* bad."

Sierra bit back a smile.

Anton rallied to Ky's defense. "What're you doin' up here anyway, Boone? Finding third graders to beat up?"

"Or smart-mouthed sixth graders. I'm makin' conversation. Now turn around or I'll tell Mrs. Craftsman you were looking down Daphne's shirt."

Anton blushed. But he turned around.

"So how long have you been here?" Boone asked. "I haven't seen you around town."

"Just since Saturday. We moved from Arizona."

"You here for good?"

I hope not. "Probably."

Boone rested his forearms on his thighs and leaned closer. "You don't seem too happy about that."

"It's not that. It's just...I don't know anyone."

"You will soon enough, trust me. Half the school will wanna get to know you a whole lot better."

She wasn't sure how to take that.

The bus started to slow down. Boone tapped Ky on the shoulder. "You'll make sure Sierra gets off at the McKay bus stop?"

"Duh."

"The McKays have their own bus stop?" Sierra asked Boone.

"The McKays could have their own *bus*." Boone stood and slung his backpack over his shoulder, flashing that dimpled grin again. "See ya around, McKay." On his way down the aisle he lightly tapped his younger cousins on the back of the head. They all complained, but she could tell they were happy to have his attention.

Aware that Kyler's and Anton's eyes were on her, Sierra tried really hard not to check out Boone's butt.

Maybe this riding the bus home thing wouldn't be so bad.

Chapter Six

September...

"Now that Sierra has started her second week at school and you have everything unpacked, what will you do this week?" Rielle asked him.

"Thought I'd try to beat my high score on Grand Theft Auto," he said with a perfectly straight face. "It'll probably take more than a week, though."

"Oh."

"Then I'll tackle Vision Quest. It's a bitch to reach the tenth level, but once you do it's worth it because the reward is an orgy. In full color. Better than porn. Or so I've heard."

Rielle's eyes widened. "Sounds...interesting."

"It's awesome to finally have all this free time. I've always wanted to sleep in until noon."

"Noon?" she repeated. "That's..."

Gavin couldn't hold back a laugh. "Gotcha."

She lightly smacked his arm. "Gavin Daniels, that's just plain mean. As if I'd believe you'd lounge around all damn day playing video games. Aren't you buying up squares of land and putting houses and hotels on them, monopolizing the market?"

"But you did believe it, Miss Up-at-the-Buttcrack-of-Dawn-Every-Morning. I thought you knew me better than that."

"I do. You've blabbed all your secrets to me, remember? Since you're constantly underfoot pestering me."

"No, I've withheld a few secrets. It adds to my manly mystique."

Rielle laughed. "As Sierra would say...you're a dork."

"You laughing at my jokes proves you're equally dorky." He reached over and brushed his fingers beneath her jawline. Her skin was so soft right there.

Rielle's pale green eyes were enormous as his fingers moved across her jaw. "What are you doing?"

"Umm...you had flour left from this morning's bake-a-thon," he lied to cover up his strange compulsion to touch her.

"Thank you."

"My pleasure." He tried really hard not to stare at her ass as she retreated and busied herself refilling their mugs with the last dregs of coffee.

"What are you really doing today?"

"Chet and Remy West are coming by this morning to show me the tentative plans for the four-car garage they're building."

"Ha ha. You almost got me twice today."

"I'm not kidding."

A moment passed and then she demanded, "When did you decide that?"

"Last week. They've promised to get it done before the snow flies."

"Where on earth are you going to put a four-car garage?"

Gavin sipped his coffee, hating that their easy banter was about to end. "On the right side of the drive. The structure will be attached to the house and be accessible—"

"Through the mudroom in the basement." Rielle looked as if she wanted to say something else but she didn't.

"As long as they'll already be doing dirt work, we're revamping the front. Since this isn't a B&B, there's no need for a full-sized parking lot. Adding a garage will fill the space and close it off, giving it a more residential feel, as well as adding symmetry."

"So the barn?"

"What about it?"

"Just wondering if you were making changes to it too."

Not just prickly, but pissy. Not that he was surprised. "The barn is new, and from what you've told me and what I've seen, largely unused."

"You sure aren't letting grass grow under your feet when it comes to making changes, are you?" She slapped her hands on the counter. "Speaking of grass...please tell me you don't intend to lay sod across the entire length of the former parking lot? That'd be a serious waste of natural resources. Water is as scarce here as it is in the desert. No one has groomed lawns in the country, Gavin, not to mention the deer and turkeys will rip it up—"

He placed his fingers over her mouth. "Don't go off half-cocked on environmental self-righteousness, hippie chick."

"Hippie chick?" she mumbled beneath his fingers.

"I figured you'd prefer that to granola head or tree hugger."

Rielle's eyes darkened.

He grinned. "Ree. I was trying for levity to make this easier on both of us. Yes, I'm making changes, but not without help. I intended to ask if you had time to talk to a landscaper. You know everything about this chunk of land and I don't. I prefer the natural look. Maintaining a manicured lawn is the last thing I'd ever do."

She turned her head, dislodging his fingers. "I'm glad to hear you aren't completely an urban idiot with visions of becoming a hobby farmer, calling your riding lawnmower a *tractor*."

He murmured, "Touché."

"If you're serious about hiring a landscaper, I know a local guy in Spearfish who is excellent and specializes in xeriscaping."

"I'd appreciate it. I'll tell the West brothers we have that part handled." He crossed his arms over his chest. "See? That wasn't so hard."

"Doesn't change the fact that now I wish you had been telling the truth about being locked away inside playing video games."

Gavin had no response for that as she walked away.

Dirt therapy worked better than scream therapy. Good thing because she wanted to scream her fool head off at Gavin.

The man drove her insane. Always so even-keeled. Matter of fact. Not to mention he was thoughtful, surprisingly funny and so unconsciously sweet that she just wanted to hug him.

And that annoyed the piss out of her.

The earth made a loud *ching* as the shovel blade connected with the crust. She put muscle into it, turning the soil over until dark chunks appeared. Rielle dropped to her knees and brushed the dirt from the clumps of blue fingerling potatoes. These were in high demand in recent years, so she'd filled one entire bed with just this variety. Restaurants in Casper, Cheyenne and Jackson Hole had already placed orders. The entire crop was sold before she'd harvested. That was a good feeling.

She stood and wiped her brow with the back of her glove. It was unseasonably warm for September—not that she was complaining. The longer the sun kept shining, the better the chances were the last crop of heirloom tomatoes could ripen on the vine.

This year she might actually get to harvest everything before the first frost. Over the past three years she'd tripled the size of her gardens. Specializing in organic vegetables had tripled her income. But she was too cheap to hire extra help, so she'd rigged up a generator and the light allowed her to harvest at night.

Gavin constantly commented about her working too hard, but the irony was he ran two businesses and she knew he worked late into the night. He wasn't exactly a stuffed shirt either; he acted more relaxed now than he had when she first met him. But he was very matter of fact. Very methodical.

Isn't that what you like about him? He doesn't pussyfoot around an issue? He comes right out and tells you what he thinks and then gives you a chance to agree or disagree?

That was a refreshing trait. Most men tried to charm or cajole her, acting offended when their bravado didn't have the desired effect, either in business or personally. Which is probably why she didn't date. Too much bullshit.

How had the subject of dating and Gavin come up together?

Because face it, you're attracted to him.

Yes, they flirted constantly. But it didn't mean anything because they were... What exactly were they?

Roommates. Friends. Tied together by a business deal that each of them regretted on some level. The potential for more was there. The question was: Would either of them act on it? Or would they just keep it comfortable and remain at the friendly, teasing stage?

Pushing those thoughts aside, she got back to work.

Sometime later, she heard, "Hey, Rielle."

She glanced up to see Chet and Remy West hanging over the fence on the far side of the tomato garden.

"What can I do for the West boys today?"

"Gavin suggested we come talk to you," Chet said.

She dropped her gloves by the tomato plant so she'd remember where to pick up. "There are benches down here." She could use a break. Standing slowly, she set her hands on her lower back, then arched back to ease the strain.

Since her hands were full with two baskets of tomatoes, Remy opened the gate for her. He wasn't a tall man, but his bulked-up body made him seem bigger. With his curly dark brown hair, warm hazel-colored eyes and sweet smile, Rielle wondered why she'd always turned him down whenever he'd asked her out over the years.

"Plants look great, Ree."

"No blight this year, thank heaven."

Chet peered in the basket of tomatoes. "Ma wants to know if you'll be at the farmer's market or if you'll be selling directly from here."

"Some of both. Next Saturday I'll be at Spearfish Park. She can always call me or stop by. I'm here most days." Rielle sat on the slate bench. "Why does Gavin think I need to talk to you guys? The house and the front section of property are his now and he can do whatever he wants with it." Including building a big damn garage. Would he fill it with boy's toys? A sports car? She tried to picture it, but Gavin didn't seem the flashy type.

Chet stared off into the distance. His height topped his brother's by an inch or two, but his physique was identical to Remy's—brawny and muscle bound. His gaze met hers. His eyes were deep brown, almost black. His blond hair also held a hint of curl. If their eye color and hair color weren't complete opposites, Rielle would swear the men were twins. "Everything is finalized on the addition and we'll start next week since we had a three-week hole in our schedule."

"Seems...coincidental the opening just happens to be the same time Gavin needs a project finished."

Remy shrugged. "Sometimes things just work out like they're supposed to. But that's not why we're here."

Rielle twisted the top off the gallon jug of water and took a long drink before she answered. "What's up?"

"After we got the phone call from Gavin, we revisited the building plans for your place since we hadn't looked at them in a while."

"And?"

"And the design is solid. We're able to design all the eco features you've asked for. However..."

Chet and Remy exchanged a look, then Chet said, "It'll be very labor intensive, which we all knew going into this project. So we updated materials costs and reworked our original estimate..."

She held her breath because this wouldn't be good news.

"The cost has gone up twenty percent."

"Shit."

"We refigured it a couple different ways," Remy said, almost apologetically, "but the price didn't change."

Due to her miserly ways, she could afford to pay additional costs, but she was kicking herself for putting this off. "Thank you guys. The cost of everything has gone up." She offered a wan smile. "Not happy, but not surprised. So that's the worst of it?"

Chet leaned forward. "Nope. With the building site location, and the time of year, and what's already on our plate, there's no way we can get to the project until next spring."

"And that doesn't have anything to do with us takin' on Gavin's garage," Remy added. "Colby and Channing hafta wait for spring for the addition on their house too."

"I should've set a firm date for the start date."

"Well, we don't blame ya for waiting. You were already taking care of a house, even if technically it wasn't yours."

"Did you tell Gavin about my building delay?"

"Nope. It's between us, Ree, you have our word," Chet said. "And no matter what you decide, whether or not to proceed in the spring, and why or why not, it'll stay strictly between us."

Her sharp gaze moved between the brothers. "Why would you think I'd back out?" She bristled. "I assure you, I may have had some rough times in the past, but I do have the money now—"

"Whoa, there, that wasn't what I was insinuating at all." Chet blushed and looked at Remy.

"You're insinuating something...worse?"

"Let's just back up," Remy said. "One of Gavin's main stipulations for hiring us was to keep this project in line with your original plans for the B&B outbuildings you didn't get to implement due to your financial situation at the time."

"Gavin respects you. It's there every time your name comes up," Chet assured her. "And we're to defer all the dirt work changes and landscaping to you. You have total control."

"Our whole point is...even before we talked to Gavin, we believed you'd be better off waiting until after calving season to break ground. A lot of things could change between now and then."

"What kind of things could change?" she asked Remy suspiciously.

Remy gave an embarrassed laugh. "Now, Rielle, darlin', don't take this the wrong way. You are a damn attractive woman, but you don't date. We know you've said no to all guys who've asked you out, not just us. Now you're living with a man who saved your bacon a few years back?"

"You think I'm interested in Gavin because he's rich?" Goddammit. Was that what everyone in the area would think? She'd assured Gavin it wouldn't bother her...but faced with assumptions, she wasn't so sure.

Both Chet and Remy burst out laughing.

"No, but the man sure is interested in you."

She stared at them blankly.

Remy nudged Chet. "Told ya she hadn't even freakin' noticed."

She had noticed how Gavin acted around her—she'd have to be blind not to see how he looked at her sometimes, stupid not to recognize the familiar way he touched her and a complete idiot to pretend to be unaffected by his attention. It just surprised her that Chet and Remy West had picked up on the undercurrent so quickly.

Or had Gavin said something to them?

No. Gavin wasn't like that. But as far as she was concerned, that topic was off limits. "The only thing I'm interested in is you guys taking some of these tomatoes off my hands. You can swing by your mama's house and earn major brownie points."

"That'd be great. You're a doll," Remy said.

"And just for that, I'll send a loaf of bread home with you guys too."

Chet groaned. "Man, I love your homemade bread. Don't suppose you've got any extra honey lying around?"

"Jesus, Chet," Remy said and smacked him in the back of the head. "Don't be such a fuckin' mooch."

"I'm not a mooch, asshole. I was gonna buy it."

Remy dodged Chet's retaliatory swat.

"Boys. There's enough to go around. Let's head up to the house." She purposely didn't say *my* house.

Gavin didn't appear until Chet and Remy were gone. He leaned against the porch support. "I see you take pity on poor bachelors and send them home with food."

She hadn't shaken off the disappointing news yet. "The bachelors I like, yes. Why? You jealous?"

"A little." Gavin started down the steps. "But since you feed me on occasion, I get the better deal, since I'm living with you and all. That seemed to interest them more than it should have." He stopped in front of her. "Is everything all right?"

The man had no concept of personal space. She considered saying something flip, but a soft, "No," slipped out and she dropped her gaze to the empty basket still clutched in her hands.

He took the basket from her. When she looked up, he curled his hands around her arms, moving closer yet. "Rielle. What's going on?"

"West Construction can't start on my house until next spring."

"Because of the garage addition? Dammit, I told them I could wait if it would affect—"

"No, it has nothing to do with that."

A calculating look entered his eyes. "If you need—"

Lightning fast Rielle placed her fingers over his lips. "Don't you assume anything and offer me money or I swear to God I will scream or...do something equally horrible to you."

His lips curled into a smile and he lightly nipped her fingers before she pulled her hand away. "I like it when you get feisty. But if money isn't the issue, what is?"

"Time. If they can't get started until spring, then that means I'll have to move into the cabin because I'm sure you don't want me living with you and Sierra indefinitely."

The immediate fierceness in his eyes made it hard to breathe. "Now who's making assumptions?"

There wasn't any sign of mild-mannered Gavin. In fact, she'd begun to wonder if that easy-going man had just been a figment of her imagination—a pencil-pushing pushover she'd never be attracted to, therefore she could keep him at arm's length. But this Gavin? No pushover. All man. All the time. And her attraction to him kept getting stronger every day.

"Listen to me. You are *not* staying in that cabin unless living with me is so heinous that you want to kill me in my sleep."

"It's not, I mean, you're not," she assured him.

"Good. So we'll stick to the original plan. Because I think it's been working great." He grinned. "So, pity a poor bachelor. What's for lunch?"

Rielle growled and smacked him playfully with the basket. "You're such a mooch."

But she made him lunch anyway.

Chapter Seven

Gavin strolled into the kitchen and poured himself a glass of iced tea. Then he peered over Rielle's shoulder, waiting for her to acknowledge him.

In the past few weeks he'd gone out of his way to pester her—not that she considered the attention of a smart, funny, sexy man a chore. Gavin was interested in everything she did workwise and asked a million questions. So Rielle returned the favor whenever possible. Showing up in his office to chat. Since the man lived on the phone, she got to hear him acting all professional and business tycoon-y. But he hadn't complained about her impromptu interruptions either.

"What're you doing?" he finally asked.

He stood so close the deep timbre of his voice vibrated against her skin and she fought a shiver. "Updating my notes on the new vegetable varieties I planted this year."

"Bad year for squash?"

"Which one? There are four genuses of squash: *C maxima, C mixta, C moschata* and *C pepo.*"

"That's what I get for trying to be funny."

"Squash is no laughing matter. So what's up?"

"Have you ever done something under...duress and wished you hadn't?"

That was random. But typical for Gavin. She kept typing. "Like telling a stranger she can live in your house until spring?"

"Funny, Ree. But I'm serious."

"All right. What did you say under duress? And who'd you say it to?"

"Sierra. And I kinda, sorta, maybe promised...to buy her a car."

Rielle looked up from her laptop. "Are you kidding me?"

"Ah. No."

"And you're telling me this...why? Because you want the parent-to-parent lecture on *not* rewarding your child's bad behavior? The girl gets herself arrested and you're buying her a car?"

"Yeah." Gavin distractedly scrubbed his hands over the razor stubble on his face.

She squinted at him. He always bounded down in the morning dressed and clean shaven. It was afternoon and he looked like a bum—

a hot bum, but nowhere near his usual put together self. "Gavin. Are you okay?"

"I don't know." He sighed. "This whole buying her a car business might seem sudden, but I had planned on buying her one in Arizona, I just hadn't told her. Then all that shit happened with her arrest. So as we're driving across country, I'm encouraging her to talk to me, and she broke down completely. Crying about her mom leaving and how abandoned she felt, how stupid she felt that her new friends avoided her and her old friends dumped her, and berating herself for letting her grades drop. We were finally really talking about that long overdue emotional stuff...and it just slipped out."

"It just slipped out," she repeated slowly. "That you were buying her a car. While she was crying and carrying on about how much her life sucked?"

Gavin bristled. "In my defense, there isn't public transportation here, unless you count the one-way bus ride in the afternoon. It's not like I'm buying her a brand new car. It's used."

And he wondered why Sierra acted entitled? Rielle focused on the document on the computer screen and scrolled down to the next page.

"What? Aren't you talking to me now?"

"You don't need my input. She's your daughter. You can give her anything she wants." Literally, since the man was reportedly worth millions—if the conversations she'd heard recently in his office were any indication.

"So you think I'm making a mistake?" Gavin pressed.

"Why does it matter to you what I think?"

Gavin leaned across the counter, forcing her to focus on him. "Because your daughter is a well-adjusted adult, attending grad school on full scholarship. You are an excellent parent and I can learn from you. So help me out here."

"Laying it on a little thick today, aren't you?" she said wryly.

"I'm not joking. I need your input. I trust your judgment."

Good thing he hadn't flashed her that charming I-get-anything-I-want-because-I'm-a-McKay smile because she hated that type of male manipulation. "Fine. I'll give you my opinion, just this one time." Rielle sighed. "Let's backtrack. Before all that crap happened this summer, were you teaching Sierra to drive?"

"We went out a few times. She learned to park at the mall. We mostly stayed on residential streets. I had her drive on the freeway once and it freaked her out."

"So she's never driven on a gravel road."

"No. Charlie has offered to teach her to drive after school and I've agreed because I know he'll be more patient. Plus, he has the time to spare."

"That's good because I doubt she had to deal with adverse road conditions in sunny Arizona. Maybe you should have Charlie give *you* a few winter driving tips too."

He lifted an eyebrow. "Funny. But what's your advice?"

"Buy her the car. But park it in the driveway. That'll be an incentive for her to bring her grades up and stay out of trouble. Riding the bus is good for her socially. Plus, she'll have a better appreciation when she's allowed to drive the car on a regular basis."

Gavin studied her.

"What?"

"You're so damn smart." He trailed his palm down the length of her bare arm. "Thank you."

A tingle started at her nape and traveled to her tailbone. She reacted to Gavin's unexpected casual affection instinctively, rubbing her fingertips over the dark growth on his cheek. "Ooh, look out. The tycoon is going native. He's already forgetting to shave."

"Wrong. I'm out of razors. Since you were a smartass—" Gavin scraped his stubbled cheek up and down her arm until she shrieked, "—you'll just have to put up with my manly scruff today."

Oh yeah, I can think of a couple other places you can rub that manly scruff on me.

The way his eyes stayed locked on hers, she swore he'd read her mind.

"You could've asked to borrow one from me, roomie," she teased, "but I'm sure you're too *manly* to use a pink razor."

"Like hell I am. Hand it over. You can watch me shave."

"Oh, right. I'm out of razors too. I haven't shaved my legs in a week." Not that she had a reason to.

"Really?" Gavin rotated her barstool and latched onto her ankle. "Let's compare, shall we?"

"What are you doing?"

"You felt my stubble; it's only fair I feel yours." His blue eyes held a wicked gleam as his palm slowly inched up the outside of her calf.

"This is..." *Crazy, sexy, hot.* How long had it been since she'd been touched with such teasing sexiness?

Forever. Maybe...never.

"See? I knew you were lying. Your skin is silky smooth."

Keep going. The hair gets a lot coarser higher up.

His hand stopped at the hem of her skirt. Keeping his eyes on hers, his fingers caressed the skin above her knee. "No hair here."

A rush of desire had her so dizzy she feared she'd topple off the chair.

Gavin's hands followed the contour of her calf down to her ankle. Then he set her foot to the chair rung and stepped back, grinning widely. "Thanks for the advice." He wandered out of the kitchen, whistling.

That was weird. Sexy as hell, but weird.

Of course Boone West was working with his uncles on a day her hair looked like total dogshit. And she was wearing ratty sweats and no makeup. And she had cramps like a motherfucker that no dosage of Midol could cut. So she was cranky. Even her dad had told her to get a grip on her crap attitude before he'd taken off with Ben. Uncle Ben. The thought of calling the intimidating Ben McKay *Uncle Ben* made her snicker.

Then Boone wandered into view again and Sierra sighed. He wore a black wife beater that showed more muscles than she'd given him credit for. His skin glistened with sweat from lugging heavy tools and lumber. Watching him, she understood that Boone was no ordinary high school boy who would slowly morph into an adult male; he was already a man. A hunky, hard-working man and she had it bad for him, even when she knew there wasn't a snowball's chance in the desert he'd ever look at her with lust in his eyes.

Especially not today.

She tapped her fingers on the windowsill, considering her options. Stay inside and continue to spy on him from the big window? Then he wouldn't know she was having a bad everything day. Or should she casually wander outside and pretend to be shocked he was at her house?

So what's it gonna be, Sierra? Hide? Or seek?

When she saw his uncles' work truck heading up the driveway, leaving Boone all alone... Seek won out.

She resisted the urge to squeeze into a pair of skinny jeans and switch her sports bra for a push-up. Grabbing the half-full garbage bag from the kitchen, she sailed out the front door.

Sadie, Rielle's sweet German shepherd, trotted along beside her as Sierra strolled to the Dumpster. The hinges squeaked as she opened the metal lid and tossed the garbage in.

"You're not supposed to throw regular garbage in there, just building materials."

Sierra manufactured a surprised look before she wheeled around. Boone had crouched down to scratch Sadie's ears. Some guard dog; her tail was wagging furiously. "Oh. Hey, Boone. Sorry. I'll take it out."

"Here, let me. You don't wanna get your clothes dirty. Mine already are."

Sierra froze when Boone sidled right up to her, close enough their arms and shoulders touched. His biceps rippled as he fished out the garbage bag. Then he jogged to the barn, tossed it in the plastic can and jogged back.

"Thanks."

"No problem."

"I didn't know you worked with your uncles."

"Only when they need a gopher and wanna haul my ass outta bed at six a.m. on a Saturday."

"You must be more than a gopher if they left you here by yourself."

"Nope. I'm on clean up duty. They went to get supplies and lunch."

"Are they bringing food back for you?"

Boone snorted. "Doubtful. I was late this morning 'cause I worked until freakin' midnight and didn't have time to make my lunch." He shrugged. "Going without lunch is supposed to teach me responsibility or something."

"Bull. It's irresponsible for them to expect you to work on an empty stomach. Mean too, since *they're* eating. I...ah...was about to make myself a sandwich and it's just as easy to make two." Had she really invited him in for lunch? *Take it back before he can refuse.*

"Thanks, but I'll be fine." His gaze swept the empty parking area, then those beautiful caramel-colored eyes locked to hers and her stomach flipped. "Is your Dad or Rielle home?"

"No."

He raised a brow.

She blushed and then pushed him. "It's not like I planned to drag you into my bedroom. It'd just be us having a sandwich in the kitchen. But whatever. Go ahead and starve."

A beat passed before Boone bestowed a grin that kick-started her heart. "Well...since my virtue is safe with you, McKay, I *suppose* you can fix me lunch."

They started walking toward the house. "Why do you keep calling me that? I'm not a McKay."

"Blood don't lie. With the way you look and act, you're all McKay."

"You say that as if it's a bad thing."

"Not always. Don't know if you're aware, but there's been bad blood between the Wests and the McKays over the years. No one talks about it, but some of it's still there even after intermarriage between the families."

"I had no idea. But there's a lot I don't know about this family."

"Ask me anything. I'm totally unbiased." He grinned.

"Says a West. So, if Chet and Remy are your uncles, who's your dad?"

"Dax. He's the oldest. As I'm Chet and Remy's only nephew, they feel it's their duty to teach me to do 'manly shit' like carpentry and cars and…other stuff."

"So who teaches you how to do 'womanly shit' like make sandwiches and set your alarm? Your mom?"

"You're sassy." Boone bumped her with his shoulder. "My mom lives in Gillette. I live with my dad."

"My parents got divorced when I was five."

"Mine never got married. My dad knocked my mom up when she was a senior in high school."

"Really? Was he in high school too?"

"Nope. He was nineteen. Old enough to know better, as he constantly preaches to me." Boone winked at her. "Which is why I usually avoid the temptation of being alone with hot females."

Was he saying she tempted him?

Get real, Sierra.

On the front porch, Sierra waited as Boone dusted off his clothes and kicked off his heavy soled boots. "Where can I wash up?"

"The kitchen sink is fine. Follow me."

Sierra pulled out a package of roast beef, sliced smoked cheddar, yellow mustard and lemon basil mayo. She turned around, getting an eyeful of the muscles in Boone's back working beneath his tank top as he thoroughly scrubbed his arms and face. Her gaze dropped to his incredibly tight butt—*thank you, Wrangler jeans.* He didn't notice her guilty look or flushed face when she handed him a towel.

"What can I do to help?" Boone asked.

"Tell me if you want tomato and arugula on your sandwich." She sliced thick chunks of Rielle's homemade herbed oatmeal bread.

"What's arugula?"

"Peppery lettuce." She gestured with the knife to a pile of greens. "Try some."

Boone popped a piece in his mouth and chewed. "I'll have that. And tomato." He leaned closer to watch her. "So do you like to cook?"

"My parents got divorced when I was five and we ate out a lot, no matter which one of them I stayed with. By the time I was ten, I never wanted to eat another McDonald's Happy Meal. My Grandma Grace taught me some basics. Then dad and I enrolled in cooking classes that forced us to look beyond canned stuff, mac and cheese and spaghetti. I experiment with food because I know my dad won't."

"My idea of experimenting with food is to put different taco sauce on frozen burritos."

Sierra sliced tomatoes. "I haven't seen you on the bus lately."

"I've got a job after school or I'm studying at the library."

"You work with your uncles during the week?" She slathered mayo on the bread and placed it over the tomato.

"Nah. I work part-time as an EMT on the Crook County ambulance crew."

Her eyes met his. "Don't you have to be eighteen to be certified?"

"I passed the course last spring after I turned eighteen."

No wonder he didn't look like a boy—he wasn't one. She slid his sandwich onto a plate and set it in front of him.

"Tell me what that little shit Kyler said about me when I haven't been on the bus to defend myself."

"He mentioned that you're...kind of mean." Not entirely true. Kyler said Boone had a bad reputation.

"Bullshit. What's he really say?"

So Sierra told him.

Boone grinned. "I'm back to being bad boy Boone, eh? Cool."

No explanation.

Sierra filled two water glasses and parked herself next to him at the breakfast bar. This was surreal. Having lunch with Boone West. She glanced at him out of the corner of her eye. God. He was so hot.

"How you like livin' in Sundance?"

"I'm starting to like it better."

"You're hanging out with Marin Godfrey, right?"

"Why? Is she a troublemaker or something?"

Boone shook his head. "No, she's cool. I saw you talking to Angie and Kara. Those two chicks have bad reputations. Don't go to any of the parties they invite you to, okay?"

She wasn't a country bumpkin waiting to taste her first beer. "Umm, no. If I actually get invited to a party, I'm going. And FYI, I went to parties *all* the time in Arizona. I've probably seen more wild stuff than you have, Boone." An exaggeration, but he wouldn't know that.

He chuckled. "Don't bet on it."

"Do you go to those parties?"

"Sometimes. So I know what I'm talking about when I tell you to steer clear."

She drained her water and felt him staring at her. She faced him and said, "What?" a little sharply.

"Don't get pissy with me. You're a pretty girl." His gaze slowly roamed her face. "Scratch that, you're a beautiful girl and I don't want to see the jerks and assholes taking advantage of you because you're new to town, looking for friends and a good time."

Had Boone really said she was pretty? Wait. He'd said she was beautiful? Get out. And she looked like shit today.

"Sierra? Were you even listening to me?"

"Ah. Yeah. Sure. Watch the parties. Got it."

After he finished his sandwich and the other half of hers, he said, "Is that your Jeep Waggoner parked out front?"

"Yeah. Why?"

"Sweet ride. I love those classic cars."

"My dad says I'm still learning to drive so he never lets me go anywhere by myself. He's being such a hardass about it."

Boone wiped his mouth with a napkin. "He should be. Driving on the gravel roads takes getting used to. We get all sorts of accident calls and that's before the snow and icy conditions start."

Talk about treating her like a kid sister. That wasn't the way she wanted him to see her at all. Maybe she should've worn that stupid push-up bra.

He rinsed their lunch plates. Then he slayed her with his high-power grin. "I'd better get back to work before my uncles see that I'm not starved to death. Thanks for lunch. It was awesome."

"You're welcome."

"See ya around, McKay."

Sierra stood by the window, watching him walking away, a plan hatching in her mind. If she ever was at a party with him, she'd show him that she could live up to the wild McKay reputation she'd heard so much about.

Chapter Eight

"No. I don't care what the policy was before. *My* management policy is the tenant's problem gets addressed the *first* time they call, not the third." Gavin paced in front of his desk. "This bullshit has been going on since I bought the property three months ago? Leave Chris a message. I'd better hear from him today, or he'll be in the unemployment line tomorrow." He hung up.

Jesus. He'd been so distracted with Sierra's arrest and the custody hearing that he'd let a few things slide in the transition to running his business remotely. Things he'd deal with when he wasn't so pissed off.

Full of restless energy, he laced up his running shoes and hopped on his treadmill. At least he'd put the anger to good use.

Gavin ran for an hour. Then he cooled down and lifted free weights. Last year his blood pressure had skyrocketed, forcing him to shed thirty pounds and take charge of his health. An exercise regimen, the right diet, the right medication and he felt like a new man. He even had a libido—something he'd never had much of until medical tests four months ago revealed low levels of testosterone.

At first he'd scoffed at taking testosterone supplements. He'd gotten by fine for years without them. But in thinking about how little interest he'd had in sex over the years, he decided he had nothing to lose.

And thinking about sex...his thoughts drifted to Rielle. The woman made him insanely hard. Just sitting beside her at breakfast, he had the urge to pull her onto his lap and kiss the hell out of her, while running his hands down her muscled arms. Then he'd hold her generous breasts before clamping his hand on her ass, bringing her pelvis against his so she'd know exactly how hard she made him. He was getting a woody right now just thinking about her.

Stop. Time for a cold shower.

Then maybe he'd wander down to the Garden of Ree and see what chores his too-tempting roomie had assigned herself today.

"Rielle?"

She pivoted in the dirt and faced Gavin. "Are you lost?"

"No. Just exploring." He sighed dramatically. "I'm lonely."

"Right. You're bored."

His low, throaty laugh was seductive. "That too. I followed the road that winds around the gardens and it ended abruptly."

"It ends to deter explorers."

"You are hilarious. So what are you ripping out, plowing up, or chopping down today?"

Rielle peeled off her gloves and set them on top of the fence before she left the fenced garden. "I'm about to check my fruit trees to see how close I am to harvest."

"Then you what? Pick them, load them and haul them to a farmer's market?"

"Some gets sold locally, but the bulk goes to restaurants across the country."

"There's a market for it outside of Wyoming?"

"A much bigger market."

Gavin fell in step with her as she headed toward the grove of trees at the bottom of a small hill.

Rielle gestured to the orchard. "These are considered old fruit trees. They'd been here thirty years when my parents bought the place thirty years ago. So they're sixty-year-old trees that've never been treated with pesticide. That's incredibly rare."

"So you just leave them be and let nature take her course?"

"I prune and water and use natural pest repellents. It usually works. But one year the trees were infested with some weird bug and had zero yield. I figured all the trees were done for because..."

"You couldn't spray them."

"Exactly. The next year, the trees came back stronger than ever, no bugs. I chalked it up to nature knowing what the trees needed better than I did."

He walked alongside her. "I am a clueless urbanite when it comes to trees—with the exception of recognizing orange and grapefruit trees."

"I think it would be cool to walk into your backyard and pick a grapefruit for breakfast." She touched a branch of the closest tree. "This is a pine sweet apple."

"Never heard of that variety." His eyes lit up. "Ah, this is the tree that lays the golden apples."

She laughed. "Yep. I have two of these. Next in line are mountain pear trees, again a rarity. These two are the fussiest of all the trees; I never count on any kind of yield."

"But when it does bear fruit?"

"I get five bucks *apiece* for them. They're so tiny, yet have such robust flavor. One chef in Chicago has a standing order to buy the entire crop. He's anxiously awaiting shipment because it's been two years since these suckers have bloomed."

Gavin whistled.

"The next two trees are golden apricot. I sell the fruit to locals or find some use for it in my own cooking and canning. After those are the plum trees. The variety is sweet water pink, another rarity. The skin is such a deep purple it's almost black, but the flesh is a very pale pink. The fruit doesn't get big, and it tastes like a cross between a blueberry and a strawberry."

"What's the going rate for a sweet water pink plum?"

"Six bucks apiece."

"Do you sell them around here?"

She shook her head. "Wyomingites won't spend that on a beer, let alone on a tiny piece of fruit. There's a Japanese fusion restaurant in San Francisco that takes the whole lot every year. My understanding is the chef slices a single fruit and plates it with single curls of white, dark and milk chocolate and charges twenty-five bucks for it."

They kept walking and she began to feel self-conscious, blathering on about trees. "You sure you're interested in this? Or are you just being polite?"

He stopped and grabbed her hand. "I'm very interested."

"Why?"

"Because I've never known anyone who makes a living off the land the way you do. I mean, yes, the McKays do, but in a different way. I've watched you nurturing your garden, slaving to harvest, exhausted but exhilarated. It's something to behold. I don't think I could do it year in, year out, being at the whim of nature and the weather."

Rielle stood close enough to him to let his eyes draw her in. That vivid blue, the same blue all the McKays had, but his eyes seemed...brighter somehow. Truer. Something about Gavin said *trust me*. This was the first time she'd ever had that gut reaction. Because she didn't trust easily, that made her attraction to him all the more acute.

"I like seeing you this way," he said in his rough and compelling voice.

"How's that?"

"In your element."

"Meaning covered in dirt?"

"You being dirty suits me just fine, Rielle."

Oh. My. God. Had he really meant it that way? Yes, if the heat in his eyes was a sign.

"I don't even know what to say to that, Gavin."

He just smiled. He dropped her hand and pointed to the last two trees. "What about those? Magic Mediterranean figs that taste like ambrosia and earn you a hundred bucks a pop?"

In that moment the sexual tension vanished and everything went back to normal between them. She was glad for it, even when she had a pang of regret for being tongue-tied when he always came up with such sexy off-the-cuff comments. "Those are just plain old red delicious apples."

"But from sixty-year-old trees."

"Yep. I don't sell many of those. I sacrifice them to the deer, hoping they'll gorge themselves on these first two trees and leave my other trees the hell alone."

"Logical. But I see you've erected some netting as extra insurance."

"That's mostly to keep the birds away. That's also why I've let the chokecherry bushes get overgrown. It's a natural deterrent and a critter barrier." She ducked under the netting and beckoned to him. "Come into my secret garden, tycoon."

A smiling Gavin followed her without question.

At the base of the plum tree, she pointed to a branch directly above his head. "I can't reach that high, so I want you to pick that plum closest to the trunk."

"Seriously? You're letting me try a six dollar piece of fruit?" His eyes took on a strange twinkle. "I'll warn you, I don't have any bills smaller than a twenty on me."

"I oughta charge you double for that crack. Go on. Pick it."

Curling his fingers around it, he tugged and promptly handed the fruit to her as if it was a bomb. "It's so small. And warm."

"That's what makes it so luscious." Rielle held the fruit between her thumb and forefinger. "I'll take the first bite so you can see how juicy and tender the pink flesh is." Keeping her eyes on his, she brought it to her mouth, using the very edges of her teeth to sink down through the skin. The instant the sweet juice hit her tongue she closed her eyes and moaned. Normally she limited herself to the damaged or near rotten fruit, not the perfect ones such as this.

When Rielle opened her eyes, Gavin was right there. He couldn't tear his gaze away from her mouth. Her voice dropped to a sultry whisper. "See how the juice coats the pink flesh when it's soft and warm?"

"Goddamn, I want a taste," he said, his voice a deep rasp. "A full taste."

"Of this fruit?"

His hot blue gaze locked to hers, broadcasting that he wasn't thinking about the plum. "Oh, I'd take a full taste of that too." Holding her hand in place, he bent forward and sucked the other half from her fingers. "Mmm." After he removed the pit from his mouth, he nipped her fingertips. "I'm thinking I need another taste."

"Gavin."

"You know what I want to do right now? Lick every bit of juice off your lips. Then I want to suck it off your tongue. So when I kiss you the first time? I'll know the sweetness and heat is all you."

Her mouth had gone desert dry, but she eked out a soft, "Do it."

Just as Gavin started to close the distance, the bushes behind them rattled. They both jumped back and a deer bounded past.

Cheeks burning, Rielle retreated, ducking out of the netting.

Gavin caught her hand and spun her to face him. "Rielle. Stop. Don't run from me."

"I'm not running."

He quirked a brow. "Did you suddenly remember you left muffins burning in the oven or something?"

"Okay. Maybe I was running."

"Why? Are you upset by what just happened?"

"Nothing happened," she said quickly.

His handsome face reflected grim amusement. "Maybe that's why you're upset? Because I am. I'm not much of a hunter, but if I would've had a rifle, I would've blasted that damn deer for interrupting us."

She couldn't help but laugh.

"That's better. I like to hear you laugh as much as I like to see you smile." His thumb swept across the pulse point in her wrist. "I really like that you urged me to kiss you and I almost did."

She tried to jerk her hand away but he held firm. "Why are you determined to embarrass me?"

"Why are you determined to pretend this is nothing?" he countered, his eyes serious. "Or is almost kissing in the orchard like giddy teenagers normal for you? Because I have to admit, it's not normal for me. Not even close."

Buoyed by his confession, Rielle smiled at him. "Me either. Come on." She walked closer to him as they strolled back to the gardens.

"How do you harvest all that fruit?"

"Get a ladder, strap on a bag and start picking."

"No, I mean by yourself. That's dangerous work."

"You know that's how it goes when you run your own business. When things need to be done, you just do them and don't think about it."

"How long does it take?"

"Not all the fruit is ripe at the same time so it varies. I'll pick the plums on Wednesday and ship them Thursday. The pears look to have at least a week left. The apples, another two weeks minimum. Why?"

"Because I volunteer my services as a fruit picker."

She wouldn't get anything done with Gavin distracting her. "Don't you have construction workers to boss around?"

"I excel at multitasking." He pointed to a small structure at the top of the rise. "What is that building used for? And is it on my property?"

"Technically, yes, it's on your property. It's a honey house."

As expected, his head whipped around and he flashed her a depraved grin. "Do tell."

"It's a place to process my honey away from the bees." She gestured to the stacks of white boxes in front of a cluster of chokecherry and buffalo berry bushes. "I'll check my bees in the next couple days."

"Checking your bees... Is that like minding your p's and q's?"

"Clever, tycoon. But no. It's a little more involved."

"Why in the hell would you want to keep bees? Don't they sting you?"

"Only if provoked. At first I started a few hives because Wyoming joined an experimental subsidy program and it paid well, especially for a single mom. But I believe in the program and honeybees are essential in pollination of one third of the world's crops. I have a higher yield in my gardens because of the bees. The ranchers that plant alfalfa reap the benefits of my bees too. Win win, right? Plus, I get to sell the product and the byproducts."

He frowned. "Byproducts...plural?"

"The honey and the beeswax. Have you ever tasted wildflower honey?"

"I don't know. Does it taste different?"

"Yes. And my honey tastes different from someone else's honey."

Gavin's hot mouth brushed across her knuckles. "Of that I've no doubt. And I can't wait to taste yours."

Her entire body heated. Was she having a hot flash? Or were his words just that sexually potent? Yeah. It was all him.

"So those stacks of white boxes scattered all over the property. Those are bee traps?"

She snorted. "Bee traps. Those are the hives."

"Square hives?"

"Technically they're called supers."

"How do you get the honey out?"

"By pulling the frames. Then slicing the wax caps off."

He frowned. "Still don't get it."

"I can go into explicit detail of honey production and harvesting or give you an overview."

"I'm more the explicit type."

I'm sure you are.

Rielle detailed the process. Inside her honey house, she modeled her beekeeper suit and showed the smoker used to calm the bees before she opened the hive to check them. Then she showed him the spinning extractor that used centrifugal force to separate the honey from the wax comb. Lastly she pointed out the big buckets with spigots for bottling the honey.

"What do you do with the bees in the winter?"

She glanced at him. His eyes hadn't glazed over yet. She tended to be enthusiastic about beekeeping, especially to the uninitiated. "Keep them in their hives."

Gavin looked skeptical. "They don't freeze up here in the arctic north?"

"There's always some loss. But honeybees winter well when they're properly protected with have enough honey to survive. I leave about seventy pounds of honey in each hive."

"That much? Does that give you much of a harvest?"

She smiled. "Oh, I get at least that. Last year I ended up with ninety pounds from each hive. And with twelve hives..."

"Honey, that's a whole lot of honey."

"Yep. I bottle it, sell it locally, and send some to stores across the state that specialize in Wyoming-made items. Skylar at Sky Blue buys a lot to use in her beauty products. Honey production is my most profitable business. I do the least amount of work. It's a sweet deal."

Gavin groaned at her pun.

"Thanks for listening to me blather."

"My pleasure. I'm interested in your life and livelihood, Ree, but I haven't forgotten about that almost kiss." He started to move closer, but stopped to pull his buzzing cell phone from his pocket. "It's time to get Sierra from the bus stop. We'll pick this up later."

Break over, Rielle returned to work.

Chapter Nine

October...

Rielle knocked on Gavin's office door.

He answered with a terse, "What?"

She poked her head inside. "Is it safe to come in? You sound grumpy."

"I am. Where the hell have you been the last four days?"

"Honey harvest time, remember? What's put the wrinkle in your brow?"

"A lot of stuff. I'm in a lousy mood. You'd best trot your little self back downstairs."

Wow. Little self? Was he trying to start a fight with her? "What happened that's got you locked in your office on a Saturday?"

"The idiot running one of my new properties somehow lost all the property maintenance records for the last three years."

"Lost? Don't you have a backup copy?"

Gavin paced behind his desk. "You'd think so. But no one can find a backup. I've had to walk him through every single step of searching programs and documents, which he should know how to do. I finally told him to take the tower to my computer guru to see if there's anything on the hard drive. But instead of taking it where I told him, he dropped it off at Best Buy because it was closer to his house. Now I suspect he purposely erased all the records because he knows I'll see shit hasn't been done on the property for a long time. I've had nothing but problems with him."

"Why keep him on if he's such an idiot?"

"Some sob story from the previous owner about the guy trying to get custody of his kids from his ex-wife."

"Which would be a trigger for you to give him a chance," Rielle said.

"And speaking of triggers..." He made an exasperated noise. "Sierra pushed all my buttons today. Every. Single. One. Which hasn't happened for a while so I guess she decided we were overdue for a fight."

She watched him beat a path across the carpet. He looked damn fine in workout clothes; a gray sleeveless T-shirt that showed off his defined shoulders and biceps and navy-colored boxing shorts that hung off his lean hips. She imagined his back muscles bunching up and his biceps rippling when he smacked the heavy bag. His sweat-dampened shirt clung to his pectorals. Would his sweat carry the clean scent she associated with him? Or something more raw and masculine?

"Rielle?"

She snapped back to attention. "Ah, yeah?"

"Why are you here?"

I missed you. "Chet and Remy need to talk to you about something."

"Great. Maybe they'll tell me why this garage project is stalled."

She sauntered behind his desk. "After seeing you so aggravated, I'm offering you the ideal way to work off some of that frustration."

Gavin tilted his head "I'm listening."

She fought a shiver at his very sexual once-over. "You offered your harvesting services. I'm here to collect. It'll be fun. It's a gorgeous day. Not many more left. The fresh air and sunshine will help you forget about your problems, if only for a few hours." She poked him in the sternum. "And if you prove to be a good worker bee, I'll even fix you lunch."

He snatched her finger. "First, don't poke me because I poke back. Second, thanks for giving *me* the chance to do *your* heavy labor so *I* feel better." He smiled. "But you know what? I accept. I will expect dessert with my lunch. Something really sweet. Think you can handle that?"

"With one hand tied behind my back." She poked him again and ducked out of his reach. "When you're done dealing with Chet and Remy, trot your little self down to the gardens."

After three hours of laboring in the dirt, Gavin sighed heavily. "How many acres of root vegetables did you plant?"

"Acres?" she repeated.

"Can't you harvest these with a tractor or something? This digging them up by hand shit really sucks."

Rielle leaned on her shovel. "A tractor? Really?"

"Tractor, plow, rake, combine, whatever. I'm tired. Aren't you tired?"

"Nope. And when did you turn into Sierra, complaining *this sucks* and *that sucks*?"

Gavin threw down his spade, tore off his gloves and said, "That's it. I can take you making fun of my lack of vegetable ranching knowledge, but when you compare my attitude to that of a sixteen-year-old girl? Well, honey, it's on. Because I am all man."

"Yeah?"

"Oh yeah."

"Prove it."

Flashing his teeth, he jumped over the spade handle and made a beeline for her.

She started to run but the soft, overturned dirt slowed her down. When she glanced over her shoulder, Gavin was gaining on her. She put on a burst of speed but it was too little, too late. His arms came around her waist, and he jerked her to a stop.

Rielle shrieked. She shrieked louder when he lifted her off the ground. "Gavin! Put me down!"

"No. You're my captive." His warm breath teased her ear. "What should I do with you? Turn you over my knee and spank you?"

"Don't you dare."

His nose drifted along her neck. "Damn, Rielle, you smell great."

"It's, ah..." Shit. She couldn't think straight when his mouth was on her skin.

"It's what?" he murmured.

"Honeysuckle."

"That fits." He pressed a kiss on her neck. "I'd like to suckle some of your honey."

The words should've sounded corny, but they were beyond sexy murmured in Gavin's throaty rasp.

He set her down and turned her around. He brushed something out of her hair and used the backs of his knuckles to outline her jaw. "Know something?"

"What?"

"I've been thinking about you. Missing you the last few days. A little pissy about it if you want to know the truth. Wondering if you missed me at all."

"I did."

"Good."

He kept stroking her face.

"What?"

"I'm a lousy worker bee. I kept looking over at you, trying to draw you into conversation and now that you're right in front of me...I can't think of a damn thing to say. These wide green eyes of yours draw me right in."

She blinked at him.

"And then there's your mouth..."

"My mouth what?" she managed to whisper.

"Your mouth is so lush. I could sink into it for days."

Rielle licked her lips.

He groaned. "You tempting me? Or challenging me?"

"Both." She snaked her arms around his neck and pulled him down for a kiss.

The move caught him by surprise but it didn't take long for him to haul her against his body and sink into the kiss like he'd warned. Opening his mouth to consume hers in a teasing, hot tangle of tongues. A kiss that changed from hungry to seductive to sweet and back to hungry.

Her head buzzed. If Gavin didn't have such a tight hold on her, she'd have a hard time standing, he kissed her with such ferocity. Like she was air, water and light.

Gavin ripped his mouth from hers and said, "Holy fuck."

That made her smile because she'd been thinking the same thing.

His hands were on her face, tilting her head back. His burning gaze moved to her mouth. Then his lips were on hers again, giving her the sweetest, gentlest kiss. The wet glide of his lips and the possessive way his hand slid down to the back of her neck, holding her in place, was undeniably sexy.

Rielle didn't know how long they stayed like that, body to body, mouth to mouth. By the time he released her, her panties were damp, her breathing was choppy and she considered tearing off her clothes so they could go at it, right there in the dirt.

She rested her face on his chest and heard his heart beating beneath her ear. His shirt was damp and she breathed in his scent.

"This changes things," he said softly, stroking her hair.

"I know. Did you ever imagine this would happen when you saved me from the evil banking empire two years ago?"

"No. But seeing you pushing that wheelbarrow the first day we arrived..."

She arched back to look at him. "I was wearing a skintight tank top and no bra that day."

"I noticed." Gavin grinned without shame. "Believe me, I've done my share of noticing lots of things about you."

Rielle couldn't keep from asking, "Like?"

"Like how sweet your ass looks in those cargo shorts you always wear."

"You're trying to make me blush." But she didn't want him to stop.

His gaze turned solemn. "No, I'm trying to tell you what's happening between us isn't just because it's convenient."

Relieved, happy—hell, she was giddy—Rielle rose to her toes and pecked him on the mouth. "Thank you for saying that, because that worried me too. The truth is, I like you. A whole lot. And what a bonus that you're an awesome kisser."

"I can't believe we're having this conversation in a beet field.

That's me, Mr. Romance."

She tugged on his shirt. "Speaking of...I have to get these roots out of the sun. Then I'll make lunch."

Gavin didn't complain for the next hour as they transferred the beets, sweet potatoes and celeriac to the root cellar.

"I had no idea this was here," he said, studying the earthen walls and rickety wooden stairs.

"That's sort of the point." Rielle clumped the beets together on a long table. "My parents weren't aware of the underground missile silos all around Wyoming before they moved here. The missile sites are gone now, but it was an issue for them, so they started building a bomb shelter."

"Seriously? Why?"

"What part of *hippie* is confusing to you?"

"I like that you can joke about it."

"What? The word hippie? Or the way I was raised?"

"Both. The word doesn't mean the same thing to me now as it did even two months ago." He wore a grimace as he handed her more beets. "You make me feel lazy and that's not something I'm used to. Usually I'm the hardest working person in the room. It boggles my mind, all the stuff you know how to do."

"It's not like I had formal schooling. It was haphazard at best. They taught me when they felt like it, what they felt like—never on any type of schedule. They preached the idea that real life lessons don't come from books. While I agree to some extent, they didn't understand how much I craved books and knowledge. My mother did a somewhat normal thing and took me to the library in Moorcroft. I devoured every type of book I could get my hands on. I would've given anything to have the regular kind of life I could only read about."

"And I would've given anything for my dad to teach me something useful, like how to use a hammer. Or change a tire."

"Isn't that human nature? To wish for something different than what we have?"

"Maybe." Gavin kissed the edge of her jaw, down the side of her neck and sucked the spot on her throat where her pulse pounded. "Right now I wish we were in a room with a bed."

"Too good for a bed of dirt, tycoon?" she teased.

"Not at all. But I'll need food for strength before I get started on all the dirty things I want to do with you."

She shivered. "Maybe we should take a lunch break now or we will end up doing it in the dirt."

Lunch was deer sausage on wheat rolls with sliced tomato and goat milk cheese, sweet potato chips and cantaloupe. Gavin ate like she'd served up a gourmet feast.

After he helped clean up the kitchen, he cornered her, bringing his body in line with hers, pressing her against the wall. "I do believe I was promised dessert with this lunch."

"If you'll give me a sec, I'll—"

"I know what I want. And I can't think of anything sweeter than your lips." He connected their mouths in a kiss so hot she wondered if she had blisters on her tongue after he released her.

Then he kissed the side of her neck, one hand gripping her short hair, the other curled around her hip.

Her eyes closed and she stopped second guessing why her body went haywire at Gavin's slightest touch. Her bones seemed to melt as his mouth tasted her skin and his thumb feathered across her belly above the waistband of her jeans.

"This is going to be dangerous," he murmured against her throat. "Now that we've started this, I don't know how I'll keep my hands off you."

"I don't want you to keep your hands off me." She slid her palms up his chest. "But we need to talk about it before Sierra gets here."

That gave Gavin's amorous attention pause.

Regretfully they both backed off.

"There's not much to talk about. We've kissed. I plan on kissing you a whole lot more. Will those kisses happen in front of my daughter? No. What happens between us isn't anyone else's business until we make it so."

"Agreed."

He crooked his finger at her and grinned. "So why're you standing so far away from me?"

"Because I heard a car come up the driveway."

"How is your hearing that good?"

"I've lived in the country forever and I am attuned to every nuance and change around me." She paused. "Or Sadie barked."

Gavin laughed softly. "I'll admit you were right. Being outside fixed my crappy state of mind. Thank you."

"You're welcome." She drained her water. "I'm heading back out."

"If this is your busiest time of year, why don't you hire seasonal help?"

Don't bristle. It's a legitimate question—one your friends ask you too. "Because it's expensive. And like your issues with your employees, I have the same problem. For them it's just a job. For me, it's my livelihood. What I earn in a three month period has to sustain me for the rest of the year. I'd rather be tired for a few weeks and know I did it right than trust someone else at this critical point and pay for it the rest of the year."

Gavin looked as if he wanted to say something but thought better of it.

Good. Gavin might be a whiz at running his business, but she didn't need his unsolicited advice on how to run hers. "I'd better head out and see who's here."

"You don't have set hours?"

"No nine to five for ranchers."

Chapter Ten

"Dad, Marin is here," Sierra yelled up the stairs.

"Don't forget I'm going to Quinn and Libby's for dinner."

"I know."

"You're still spending the night at Marin's?"

"Yes. God. You've already talked to her parents about it." How embarrassing. Who did stuff like that? "Can I go now?"

"Yes. But—"

Before she bounded out the door she vaguely heard him say her midnight curfew still applied and she had to clean her room tomorrow. She hopped into Marin's Chevy Blazer and threw her duffel bag in the backseat. "Thanks for picking me up." She could not wait until she could drive and didn't have to beg for rides.

"No problem. So you ready for your first Tri-County football game championship?"

"I guess. How is it different from any other high school football game?"

"There's tailgating. And cowboys fighting. It's awesome." Marin cranked the radio and belted out the words to some annoying country ditty. Then she looked over at Sierra. "I just love this song, don't you?"

"I'm not really a fan of country music."

Marin gasped. "Oh, Arizona, I'm gonna love getting you countrified." She scrutinized Sierra's outfit. "What's up with the parka?"

"It's freakin' cold here." Sierra paused, unsure. "Truth: do I look ridiculous?"

"Ah, *yeah*. It won't be that cold out tonight, so leave it in the truck. Plus what you're wearing is cute!"

Cute, but she'd freeze her ass off. She should've stashed a hoodie in her duffel bag. "Did you finish the English assignment?"

"Yep. I plan to write the report Sunday night. But we're not talking about homework tonight. We're gonna get wild."

Wild? Right. Wild for Marin meant using ketchup and ranch dressing on her fries. Not that Sierra didn't like her; she liked Marin a lot. They had fun together.

"So...you've been here for almost a whole quarter. You got your eye on any guy at school?"

Boone West's face popped into her mind. He was so unbelievably hot. Those smoky eyes. That hank of hair that fell just a little too far down his forehead. Sigh. That sweet and devilish smile. Not to mention his rocking body.

"Ah hah! I recognize that dreamy look," Marin accused. "Come on. Spill it. Who?"

Sierra's thing for Boone wasn't up for discussion. Not only because she didn't have a chance with him, but she'd die if Boone ever found out she was crushing on him. She hadn't told Marin about fixing lunch for Boone or how pervy she'd acted, peeking out the window, watching him work those muscles. "I saw this guy at the C-Mart the other day," she lied. "He was older. A total cowboy. He flirted with me a little and left before I asked his name."

"Shame. I'd like to know who he was so I could tell you all about him. Or tell you to avoid him."

That was another problem she'd discovered living in Sundance. Everybody seemed to know everybody else's business. "Maybe I'll get lucky and see him tonight."

"Cool. So it's your turn. Ask me who's been flirting with me nonstop since the last FFA meeting."

"Who?"

"Mitch Michaels!"

Sierra turned down the radio. "Seriously, Marin? You're just telling me this *now*?"

Marin bounced in her seat and squealed, "Yes! I mean, I don't know if it'll come to anything, but we're on the same sales team, selling raffle tickets for the quilt fundraiser."

"Think he'll be here tonight?"

"Maybe."

Hopefully Marin wasn't the type of friend to ditch her as soon as she hooked a guy. Sierra would *never* do that to a friend. Not that she'd ever had a real boyfriend. She'd kissed a few guys but none had been worth bringing home to her dad.

"What are we doing after?" Marin asked, tilting the rearview mirror so she could add a coat of lip gloss.

"Have you heard if anything is going on?"

"Dave Darling is having a party at his house. But he's charging ten bucks a head to cover the booze and you have to pay even if you don't drink." Marin didn't drink, but she didn't preach about it.

The parking area was packed and Marin ended up parking in the pasture across the road.

Welcome to Wyoming. What would her friends in Arizona say if they saw her now?

What friends? She hadn't heard much from anyone except a few random Facebook comments and texts.

Sierra shivered as they walked toward the stands. A huge crowd had gathered for the game. When Marin stopped to talk to her parent's friends about someone with terminal cancer, Sierra turned away and looked around.

That's when she saw him.

He stood beside the ambulance. Looking bored. Okay, looking awesome in his EMT uniform. But as she watched, she noticed he wasn't alone for long. A group of girls approached him. He smiled, flashing those dimples, but the girls didn't stick around. Then a group of cheerleaders from the rival high school sauntered up. Same routine: a quick smile, a fast chat and they were gone. When a couple of pretty, college aged women invaded his space, she expected he'd pay more attention to them, but he didn't act any differently.

Weird. Boone West could have his pick of any girls or women he wanted. So why did he look relieved when they left?

Then Marin dragged her to the school cheering section. They squeezed in behind the band, standing with some people from her class. Immediately after the national anthem was the kickoff. Marin clapped along with a crowd cheer. "The cheerleaders are so much better this year than last year. The new coach is whipping them into shape. I'm thinking of trying out for the squad."

"Who's the coach?"

"Some woman who used to live here and was a super-cheerleader in high school." Marin pointed. "That's her. The little dark-haired one with the clipboard."

Sierra squinted at the sidelines and saw a tall, dark-haired man beside the cheerleading coach. He seemed familiar. "Hey. I think I know him."

"Know him? Arizona, you're related to him. That's Tell McKay. He's your cousin."

"Am I related to every freakin' person in town?"

"Just about." Then Marin grinned. "But if the coach is doing your cousin, you'd totally get on the team, no problem and as your bestie you'd get me on too, right?"

"Right. Except I don't know the first thing about cheerleading."

"Last year? Neither did they."

Sierra laughed. But could she really see herself in a short skirt and a tight top, shaking pompoms and yelling at the crowd? Maybe. Might be fun. It'd beat sitting at home watching her dad watch football and yell at the TV.

Mitch Michaels showed up after halftime. He kept turning around to talk to Marin, so Sierra decided to leave them alone for a little while.

She ducked under the stands and cut to where the food vendors had set up. Next to the ambulance.

Don't do it. Don't try to talk to him. You saw how dismissive he was with all the others. He'll be dismissive with you too.

Her feet kept shuffling forward even as her head screamed *stop.* "Boone?"

His head snapped up and his eyes zoomed to her. "Hey, Sierra."

"So you do know my name."

"McKay fits you better."

Okay. This was good. Just keep talking. "How'd you get stuck working?"

"I volunteered for this shift. It's probably wrong for me to hope I get to see some action tonight." He rubbed his hands together. "A broken bone would be cool. Even a broken nose if it's gushing blood."

"Eww."

He laughed.

"So then do you get to set the bone or whatever?"

"Hell no." He jerked his head to the uniformed guy talking to an elderly woman. "He's the head EMT. I'm just the gopher, driver and the muscle if we have to load an injured person. The docs do all the real work. We just try to keep 'em alive on the ride to the hospital."

"Is it a rush, racing around, dealing with life or death situations?"

"It's a serious fuckin' rush."

"Is that why you do it?"

"Partially." Boone picked up his book and scooted over. "Sit down. Chill out for a bit. Unless you wanna get back to the game?"

She about lost the ability to breathe when he pinned her with that hooded brown-eyed gaze. "No." Then she was sitting thigh to thigh, arm to arm and shoulder to shoulder with Boone West.

Be cool. "What are you reading?"

Boone flipped the book over and showed her the cover.

She read, *"Mental Preparedness: Pushing Past Your Limits.* Not what I'd expected."

"Oh yeah? What did you think I'd be reading?"

His tone had gotten sharp. "I honestly had no idea since I don't know you. It could've been a carpentry or medical book. Maybe a manual on how to keep the family peace on a school bus."

Evidently that was the right answer because he smiled. "I forget you haven't been around forever to pass judgment on me."

"Who passes judgment on you?"

"Everyone. A few years back, I got into some trouble."

"Is that why Kyler made the crack about you being in the principal's office?"

"Probably. My dad pulled me up by the short hairs before the stupid shit I was doing became *dangerous* stupid shit. He said he wouldn't let his only kid go down that path and waste a promising life. He sent me to forestry camp for the entire summer. Straightened me out."

"Did you hate it?"

"No, I liked it. Part of the program was taking an aptitude test. I scored high on strategy. So I'm working my way down the reading list my counselor suggested." He paused and swigged from a bottle of water. "What about you?"

"What do I read? Nothing outside of assigned homework and even then only enough to pass my classes. Reading isn't really my thing."

"But I'll bet you read cookbooks," he pointed out. "Man. I still think about that sandwich."

So in a way he had been thinking about her. Cool. "Do you read only during slow times on your shift? Or do you read at home?"

"Most nights after I work I'm wiped out and I just go to bed. But my dad is home this weekend and he mentioned hanging out."

Didn't it just figure? There went her hope they'd run into each other at a party tonight after the football game.

"My dad never says, *stick around son, we're gonna drink beer and fix that piece of shit Mustang we've been working on for four years.* But last night he made a specific point of telling me to make myself available."

"What do you think that means?"

Boone shrugged. "Maybe old Dax wants to break it to me that he found himself a girlfriend."

"How old is your dad?"

"Really old. He just turned thirty-eight."

"Can you imagine having a kid right now like your dad did at your age?"

"Way to ruin my happy buzz." He raked his hand through his hair. "That'd be a freakin' nightmare."

"Tell me about it. There was this girl in my class last year who got pregnant and kept the baby. Rielle got pregnant at sixteen and kept her daughter. Then there's my Grams who gave my dad up for adoption. Seems like you're screwed no matter which option you choose."

"Sometimes I wonder if I'da been better off if my mom had done that. No doubt Dax would've been happy to be off the parenting hook. Maybe I would've ended up with rich adoptive parents like your dad did."

Took a second for that to sink in. Then she stood in front of him and glared. "That was a shitty thing to say. How would you like it if you'd been given up and found out years later that your biological parents ended up married anyway? Oh, then they had more kids together? But after my dad found out years later, he's come to this family to try and sort it out, where he's so obviously a McKay as you like to point out with me, but yet he isn't. He chose to face her choice every day instead of ignoring it and going about his...*rich man* business—which is just another thing you assume and that pisses me off because my dad earned what he has by working his ass off. So I know this situation has to bother him because it bothers me." With her angry eyes locked to his the cold seemed to hit her all at once and she began to shake.

"Hey." Boone's strong fingers circled her wrists, staying her retreat. "I'm sorry. I wasn't thinking and I just said the first stupid thing that popped into my head."

Her gaze dropped to his mouth. Lips that full should look girly, but didn't on him. Yet she couldn't help but think, pretty mouth; not so pretty words spilling from it.

"Sierra?"

"What?" she snapped.

"Don't be pissed off at me."

"Don't expect me to forgive you for that total dick comment."

Boone tugged her closer until the outsides of her legs were wedged between his knees. "You so mad you're shaking?"

"Maybe." Sierra could feel his body heat, but it didn't warm her; it caused her to shiver again.

"I *am* sorry."

She looked at him and saw real remorse in his eyes. "I can see that now."

"Good." His fingers slid down and he clasped her small hands in his larger ones. He frowned. "You're not mad. You're freezing." His assessing gaze moved across her upper torso. "Where's your coat?"

I left it in the truck so I didn't make a bad fashion statement. Like she'd admit that to responsible Mr. EMT. "Uh. I forgot it."

"Christ. Don't you know how fast it gets cold here?" Boone released her hands and shrugged out of his flannel-lined corduroy jacket. Then he draped it around her shoulders, pulling it around her arms and chest. "Better?"

Sierra stared at him, resisting the urge to sniff the inside collar of his jacket, where his scent was the strongest. "Thanks."

Then he gently freed her hair from beneath the collar. Nothing about his movements was flirtatious, but her heart raced when his fingers brushed her skin. Especially when his hands smoothed her hair back from her face, slowly, from her scalp to the ends that stopped above the jacket pockets covering her breasts. "You warming up?"

She was practically hot now. Mostly in the face. "Yeah. I'll give it back before I go."

He waved her off. "Keep it. I've got another one in the cab. I'll swing by and pick it up sometime." He grinned. "Maybe you can fix me lunch again."

"Okay."

"I'm glad you came over to talk to me. You're different than the girls around here."

She blinked at him.

"I recognize that have-I-just-been-insulted? look. I definitely meant that as a compliment. I've had more real conversations with you in the last few months than I've ever had with anyone else in this town."

Sierra did a mental fist pump, but managed a droll, "Cool. I suspected you only wanted to hang with me to give your uncles the middle finger for being friends with a McKay."

He laughed. "Nope. I like you despite your family heritage. You're funny. You don't bullshit me. You don't try that fake come-on crap." His voice rose an octave. *"Oh Boone, you're an EMT? I'll play doctor with you anytime."* He rolled his eyes. "Lame, huh?"

"Really lame." Good thing she hadn't said it, because she'd definitely been thinking it.

"West! We've got an injury, let's go!" the other EMT shouted.

Boone's boots hit the dirt. "See you around, McKay." And he was gone.

Back in the stands, Marin was so enamored with Mitch she didn't even notice that Sierra had returned, wearing a borrowed jacket. Not that she'd tell her friend where she got it. Some secrets were just too good to share with anyone.

Chapter Eleven

"Rielle!"

Gavin winced. Why couldn't Sierra walk downstairs instead of yelling down the stairs? He should install an intercom system.

"What?" Rielle yelled back.

Then again, these two didn't need one.

"Come up and watch a movie with us. I made popcorn."

"Be right there."

Sierra gave him a smug look. "It's on."

"Don't be so cocky," he warned. "I still say she won't want to watch the movie you picked."

"We'll see, won't we?" She ripped open the bags of microwave popcorn and filled two bowls.

Rielle walked in. "Hey guys."

Gavin pretended not to notice how the V-cut of her T-shirt made her breasts look completely lickable. Or that her cargo shorts were too baggy and hung low on her hips, providing a peek of her flat belly. Or that her smile seemed to light up the whole damn room.

She frowned at the windows. "I don't know if I'll ever get used to those blinds. Makes it dark as a cave up here."

"Which is perfect for watching movies," Sierra said. "You've got two choices."

"Why do I get to pick?" She looked at Gavin. "And isn't Sunday night sacred football night?" His love of sports baffled her.

"I set the DVR to watch it later."

Sierra handed Rielle a bowl of popcorn. "Dad and I can't agree on one."

"What are the choices?"

"*Ten Things I Hate About You* or *Seabiscuit*."

"Definitely the one with Heath Ledger."

Sierra did a little happy dance. "Told ya. And I want cherry."

Rielle's gaze winged between them. "What'd I miss?"

"We bet on which one you'd choose. *Seabiscuit* was Dad's idea. It's the best movie in the history of movies—according to him—and he's always trying to get me to watch it."

"Only because you've never made it through the whole thing so you can't know how great it is."

"That's because it puts me to sleep." Sierra stretched out on the loveseat and asked Rielle, "Have you seen it?"

"No. I fell asleep too. But Heath Ledger definitely keeps me awake."

Gavin put the disc into the DVD player. He turned around. Sierra had snatched the remote. "Where's my popcorn?"

"You're sharing with Rielle."

He'd be suspicious his daughter suspected something was going between him and Rielle if he didn't know how selfish Sierra was about her popcorn.

Rielle already had her feet on the coffee table.

He dropped beside her so they were hip to hip. He stretched his left arm across the back of the couch and grabbed a handful of popcorn.

"Your new furniture is comfy," Rielle said.

"I must've sat on two dozen sofas until I found this one. It's a little bland bachelor-ish as the fashionista pointed out, but comfort is more important than style."

"Definitely plenty of room for guests."

"Not if we invite all the McKays," Sierra said.

Rielle laughed.

So while she watched the movie, Gavin covertly watched her. The curve of her smile. The way she grabbed a handful of popcorn, then ate it delicately—a kernel at a time. He liked that she gradually snuggled closer to him. Not in an obvious lover's clinch that would raise Sierra's eyebrows.

When her eyes started to droop, he didn't jostle her awake. He let her sleep so he could watch her without guilt.

He brushed loose strands of her hair back. His gaze encompassed her face, from the frown lines between her eyebrows even in sleep, to the smattering of freckles across her nose, to her fantasy-invoking lips.

It was only a matter of the right timing until they became lovers. The spark between them had burned a little hotter every time they were together. As much as Gavin wanted that explosion, he was a patient man.

Rielle opened her eyes and blinked sleepily. "Sorry for crashing on you. Guess I was more tired than I thought."

"Sierra conked out too. You'd think we were watching *Seabiscuit.*"

She smiled and her gaze cut to Sierra sprawled on the couch. Then she tried to squirm away, but Gavin held her in place.

"No worries. She's snoring." Gavin kept stroking her cheek, gauging her reaction.

"What are you doing?" she whispered.

"Nothing. Yet. But I can think of a whole lot of things I'd like to do with you." He caressed her face. "So pretty."

Rielle blushed. "You don't have to say that."

"But it's true." His eyes searched hers, hating to see such wariness. "Why don't you believe it?"

"Because guys never say stuff like that to me. Even casually. Or jokingly."

"I'm not joking. I'm not the guy who only compliments a pretty woman because I want to get into her pants."

"So you're not a player like the rest of the McKays?"

Gavin wanted to laugh. If she only knew he spent more time on the bench than in the game. "I've been here two months. Have you seen me with a woman or five?"

She shook her head.

"That's because I'm not that guy."

"I'm glad."

He moved his hand down to outline those lush lips. "Goddamn your mouth drives me crazy." He leaned closer, intending to kiss her.

"Gavin, we shouldn't."

"But we're going to anyway. Close your eyes."

She looked unsure for a moment and then she lowered her eyelids, her long eyelashes dark against her skin.

Gavin breathed a sigh of relief that she hadn't balked. Since he wasn't any kind of lady killer lothario, he was completely winging it with her. Apparently she liked when he took charge.

He teased her mouth, using his lips to nibble on hers. Drawing his tongue across the seam of her velvety lips, feeling the edge of her teeth and the quick dart of her tongue.

Rielle opened wider on a soft moan, and Gavin dove into the wet warmth of her mouth. Immediately the kiss caught fire. She arched up to meet his plundering tongue, her breasts mashed to his chest. He pinned her right arm above her head and his hand drifted down to the outside of her breast. He caressed the generous swell, each stroke getting closer to her nipple.

At this angle his cock pressed painfully against his zipper. Gavin shifted slightly, cupping her whole tit in his hand. He broke the kiss, scattering tiny biting kisses to her ear. He murmured, "I have to stop or I won't be able to."

"I know." Her hand brushed his scalp, sweetly, tenderly and then she pushed him away and sat up.

Their gazes connected. She smiled. "Heck of a goodnight kiss, Gavin."

"Wish it could be more."

"Me too." She stood and stopped in front of Sierra. She gently pried the popcorn bowl out of her hand and set it on the coffee table.

She pulled the edge of the blanket off the floor and draped it over her feet. Then she quietly disappeared down the stairs.

He remained there, not watching TV, just thinking about Rielle's sweetness and fire. A potent combination. And he'd started to realize he wasn't such a patient man after all.

Gavin had been expecting Vi Tuesday afternoon, but the doorbell chiming like the clang of a dinner bell startled him.

He opened the door and saw she held a big box. He immediately took it from her. "I could've carried this in for you. There's fresh coffee in the kitchen."

She unbuttoned her wool coat and unwound a vibrant scarf. "It is so damp out today. Coffee sounds heavenly."

After he dumped the box in the dining room, he saw Vi sitting at the breakfast bar, poking buttons on her cell phone.

The glob of dough on the marble countertop hadn't magically transformed itself into pie crust. He grabbed the rolling pin, determined to get the damn crust to roll out evenly before his snarky daughter returned home.

When the rolling pin squeaked, Vi glanced up and scrutinized the mess. "You're making a pie?" she asked with surprise.

"*Attempting* to make a pie is more like it."

"Why?"

"I lost a bet. Sierra challenged me to bake a pie and I had to swear that I wouldn't get Rielle to help me."

She drummed her fingers on the counter. "What kind of pie?"

"Cherry. I don't have to make the filling from scratch. I'm having a hard enough time with the crust. The dough is sticky."

"It gets that way after it's been at room temperature for a while."

"So it's not necessarily my bad technique?"

She laughed. "No. Throw it in the freezer for a few minutes and it'll be fine."

"Thanks." When Gavin turned around, Vi was giving him a thorough inspection. "Do I have flour all over my clothes or something?"

"No. Sorry. It's just...we've never been in the kitchen together like this and I wondered if your...if Grace taught you to cook."

"Not really. I learned in a helluva hurry when my ex wouldn't touch the stove and Sierra's first word was McDonald's. Did you teach your sons to cook?"

"I cooked for the all the boys growing up. I figured their wives would cook for them after they got married. That worked for Quinn since he and Libby tied the knot pretty young. Chase...I suspect he ate fast food all the time he was on the road. Now he and Ava have a personal chef, which boggles my mind." Vi fussed with her ruffled shirtsleeves. "However Ben is a good cook. He grills a mean steak. Sad to say he didn't learn that from me. I tend to char meat to the point it's inedible if I cook it over an open flame."

"Same here." Gavin removed the dough from the freezer. He reached for the rolling pin, trying not to feel self-conscious that Vi—who was probably a blue-ribbon-winning pie maker—scrutinized his every clumsy move. When the dough gummed up yet again, he was tempted to whip the blob into the sink and flip on the garbage disposal, conceding defeat.

"Gavin, would you be offended if I offered to help you?"

"God no. I'd be grateful. And Sierra only said *Rielle* couldn't help me, so that leaves us both in the clear."

Vi snorted and pushed up her sleeves. After she washed her hands, she tackled the dough like a pastry chef, expertly rolling out two perfect dough circles. "Is the filling ready?" She peered over the tops of purple zebra print eyeglasses. "I assume Little Miss wants a double crust pie?"

Little Miss was an apt description. "Yes, although technically, I think that should count as two pies."

She snickered and transferred the dough into the pie tin.

Gavin opened a can of cherry pie filling. Before he dumped it into the shell, Vi placed a hand on his arm. "You know what would jazz that up? Almond flavoring. I'll bet there's almond liquor in the bar."

He returned to the kitchen with a bottle of amaretto. She handed him a measuring cup and he stirred the liquor into the pie filling, then spooned the mixture into the pie shell and slid the pie tin across the counter.

He found her pie-making skills fascinating. His mother had never baked. Vi stretched the dough over the top, slicing away the extra and pinching the edges together. She brushed egg wash over the dough and cut three long slits in the top before popping it in the oven. "I know I'm not supposed to covet things, but I really want an oven like this. And as long as I'm making confessions, I haven't made my own piecrust in years. I buy the frozen ones. No one knows the difference."

Gavin grinned. "Your secret is safe with me."

Vi arranged the extra scraps of dough on a cookie sheet and sprinkled cinnamon and sugar on each piece. "This will make a good afterschool snack. I know Sierra doesn't need the information for her history project for a while, but I thought I'd bring it over early. If she wants more information on the McKays, she can ask Carson and Carolyn. They have all the family archives, dating back to when the McKays bought the first piece of land in Wyoming in the late eighteen hundreds."

His eyebrows rose. "The McKays have been here that long?"

"Yep. The McKay ranch is one of the oldest working ranches in Wyoming. Of course, the original land is a tiny cow pasture compared to what they own now."

He and Sierra shared the same love of history. She'd been itching to get her hands on documented family history. "I'm sure Sierra will be in touch if she has any questions."

"There wasn't a whole lot to give her on the Bennett side. We moved a lot and my father was very clear on the evils of material goods because you couldn't take them to heaven."

"I remember you mentioned your father was a preacher."

"He preferred the term *man of God.*"

"Sounds like you had a rough upbringing."

"I did."

"I'd like to hear about it." That wasn't so hard to admit.

"Well, then I'll need something stronger than coffee to have this conversation." She poured a shot of amaretto into her coffee cup. "Elmore Bennett was a Baptist minister. We didn't travel to exotic locales spreading the word of God—although Wyoming seemed exotic after living in the South. My father was a difficult man." She tossed the booze back. "Correction. My father was a pious man, but verbally abusive. He utilized the fire, brimstone and punishment part of religious teachings to keep us in line."

"What was your mother like?"

"The perfect preacher's wife. I don't think she had a thought in her head except for the ones my father put there. She loved me and my brother and sister, but she'd always save her own skin first when it came to dealing with my father."

"I take it he's dead?"

"They both are. Daddy died of a heart attack when Quinn was two. Mama lived with her sister in Mississippi after that. She wasn't in good health. I went to her funeral when Chase was a baby. I haven't seen my siblings since. I'm the black sheep of the family."

Hard to believe. Vi McKay looked like a sweet-faced grandma, but there was an aura of tension surrounding her. A tension that Gavin suspected had a lot to do with him. "Why are you the black sheep?"

"I was a young, unwed teenage mother who gave her baby up for adoption. I turned my back on the church I was raised in. Then I married a man my father hated." She waggled the empty glass. "And I like to drink. It's taken me years to learn to deal with much of this stuff. But some of it...I'll never come to terms with it."

Ask her. Here's your chance to get answers to all the shit that's been bothering you since you found out the truth about your birth parents.

But he couldn't force the words past his tightly closed lips.

"I don't want to make you uncomfortable, Gavin, but I'm so happy you're here. And I won't push for more than you're willing to offer. I just...thought you should know."

"I appreciate it, Vi. This is still overwhelming for me."

"I imagine it is." Vi smiled sadly and slid from the chair. "On that note, the rest of the McKays are asking about you and Sierra. Now that you're settled in, would you consider hosting a get together?"

"I don't know...that's not really my thing."

"I understand. But it's something to think about. You could have them all over here for a few hours and be done with it. Now I need to get home. I have an urge to bake Charlie a pie."

"I hate this class."

Gavin glanced up from *Kiplinger's* magazine and looked at Sierra, sitting at the dining room table with papers spread out. Strange to see her there. She always did her homework in her room, music blasting from behind the closed door. "Which class?"

"Anatomy. Why do we have to memorize all the stupid muscle groups? It's not like I plan to be a doctor or anything."

"Anything I can do to help?"

Sierra puckered her lips with distaste. "Not unless you wanna take the test for me."

"Sorry, sweetheart. There's no way I'm prancing around pretending to be you, wearing sweatpants with *Juicy* written across the ass."

"Ooh. You said ass. I remember when you never swore around me."

"I'd be happy if cussing was the only bad habit you pick up from your parents."

"True." Sierra tapped her pencil on her notebook. "Have you heard from Mom?"

Speaking of someone with bad habits... "No. Have you?"

"Yeah. She called me at like three in the morning. Said she 'forgot' about the time difference."

Gavin waited for her to continue, understanding why she'd chosen to study outside her room.

"That's such a load of bull," she sneered. "She just doesn't care about anybody's life but hers."

"What did she have to say?"

The pencil tapping grew louder but she didn't look at him. "I don't remember. I was pretty groggy."

This was the worst part of having a teenage daughter: not knowing when to push her to talk or when to ease off and wait until she was ready to talk. He'd given up predicting which approach worked better, because her responses were always mood dependent.

He slowly flipped through the magazine pages, not really seeing the text.

Sierra slammed her notebook down. "Do you know she didn't ask me anything about how I liked living here? No questions about school, or if I have friends, or if I'm driving. Nothing. She went on and on about how *fantastique* Paris is. How fluent she's becoming. How she spends the days soaking up culture and the nights hitting the hottest clubs and restaurants with Vince." She pulled her knees up, wrapping her arms around her calves as she curled into a ball. "I hate her."

Gavin moved to sit beside her, ignoring her closed off vibe, and gently rubbed her back. "You don't mean that."

"No, I don't. It's just...she's so selfish."

He bit back the comment *like that's news*, and continued soothing her with the same soft touch he always used.

Several long moments passed before she spoke again. "And wanna know what I really hate? That I know sometimes I act just like her. No wonder I'm not making friends at school."

Another prickly situation. Sierra became defensive when he offered suggestions or even tried to talk to her about her problem making friends. He didn't understand why it'd always been so hard for her.

She shivered. "I don't want to be like her. Ever."

"You won't be. I won't *let* you be."

She raised her head and looked at him. "Promise?"

"I promise. But understand that you might not like my methods of ensuring that won't happen."

"Someone's gotta be the taskmaster hardass in our family." She kissed his cheek. "Thanks, Dad."

"No problem. So I came up with a surefire way for you to learn your anatomy terms."

A horrified look crossed her face. "No. *No way.* Don't even say it."

He grinned and waggled his eyebrows. "Flashcards."

"Dad!"

"I'm serious. Making a set of flashcards will help you."

"I am not in third grade trying to memorize my multiplication tables," she retorted.

"True." He tugged on her hair. "But it worked. And it worked when you had to memorize all the state capitals. And it worked when you had to memorize musical terms. It's a tried and true method."

Sierra sighed. "Fine. But I don't have any index cards. And I doubt the stores in Sundance are open."

"They do roll up the sidewalks early." He stood. "I'd bet Rielle has recipe cards. I'll go ask her."

Rielle scrambled away from the swinging door. She hadn't meant to eavesdrop. She'd been heading to her bedroom and stopped outside the door when she heard Sierra talking about her mom and hadn't wanted to interrupt.

Gavin strode in, lost in thought. But his focus changed the instant he set eyes on her. "Just the woman I was looking for."

"What can I do for you?"

"This first." He crowded her, bent his head and kissed her in that sure and steady way of his. And just like every other time he'd kissed her, her stomach bottomed out.

How long before these randomly stolen kisses pushed them to the next level?

Almost as if he'd read her mind, his mouth drifted over her ear and he whispered, "Soon."

"Like how soon? Because I'm not busy right now." She sank her teeth into his earlobe.

Gavin groaned softly. "If my daughter wasn't sitting in the other room, I'd take you up on that." Another whisper-soft kiss across her ear. "I've started carrying a condom in my pocket, just in case."

"Better put one in each pocket." Rielle gently pushed him back. "Was there something you needed?"

"Ah. Yeah." He scrubbed his hands over his face as if he was trying to remember. Good to see she wasn't the only one sexually frustrated. "Oh. Right. Do you have extra blank recipe cards we can use?"

"I'm sure I do." She grabbed her recipe file box from the pantry, rummaging through the mishmash of papers until she found an unopened pack of plain index cards. "Here you go."

"Thanks. You're a lifesaver."

"Happy to help. If you don't need anything else, I think I'll head to bed."

Gavin set his hands on her shoulders. "You mad at me?"

"No. I'm just..." *Horny. Which is a totally foreign feeling.* "Antsy."

"Me too. But I don't want to rush this, Rielle. With the construction guys around during the day I get interrupted, or you get interrupted by your customers, or Sierra is under foot and we're hardly ever alone. Might sound corny, but I don't want anyone around or any distractions the first time we're together. I want it to be just you and me. Completely focused on each other."

This man was too good to be true. But had he come up with those parameters because he could tell how skittish she was? How little experience she had?

He stroked the side of her cheek. "You okay with that?"

"Very okay." She lightly pecked him on the mouth. "See you in the morning."

Chapter Twelve

"So Vi suggested something to me yesterday and I immediately dismissed it." Gavin refilled Rielle's cup and Sierra's before topping off his. The kid had kicked her addiction to Starbucks, but she was still a morning caffeine junkie. "But then I got to thinking about it and I realized it's not a bad idea."

"What was her suggestion?"

"That I have a family housewarming party." He knocked back a slug of coffee. "Here."

Rielle's hands tightened around her mug. "When?"

"I think we should get it out of the way tomorrow night."

"Tomorrow night?" Sierra repeated.

"Yeah, why? Is there something else going on?"

She paused. Opened her mouth. Closed it. Then shook her head.

"And get this—Vi believes I ought to invite all the McKays."

"All the McKays?" Rielle repeated. "At one time?"

Sierra snickered.

"What's so funny?"

"The look on Rielle's face as she's thinking about Ky, Anton and Hayden playing football in the living room."

Gavin scowled at her. So much for his daughter backing his play.

"This is your house. If you want to have a party, have a party. But I will remove all my breakables out of the great room and any other areas the wild McKay clan might vandalize."

Vandalize? That was a harsh assessment.

"Will this be a potluck?" Sierra asked.

"Hell if I know." He looked hopefully at Rielle.

She threw up her hands. "No way. I don't want any part of this party."

"I'll help you, Dad. I'm sure Vi will pitch in and bring food since it was her idea. We'll just have munchies and drinks. Paper plates, plastic cups, easy stuff. Pick me up after school today and we'll hit Wal-Mart in Spearfish."

Why was Sierra being so helpful?

Stop looking for motives. You should be overjoyed she's pitching in and wants to be around her family.

"Sounds like a plan." He glanced at the clock. "Better get your stuff. It's about time to leave."

As soon as Sierra was out of the kitchen, he leaned closer to Rielle. "I'll help you move anything you want out of the great room. And I'll try to keep everyone in the kitchen and dining room."

"That's...thoughtful. Thank you. But if it's all the same, I won't stick around tomorrow night."

Gavin laid his hand on the side of her face. "I'd like it if you'd stay. Not to keep the appetizers supplied, or pour drinks, or even to run herd on unruly McKay munchkins."

"Then why?"

"Honestly? Because I'm related to the McKays, but you know them way better than I do. I'll probably need you to prompt me on some names." *Such a lie. Why don't you tell her the truth?*

"So I'd be a crutch."

His gaze fell to her mouth. The woman had the most enticing lips. He adjusted his hand and his thumb followed the swell of her lower lip. "Fuck. I want to take you to bed in the worst way."

Rielle shivered delicately.

The sound of heavy equipment rattling up the drive broke the moment.

Gavin retreated. Or tried to. Rielle wrapped her fingers around his wrist, holding his hand in place.

"I asked you a question. If I stay for the party tomorrow night, will I just be a crutch for you?"

"No. You'd be a lifeline."

Rielle offered him a shy smile and pressed a soft kiss to the base of his thumb before she released his hand. "Then I'll stay."

Sierra yelled, "Dad! *Come on.* I'm gonna be late."

Gavin kissed Rielle hard. "Later."

What the fuck had he been thinking, having a fucking party?

There were approximately ten billion people in his house and the majority of them were less than two feet tall. And yelling. Or crying. Or doing both.

In the kitchen, Vi sidled up with another veggie plate. "Scoot a cheek, son, so I can put these down."

"Sorry. Have you seen my co-host?"

"Rielle?"

I wish. "No, Sierra."

"Last time I saw her, she was looking for Keely." Vi tugged him down and whispered, "Maybe you'd better track her down. Who knows what kind of wild ideas Keely is putting in her head. That girl was hell on bootheels from the time she was two years old."

"Thanks for the tip. Can you keep an eye on this for a few minutes?"

"It'd be my pleasure." She smiled at Ben and Ainsley. "Look at all this food! Isn't it great Gavin and Sierra did this all themselves?"

Ben caught his eye and mouthed, "Run."

Just inside the dining room, something smacked into Gavin's leg. And held on. The dark-haired boy looked up at him and grinned.

Jesus. All these kids looked the same. He couldn't remember this kid's name. "Ah, hey there, little guy. Thanks for the hug, but you gotta let go now."

The kid didn't budge. He grinned wider and held tighter.

Gavin figured if he started walking the rugrat would slide off.

No such luck. This kid had an iron grip. Like a bull rider. Had to be one of Colby's sons.

Maybe he could bribe him. "I'll give you candy if you let me go."

He shook his head, wiping his wet mouth on Gavin's jeans.

"Beau," a male voice said sharply. "Let him go."

The kid dropped his arms, looked up at Gavin and said, "Now gimme candy."

"What? No way."

Cord scooped the boy up, cocking him on his hip. "Sorry. He's a little ornery tonight."

Ya think?

Cord's focus dropped to the wet spot on Gavin's knee. "Did he bite you?"

Bite him? What the hell? "No."

"Good. This one's a biter, much to his mama's dismay."

Gavin had no idea what to say to that.

"Anyway, AJ wanted me to relay her thanks for the invite and she's sorry she couldn't make it tonight."

"Is everything all right?"

"It will be when she has the baby. I wanted to tell you to swing by for a beer sometime. Our door is always open and if you need anything, just holler."

"Thanks, Cord. I appreciate it."

He skirted two girls chasing each other and a third twirling in place like a ballerina. He saw Dalton, leaning against the wall, a baby cradled in his arms while Brandt and Jessie were eating.

Dalton smiled. "Great party, cuz."

"Thanks. Glad you could make it. Where are Tell and Georgia?"

Jessie answered, "Cheerleading tryouts for winter sports are at the school tonight. And of course Tell had to go and help, since he and Georgia are joined at the hip."

"Tonight?" Vi said from behind him.

He turned around. Why was she following him everywhere? Then he saw her wiping down the opposite end of the table.

Don't be an ass. She's just being helpful.

"I thought Sierra wanted to try out for cheerleading," Vi said.

That surprised Gavin. Sierra hadn't even mentioned it.

"It's too bad," Jessie said. "Georgia would've loved to have her on the squad."

Why hadn't his daughter said something? Did she think he'd say no? Just another reason he needed to track her down. Before he made it to the hallway, he was stopped five times. Once by Colby, who said pretty much the same thing Cord had. Ditto for Kane and Kade. Colt managed to repeat the offer before the girl child in his arms screamed like a banshee and he hot-footed it outside.

His gaze swept the great room where the McKay wives were clustered with still more kids. Libby winked at him and he smiled back. He'd gotten to know her a little better in the last few months and she was such a sweetheart.

Carson and Carolyn each had their hands full with a dark-haired grandchild, but Carson invited him over to skeet shoot, which was unexpected. Calvin called out to Carson and he wandered away.

Gavin must've looked overwhelmed because Carolyn reached over and rubbed his arm.

"You didn't know what you were in for with this bunch, did you?"

"Not really. The McKays are...a fertile lot."

She laughed. "And a loud lot. Just think, Cam and Domini aren't here with their six kids. Neither are Carter and Macie and their four kids."

"You have ten *more* grandkids?"

Carolyn kissed the sleepy, dark-haired girl's head. "Yes, we are very blessed. And we all feel the same way about you, Gavin. Blessed to have you as part of the family."

"Thanks. Have you seen Keely? I heard she was with Sierra."

"No." She scanned the room. "Hmm. I don't see Jack either. Those two probably snuck off somewhere. They're trying to have a baby and I swear Keely wants bragging rights that she got knocked up in the bathroom or something."

That was pretty...intimate stuff to share.

Carolyn chuckled. "My wild-child daughter loves to shock her father, her brothers and her cousins with that type of information, so I thought I'd forewarn you."

"Good to know. If you'll excuse me, I've got to find my daughter."

He walked past the guest bath and saw two boys filling squirt guns. He shook his head. "Take 'em outside."

"Told ya, Gib."

Gib. Colby's oldest. Since the boy in the mirror looked nearly identical, they had to be brothers. When another, smaller boy leaped out from behind the shower curtain with a loud, "Rawr!" Gavin jumped.

The boys broke into bouts of gut-holding laughter.

Then Gavin heard Sierra's laugh and he spied her at the end of the hallway chatting with Keely. He did a double take. Seeing them standing so close together the family resemblance was a little spooky. Same height, same dark hair, same build. Same sort of scheming smile.

Lord help him. So far boys hadn't started sniffing around his daughter, which made him wonder what the hell was wrong with boys these days because she was a beautiful girl; yet, he was damn happy she wasn't boy crazy like so many girls her age.

"Hey, sweetheart, did you forget you were my co-pilot for tonight's festivities?"

"It looked like everyone had gone through the food line."

"Vi is in the kitchen restocking everything. Go help her."

Sierra sighed. "Fine. See ya, Keely."

As soon as Sierra was out of sight, Keely said, "Shit. That was close." She opened the door to the spare bedroom and her husband Jack leaned against the wall just inside the doorway.

Jack's hair was a mess, his shirt was unbuttoned, his belt was buckled but his fly was undone. And he didn't seem a bit concerned that Gavin saw his state of undress.

"Sorry." She gave Gavin a sheepish look. "We, um, *borrowed* your room for a few minutes. Sierra was coming out of that room the same time I came out of this one. So I thought it'd be best if Jack stayed hidden."

So they had snuck off for a quickie. In the midst of all this chaos? In a house filled with family members?

Yeah, Gavin planned to keep Sierra far, far away from Keely.

Keely was already focused on Jack, smoothing the wrinkles from his shirt. "GQ, we have to straighten you up before you go out there. You look like you've been rolling around in bed."

"Or more accurately, on the floor." Jack made a low noise and wrapped his hand around the back of Keely's neck, pulling her closer. "Since I'm half-dressed...it's your wifely duty to get back in here and make sure I don't miss any buttons."

"But we already—"

"That one was for you. This one? For me." She squeaked when he tugged her into the room.

The last thing Gavin heard: "Lock the damn door, cowgirl."

At least someone was getting laid in this place.

He shot a look at Rielle's closed door. He knocked. No answer. He started back down the hallway. When he reached the entryway, Quinn walked in through the front door.

"Hey. I wondered what happened to you."

"Just enjoying the fresh air. You look like you could use some." Quinn smiled. "Dad—Charlie—is outside. I was getting him a beer."

"I'll take it to him."

Quinn reached into the cooler and pulled out a Miller Lite. "Have at. Better see if Libby needs my help with the kids anyway."

Gavin grabbed another beer and stepped onto the porch. He took a second to breathe in the cool night air and take in the blessed quiet. He saw Charlie sitting on the steps and walked over, dropping beside him. "Miller Lite, right?"

"Gavin." Charlie didn't hide his surprise. "Wasn't expecting you." He quickly added, "But I'm glad you have time for a beer."

"I needed a break. I left the kitchen in Vi's capable hands."

Charlie twisted the top on his beer bottle. "She's in her element. Thanks for asking her to help. It means more than you know."

"Help? Hell, it was her idea."

He chuckled. "I ain't surprised to hear that. So how're the West boys comin' with the garage? I couldn't see much of it in the dark tonight."

"They do great work, but they had to stop for several weeks and finish another project. It's almost done. You should swing by during the day and check it out. They don't mind having people around."

"I'll do that. I guess my question is do you mind havin' me around?"

Gavin released a slow breath. "I'll admit even after being here a while I don't know how this living close to family thing works. What are the parameters? Do you just drop by Quinn and Libby's? And Ben and Ainsley's?"

"We used to. Not so much anymore. We call first." He took another pull off his beer. "Vi...God love the woman, but she overstepped her bounds with Quinn and Libby from the moment they got married. Things went south for them for a while and they ended up mending fences. Quinn warned his mom to butt out. Then she made a pledge to all the boys she wouldn't try to control them, or guilt them, or nag them. And she's even stuck with that promise—for the most part."

"I remember the first time I showed up here and Vi said that situation with Quinn and Libby was a wakeup call for her?"

He nodded. "Vi had one of those moments where every damn thing you've done wrong just smacks you square in the face. That's when she finally told me about you."

Gavin didn't have the balls to ask if Charlie felt what Vi had done—giving him up for adoption—was wrong. Because one thing he'd noticed about Charlie? The man had fierce loyalty. If he disagreed with his wife, he never said so in public. He held Vi in the highest regard. Whereas Gavin's father, Dan, was the complete opposite. While a shrewd businessman, he made a lousy husband, and Gavin's mother had turned a blind eye to her husband's many affairs.

"I ain't gonna pretend I wasn't mad. I was mad as hell. And don't take this the wrong way, but my anger was directed at her—not that she'd given a baby up for adoption, but that it'd taken her so damn long to tell me about it."

"Would it have made a difference if she'd told you ten years earlier? Twenty years earlier?"

"I can't answer that. Sweet baby Jesus her father was a mean bastard, so I never doubted for a second that shaming her into an unwed mother's home was solely his doing." Charlie tipped his bottle up and drank. "I argued with her for even wanting to name our second son Bennett because I didn't want anything to do with that SOB." He sighed. "Sorry. I've started doin' that old man rambling thing. I'm sure this had a point, but I'll be damned if I remember what it was."

"I asked about your family policy on drop-ins."

"Ah. Policy. Well, remember that I ranched with Quinn and Ben, so we were at each other's places every day. Chase hasn't lived around here for any length of time since he started ridin' bulls. This thing with you...is a new situation for us. We don't wanna crowd you, but you oughta know that we both consider it nothin' short of a miracle that you're even here, livin' a few miles up the road from us. It's more than we ever had hoped for."

"I fear the reality won't match up to the hype."

"You mean living in Wyoming? Or living around family?"

Both. Neither. "I don't know what I mean. I appear to be rambling too." He changed the subject. "The driving lessons with Sierra are going well?"

Charlie smiled. "I'll admit it's a lot different teaching a girl to drive. I don't recall that I ever taught the boys much. They just seemed to know it. She's eager to learn, that's for damn sure."

"She listens to you?"

"Mostly. The girl does ask a lot of questions. And she likes to talk."

"Bet that's a different experience."

Charlie looked at him. "'Cause Quinn is quiet?"

"Ben is too, for the most part, unless it's one on one."

"Guess we all feel there's no reason to waste air sayin' something that don't need to be said."

The door slammed and half a dozen kids raced out.

Adam climbed onto Charlie's lap. "Bet your daddy doesn't know you're out here." Charlie looked at Gavin. "This boy wears his shoes out he's constantly on the go, aren't you, buddy?"

"Gampa, I hungry."

"Grama's probably got some cookies with your name on 'em, though I suspect your mama would rather have you eatin' carrots."

"Cookies!"

The door slammed again and Quinn clomped down the steps. "Adam, what'd I tell you about running off?"

The boy started to cry and wouldn't let go of Charlie.

Gavin took that as his cue to leave. He was completely off balance anyway, in unfamiliar territory on so many levels. He needed something familiar to hold onto. And Rielle was the first thing that came to mind.

Where the devil was she? He hadn't seen her for at least an hour. No one waylaid him when he checked her room. No sign of her. He scoped out the ladies sitting and chatting in the great room. She wasn't here either.

Ainsley was in conversation with Libby so Rielle hadn't snuck off with her partner in crime for a drink. She wasn't helping Vi and Sierra in the kitchen, although it must've driven her crazy leaving it to chaos.

Chaos. As someone used to solitude, she'd want to go someplace quiet.

He snuck up the back stairs and opened the door to his bedroom. Everything in him settled, seeing her silhouette against the French door.

Chapter Thirteen

"Rielle?"

She whirled around guiltily. She hadn't heard Gavin enter. Right. She couldn't hear anything over the pounding in her head. "Oh. Ah. Hey. Bet you're wondering what I'm doing in your bedroom."

Gavin shut the door and silently leaned against it.

"I'm sorry. There were just too many people. Too many kids. My God, what is it with the McKays? Are the women who married into the family having a contest to see who can pop out the most babies? And didn't it seem like all the babies were screaming at one time? Guess what, they were. I timed it. There was a two minute window when no kids were yelling. Two minutes. That's all. In the last two hours. So naturally a pause in the collective noise pollution was a signal for the adults to get louder. Laughing and chatting like they hadn't seen each other in years, when I'm pretty sure they have some kind of crazy McKay gossip fest every couple of weeks.

"Then there were all these toddlers and school age kids running around. Climbing on the furniture like monkeys. Did the parents make the older kids go outside? No. They let those adorable, monstrous children race up and down my hallways. Up and down my stairs. Around and around my dining room table like it was a race track. All the while these kids were dropping potato chips and fruit and spilling ranch dressing on the rugs. I tried to stay out of the way and embrace the *kids will be kids* philosophy, but I wanted to run screaming out of my own damn house. But I couldn't. So I came to the one place that's always been my refuge.

"But when I got up here, I realized, this place no longer is mine. This is your private space and I'm sorry I violated it. But where am I supposed to go? So I stayed because I just needed a minute to breathe."

Rielle placed her hands on her cheeks. Her skin was on fire. Or maybe she was having a hot flash. Better that than a panic attack. She vaguely remembered her parent's advice about breathing techniques and visualization exercises to calm down.

Why the fuck couldn't she remember how to calm the fuck down?

Her heart galloped and her pulse throbbed...maybe she was having a heart attack.

She grabbed the bottle of whiskey off the dresser and swallowed two huge mouthfuls before she set it back down.

That didn't help. It just increased her feeling of burning up from the inside out.

Hot. Too hot. On fire. Can't breathe. Skin is suffocating. Must get out of my clothes so I can get air to my skin...

Rielle unbuttoned the top two buttons on the sheer white blouse and pulled it over her head, leaving her in a floral patterned camisole and a gauzy skirt that hit below her knee.

She waited for a sense of relief to settle in.

Nada.

I need to take all my clothes off. Nothing constricting my skin.

When her fingers curled around the bottom band of the cami and she started to pull it up her torso, a hoarse male voice barked, "Jesus, Ree. Stop."

She froze and glanced at Gavin, still plastered to the door.

Oh. My. God. In her panicked state of mind she'd started to strip in front of him; she'd forgotten he was even there. What must he think of her? Some crazy woman muttering and ripping off her clothes, sucking down his high-end booze after hijacking his bedroom to have a mental breakdown.

That's when she started to hyperventilate for real.

Spots danced in front of her eyes and she swayed.

"Shit." Then Gavin was right in her face, holding her upright. "Are you okay?"

She couldn't speak.

"Rielle! Talk to me."

"Too. Hot," came out whisper thin.

He shook her a little. "Goddammit, what is going on?"

"Need. Air."

He hauled her against his side and flung open the French door, dragging her onto the balcony.

She vaguely heard the door bang and hoped he hadn't locked it, trapping them out here.

Gavin stood behind her, his strong hands firm around her upper arms, his mouth against her ear. "Breathe."

Feeling lightheaded, she started to fall forward.

He made a grunting noise and placed her hands on the metal railing. "Hold on."

The metal felt cool on her hands and some of the tension left her body, allowing her to sag against him.

"Huh-uh. Stay on your feet. Come on, honey. Smell that fresh mountain air? Suck it into your lungs."

She opened her mouth and choked on the deep gulp of air.

"Through your nose. Nice and slow. That's it."

Rielle closed her eyes.

"Dammit, don't hold it in. Let it out so you can take more in."

Inhale like sipping water through a straw; exhale like you're blowing in a lover's ear.

Rielle didn't know where that advice came from, but she focused on it. Practiced it. Used it. Imagined turning her head and breathing in the scent of Gavin's skin. Then angling her mouth up to send a stream of air across his ear.

"Just like that. Good. Keep going. Breathe in slow."

Finally, after heaven knew how long, she was breathing almost normally.

Gavin still had hold of her. But instead of having a firm grip on her biceps, his palms skated up and down her arms, a barely there touch that sent goose bumps cascading over her flesh.

She shivered.

"You're cold. Let's go in."

"No." She pressed back against him. "My breathing is better but I'm still hot. I want to stay out here."

"Okay."

He was a talker, so she expected he'd grill her on why he'd found a near-hysterical woman in his room.

But he didn't. He just wordlessly stroked her. Soothed her.

No man had ever done that for her. Largely because she didn't allow it. She was self-sufficient with a capital S.

Rielle remained against his body, her back to his chest. Gavin was solid. Not ridiculously muscle bound, but toned. His expelled breath flowed across her bare shoulder and he kept up those teasing caresses.

She tipped her head to look at him, but his eyes were squeezed shut. "Gavin?"

"Hmm?"

"I like your hands on me."

His eyes flew open. "What?"

"I like the way you touch me."

His fingers circled her wrists. "So it calmed you down?"

"Yes." Her heart beat hard for an entirely different reason. "But it's also revving me back up."

He seemed to consider her response. "So what does that mean? Do you want me to keep on touching you?"

"Yes."

"Like this?" His warm lips connected with the ball of her shoulder and he dragged a painstakingly slow kiss up the side of her neck, stopping at the start of her jawline. Then his breath tickled her ear. "Want me to stop?"

"No." Rielle turned her head and nuzzled his cheek. "Please, keep going."

His deep groan reverberated through her entire body. Then his hands landed on her hips and he slid his palms up her belly and over her rib cage while his lips and tongue tasted the skin at the base of her neck.

She felt him bump his hips forward, showing her how hard he was. For her. She wiggled her backside and he sucked in a swift breath.

Gavin pulled the stretchy cami down, exposing her breasts. Then his hands were on her, his thumbs stroking her nipples, his mouth leaving biting kisses down the slope of her shoulder.

Rielle ground her ass into his erection, her breaths short once again, her skin on fire from where his hot mouth worked her, and that heat arrowed straight between her legs.

Then he spun her and pushed her against the side of the house, his wet mouth suckling strongly on her nipples, moving back and forth, squeezing her breasts as his tongue licked and laved the tips, and driving her insane with need.

Clamping her palms on his head, she stopped those deep sucks that made her breasts ache, and tilted his face up to look in his eyes. "Gavin. Please."

"One step ahead of you." He fished the condom out of his pocket and held it between his teeth as his fingers worked his belt. The sound of his zipper was loud in the still air. His jeans and boxers hit the pavement. He ripped open the package and rolled the latex down. His hands were on her ass and he panted, "Hang tight," in her ear.

A little squeak escaped as Gavin picked her up and pressed her back against the siding. Rough-tipped fingers followed the curve of her ass and the backs of her thighs, then the insides of her thighs.

Gavin's mouth was attacking her neck as he maneuvered their lower halves. He bit off, "Move the skirt."

Rielle couldn't think straight, but somehow she yanked the material up around her waist. Immediately something brushed over the crotch of her thong.

"Jesus, you're wet."

She blushed.

He jerked the tiny scrap of fabric aside and took her mouth in a hungry kiss as he steadily fed his cock inside her and stopped.

Holy shit that burned. It'd been a long time. She felt Gavin shaking and then all that hardness slipped back out fully and slammed into her again.

The fabric of her thong was stretched tight across her clit, the edge rubbing perfectly on that hot spot, so by his fifth thrust, she was coming.

Rielle came in silence as Gavin kissed her crazily. Her fingers digging into the back of his neck was the only outward change, because she'd make damn sure nothing took this moment away from her.

A few more long, deep thrusts and Gavin's body stiffened. He broke the kiss abruptly, letting his head fall forward as a long, "Fuck," drifted from his mouth.

Breathing hard, bodies shaking, they remained locked together. Then he sweetly pressed his lips to her temple.

If they hadn't been so still, they might not have heard, "Dad? Are you up here?"

She squirmed to be let down in case Sierra stepped onto the balcony, but Gavin rasped, "Don't move," directly into her ear.

Loud knocks sounded on the bathroom door and Sierra raised her voice. "Dad? People are starting to leave. You need to come say goodbye."

Gavin didn't move until he heard the bedroom door slam. He carefully lowered Rielle to the ground and eased out of her body.

She sucked in a sharp breath at the sudden stab of pain and Gavin finally looked at her. Guiltily.

He broke eye contact and yanked up his jeans, which he left unzipped and unbuckled because he still had to ditch the condom. "Sorry. I have to go."

"I heard." Keeping her head down, she fixed her thong and straightened the layers of her skirt.

"I... We'll... Dammit. We'll talk about this later, okay?"

Rielle nodded.

After Gavin left the bathroom, she snuck back into the room and picked up her blouse. She checked herself in the mirror in case she ran into anyone.

Yeah, try and explain why you're coming out of Gavin's room looking like a train wreck.

That'd feed the McKay gossip coffers for a few weeks.

Her mouth was a little puffy. Her hair a lot unruly, but besides that she didn't look like she'd been fucked hard and fast against the wall on her balcony.

How could the best sex of her life also be the most humiliating?

Chapter Fourteen

"I suck at sex."

Ben stiffened at Gavin's announcement and reined his horse to a stop. "You wanna explain that?"

This would be one of the most embarrassing discussions he'd ever had. Now that he'd brought it up, maybe he shouldn't have. Maybe he'd freaked Ben out.

The man had been a Dom in a sex club for a decade. Chances are high he's seen it all and done it all.

Gavin tried to get his horse to stop but the damn mare just kept moseying along.

"Gavin? Where you goin'?"

"Nowhere, but this horse won't obey."

Ben trotted up alongside Duchess and said sharply, "Jerk the rein back hard. She'll think she's in charge until you prove otherwise. Go on."

He pulled the reins much harder than before and Duchess immediately stopped.

"See? That's the first step of mastering her. Get her to do exactly what you want with a combination of firmness and praise."

Gavin had a strange feeling Ben wasn't only talking about horses. "Thanks."

"So, back to your comment. Did some chick say you were bad in bed or something?"

"Not exactly."

When a moment of silence passed, where Gavin couldn't even look at Ben, Ben sighed. "You know I'm the last guy who'd pass judgment on anyone. I assume that's why you wanna talk to me?"

Come on, Daniels, don't be a pussy. You've been a pussy your whole life, which is why you haven't gotten any pussy. Own up to all you don't know.

"Yeah. Remember when Dalton staged that intervention after the incident at the club and I said if I ever found my balls again and started dating that I'd come to you for advice? Here I am."

Ben gave Gavin a considering look. "I ain't much help on dating, but sounds like it's sex advice that you're after anyway."

"It is. And I have to admit, this is so far out of my comfort zone I may as well be on another planet." He inhaled slowly. "But I'm ready to figure out a way to fix it."

"You want my help, I'm gonna expect you to be completely honest about everything—and I mean everything, Gavin. Good shit, bad shit, the shit that you've kept bottled up inside, the shit you don't think anyone will understand, the embarrassing shit. All of it."

"I can do that."

"Start at the beginning."

Gavin frowned. "Of what?"

"Of your sexual history," Ben clarified.

Seriously? Gavin wanted to ask why that was relevant, but seeing the hard set to Ben's jaw, he decided to start talking. "This'll probably shock a guy like you, but I've never been that into sex. I had my horny teen years where I thought about sex twenty-four/seven and jacked off that many times every day. Got my first girlfriend, we had sex a few times but she wasn't that into it. Of course, at that age I never imagined it could be *my* lack of experience which caused that reaction in her."

Ben chuckled.

"By then I'd started college. I focused on academics and when I wasn't in school, I worked for my dad, learning the real estate business. Prime time for my sex drive, right? Well, I was more interested in spreadsheets than finding a girl who'd spread her legs. After I graduated, I was even more driven to prove myself. I didn't date, didn't do anything but work."

"Didn't your family encourage you to find a woman and settle down? God knows the McKays are all about that."

Gavin shook his head. "My dad married later in life, so as far as he was concerned, I was following in his footsteps." He paused. "Then I met Ellen at a party. This young, gorgeous woman was all over me. It's fucking pathetic, but I'd never been the guy the women look at and say *I wanna get with him because he's so fucking fine.* Ellen's attentions were beyond flattering; she slept with me the first night we met. Then she kept coming back for more. At that point in my life, having sex with her twice a week felt like I'd hooked up with a nympho. I fell for her hard, not seeing her for the manipulative, psycho bitch she was. After dating six months, she told me she was pregnant. Even then I hadn't known I'd been set up from the start."

"Lemme guess. You did the right thing and married her."

"Yes. I thought I'd had it all. A job I loved, a hot wife who loved me and was pregnant with my child." His hands unconsciously tightened on the reins. "Before Sierra was even born Ellen demanded we buy a bigger house. I wanted to make my wife happy so I opened my wallet and she proceeded to empty it. Sounds corny, but when Sierra was born my world changed." Gavin remembered the instant the nurse placed the screaming and pruny-looking thing in his arms. He'd also had a moment of anger, imagining his birth mother just handing over a helpless baby to a stranger.

Focus on the here and now.

"I never doubted that Ellen loved our daughter. But from the time we brought Sierra home from the hospital, I saw Ellen had no desire to learn to be a parent. If she couldn't deal with Sierra, she hired a babysitter or called my mom and went shopping. Then Ellen started screwing around on me. By the time Sierra was five, I'd had enough of the bullshit and lies and divorced her."

"So how was sex after you got married and after Sierra was born?"

Gavin shrugged. "Ellen claimed exhaustion a lot, which I forgave because I was tired too, so we were having quick, no-frills sex about once a month. Then it tapered off to once every two months and then the last year, no sex at all."

Ben cocked his head. "Did it ever occur to you to cheat?"

"No. Any sexual urges I satisfied with my hand. And it wasn't like the ladies were propositioning me anyway."

"So you haven't had sex since you were with your ex?"

"I slept with a woman at a weekend conference a few years after the divorce. Then after my mom died, there was a friend I ended up with for a few months, but she stopped calling. Now I look back and I wonder if it was because the sex sucked."

Ben held up his hand. "First off, the past is the past. None of that matters. Is there someone specific you're lookin' at around here that you wanna impress with your sexpertise?"

"Rielle."

"You're with her? Or you want to get with her?"

"We've been together."

That caught Ben by surprise. "How long's it been goin' on?"

Gavin blushed and felt like an idiot for it. "After I moved here, things started out slow, us talking and hanging out. Then we found an excuse to touch each other. Then we were making out like crazy whenever we were alone. And the night before last...we had sex. It happened so damn fast. Too fast."

"Did Rielle complain?"

He groaned. "No, but she's been avoiding me, probably because it lasted like a minute."

"You afraid she was disappointed?"

"Yeah."

"Were *you* disappointed?"

"God no. It was intense and spontaneous. I've never acted that aggressive with a woman. I fucked her up against the damn wall.

Outside. On the balcony."

"And Rielle gave you the go ahead?"

Gavin's eyes cut to Ben. "Completely consensual."

Ben chuckled. "Here's the truth. Women love that shit. You getting her turned on and then fucking her hard and fast right where she stands. I'll bet Rielle was just shocked because *you* acted that way and she hasn't seen you in that role."

"It gets worse. I got put back into the 'Dad' role because Sierra came in right after the spectacularly fast finish."

Ben's eyebrows rose. "Sierra caught you?"

He shook his head. "We were on the balcony outside of my room and it was dark."

"Wait. Was this the night of the McKay party?"

"Yep."

"So that's where you were. I gotta say, bro. I'm impressed. Getting some with all the family around."

The horses were getting restless. Ben urged his horse into a walk and Duchess followed.

Gavin tried to focus on the scenery; the crisp air and the shadows skittering across the ground as clouds clustered and broke apart overhead. Rielle would be outside, doing ten thousand things at once. "Thanks for bringing me out here, Ben. This is gorgeous country."

"Have you explored much of the land you bought from Rielle?"

"No. Ree says the terrain is rugged and I needed a horse on the unbroken trails rather than an ATV."

"She has a point. But I'll also remind you it's your land. The Wetzlers were always weird about letting people onto that section. It's yours now. You can do whatever the fuck you want with it. If you wanna clear all the damn trees and make a trail for four-wheelers, do it. If you're nervous about setting off alone, just call me. I'd be happy for the chance to get a look around."

"I'll think on it and let you know."

"Fair enough. Let's head back."

They turned the horses around.

"Bet you're waiting for my advice," Ben said after a bit.

"Do you have some?"

"Yep. Fake it 'til you make it. Next time you're with Rielle...act like you've got the hot sex moves and she'll believe you've got them. You will too."

"You think that'll work?"

He grinned. "It already did once, didn't it? You have the woman so flustered about you going all caveman on her ass that she's hiding from you. That ain't the Rielle I know, trust me."

"I guess that makes sense." Maybe. Hopefully. Fuck. How was he supposed to know?

"That wasn't very convincing." Ben pushed up his hat a notch. "Tell me what your other option is?"

Gavin blinked.

"For the love of God, please don't tell me you planned to confess your lack of sexual experience, hoping she'd understand and you could discuss what to do about it." When Gavin didn't respond, but must've looked guilty, Ben said, "Jesus, I can't fuckin' believe you were actually considering that! Screw that. You need to fuck it out, not talk it out."

"So I shouldn't talk to her at all?" Gavin said skeptically.

Ben muttered something. Then he sighed. "Talking is important, especially in the type of sexual activities I prefer. But in your case? Save the talking for after. First, act like you're gonna rock her world in bed and then follow through with it. Besides, it's not like women come with an instruction manual."

No way could Gavin confess he'd bought the book *Amazing Sex for Dummies*. And *How To Go Down On A Woman*. And *Sex Secrets from Porn Stars*. And *Making Love 101*. Ben would laugh his ass off.

"Come on, bro, you've got a guilty damn look on your face. Tell me what you're thinking."

"I've lived my life by honesty is the best policy, Ben. This feels dishonest."

"But it's not like you're lyin' to her." He brooded for a moment. "Lemme ask you this; how do you feel when you see Rielle?"

"Like stripping her bare and taking her right that second. Christ. All she has to do is walk past me and I'm hard. I think about her constantly. Fantasize about all the things I wanna do to her."

"Make those thoughts reality. Let your lust for her be your guide. Women want spontaneity. They want the sole focus to be what the two of you are doin' to each other right at that moment. The rest is just mechanics." He held up a gloved hand. "With the exception of BDSM. That takes some skill if you wanna go that direction. Even if it's not, it's fun to dabble."

Dabble in tying Rielle up and spanking her ass? Yeah, that might be out of her comfort zone. Or...out of his.

"And if you're lookin' for inspiration or ideas or whatever, watch porn."

"I can just see Sierra walking in when I'm taking notes on different positions." He sighed. "Am I just kidding myself that this will work even if I do figure out how to rock Rielle's world? Do I smuggle Rielle into my room? Or sneak into hers? And doesn't it make me a hypocrite to tell Sierra to wait to have sex when I plan to fuck Rielle nine ways 'til Sunday?"

"Maybe it makes me a dick, but I'll point out that you deserve to have an adult relationship. You're forty-three. Sierra is sixteen. Different expectations, bud. Should Sierra find you and Rielle fucking on the countertop? Nope. Does that mean you and Rielle shouldn't fuck on the countertop? Nope. It's all about timing. Including when you and Rielle decide to tell Sierra that the two of you are romantically involved."

"That'd be another first."

"I suspect it'd be a first for Ree too. But if you're intimate with her, at least give her the courtesy of owning up to it. Don't treat her or what the two of you are doin' behind closed doors as a dirty secret."

Gavin considered that and nodded.

"Anything else?" Ben asked.

"No. Thanks. I really appreciate your advice."

"Happy to help."

He adjusted his seat on the saddle and his ornery horse decided to take advantage of the slack in the reins. Gavin pulled Duchess to a stop with a firm tug and a sharp warning.

"That's it," Ben encouraged. "If she gets it in her head to lead, you show her who's boss right quick."

Again, Gavin understood his brother wasn't just referring to horses.

Chapter Fifteen

Needing fortification, courage, balls—whatever, Rielle tossed back half the lemon-drop martini. "I need some advice."

"I hope it's not medical advice, because Doctor Monroe is not in tonight," Joely said.

"It's personal. And slightly embarrassing."

"Embarrassing? Interesting." Joely sipped from her martini glass, shrewd eyes focused completely on Rielle. "Spill it."

She blurted out, "I had sex with Gavin Daniels."

"Girlfriend, are you serious?" Joely grinned and lifted her glass for a toast. "That is awesome!"

"Except it wasn't."

"It wasn't awesome? Explain that. In detail."

Her cheeks flamed. "Long story short. Thursday night Gavin had a party for the McKays. I freaked out and hid in my former bedroom. Gavin found me and tried to calm me down. So we're out on the balcony and he's touching me and the next thing I know, he hoisted me against the wall and fucked me."

"And this is bad...how?"

Rielle angled across the table. "It was fast."

"For you? Or him?"

"For both of us. I had an orgasm within about fifteen seconds and I was so embarrassed about it I didn't make a sound. Then afterward, I realized I hadn't touched him at all. I just set my hands on his shoulders and let him fuck me."

"Sweets, I gotta ask this. Did Gavin notice you didn't participate very much?"

"That's what I'm worried about. We haven't seen each other since. And we live together so I'm pretty sure he's avoiding me because I proved to be a lousy lay." She finished her martini and slid the empty to the edge of the table. "Or worse, he immediately figured out how little sexual experience I've had."

Joely held up her hand. "Hold on. Back up. Tell me how it played out from the time Gavin found you in his bedroom."

As Rielle relayed the events, she remembered how awesome that buzz of sexual anticipation felt. How much she liked having Gavin's hands on her. His mouth on her. And how wet he'd made her in such a short amount of time. She sent Joely a panicked look.

But Joely was deep in thought. Then she smiled. "Okay. Let me put on my stethoscope for a bit. Hot, spontaneous sex isn't the norm for you. Let's talk about your sexual history."

God. No. This was exactly what Rielle was trying to avoid.

Wrong. This is exactly what you need.

Joely squeezed her hand. "Hey. It's me. I'm thankful for our friendship, Ree, and I'd be the last person to pass judgment on you. I want to help, 'cause, sugar, I think you need it."

She blew out a slow breath. "Sexual history. Right. I got pregnant at sixteen the first time I had sex. The guy..." Rielle closed her eyes. She couldn't even remember what he looked like. That guilt ate at her, this disconnect with the man who was the father of her child.

Cool fingers wrapped her fingers around the stem of a martini glass. "Drink this. It'll help."

Rielle opened her eyes and smiled. "Thanks."

"Take your time. We can get hammered tonight because I have designated drivers on call."

Not the first time Joely had mentioned that. After a minute, Rielle said, "You know I was raised by hippie parents with the live-off-the-land, make-our-own-way, screw-the-man attitude."

"That sounds familiar. Wouldn't it be hysterical if your hippie parents knew my hippie parents? Or had spent time in the same peace, free-love and no nukes commune?"

"That'd be a total trip, man."

Joely laughed. "Keep going. We'll compare notes later."

"Our doors were open for anyone who would work for food and shelter—very much a commune-like vibe." She allowed a small smirk. "Rumors flew that my folks grew pot on their funky little piece of land in McKay country. Untrue. They'd grown it in California, and surprisingly, they had a profitable business. My mother, the smarter of my parents because she hadn't smoked all the profits and the product, sold their operation. We moved here when I was eight. They didn't believe in formal education so I was home schooled. None of the transients who crashed with us had kids, so I grew up isolated, from kids my own age and society in general." Feeling like a freak, she looked at Joely. "Was it like that for you?"

"No. I lived in a commune where all kids were raised by the community. We called everyone mother and father. I had thirty siblings. We were dressed the same. We didn't even sleep in the same bed every night, lest we get attached to material objects. I had nothing of my own; everything was shared. But they did at least educate us, which allowed me to get the hell out." Sadness passed through her eyes. "But enough about that. This is about you. Keep talking."

Rielle hoped someday Joely would fill in the blanks of her life before she became Doctor Monroe. "Given that history you can imagine how a sixteen-year-old-girl, starved for attention, and just discovering sexuality, would react when an older guy started paying attention to me. Talking to me. Listening to me. Touching me. I craved that touch because my parents were unaffectionate."

"With each other too?"

"Yes. They had an open relationship. I remember seeing Mom sleeping on the couch when Dad was in their bedroom with someone else. Same with my dad sleeping on the couch when Mom was *having a meeting* with some dude in their bedroom."

"At least it was equal opportunity 'meetings' for them."

"True." She smiled. "You'd think I'd have picked up the basics on sex, but I was so damn naïve. When 'John'—" she made air quotes, "—kissed me and touched me and told me it was okay, it was natural, I believed him. But the night he came into my room and took my virginity? There wasn't sweet words or kisses or anything but the smell of pot smoke clinging to his clothes as he crawled on top of me." Rielle felt Joely's piercing stare, but she needed to get through this part to get to the heart of the matter. "I ended up pregnant. I had no idea I was pregnant until about the fifth month and I kept feeling all this stuff going on inside me and I'd put on weight. My mother figured it out. Four months later I gave birth to Rory, at home, with some whacked-out midwife and my mother in attendance."

"Oh sugar," Joely said. "You were just a baby yourself."

"I know. But I loved my baby so much. She was perfect and all mine. I didn't have sex again until the night of my twenty-first birthday. I ended up doing it with some sweet-talkin' cowboy in his pickup. I went home with him afterward and we had sex again. I tried oral. Received oral. But it wasn't great. I thought there was something wrong with me and decided sex wasn't worth the hassle. Plus I had that whole 'young, single mother' stigma and I didn't want to have a reputation that Rory would have to deal with. The two other times I've been attracted to a guy and we ended up having sex, it's always been a disappointment. So, like I said. I've always figured it was me."

"Was it a disappointment with Gavin?"

"Only in how I reacted. I was shocked because I've never had an orgasm with a man during sex. During oral? Yes. I can get off by my own hand, so I know I'm not incapable. I'm just..."

"Inexperienced," Joely finished.

"At age forty. Gee, wouldn't you wanna get all up in this?"

"I totally would, if I didn't have a serious love of cock."

Rielle choked on her drink.

Joely grinned. "I love shocking you."

"No shit. So, tell me, Doctor Love, what should I do?"

"First off, do you want a sexual relationship with Gavin?"

"Yes."

"Then I'm writing you a script for birth control pills." She pulled a pad out of her purse, filled it out and passed it over. "Get that filled tomorrow, you hear me? Use alternative birth control methods for a month."

"Yes, Doctor Monroe."

"Do you think your inexperience will scare him off?"

"Maybe it already has. How do I convince him to give me another try?"

"Besides getting on your knees?"

"Joely!"

She laughed. "That would work, trust me. But in all seriousness, come on to him. Tell him he made you come so hard that night you were speechless. Tell him you can't stop thinking about him. Tell him you want him. Then prove it. Seduce the fuck outta him."

Rielle considered that advice and polished off another martini. She had a decent buzz going. "How many of these have we had?"

"Three. Each. And now that one is empty." She signaled to the cocktail waitress for another round.

"I'm hardcore tonight."

"Damn straight. Besides, you wouldn't have the guts to talk to me without a little liquid courage."

"True. Now I'm mulling over your advice and it's your turn to confess how Joely gets her jollies."

"Hilarious. Like you, I can only admit what I really want when I've put away several of these babies."

"Wanna explain that?"

She ran her hand through her short red hair. "I can't explain it to myself. It's so fucked up. Every time I swear I'll never do it again...I do." She scowled over her shoulder. "Where the hell is my damn drink?"

"Hey, look at me." When she had Joely's attention, she said, "This road runs both ways, girlfriend. I'm as good at keeping confidences as you are. Any time you're ready to spill, I'm here."

"I appreciate it, Ree, I really do."

"But you'd rather help other people than yourself."

"Yep."

The cocktail waitress dropped off the martinis.

Joely plucked hers up. "Right now, I'm helping myself to another drink. Cheers."

Rielle knew the subject was closed. So they switched gears, talking about cooking and yarn, since Joely was an avid knitter. Then out of the blue, Joely said, "So what are you going to do about Gavin?"

"Taking your suggestion to *seduce the fuck outta him.*"

Joely raised an eyebrow and grinned. "Good. 'Cause sugar, he just walked in the door."

The Golden Boot was packed on a Saturday night. Gavin wasn't much into the bar scene, but sitting home by himself was borderline pathetic. He'd headed to the closest honky-tonk to soak up some atmosphere after Ben and Tell both had mentioned a good local band played some weekends. But with the dark stage it didn't appear to be this weekend.

He found a spot at the bar and ordered a whiskey, neat. He felt a little out of place wearing jeans, a wool sweater and loafers amidst all the cowboy hats and boots, but no one glared at him like it was a hanging offense.

After ten minutes or so, the guy on his left struck up a conversation. He'd just settled in when the guy's eyes locked on someone behind Gavin. He turned and his heart rate spiked at seeing Rielle. For the first time in two goddamned days.

She offered him a little finger wave.

His new buddy from the bar gave him a huge grin and took off.

Rielle moved in. Right in. Slid her palms up his chest and snuggled her body into his. She tipped her head back and smiled at him. "Hey, roomie."

She looked so good and her sexy little body felt so good against his that he bent down and touched his lips to hers. She tasted like lemons and smelled like heaven. "Hey, yourself. Fancy meeting you here."

"Joely picked me up for a few cocktails. I was about to order coffee to sober up before the ride home. Then I saw you and thought I'd ask if you wanna give me a ride?"

I'd like to ride you like you wouldn't believe.

"But I wouldn't want to tear you away from anything...pressing." Keeping her eyes on his, she pressed her pelvis into his, adding a tiny grind of her hips.

Gavin instantly went hard.

But Rielle wasn't done. She dug her fingers into the back of his neck and pulled him closer to whisper in his ear. "Are you avoiding me after the other night?"

"No. Why?"

"I thought maybe you were since I might've come across a teensy bit of a lousy lay."

He froze. "What? God no, Ree, I'm the one—"

"But here's the secret I tried to keep from you. Why I might've seemed so motionless and quiet."

"What?"

"You made me come so hard, so fast that I forgot how to breathe."

Gavin curled his hands on the side of her face and tilted her head back. "How much have you had to drink?"

"Enough to give me the courage to talk to you but not enough to make me forget what I want to say," she said softly.

"What do you want to say to me, Rielle?"

"I want more of you. More of us. But naked this time. I wanna feel your hands on me. I wanna feel your mouth on me. God, Gavin, I'm dying to feel every inch of your body rubbing on mine. Like at least four times tonight."

Jesus fucking Christ.

"What do you have to say to that?"

"We're leaving. Right. Now." Gavin didn't even finish his drink. He grabbed her hand and towed her out of the bar. He didn't stop moving until he reached his car.

Then he pressed her against the passenger's side door and slammed his mouth down on hers. Taking the kiss that he'd wanted for two damn days. Pouring passion into it. Licking and sucking and biting at her succulent mouth, then easing off. Stroking her tongue with his. Pulling back a fraction of an inch, feeling her stuttered breaths as he teased her with a soft, barely-there glide of his lips. "Ree."

"Don't stop kissing me."

"I'll kiss you all you want, just not here. Let's go."

She blinked. "Where?"

"Home."

"But Sierra—"

"Is staying over at Marin's tonight."

"Oh." She smiled. "So we have the house to ourselves?"

"All night." He dropped another kiss on her mouth. "Get in the fucking car before I throw you on the hood and fuck you right now and prove to you that you're nowhere *close* to a bad lay."

Rielle got in the car.

Gavin was giving himself a stern talk about being a man and lasting longer than one goddamn minute this time, when Rielle grabbed his right hand and shoved it between her legs. "What are you—"

"Get me off. Please." She rubbed the side of her face on his arm and squeezed her thighs together. "I'm wet. Just from that damn kiss. Stick your hand in and see for yourself what you do to me."

His first thought was to tell her to keep her pants on; it'd wait until they got home. His second thought was, what the fuck was wrong with him? Rielle was begging him to touch her. No woman had ever begged him.

That was fucking hot.

He briefly took his focus off the road. "Take your jeans off."

Her eyes widened. Then she released a little moan and unbuttoned and unzipped her jeans. She shimmied the denim down her legs, revealing a tiny pair of pink panties. So unexpectedly girly. So unbelievably sexy.

When Gavin glanced up, he saw he'd drifted clear into the other lane. This was too damn dangerous. He pulled onto the shoulder and cut the headlights. The lights from the instrument panel cast a golden glow over her half-naked body.

"Gavin?"

He unbuckled and leaned over to run his fingertip over the lace band stretching between her hips. "I want to see you. All of you. Off. Now."

Rielle didn't hesitate.

This being in charge was heady stuff. "Lower the seat. Top button on the side. That's it."

Her teeth were digging into her lower lip; those beautiful pale eyes didn't venture from his face.

Gavin caught her scent; sweet honey. Like her hair, like her skin, like her mouth. He ran his index finger up and down her slit. "You are wet."

"Yes."

"What should I do about that?"

"Touch me. Make me come."

"With my hand?"

"Yes," she moaned.

"Or..." He swirled just the tip of his finger over her clit, backing off when her hips bucked up. "Maybe I should make you get yourself off and I should watch."

He could almost feel the heat from the way her body flushed. So she had no problem being naked from the waist down, but masturbation made her tense. Gavin didn't blame her. Had the situation been reversed, his face would be cherry red if she demanded he whip out his cock and stroke it until he came.

"Or...I could get you off with my mouth." He brushed his lips over hers after he heard her swift intake of breath. "Put one foot on the door and one foot on the console. Spread your legs as wide as you can. That's good. Now slide up. That's perfect."

Her ass was a little more than halfway up the back of the seat, which put her pussy within range. He leaned across the console, biting back a wince at the painful position of his cock. He breathed her in. Flicked her clit with his tongue. Just one time.

Rielle moaned.

Then he gave her one thorough lick, getting his first complete taste of her. Goddamn, she tasted so fucking sweet. He could suck up her cream all night. He worked her with his tongue, lips and teeth. Losing his mind in the fact that he was going down on Rielle, in his Lexus, on the side of the road.

"Oh God."

He traced her hot folds with his tongue, top to bottom. He drew lazy circles, broad circles, stilling her hips with a firm push of his hands when she tried to grind upward.

"Gavin."

"Mmm-hmm?" he answered, the sound vibrating against her blood-engorged tissues.

Her whole body quivered. "Please. I can't take any more."

He heard the words, "Hold on," rumble from his mouth in an animal-like growl. He grabbed her left ankle and swung her body around, almost clipping himself in the head with her heel as he wrapped her leg around the back of his seat. Slipping his hands under her butt, he pulled her closer and buried his mouth in her juicy sex.

She gasped when he wiggled his tongue inside her opening. After a few fast flicks over her clit, Gavin enclosed that swollen flesh between his lips and sucked hard.

Rielle exploded. She clamped her hands over his ears and wrapped her right leg around his shoulder, holding him in place while she came in violent waves against his mouth.

Gavin watched pleasure overtake her. It was one of the hottest experiences of his life.

When she finally went limp, he released his hold. He nipped the inside of her thigh, earning a sharp, surprised yip from her. Although his cock was smashed against his belly and constricted by his jeans, he took a second to burn the image into his brain. Beautiful, sated woman sprawled in front of him, bared to him fully, breathing hard and peering at him from beneath lowered lashes. He unhooked her leg from his seat, kissed the outside of her ankle and swiveled her around to face forward.

He did the same. Then he smiled at her as she just sat there, unmoving, sort of stunned. "You getting dressed?"

"Oh. Right. Although, I'm pretty sure I won't be wearing these clothes long when we get home."

"That'd be a sure bet."

Chapter Sixteen

Gavin kept hold of Rielle's hand on the drive home. Stroking his thumb on the inside of her wrist. Moving his palm up and down to rub the tips of his fingers between the webbing of hers. Then he brought her knuckles to his mouth. Kissing and nipping, drawing the backside of her hand across his goatee.

Rielle broke their handhold and twisted in her seat, rising on her knees. Leaning over the console, she placed her lips on his ear and said, "You always smell good."

"If you keep that up I'll wreck the car."

"No, you'd wreck if I put my hand on your crotch. You can handle this, Gavin." She rubbed the side of her face over his. Her mouth would randomly connect with his cheek, the spot below his earlobe, the shell of his ear, his temple, above his eyebrow.

The sweet nuzzles and soft kisses fired his blood. It was damn hard not to close his eyes and just enjoy her attention.

Finally the turnoff was within view. "Rielle, honey, sit. I don't want you to go flying when I take the corner on two wheels."

"In a hurry?" she purred in his ear.

"Like you wouldn't believe."

She laughed and the soft, seductive sound burned a path through his ear canal straight to his dick. "Me too."

Gavin parked in his usual spot. They both scrambled out and met in front of the car. His mouth crashed down, her arms circled his neck and he was lost to the kiss. He'd thought passionate soul kissing was for teens and youngsters, so clearly he'd never experienced that overpowering rush of need to have her lips on his. To feel her tongue stroking and sucking, mouths open to give and receive.

He'd intended to clamp his hands on her ass and drag her closer to his body, but instead, he slipped his arm behind her knees and cradled her against his chest.

Rielle gasped. "Gavin."

He started up the steps, but kept his heated gaze on her face. "Might be over the top to carry you up the stairs to my bed. But I owe you a little romance for the way I fucked up our first time. So indulge me."

Her beautiful green eyes softened and she brushed a kiss on his neck.

He opened the front door and cut down the hallway to the staircase. Sustaining a kiss was difficult as he scaled the stairs, so he filled his lungs with her honeysuckle scent. Tightening his hold on her until he had her in his bedroom.

She laughed when he kicked the door shut.

Gavin set her on her feet at the end of his bed. Then he indulged in a long, deep, slow kiss and by the time they broke apart, they were both breathing hard and he saw the pulse point in her neck pounding as rapidly as his heart.

"Stay right here for a second." He locked the door, turned on the lamps for ambient lighting and rolled the comforter to the foot of the bed.

She watched as he took four condoms out of the package and set the strip on the nightstand.

Then he was standing in front of her again. Gavin couldn't think of any pretty words as his fingers started with the top button of her blouse. Her gaze remained on his face but he didn't look into her eyes until her shirt hung open. He kissed her and pushed the soft fabric off and it fluttered to the floor.

He was used to seeing her in a camisole or tank top, so the lacy bra that matched her sexy underwear was a bonus. His finger traced the plumped curve from the top of her bra down to the deep valley of her cleavage, and back up the other side. He planted a kiss on her right breast.

A shiver worked through her.

He murmured, "Take off your jeans, Rielle," as he nuzzled the abundant flesh.

She peeled them away.

"Now your bra."

Her face flushed and she tipped her head forward as her hands circled around to jerk on the clasp. Once the straps and cups loosened, he put his fingers under her chin and looked into her eyes.

"I got this part."

Rielle smiled shyly.

Gavin hooked his fingers inside the bra cups and pulled. The straps slid down her arms and the bra dropped to the floor. Her breasts were full, round, with dark rose-colored nipples. Just for a second, he forgot to breathe. "God. You're gorgeous." Then his hands squeezed as he buried his face in all that perfect white flesh.

She arched into him, her hand at the back of his head.

He dragged his mouth from side to side, teasing her. Rubbing the rim of his lip across the tight peaks.

A soft moan drifted from her.

Gavin's lips blazed a path up her throat to her mouth. He played with her breasts, squeezing and rubbing as he kissed her. She was so sweet and hot.

Rielle rolled her hips, grinding into his erection. She moved her lips to his ear. "You still have your clothes on. I wanna feel your skin against mine, Gavin."

The former chubby guy part of him balked at the idea of getting naked with her, afraid she'd be judging him.

You shouldn't have started this if you have no intention of finishing it.

Oh, he'd finish it all right—a spectacular fucking finish this time.

"I want that too." His hands followed the contours of her breasts down to her hips. He squeezed once. "Hop up on the bed."

"But." Indecision warred on her face before she boldly reached for his belt buckle. "Don't you want me to undress you?"

"Next time, okay?"

"Okay." She backed up and sat on the end of the bed.

Gavin kicked off his loafers, pulled his sweater and T-shirt over his head. Unbuckled, unzipped, he tugged his jeans down and ditched his socks. Wearing only his boxers, he moved toward her.

Rielle's eyes flicked over his body, zeroing in on his crotch. "Naked, means naked." She gestured to his underwear. "And that's not naked."

"You're still wearing underwear," he pointed out, stalking her.

She crab crawled to the center of his bed. "I'll take mine off, if you will. But you've gotta go first."

Right then Gavin wished he was packing a solid ten inches. But he was also just damn glad he could get a hard-on without the help of Viagra. He slipped his fingers beneath the waistband and dropped his boxers.

She grinned.

"What?"

"It's just weird to think that's been inside me and this is the first time I've actually seen it."

Gavin hadn't ever been the type to tease in the bedroom, so he wasn't sure what possessed him to grin and fist his cock, stroking it slowly. "It's more than ready to get reacquainted. Just as soon as you lose the panties."

She stripped and threw them over the end of the bed.

He walked to the nightstand, tore off a package and ripped it open, watching her eyes as he rolled it on. Then he climbed onto the bed and pushed her thighs apart, making room for himself.

Rielle laid flat on the mattress, as if expecting him to mount her right now.

110

Why wouldn't she think that? You're wearing a condom.

Only so he didn't have to fumble with the damn thing at the moment of truth.

Gavin kissed the blond hair at the top of her mound. Her belly button. Her sternum. Then those perfect breasts were in his face again. He sucked on her right nipple. Played with the rigid point with his teeth and tongue. Making her squirm. He switched to the other side, worshipping her breasts as they deserved.

Her nails were digging into the back of his neck and she lifted her pelvis, trying to connect with something solid.

He looked up, seeing her face flushed and her breathing ragged. "Ree?"

"Don't stop. I'm about to..."

"Just from me sucking on your nipples?"

"Yes. They've always been sensitive. And what you're doing...is really, really doing it for me, so don't stop."

He latched on with renewed vigor and she almost shot straight off the mattress. He pinched her other nipple hard, then palmed her pussy, while strongly suckling the taut peak.

Rielle cried out, "Yes!"

Gavin could feel the pulsing beneath his sucking lips and beneath his palm. He watched her face as she climaxed—she was something lost in pleasure. Softer somehow. He wanted her so bad his balls ached.

As soon as she relaxed, he aligned his cock and propped himself above her.

She opened her eyes and rose up to kiss him, her hands sliding down to grip his ass, letting him know she was in the moment.

He eased in slowly, kissing her softly until they were fully joined. Staying right there, her pussy hot and wet and tight around his shaft.

Then he moved on her, in her, keeping a steady rhythm that allowed him to sustain the kiss.

Rielle's legs were splayed wide and her chest rose to meet his every rolling thrust. The cushion of her breasts rubbed against the thatch of hair on his chest.

Gradually he pushed into that channel a little harder. A little faster. His heart rate kicked up and sweat beaded on his brow.

Her lips slid free and she kissed his chin, the side of his neck, his Adam's apple, the hollow of his throat. She clamped both hands on his butt.

Fuck. This was so good. And with her biting his neck like that and blowing in his ear, he was already riding that edge. So he slowed to a stop and pressed his lips into her hair.

Rielle tipped his head to meet her gaze. "What's wrong?"

"Nothing. It's perfect. Being with you, is amazing. I just want to take my time."

"You don't have to do that on my account, Gavin." She whispered a kiss across his lips. "Move faster, harder, whatever you want. I'm right here with you."

"You sure?"

"Yes."

Gavin ramped up the pace. Rising into a pushup position to drive into her tight cunt harder. Faster.

She clung to him, frantically kissing his neck, undulating and arching beneath him with every snap of his hips.

Then he had that short warning tingle down his spine. He switched to short, quick jabs.

He groaned when his balls pulled up. His head fell back as his dick spasmed; each hot pulse shook him with a full body shudder. His hands curled into the sheet and he groaned again, longer, louder as the climax reached the apex. White and black spots danced behind his eyelids and a dull roar filled his head.

Yeah, that made up for the quickie on the balcony.

He looked down at her.

No smile. A somber face.

"Ree? Honey, what is it?" Had he hurt her somehow?

She lifted up to kiss him fiercely.

Gavin nuzzled her ear. "You okay?"

She shook her head.

His stomach dropped.

Then she buried her face in his neck and he realized she was crying.

Chapter Seventeen

Embarrassed, Rielle tried to roll away from Gavin—wishing she could crawl under the bed—but he wouldn't allow it. He tucked her against his body, acting as if it were perfectly natural for a woman basking in the glow of two outstanding orgasms to be teary-eyed.

He didn't push her to talk; he just held her.

Once she regained control, she got brave enough to lift her head. "Thank you. That was the best sex I've ever had. Well, except for the other night out on the balcony."

"Really?"

She could hear the smile in his voice. "Really."

"So why the tears?"

"Because I feel like a freak." She expected he'd force her to look at him after that statement, but he didn't. "I've spent my life as a single mother, Gavin. I don't have the sexual history most women do."

"Why on earth would you think that'd be a problem for me?"

"Because it's always been a problem for me," she said softly.

Then he did tip her chin up to study her face.

"The tears caught me by surprise. I'm so not a crier. But being with you...I got this rush of happiness, followed immediately by fear."

"We should've talked about this before. But the instant I put my hands on you, I lose any coherent train of thought." Gavin's fingers traced the line of her spine and he smoothed his palm over her buttocks. "See? I already forgot what we were talking about."

"Me being practically a forty-year-old virgin."

"Hey. No more thinking you're a freak. You're perfect, Ree. And I'm not exactly such a..." He snapped his mouth shut.

"Not exactly such a what?"

"Never mind." Gavin got up and ditched the condom. Then he took her in his arms again. "This is a clean slate for both of us. Nothing we did or didn't do before matters." His eyes glowed with pure male intent. "So if there's a position you're dying to try, or some fantasy you have, feel free to share and we'll act it out in explicit detail."

"This feels like a fantasy, lying in bed with you after we had awesome sex." She fought a blush at confessing, "I've been thinking of quite a few things I'd like to try with you." She brushed her mouth over the smooth section of flesh above his nipple. "And you promised me four times tonight, remember?"

"*You* said you wanted me to fuck you four times. I never agreed because I don't promise what I can't deliver."

She loved it when the smooth businessman veneer slipped, revealing his raw masculinity. "I like it when you say crude sex things."

Gavin flashed his teeth. "So noted."

Rielle rolled and straddled his groin, sitting on top of him. She placed her hands by his head, leaning over him. "Know what else I like?"

"Please tell me it's giving blowjobs."

She threw her head back and laughed.

"You don't do that enough."

"What? Give blowjobs?"

"No, smartass. Laugh. I love to hear you laugh." He dragged his finger from the tip of her chin down between her cleavage.

"I laugh more with you than anyone else."

"Also good to know." Gavin traced a circle around her nipple until it drew into a rigid point. "Now you were about to tell me something else you liked."

"Kissing you. I get a little dizzy when you kiss me. I feel like a teenager saying that, but it's true."

He wrapped his hand around the back of her neck and kissed her. After he thoroughly ravished her mouth, he murmured, "Dizzy yet?"

"Very."

"Me too. And hard. Grab a condom."

Rielle tore the package open, taking time to enjoy his every hiss and moan as she touched him.

"Push back and lift up over me. I want to watch your pussy swallowing my cock."

As soon as every inch of that hard shaft filled her, he reached for her. "Ride me hard. I want to see your tits bouncing. Oh yeah, just like that. Fuck me."

Who knew she liked a bossy, dirty-mouthed man in bed?

Rielle's internal alarm clock woke her up even on the weekends.

So...what to do, lying in the arms of a naked man, in the early morning hours?

Be bold like you were last night, putting his hand between your thighs in the car. Seduce him.

But what if he was one of those cranky morning guys? Grumbling about being woken up and thrashing away from her?

She'd be better off surprising him with breakfast. Rielle pressed her butt into his groin and arched her spine away from his chest, expecting he'd release her and turn over.

Gavin's throaty, "Mmm," rumbled in her ear, sending a shiver down her spine. "You going somewhere?"

"I can't sleep. I didn't mean to wake you."

"Is it like five in the morning or something?"

"Six."

He groaned. Then he pressed a hot kiss on the side of her neck. "So if I let you up, what are you going to do? Wash windows? Knit socks for every needy kid in Crook County? Bake muffins for the rest home?"

"No."

"Not ambitious enough for you?" he murmured against her throat.

"Funny. I'm not *always* working."

"True. You're always *slaving*."

"Is that how you see me?"

"You are one of those busy worker bees in your hive. Mind focused on finishing one task so you can fly to the next one before your buzz wears off."

Did he think she was incapable of kicking back? "That's not all I am."

"So prove it." His mouth teased her ear. "Let's play a game."

"What game?"

"Honeypot."

She snickered. "Really, Gavin? Honeypot?"

"Yep. This morning you are the queen bee and I'm your drone, servicing your every need."

"You do realize that immediately after a drone mates with the queen bee midair his penis is snapped off and he plummets to his death?"

Gavin went motionless. "You're kidding me, right?"

"Nope."

"Jesus. That is just plain nasty."

If Rielle hadn't felt both his hands on her body she'd swear he was cupping his junk.

"Speaking of nasty...how about if I do naughty things and make you forget everything except my hands and mouth?"

Another shiver tightened her skin, but she managed a droll, "Well, you can *try*...but my to-do list is pretty extensive."

"Oh, so you'll be composing a *to-do* list while I'm doing this?" Gavin sank his teeth into her nape and pinched her nipples. "Or how about this?" Rielle gasped when he pulled her outer leg over his hip and stroked her slit.

His chest was hot against her back. His mouth was everywhere; on her neck, her shoulder, her ear. Then his fingers were inside her, stroking her. He murmured, "You're wet. I like that you're wet."

Rielle arched into him. "You're hard. I like that you're hard."

"Hold that thought." Gavin eased his fingers out and she heard the crinkling of a condom wrapper. He hooked his arm behind her knee, lifting it for better access to her pussy. The head of his cock circled the mouth to her sex and he slowly pushed his shaft inside. "Okay?"

"Very okay." In this position she felt a deeper penetration. She felt stuffed full.

"Good." His tongue traced the shell of her ear. "I'm not feeling sweet and romantic right now, Ree."

A shiver of want, of anticipation, rolled through her and he felt it.

"You like that."

"Yes."

"You are a naughty little thing, aren't you?" Gavin shifted his upper body and then his hand was tightly, almost painfully, gripping her short hair.

Rielle gasped softly. Wow. That was sexy hot, how he just held her head where he wanted it.

"Touch yourself. I don't have enough hands."

She blushed.

"Do it." He sucked on the skin behind her ear. "I want to look down your body and see your fingers moving as I'm fucking you."

She slid her right hand down her belly, following the rise of her mound to her clit. As soon as she started to stroke, so did he.

Sweetness became body-pounding passion as he thrust into her so hard the bed jiggled. His mouth found all her hot spots on her neck and shoulder and nape—he zeroed in on the one that caused her to moan and try to twist away but he held her in place.

The combination of his deep, hard thrusts and the constant pressure of her fingers on her clit sent her headlong into orgasm. A throbbing, pulsing, blinding surge of pleasure.

Gavin's cock hammered into her and then he growled in her ear as his release followed on the heels of hers.

She hadn't opened her eyes or leveled her breathing when he whispered, "So...how's that to-do list coming?"

Rielle and Gavin made breakfast together—unlike other times they'd cooked together. He continually touched her. Nuzzled her. Kissed her. By the time the bacon was finished, his sweet eroticism had her so worked up she would've let him take her right on the counter. A shocking scene for Sierra to stumble upon on a Sunday morning.

Which was a pointed reminder she and Gavin needed to talk.

He rinsed the plates and refilled their coffee. "So what's on your mind, Ree?"

Damn perceptive man. "I'm new at this morning-after stuff."

"I know. You avoided me Friday and Saturday morning after our Thursday night."

"You noticed that, huh?"

Gavin leaned forward, sliding his knee between hers and placing her left hand between his. "This conversation is about the start of something between us, not the end, right?"

"Right." She sipped her coffee. "Let's deal with the elephant in the room first thing. Sierra."

"Part of me thinks that my sweet, but self-absorbed teen won't notice the change in our relationship. The other part of me thinks she's already sensed the shift in the last few weeks. Not that she's said anything to me."

"Her suspecting we're involved and her seeing us groping each other on the couch...two different things."

He nipped the tips of her fingers. "Will you let me grope you on the couch now?"

"Maybe. But my point is I'd prefer to keep this between us for a little while longer."

"Why? You think it'll burn out?"

Rielle set her hand on his cheek. "No."

Gavin kissed the inside of her wrist. "I don't want to hide what I feel for you. I want you in my bed some nights. But I don't want you feeling like you have to tiptoe down the hallway so my daughter doesn't see you sneaking out of my room."

"Or see you creeping up the stairs from my bedroom at the crack of dawn," she countered. "But that does bring up my other point, Gavin. I want to spend time with you, but not at the expense of the time you spend with Sierra. And I don't want you suddenly inviting me to do family things. We both know she'd resent that and me. I won't put you in that position, nor will I put myself in that position."

"Without pissing you off, this is exactly why I've avoided relationships. Why does it have to be so complicated?"

"It doesn't." Rielle pressed her lips to his, coaxing his mouth to open to her kiss. She loved this intimacy. The give and take. The taste of him. The feel of his breath on her face, sometimes fast and short, sometimes soft as a sigh.

He eased off first, then kissed the corners of her mouth, the apples of her cheeks, her temples and between her eyebrows. "So we can only be like this...openly affectionate...?"

"During the day when Sierra is at school. Or at night when we're alone." She gazed into his eyes. "Not forever. Just for a little while. You'll know when the time is right to tell her."

"*I'll* tell her? Not *we'll* tell her?"

Rielle shook her head. "She's your daughter. I'm just a woman who lives here." She slipped her arms around his neck. "Who is wildly attracted to her father."

He lifted an eyebrow. "Wildly?"

"Uh-huh. And I'll prove it." She nuzzled his ear. "Did you happen to bring a condom with you?"

"Nope. I brought two."

"Always prepared. I like that about you."

"Ree, I know you haven't been with anyone for a long time. I haven't been either. Can we skip the condoms?" He caressed her face. "I'd like to make love to you without latex between us."

"I, ah...talked to Doc Monroe last night, and she wrote me a prescription for birth control. But even if I get it filled today, it'll take a month for the pills to be effective."

Gavin had a pensive look on his face.

"What?"

"There's no chance I'll ever get you pregnant. I had a vasectomy nine years ago."

Her eyes searched his. "Really?"

"After the divorce and dealing with Ellen using Sierra to manipulate me...I never wanted to give a woman that much power again or to do that to another child of mine. So I scheduled the procedure. I love my daughter. She fills my life with enough joy that I'm content with having one kid. Are you all right with that?"

"Do you mean was I hoping to get pregnant at age forty when I have a twenty-four-year-old daughter?" She shuddered. "That boat has sailed for me. But I already had one unintended pregnancy in my life. I wasn't keen on taking chemicals to prevent that from happening again at my age, but I'd do it." She kissed him. "So I'm very happy I don't have to."

"Me too."

She hopped off the barstool. "Race you to my room. Whoever wins gets to be on top."

The man had such a competitive streak. He nearly knocked her on her butt as he raced down the hallway and jumped on her bed.

But he let her be on top anyway.

Gavin's cell phone rang early Monday morning. "This is Gavin Daniels."

"Gavin! Good to hear your voice. This is George Krebs. I'm with the Bracken Investment Group?"

He tried to put the name with a face but couldn't. "You have me at a disadvantage, George. Have we met?"

"Once, briefly, last year. At a Shout It Out fundraiser."

"Natalie, my media coordinator at Daniels Development Group, handles donations for those events—"

"No. This call isn't about a fundraiser, but we do appreciate all your support. The reason for my call is...a little odd. So bear with me."

"Okay."

"My understanding is you've stepped down from the day-to-day running of Daniels Development Group?"

"Technically I'm still running DDG, but not from the Phoenix office. I've relocated."

"Permanently?"

"Why don't you tell me why you're so interested in who has control of my company?"

"One of our clients is interested in buying the Golden Valley property recently listed with DDG. I assume you're familiar with it?"

"Very familiar." That was the last chunk of undeveloped land his father had purchased fifteen years ago, prior to his death. Gavin had been holding onto it, waiting to see what type of development sprang up in that section of Maricopa County. It'd been completely unzoned at the time of purchase, which meant it could end up residential or commercial. Now the surrounding area contained medical complexes and high-end high-rise condos. With the possible shift in the commercial real estate market, Gavin had decided to list it right before they'd left Arizona. And if his assessors were correct, the sale of this chunk of dirt would be the biggest financial payout of his career.

He inhaled a deep breath. "So what seems to be the problem?"

"You're the listing agent. Our client has tried several times to get in contact with you, but your office staff at DDG has been very vague as to your whereabouts." He paused. "Have any messages gotten through to you about the interest in this property? Because make no mistake; our client is *very* interested."

Gavin swore and paced to the window. "No. I haven't heard anything and I apologize for that, George." Speculation about his diminishing role in his businesses could have serious financial repercussions, so he had no choice but to explain. "Four years ago after my mother's death, I split DDG into two companies. Technically I'm still the CEO of DDG, but in the last year I've taken a more active role in Daniels Property Management. The DDG office staff apparently misinterpreted my personal contact instructions and I will get that handled immediately."

"Good. I'll admit we were concerned you might have health issues, as one of our event planners mentioned you'd lost some weight in the last year."

"That was intentional, not health related. And to allay your concerns as to my whereabouts, I'm currently living in eastern Wyoming, while my daughter finishes high school."

"Eastern Wyoming? Oh. That seems sudden."

"I discovered I had family members in this area. I've visited several times over the last few years and ended up buying land. Naturally, I wanted my daughter to be raised around family." That wasn't too far from the truth.

"I'm happy to hear that. But that still leaves me with what to tell my client."

"Tell him I'll apologize in person tomorrow for the miscommunication. Shall we meet in my office at DDG, say, around ten a.m.?"

"That sounds perfect, Gavin. Thank you."

"Thank you for tracking me down. I'll call you at this number if I run into travel delays. If not, I'll see you in the morning."

Gavin had known he'd face last minute trips to Arizona when he'd opted to move to Wyoming. He called his travel agent and winced when he heard the price for a ticket to Phoenix in the economy section would set him back fifteen hundred bucks.

A drop in the bucket if you can sell the land for the assessed value of thirty-five million dollars.

Gavin rearranged his schedule. He called Charlie and Vi, texted Sierra and left her a voice mail. Lastly, he dragged out his suitcase and picked three suits to get him through the week. The suits had been in dry cleaning bags since the movers had packed them in Arizona. Not much occasion to wear a suit and tie in Sundance.

Maybe there should be. You should take Rielle out for dinner when you get back from this trip.

Great plan. Ben had warned him not to treat Rielle like a dirty little secret. He'd love to show her this wasn't a fling by taking their relationship public. But she'd given him the impression she wasn't ready for that.

Now he had to ask a huge favor. He tracked her down and the instant he saw her, he wanted her. So he dragged her to bed.

Afterward, being naked, tangled up with her, hearts pounding and flesh damp, he realized he didn't want to hide this affection he felt for her. He didn't want to hide anything from her.

Gavin kissed the small of her back. "I could stay here all damn day, but I've gotta go."

She rolled over to face him, still modest enough that she'd pulled the sheets up to cover her breasts. "I saw your suitcases in the entryway before you carted me off to bed, tycoon."

"I wanted to give you a proper good morning and goodbye."

"Mmm. I did come two times so you got me coming and going."

He grinned. "Love that dirty mouth. I have to go to Arizona for business for a few days."

"What's going on?"

"Possible land deal sale. Possible *huge* land deal sale."

Rielle cocked her head. "How huge? I'm not asking for a spreadsheet, but I hear you wheeling and dealing on the phone, so I'm interested how this came to pass." She poked him in the chest. "You always ask me for explicit details about my businesses. So I want you to know I'm interested in your professional life as well."

"Really?"

"Yep. Your real estate tycoon-y side formed you as a man. And since I like your man form...I want to know more."

He kissed her forehead. "Basically, I've been holding on to a chunk of land that's worth a lot of money. There's some confusion in my office as to why the potential client couldn't get in touch with me. So I need to straighten out office snafus and hopefully cash a really big check."

"Better than six bucks apiece for plums?"

"Let's just say this land deal could be worth...five point eight *million* six dollar plums."

Her eyes rounded. "Wow. That's a plum sweet deal."

He groaned at her pun. "Anyway, I can't take Sierra."

"No problem. You go make your bajillion dollars and I'll crack the whip on your daughter. Not that she needs it."

"You sure?"

"Positive. Just bring me back a suitcase full of—"

"Money?" he supplied.

Rielle elbowed him in the gut as she rolled out of bed. "I'm not interested in your money, Gavin Daniels. Bring me back a suitcase full of grapefruit and oranges. They want like four bucks a pound at the grocery store and I'm too cheap to pay it."

He laughed.

Fifteen minutes later he stood next to his car, saying goodbye to Rielle. "Are you sure you'll be okay staying with Sierra?"

"If you're okay with me letting her throw a Halloween party and providing an open bar and condoms for her friends, then we're good."

Gavin tapped Rielle on the butt. "Not funny."

"Relax. Vi and Charlie are getting her to and from school. She's self-sufficient for breakfast and I cook myself supper so it's no biggie to make extra. You'll be gone what? Four days? She'll be fine."

"I'm not asking about her. I'm asking about you." He caressed the side of her face. "Sierra can be a pain."

"Are you trying to get me to change my mind?" Rielle said lightly. "Because I can."

"No. I feel I'm taking advantage of you, especially after you gave me the whole, *just because we're sleeping together doesn't mean I'm helping you parent your daughter* speech."

"I volunteered, which is different than you assuming I'll deal with childcare in your absence." Rielle stood on tiptoe and pecked his lips. "Go. Don't worry."

Gavin kissed her longer. Hotter. Then sweeter. "For the thousandth time, thank you."

"For the thousandth time, you're welcome. Now go, before you miss your flight."

"I'll see you Friday." After Gavin climbed in his car and buckled up, Rielle tapped on the window.

"Yes?"

"Don't get sunburned."

Chapter Eighteen

November...

The first three days with Sierra were almost too easy. She came home from school and retreated to her room until supper. She wasn't surly, just preoccupied with a school project.

So after Charlie dropped Sierra off Thursday, Rielle was surprised when she hung around the kitchen. In Rielle's experience with teens, that meant Sierra had something on her mind.

No reason you can't listen.

Sierra rested her chin on her hand. "Don't take this the wrong way, but it's cool that you know how to do so many things most people don't."

"How could I take that the wrong way?" Rielle asked, stirring the bundle of raw wool soaking in beet juice.

"Because my mom was almost...proud of being helpless. She couldn't cook, she couldn't sew, she couldn't garden. She hired this Mexican woman and paid her cash to clean her house and wash her clothes."

Rielle couldn't fathom that type of lifestyle. "What did your mother do all day?"

Sierra shrugged. "I'm pretty sure she went back to bed after she dropped me off at school. She watched TV or went shopping or to the salon or out to lunch with her friends or was at the beck and call of whatever boyfriend she had at the time."

Before Rielle asked specifics, Sierra said, "So I bet Rory can do all sorts of cool life skill stuff like that, huh?" She pointed to the various jars of dye that held small bunches of yarn Rielle had opted to dip-dye.

"I taught her how to cook, bake, garden, raise various things for food and how to make things to sell, if that's what you mean. Does she do any of it now? Very little."

That surprised her. "Why not?"

"She's busy in grad school and her landlord frowns on her keeping bees, chickens and goats in her apartment."

Sierra snickered.

"I'd like to think she'll get back to utilizing some of the skills she learned growing up, but I won't be upset if she decides homespun activities don't work for her. Heaven knows I don't do all the things my mom used to.”

“Like what?”

“Like raising chickens. I miss the fresh meat, but I hated butchering. And I never liked gathering eggs because chickens can be nasty creatures. At the time, selling organic eggs wasn't profitable. I didn't replace our dairy cow after Rory developed a milk allergy. I never sold any milk products; it was strictly for our own use anyway. As much as I like goats, I don't keep them, either for their angora or their milk. I love goat cheese, but goat milking is one of my least favorite things to do.”

Her nose wrinkled. “I've never milked anything.”

Rielle twisted the wet bundle until the water ran clear. “It's not fun. My mom used to make goat cheese, but Chassie Glanzer has a thriving business with excellent milk and cheese so I support her. Also, my mom handcrafted soap, but with Sky Blue creating unique products from natural ingredients, I'd rather buy from them than make anything myself.”

“That's my dad's business philosophy too. No reason to compete with a business that's providing a service better than you can offer.”

“Smart man, your father.”

“Yes, but if you tell him I said that or that I was quoting him, I'll deny it,” she said with a grin. “He lives to explain things; in other words...lecture.”

Rielle laughed. “You sound like Rory.”

“Selling all of this—” she gestured to the piles of fiber, “—is how you get paid?”

“Yep. I chose to make my living this way, in spite of some people believing being self-sufficient with self-sustaining products is an outdated concept. It's hard work and I know I'll never get rich. Growing up, Rory had to pitch in. If we didn't get a good harvest—whether it was veggies, fruit, honey—then we'd have a lean winter, finance-wise and food-wise.”

“But you got to spend time together.”

“True. It wasn't all work. We had fun too.” Probably not the type of fun Sierra knew—shopping, mani-pedis, spa treatments and fancy luncheons.

Stop assuming and ask her. The admiring way she talks about her father makes it obvious her mother isn't the only one who influenced her life.

“What about you? What did you do for fun?”

Sierra pressed her finger into the poppy seeds on her plate, left over from her lemon poppy seed muffin. “When I stayed with my mom, we did what she wanted. Sometimes she'd let me choose.”

“And when you were with your dad?”

"My dad worked a lot. But when he came home, he didn't flop on the couch and ignore me like a lot of my friends' dads did. He's a sports guy, but he taped all the games so we could do stuff together. Some fun, some that were supposed to teach me a lesson. Dad was big on learning life lessons."

That remark piqued Rielle's curiosity because Gavin had stuck to his guns with not letting Sierra drive until he felt she was ready. "Like what?"

"When I was ten I begged for a puppy and he kept saying no. Finally after a year, he said if I proved to him that I could be responsible with an animal, he'd let me have a pet."

"What did you have to do?"

"Volunteer at the animal shelter for two months. I learned to take care of all kinds of dogs and cats. I scrubbed cages. Emptied litter boxes. Helped with flea baths and combed matted fur. I fed the animals and filled water bowls and cleaned up after them. I saw what an abused and neglected animal looked like and acted like. It was so freakin' sad."

Not the type of parenting reaction she'd expected from Gavin; Rielle thought he would've given his daughter anything without restriction. "Did you end up getting a puppy?"

Sierra shook her head. "Learning all that changed my mind. Especially when my dad said I'd have to take my dog everywhere with me, even to friends' sleepovers, because he had a life that didn't entail babysitting my pet. Of course, my mom offered to buy me any kind of puppy I wanted, mostly to piss my dad off."

That behavior wasn't shocking after what Rielle had learned about Gavin's ex-wife. "Well, for never having a dog of your own, Sadie is sure taken with you."

"Probably because she misses Rory, huh?"

"Nope. I got Sadie after Rory went to college, so she's pretty much my dog."

"I thought my dad said you had, like, a pack of dogs?"

Rielle transferred the dyed fiber from the pint-sized glass jars into individual plastic grocery bags. "That was true the first time he stayed here. We had three dogs. Spuds died last year. Rory's dog, Jingle, is around if she is. I take care of Ben's dogs, Ace and Deuce, whenever he and Ainsley go out of town. So maybe that is a pack."

Sierra watched her tying off the plastic bags. "Now what do you do with that?"

"Heat it in the microwave to set the dye." She set two bags in the microwave and set the timer. "Then it cools, I rinse it, spin out the excess water and hang to dry. The immersion batches on the stove are left to cool to room temp. Then I rinse it, spin out the excess water and hang to dry. Sense a theme?" She pointed to the piles of raw, combed wool. "That is called wool roving. Sometimes I dye it whole, or tie it off and tie-dye it. But this batch I'm hand painting. It's a messy process and I like to use several different colors. The dyed fiber looks weird, but once I spin it into yarn, it is amazing. I can't keep it in stock and I have ten batches to finish."

"Where do you sell it?"

"I've been working with several stores over the years who know my quality is good and I'm not afraid to experiment with different fibers, so that keeps me in a higher paying niche market. I also sell directly to experienced knitters I've met over the years. I supply all sorts of different spun and dyed fibers to a woman who knits projects specifically for publication in how-to books. It's cool to see the patterns she creates from the yarn I've hand-dyed and spun."

Sierra peered in the pot. "That's a really pretty color. It would be so awesome to wear something you've made."

"I've got so much of this burgundy hue; I'll keep some and work on a project over the winter."

"Could you teach me how to knit?" Sierra blurted. "I know you're busy, but if you're just sitting by the fire some night, maybe I could watch you and take notes?"

Rielle was absurdly touched by the request. Sometimes when she looked at Sierra she saw a privileged, world-weary teen. But other times, like now, she saw a sweet girl who was eager to learn something out of the norm because it interested her. "I'd be happy to teach you."

"Really? Cool!"

"Vi won't get upset? I know she likes to do crafty type activities with you."

Sierra shook her head. "Grams crochets, just like my other grandma did. It doesn't interest me because you can knit much cooler things."

"Okay. I've still got a pair of beginner's knitting needles around someplace."

"Yay!"

Rielle took the bags out of the microwave, checked to see if all the dye had been absorbed and set the bags on the cooling rack. Then she put in the next two bags and set the microwave timer.

"Now I know you're big on the barter system, so you have to let me teach you to do something."

"Sierra, that's sweet, but not necessary."

"Fair's fair. And there's one thing I'm good at, because I've been doing it since I could hold a brush."

Please. God. No.

"I'll give you a makeover!" Sierra jumped off the barstool. "This is gonna be so awesome!"

Shit. "Well, I need to finish setting the dye in the last two batches. And clean up."

"It'll take me ten minutes to get my stuff together anyway. Then I'll meet you in your bathroom."

The enthusiastic teen was through the swinging door before Rielle could reply. How did she tell Sierra she wasn't interested in a makeover?

She couldn't. She'd always considered herself lucky that Rory hadn't forced her love of all that girly stuff on her. Although...Rielle could admit her new hairstyle had made a world of difference in how she viewed herself.

What did she have to lose except for a few hours? Nothing.

But she poured herself a big whiskey Coke anyway before she wandered down the hallway.

Sierra had already set up in Rielle's bathroom. She pointed to the toilet. "Sit. Get comfy."

Rielle sat, drink in hand.

"Where is your makeup?"

"Drawer on the right. There's not much."

Sierra cleaned Rielle's face with a warm cloth, which was really weird. She asked questions about Rielle's skincare regimen, which consisted of washing her face with Ivory soap and moisturizing with Lubriderm lotion.

Surprisingly, that didn't earn a heavy sigh like it would've from Rory.

Rielle kept her eyes closed and took the occasional sip of her drink as Sierra discussed skin tones, the best way to mask her under eye circles and cultivate the natural look. Which prompted her to ask, "So not wearing any makeup isn't an acceptable natural look?"

"It's fine when you're working outside, as long as you're wearing skin protection with at least thirty SPF." She smeared something beneath Rielle's eye. "But you don't want to look like you just whipped off your gloves and sun hat when you go to town, do you?"

That's exactly what Rielle had always done. So she deflected. If Sierra was anything like Rory, she'd love to talk about boys. "I haven't heard you mention any cute guys at your school."

"I try to avoid talking about guys around my dad. He gets a little uptight and lecture-y about it."

"Your dad isn't here. Since you're avoiding my question, is there some guy you're interested in?"

Sierra sighed. "There's one guy. He's nice and funny and bossy and kind of quirky. I see him at the library or around school and we talk and stuff. But he's made it clear that he just wants to be pals."

"Huh." Rielle stayed still as Sierra's fingers dotted something cool on her cheeks, nose and forehead and gently smoothed it in. "Doesn't the new girl catch guys' interest?"

"Two guys offered to break up with their girlfriends to go out with me. But I don't need any more crap from the girls at school."

Rielle opened her eyes and looked at Sierra. "Are you having a hard time and can't talk to your dad about it?"

"No. Close your eyes. Well, I mean yes. Girls at school aren't mean, they just ignore me. Marin is fun and we have a great time together, but now she's got a boyfriend. Two other girls ask me to do stuff, but they both drive and I feel like a...loser because they'd have to pick me up and bring me home. I'm thinking about asking my dad if I could be home schooled."

Her eyes flew open. "God, no, Sierra, don't do that. Home schooling sucks. Trust me. My parents didn't give me a choice. And if you think it's tough not being able to drive, imagine how much harder it'd be if you didn't see anyone but your dad, me and your grandparents."

"Keep your eyes closed," Sierra reminded her. "You didn't consider home schooling Rory?"

"Not for a single second. I won't say her school years were easy, especially not after she started middle school and hit the six-foot-one mark, making her taller than all the girls in her class and most of the boys. But she had a couple of good friends, she earned the highest GPA in her graduating class and she's socially well-adjusted. Without making generalizations—because I know what that's like—home schooled kids are awkward in normal society."

"You're not awkward and you were home schooled," she pointed out.

"Really? You sure? I can't even put on my own damn makeup."

Sierra snickered.

"I'm also forty. An old forty." Sierra dragged something wet close to her lash line and Rielle flinched.

"Hold still. Geez. I'm not gonna jab you in the eye unless you do that again."

"Sorry." Sierra lightly brushed Rielle's entire eye area and she tried not to wiggle because it tickled.

"You said that you knew what it was like when people made generalizations. What did you mean?"

"I had a baby at sixteen. So people around here assumed I was a slut. Or that I was on food stamps and all sorts of government assistance because I was the daughter of pot-growing hippies."

"Wow. Really? People said shit like that to you?"

"All the time."

Sierra touched the apples of Rielle's cheeks with a soft brush. "People are assholes. You're not any of those things. They should follow you around one day and see how hard you work."

Again, she was reminded Sierra was a lot more observant than she'd given her credit for.

"Okay. Open your eyes."

She did.

Sierra grinned at her. "Looking good, Ree. Time for mascara. I can't stand when someone else puts it on me, so I'll let you put it on yourself, just as long as you can do it without the mirror so you don't ruin the big reveal."

The big reveal. Funny girl. "Fine. I'll do it."

Sierra slapped a blue and neon pink tube in Rielle's hand. "Start at the lash line. Sweep up twice. Then only touch the very tips of your lashes. That really makes them pop."

"I'll be lucky if I don't pop out my eyeball doing this without a mirror."

"Ha ha. You're funny and not nearly as cranky as you like to think you are."

That caught Rielle's attention. "Cranky?"

"You. Thinking you're old. Acting like such a hard-ass. Like you've got no time for anyone. But I see you with my dad. You smile a lot. So does he."

This intuitive kid reminded her so much of Rory at age sixteen she ached, missed her insightful, stubborn and sweet daughter. She finished with the mascara. "Now can I look?"

"Nope. Last thing. Lipstick."

Rielle groaned.

"Oh, don't be such a baby. It's not like I'm painting your lips with goopy stuff. Now pucker up. Hold it." She outlined Rielle's mouth with a thick pink-colored pencil. "You have the most perfect lips. My mom pays a fortune to have full lips like these." She sighed. "You need to play them up. Even if you just put on hydrating shimmer gloss."

"Uh, Sierra, no offense, but I don't even know what the hell that is."

"Ree. Stop talking, you're smudging it. I'm almost done."

Guess finishing her drink was out of the question.

"There." Sierra peered at her like she was a science experiment. "Okay, I lied. There is one other thing I want to do."

"What?"

"Where's your hair spray?"

"Under the sink."

"Close your eyes again. And umm...tell me if I pull too hard."

Jesus.

Sierra fogged the bathroom with hairspray and Rielle bit back a cough. The kid did pull and twist her hair harder than she was used to. Well, with the exception of Sunday morning when Gavin had become that sexy hair-pulling beast who drove her insane with lust.

Probably not something she should be thinking about with the man's daughter right in front of her.

"All right. You're done with this phase."

This phase?

Sierra pulled her to her feet.

"No peeking until I tell you." She spun her forward and to the right. "Open your eyes."

Rielle mentally practiced her *wow* face, hoping it reflected in the mirror before her *what the fuck?* face. She slowly opened her eyes.

And her wow face was real.

Sierra hadn't caked on makeup, or given her a look that was too old, too young, or too sophisticated. The effect was very natural. Like Rielle always looked, but better. More polished.

"So? What do you think?"

Rielle met Sierra's gaze in the mirror. "You were right. This really makes my eyes pop. And I love the lip color."

"You have the prettiest eyes. Kind of like all the green things you grow are reflected in them."

She squeezed Sierra's hand. "Thank you. You are a miracle worker."

Sierra squeezed her hand back a little harder than Rielle expected. "Stop saying shit like that. Now. What do you think of the hair?"

With her hair spiked every which way it sort of looked like she'd stuck her finger in an electric socket. But it worked. Conveyed a hip, edgy vibe without it seeming like she was trying too hard to be hip and edgy.

"It's kind of funky, but you need to have a different way to fix yourself up, for when you go out."

"I do like it." She touched the top. "It's easy?"

"Just as easy as what you do now. And when you're feeling really daring? I'll show you how to curl it so you look like an angel."

Now that she'd pay to see. "I'll take you up on that."

Sierra's hands landed on her shoulders. "Don't get defensive on the next phase. Bear with me." Then she steered Rielle toward her closet door.

"Oh hell no. You are *not* rifling through my closet, Sierra."

"True. You are."

When Rielle tried to spin around, Sierra held her in place in front of the full length mirror. "We are doing this. First, pick ten or fifteen pieces of clothing you love. Mix it up between jeans, pants, skirts, tops, shorts, dresses and sweaters."

"Okay. I can do that."

"Second, pick as many accessories as you want. Belts, scarves, leggings, shawls, jewelry."

That'd be easy since Rielle had few of those items. "Is that it?"

"Yep. I've gotta check something and I'll be right back."

She was overcome with guilt opening the closet door because she'd packed so much shit in here after relocating from the upstairs master bedroom. Most of it she didn't wear, but couldn't part with because it was so damn ingrained in her not to be wasteful.

Then she felt resentful she was letting a sixteen-year-old fashionista boss her around.

But she's hit the mark with the makeover so far. Admit you're having fun. What else would you be doing? Working? Moping because you miss Gavin?

That put Rielle into the spirit of the moment and she tracked down her favorite pieces.

Sierra returned with a half-full garbage bag. The girl didn't actually believe Rielle would throw away her clothes like on those TV shows?

"Show me whatcha got."

Sierra nodded approvingly at the pieces Rielle had chosen. "When you're done in the garden, or taking bread into town, or selling your stuff at market, what do you wear?"

Work clothes. Sometimes the same jeans or shorts she'd worn picking fruit or veggies. She'd wash her hands and put on the first clean T-shirt she could find. She flopped back on the bed. "You're telling me to stop dressing like a bum?"

"Maybe. You're hiding behind grungy clothes." Sierra leaned over her. "Let me help you change that. It's what I'm good at. And you won't have to buy anything new unless you want to. We'll work with what you already have. So what do you say?"

"I say, amen, sister, it's way past time," echoed from the doorway.

Rielle sat up and her mouth dropped open. "Rory?"

"In the flesh. But I have to admit when I decided to come home and surprise you, the last thing I expected was to see you getting a fashion makeover."

She hurled herself off the bed and hugged her daughter. "What a great surprise! I was just thinking about you and here you are. So how long are you staying?"

"All weekend." Rory hugged her back, but her focus shifted. "Hey. You must be Sierra. I'm Rory."

"Hi. Wow. You look exactly like your mom. And she, uh, talks about you all the time."

Rielle noticed Sierra acted nervous, twisting her fingers in the plastic garbage bag handles.

"Look, I'm sure you guys have stuff to talk about so I'll go."

But Rory stepped in front of her and shook her head. "No way. You're staying. After I snuck into the house, I listened in the hallway and I have to admit I'm impressed that you've accomplished something I've been trying to do for years." She mock whispered, "You'll be my hero if you can get rid of all the tie-dyed clothing."

Rielle flapped her hand at Rory, but she and Sierra were too busy laughing to notice.

"So the makeup and hair is your doing?" Rory asked Sierra.

"Uh-huh. Ree is gonna teach me to knit and I wanted to teach her something useful. This is the only thing I can do that can be considered a skill."

"You're what? Sixteen? Plenty of time to develop other skills." Rory settled cross-legged on the bed. "Pretend I'm not here and finish what you started."

Since she so rarely got to see Rory, Rielle wanted to blow off the fashion show. But she wasn't surprised her thoughtful daughter wouldn't let Sierra feel left out.

"Okay. Here goes." Sierra used the pieces Rielle had chosen and put together a dozen different outfits. All casual and unique without being weird. She changed an outfit from professional to funky just by mixing and matching accessories.

With the back and forth between Rory and Sierra, Rielle started to feel like a third wheel, even when she was amused by their fashion banter.

Finally, Rory asked, "What's in the bag?"

"Stuff I had in my closet I never wear," Sierra said. "I wasn't sure if she'd like any of it, or if she'd think it was—"

"Too young for her," they finished at the same time.

Was she really that predictable?

Rory's gaze zipped over Sierra. "It'd probably fit me better than her anyway. How tall are you?"

"Five ten." Sierra fished out a few items at a time, trying each piece with each outfit to see if it'd add impact. A slim fit white rayon blouse went into the keep pile along with a tweed jacket and a butter-yellow-colored turtleneck.

"You sure you want to get rid of this stuff?" Rory asked, fingering an orange sequined tank top.

"Take it if you want it. A hand-me-down is recycling—the responsible, green thing to do."

Rielle grinned. "Ooh, Rory, she totally has your number."

"Which is awesome, because I'm gonna be the belle of Laramie in this tank top on New Year's Eve." She pawed through the bag. "What else do you have that's too young for my mom?"

Rory ended up with more clothes from the bag than Rielle did. Her thoughts drifted and she wondered what Gavin would think if he was here, seeing how well their daughters were getting along. She missed him, more than she imagined she would and she didn't know how to feel about that. She had a sense of unease that Gavin hadn't thought about her at all since she hadn't heard from him, but she knew he'd kept in contact with Sierra.

"...with a strap-on."

Her gaze flew to her daughter's and both Rory and Sierra laughed.

"You weren't listening to us at all," Rory complained.

"Sorry. What?"

Sierra's gesture encompassed the bed. Then she shook her finger at Rielle. "I'd better not see you heading to town in your gardening clothes. You aren't a bag lady. You are an entrepreneur. You have several chic outfits to choose from. And you need to own the fact you're still young and hot."

Rory laughed. "Yeah, Mom, she's got your number too."

"My work here is done for tonight." Sierra bowed and slipped out of the room.

Rielle hugged Rory again. "I'm so happy to see you."

"Let's have a drink and you can tell me all about Gavin Daniels."

She stiffened. How had Rory known she'd gotten involved with Gavin? "What?"

"Gavin and Sierra. They've been living here months. Are you ready to move into my cabin yet?"

Not even close. In that moment, Rielle decided not to tell Rory about her relationship with Gavin. Luckily, her daughter was easily distracted. "You'll never guess who I ran into at the hardware store last week."

"Who?"

"Remember Connor? The cute guy who installed the replacement electrical line in the barn?"

"Oh yeah. Definitely some electricity there."

"Funny you should say that, because he asked about you."

"Really?" Rory went off on a tangent and Rielle had a reprieve.

Chapter Nineteen

After four days attending to business in Phoenix, Gavin was damn glad to hit the wide open spaces of Wyoming. He called Charlie, letting him know he'd fetch Sierra from the bus stop. He'd missed his daughter, but her random texts amused him.

He'd missed Rielle too. It was a new feeling, missing a romantic partner. Missing the whole of her, the way she smiled at him, their conversations, the way they'd end up twined together. He hadn't texted or called her. Would she be annoyed with him?

Maybe you oughta ask Sierra for advice since you're acting like a teenaged girl.

Gavin waved at the assorted McKays, huddled in big pickups at the bus stop as they waited for their kiddos.

Sierra hustled to the car, fighting the fierce Wyoming wind. He remembered when his little girl threw herself at him, assuring him she'd missed him. In recent years he'd considered himself lucky if she even acknowledged him in public.

"I didn't think you got back until later tonight."

"I switched to an earlier flight."

"I'm glad you're here."

He smoothed a wisp of her dark hair from her cheek. "Me too, sweetheart."

"Can I drive?" she asked hopefully.

"In this wind? No."

"Damn."

Gavin laughed and pulled onto the highway. "I imagine Charlie let you drive?"

"Every day. I practiced parallel parking, which he says I rock at. Then we had hot chocolate and pie at the diner before we drove home on the back roads. He's so sweet and funny."

"So it's not awkward?"

Sierra frowned at him. "What? Spending time with Charlie?"

"Yeah."

"No. At least he wants to spend time with me."

Gavin shot her a sharp look. "Was that a dig at me?"

She rolled her eyes. "God, Dad, paranoid much? I just meant if it wasn't for the McKays, I'd never get to see anyone or do anything. It sucks being stuck in the middle of nowhere with no way to get around."

Never failed—she found a way to poke at him about the fact she still wasn't driving on her own. He knew better than to take the bait. "How was school this week?"

"Crappy. I got a hundred percent on my math quiz and blew the curve for the rest of the class so my classmates are pissed at me. Which is probably why I'm spending *another* Friday night alone. Yay."

"Never feel guilty for using your brain, Sierra. I'm proud of you for getting the top grade."

"Did you see anyone I know when you were home?" she asked.

"Just the people in the office."

"I wouldn't even mind listening to Manny complain about the heat and everything else." She sighed. "Can I go with you next time?"

"I don't know when that'll be." He glanced at her again, seeing that brooding look settle on her face. "Back up. Why don't you have plans for this weekend? Is there something going on?"

"Besides the fact I don't have any friends except Marin and she's busy all the time? Besides the fact the weather always sucks so I can't drive? No. Besides that, everything is awesome."

And...there was the sarcasm. He counted to ten. "But didn't you just say if not for the McKays—"

"Read between the lines, Dad," she snapped. "As much as I try to convince myself everything is fine, it's not. When you're gone it just reminds me that I want to go home. I hate it here."

She hated it today. Didn't mean she'd hate it tomorrow. Or next week. She changed her mind as often as her nail polish color.

Gavin parked in front of the house to unload his luggage, which included a token he'd picked up for his daughter. Surly girl would probably throw it at him, so he'd save it.

"So what? You're not talking to me now?" she demanded.

"It's pointless to argue with you, when you'll pick apart anything I say."

"That's because you know I'm right. Not that you ever listen to me." She scrambled out of the car and...yep. Slammed the door hard enough to rock the entire frame.

Welcome fucking home.

Screw that. He wouldn't let her shitty attitude sour the fact he *was* glad to be home.

Gavin left his suitcase in the entryway and hung up his coat. He loosened his tie on his way to the kitchen, searching for Rielle.

He pushed open the swinging door and there she was.

His damn heart skipped a beat. His stomach performed a happy flip. His cock stirred. He needed to wrap himself in her warmth,

135

softness and light.

"Goddamn, Ree, you're looking mighty tasty today."

She flashed him an unsure smile. "I thought you'd be here later."

"I couldn't wait to get back." He stalked her until her back connected with the refrigerator.

Rielle's eyes softened. "Really?"

"Really." He pressed his body to hers, curling one hand around her face and the other around her hip. He whispered, "I missed you," against her lips.

"Gavin. Wait."

"I can't." Then he took her mouth. Kissing her with pent up need, proving his desire for her with every hot and hard stroke of his tongue. Losing himself in the rush of her lithe body arching against his. Filling his senses with her taste, her scent. Swallowing her sexy little I-want-you-now moans that drove him fucking insane.

"Bed. Now."

"But—"

She needed convincing? Fine. He'd convince the hell out of her. He growled, cranking up the intensity of the next kiss. Sliding his hand into her hair and pulling slightly, angling her head, to dive deeper into the soft draws of her mouth.

The sound of a loud, pointed throat clearing came from behind him.

Gavin froze. Then he lifted his mouth and his gaze collided with hers.

She bit her lip.

His hands fell away and he slowly turned around.

A blonde amazon version of Rielle gave him a little finger wave.

His eyes narrowed. Or was she just giving him the finger?

"Gavin. This is my daughter, Rory," Rielle said behind him.

He'd just attacked Rielle in front of her daughter? Classy.

Wait. Did Rory know about them?

Rielle slipped her arm around his waist and rested her head on his chest. That move shocked the heck out of her daughter.

Guess that answered that question.

"So, you two are...dating?" Rory asked incredulously.

"Yes, we're involved."

"Have you been involved—together, dating, whatever—since he moved in with you?"

"Technically, I'm living with him," Rielle said evenly.

Annoyance crossed Rory's face. Her posture remained belligerent. "Oh, we're playing the word definition game. Fine. So, technically what you're really doing is sleeping together."

"That is none of your business."

"Is it Sierra's business? Should I ask her if you two share a bed every night? Or is she in the dark too? Or maybe that's why she was making you over? So you'd be what he wanted?"

"I cannot believe you just said that. What is your deal, Rory?"

"My deal? Really, Mom? You don't understand why I'd be upset that you didn't tell me you're having sex with Gavin Daniels? And apparently it's more than sex? It's some kind of...relationship?"

Rielle stiffened, but she didn't move away from him. "I don't tell you everything that goes on in my life, Rory."

"Bullshit. That's because there's nothing *to* tell since I've never known you to be involved with anyone."

"Or maybe I don't tell you because you blab any damn thing that pops into your head, regardless if it's my personal business," Rielle shot back.

Rory had the grace to look embarrassed, but it didn't last long. "Ouch. All this secrecy does is make me wonder if you didn't tell me about you and Gavin because you're ashamed about what this really is."

"And of course, you know what it really is."

"A convenience."

Gavin ground his teeth together, understanding how difficult it must be for Rielle to hold her tongue when Sierra got mouthy with him.

"Wrong. You want to know why I didn't tell you?"

"Let me guess. Because it proves me right? That he's—"

"Don't say it," Rielle warned.

"Just like the rest of the McKays," Rory finished. "He'll fuck anything that walks like it's his due and then he'll walk the fuck away. That's really the guy you want to have a relationship with?"

"That's enough," Gavin said to Rory. "I don't know what chip you have on your shoulder about the McKays, and frankly, I don't give a shit."

"Big surprise there," she interrupted with a sneer.

"But I do care that you think you can waltz in here and pass judgment on your mother, when to be blunt, you don't know fuck-all."

Rielle didn't chastise him, nor did she jump in and apologize for his harsh response.

"This is just fucking great. He's already got you under his thumb." Rory pushed off the counter. "Screw this. I'm outta here."

That's when Rielle planted all five feet five inches in front of her six foot tall daughter. "Cool off that hot head of yours, Aurora Rose. You don't get to go off on a tear, do you hear me?" Rielle drilled Rory in the chest with her index finger. "I slaved making *your* favorite supper at *your* request, so you damn well better have *your* butt parked at the dining room table at six-thirty, wearing a goddamned smile."

"Will it just be you and me? Or will they be here too?"

"Yes, Gavin and Sierra will be here, since it's a family dinner in their house."

"Whatever." Rory tried to sidestep Rielle.

But Rielle wouldn't budge. "You will be here."

"I said I would, all right? Jesus. Move. I gotta get my dog." Rory all but stomped off.

Gavin wasn't aware he held his breath, waiting for the door to slam, until it actually did—with enough force to rattle the dishes in the cupboard. He chuckled.

"Glad someone sees humor in this."

He circled his arms around Rielle. "I don't know whether to be impressed that Rory can slam the door harder than Sierra, or scared my daughter won't outgrow this stage and she'll be testing door hinges for the next seven years."

Rielle smiled wanly. "It's been a while since Rory has reminded me of her door-slamming expertise."

Gavin ran his hand down her back. "Are you okay?"

"No. I hate fighting with her."

"Must be the day," he murmured. "Sierra lit into me the second she got in the car today."

"I wondered what triggered *her* spectacular door slam. And why she'd ignored me when I called out to her, after we'd had so much fun last night."

"Doing what?"

"Sierra insisted on making me over. Rory showed up and the two of them conspired against me. They got along surprisingly well."

"Were you expecting Rory this weekend?"

She shook her head. "She hasn't gotten around to telling me why she showed up out of the blue, which is probably why she acted so bratty."

He sat on a barstool, bringing Rielle between his legs, close to his body. "What can I do?"

"Nothing. You know what it's like to have an only child. They expect immediate attention. That hasn't changed even when she's in college. Last night, she had to share me with Sierra. She assumed she'd have my undivided attention today, but Ainsley needed to talk so I met her in town for a long lunch. Then you show up and kiss the shit out of me, throwing her *mommy and me* world into turmoil. She won't have my total focus this weekend. That's never happened to her before."

"Why didn't you tell her about us?"

Rielle smoothed her palms over his cheeks. "Not because I was embarrassed. But..." She outlined his face with her fingertips, from his hairline to his jawline, to the curve of his lips. "You really are a handsome man. Such a McKay."

Gavin growled. "Answer. The. Question."

"I didn't tell Rory about you, because I have so few things that are mine. Not in an ownership way, but in a personal way. I've lived my life as an open book with her. I don't regret that." Rielle caressed his face. "So what you and I have? I've never had. I don't want to share it with her or anyone else, because it belongs only to us."

That's when Gavin fell in love with her. He couldn't tear his gaze away from this beautiful and complex woman who had swooped in and stolen his heart.

"You look so serious," she said softly. "Did I say something wrong?"

"No, honey, you said everything right." He brushed his lips up the strong line of her jaw, to the sweet spot in front of her ear. "Have I mentioned that I missed you?"

"Mmm-hmm. But you can tell me again."

Following the curve of her hips, he grabbed two handfuls of that sexy ass. "I thought about our goodbye in the wee small hours of Monday morning. A lot." He blew in her ear. "It's such a fucking turn-on when your body is squeezing me so hard I can't even fucking breathe."

"Gavin."

"But we're more than just body heat and movement beneath the sheets in the darkness." He nuzzled her neck. "I thought about how perfect it feels when I slide into you. When I hear that catch in your breath and I know in that moment, you're only mine."

"You been reading books on how to seduce a woman with pretty words, tycoon?" Rielle turned her head and nipped his ear lobe.

"Maybe. Is it working?"

"God yes."

Gavin's hands squeezed her butt, urging her closer. "I want you."

Their lips connected and he forced himself not to inhale her. He forced himself to temper his explicit words with the tenderness and sweetness of his kiss.

A *whoosh* sounded, followed by, "Seriously? God. Get a room!" Then stomping, followed by another *whoosh*.

Rielle pulled back. "And Rory breaks the moment yet again. Have you told Sierra about us yet?"

"No. I guess I'd better do it now." He kissed her cheek. "We'll pick this up later?"

"Definitely."

Rory and Sierra conspired together to keep their parents apart.

Sierra desperately required Gavin's help with biology homework. On a Friday night. For two hours.

Then Rory demanded Rielle's help to find a specific knitting pattern. Sifting through pattern books and printouts lasted two hours.

Consequently, dinner was served later than she'd planned. When Gavin offered to help, Rory made a comment about him helping himself to another make out session with her mother while the food got cold.

Rielle and Gavin were seated across from one another. Too far away to even casually touch—obviously intentional. And Rory insisted they eat each course separately, reminding her mother that the goal was to enjoy the food it'd taken her *so long* to prepare.

The appetizer course—a caramelized apple and onion tart topped with brie—was followed by the chopped salad course and ended with chicken and noodles—Rory's favorite.

Every time Rielle glanced at Gavin, that hungry look entered his eyes. A look that said he'd only be satisfied if she was his four-course meal. He'd barely touched his wine. She knew his gaze was on the clock as often as it was on her.

Rory and Sierra left them alone while they prepared the dessert course. As soon as the door swung shut, Gavin shot out of his chair.

Rielle's heart rate spiked when he moved in behind her with deliberate leisure. He set his hands on her shoulders. His thumbs lazily stroked her collarbone. Shivers spread into gooseflesh, traveling down her belly and her spine.

He pressed his warm mouth to her ear. "I want to fuck you."

"Gavin."

"I need to fuck you."

Yes, please.

"These girls can try and keep us apart, but they have to go to bed sometime. And as soon as that happens? You will be naked, underneath me."

She turned her head, almost desperate to feel her lips on his skin.

But he stayed her movement, his hand sneaking up to cup her chin, holding her in place as he licked the shell of her ear. "Remember that every time you look at me. Imagine my mouth sucking on your nipples. Imagine my hands on your ass as I'm thrusting into your hot cunt."

Rielle just about came right then.

Gavin was back in his seat by the time Rory and Sierra returned with the strawberry lemon shortcake. They chattered, seemingly oblivious to the increased sexual tension.

"So Sierra and I were talking about our after-dinner plans," Rory said as she set a dessert plate in front of Rielle.

"We thought it'd be fun to have a game night," Sierra added, sliding a slice of shortcake in front of her father.

"How about Scrabble?" Rory asked.

"I'd rather play Clue," Sierra countered.

They argued the merits of various games. Rielle cut into her dessert but she couldn't eat a bite. Her mouth was too damn dry from the heated gazes the wicked man across the table kept throwing her way.

"Mom? What do you think?"

Startled, Rielle looked over at Gavin. The lust in his eyes made her stutter, "I d-don't know." *Breathe, idiot.* "Gavin?"

"Am I up for playing a game? Absolutely." He wrapped his lips around a strawberry on the end of his fork and sucked it into his mouth.

She was so flustered she dropped her knife.

Silence.

No mistaking that for anything but sexual tension now.

Then Rory tossed her napkin on the table. "That's it. I'm done. You two wanna blow off our plans for family night, because you want to lock yourselves in the bedroom? Knock yourselves out. But I won't stick around to hear the headboard banging."

"Rory! What a rude thing to say." Her cheeks burned as she glanced at Sierra—even her mouth was open in shock.

"I'm headed back to Laramie tomorrow. But tonight, I'm going to town." A calculating look crossed Rory's face. "Come on, Sierra, let's go out."

Sierra looked even more shocked. "Ah, sure." She pushed back from the table.

"Just where do you think you're going?" Gavin asked Sierra.

"Out. With Rory."

"And where's that?" Gavin demanded from Rory.

"The Golden Boot."

"What makes you think I'll let my sixteen-year-old daughter go to a bar with you?"

"It's a restaurant. Do you think that's worse for her than being in this house, listening to the two of you get it on?"

Silence.

"Sierra's curfew is midnight. Have fun."

Chapter Twenty

Rielle waited until the front door slammed before she looked across the table at Gavin.

His steely-eyed gaze was focused entirely on her.

"Did they really think we'd pitch a fit about them leaving when we haven't been alone for four goddamn days? Did it even cross your mind to ask them to stay?"

"No." The lustful glimmer in his eye served as a warning. He'd have her stripped, bucking beneath him, lost in the pleasure his body brought to hers if she didn't snatch control right now.

Rielle pushed back from the table and moseyed over to him. Gavin watched her with the heavy-lidded gaze that caused her pulse to skip.

"Something on your mind, Ree?"

"You." She straddled his lap and fingered the collar of his black dress shirt. "I'll admit disappointment you took off that sexy tie. I had plans for it." She pressed an openmouthed kiss on his neck. "You ever been restrained, tycoon?"

"Ah. No."

"Might be fun." Rielle sucked on his throat, then whispered, "Imagine how the silky fabric would feel floating over your skin. On your chest." She eased back far enough to slide her hands down his pectorals. Then lower. "On your belly." When she found his hard shaft through his dress pants, she stroked it. "Wrapped around this. Such softness against hardness. Coolness on such heat."

"Jesus," he hissed.

Rielle kissed him. Slowly. Savoring him. Licking and sucking on that pouty bottom lip. Her hands clamped onto his head as she rolled her hips. She cranked up the intensity, making his tongue chase hers. Trapping his head as she ravished his mouth. She broke free and arched her back.

He blinked at her abrupt departure, but the sleepy haze of lust remained in his eyes.

"Undress me," she said softly. His palms slid down her back. "Take off my camisole."

A soft groan escaped after he tossed the stretchy top to the floor and her breasts were shoved under his chin.

"You want to touch me, Gavin?"

"Fuck, yes."

"Show me."

Then his hot mouth enclosed the peak of her nipple. Another groan reverberated against her flesh as he suckled more strongly. His hands caressing, plumping the globes together to better access the tightened tips. He'd push them apart, licking and burying his face in her cleavage. His fingers pinching and twirling her nipples, skating close to the edge of pain.

Rielle wanted to leap over that dividing line between pleasure and pain right now. "Gavin. Wait."

"Goddamn, don't make me stop." He scraped his whiskered cheek over the hard nub. "I love your tits. I could spend all night seeing how many times I can make you come."

She bit the shell of his ear harder than he was used to. He froze. "Do that to me."

His gaze snapped to hers. "Is that really what you want?"

She nodded.

"Say it."

"Use your mouth on me harder. Use your teeth."

A sexy growling noise escaped and then it was on. Gavin unleashed the beast. Lashing tongue and sucking lips interspersed with hard nips. Each time he used his teeth, she swore her skin would give way to the bite. Then he'd back off. Nuzzle and nip. Tease and tantalize. Rendering her so wet and needy her thighs were soaked.

His deep whisper in her ear sent a tingle down her spine. "There's no one here but us, Ree," he murmured against her throat. "No need to be quiet. I want to hear you come." He bit down on her right nipple, using the perfect erotic combination of pressure, suction and air to propel her higher and hurl her off the ledge, straight into bliss.

Her orgasm was beyond explosive. She gasped, shocked that the insistent tug of his mouth on her nipple traveled in an electric line straight to her clit. Her pussy muscles clenched and she held on through each forceful throb.

After the last pulse faded, she realized she'd dug her fingers into Gavin's biceps so deeply her hands had cramped. Her vision was still a little spotty when she looked at him.

He smiled cockily.

Pushing upright, she unlocked her fingers from his arms. "Sorry. I hope I didn't leave marks."

"I hope you did." Gavin placed a kiss on her palm and the tip of each finger. "Because that would be fucking hot as hell. Looking in the mirror in the morning and being reminded of this."

For claiming not to be a smooth talker, Mr. Daniels certainly could teach his sweet-talkin' McKay cousins a lesson or two. Rielle unbuttoned his shirt. "You look good in black." She undid the last button and peeled the fabric down his arms. "But you look even better like this." She curled her hands around his rib cage and strummed his nipples with her thumbs.

"You going to let me take you to bed now?"

"No. I decided I'd better teach you a lesson about snatching control when it's not yours to take." She pinched his nipples.

Gavin sucked in a sharp breath. "Honey, I didn't take control, you lost control the instant I put my mouth on you. No shame in that." He drew a line across the tops of her breasts.

Rielle knocked his hands away and shimmied down his thighs, dropping to her knees.

His body went rigid.

She flicked open the button on his dress slacks and unzipped him. "Stand and take off your pants. Boxers too."

Gavin stood so fast he knocked the chair over.

She bit the inside of her cheek to keep from laughing.

Then he was completely naked. Were her eyes deceiving her, or was Gavin a little unsure about being stripped bare in front of her, with all the dining room lights on?

He shouldn't be. He was all man, wonderful sexy man, and she'd do everything in her power to assure him she liked what she saw. "Your body rocks my world, Gavin."

"This old thing?"

She laughed softly. Odd to think she'd never had the opportunity to explore her lover's reaction to her touch. Sexual encounters prior to Gavin had been done quickly and in darkness.

Time to change that. She'd learn every inch of him, learn what he liked, learn what made him shake with need. Starting here and now. Her hands followed the outside of his thighs; the crisp hair on his legs abraded her palms. She mapped the hard, defined quads. His slender hips were a frame for his flat belly. She probably could've gone on in more detail, but that pretty cock, directly in front of her face, distracted her. Thick, smooth and hard, rising out of the dark, curly tufts of hair between those impressive thighs.

Rielle glanced up and saw Gavin watching her with molten eyes. She licked him from root to tip in one long, slow, wet swipe.

"Jesus. This might kill me, you know that, right?"

Smiling, she flicked her tongue beneath the cockhead. "I'm thinking you'd better hold on to something solid. Brace yourself against the table."

Gavin shifted, keeping his stance wide and his hands gripping the table's edge. He wore a look of hopeful panic, which amused her. Maybe the book she'd read had it right; men cared less about a great oral technique than great enthusiasm.

She enclosed the base of the shaft in her right hand and lowered her mouth over the tip. The taut skin was smooth against her tongue. She sucked, getting a little taste of the glistening wetness leaking from the slit.

"Damn. That feels good."

She pulled back and looked up at him. "You'll tell me if I do something you don't like?"

"Honey, I can promise you I'm gonna like it all, trust me."

"Ah. Well...I probably won't swallow since I—" *just tell him the truth,* "—haven't done it before. You okay with that?"

Gavin blindly reached behind him and came up with a napkin. He passed it to her. "Problem solved."

Rielle kissed the crown. Then she let the head pass between her teeth. Over her tongue until the shaft filled her mouth and her gag reflex kicked in. She backed off and started again, sucking him in a little deeper with each pass.

He groaned.

She circled her right hand around the base, stroking up to meet the downward plunge of her mouth. She flattened her free hand against his abdomen. Intoxicating to feel those muscles rippling beneath her touch.

Her mouth created so much wetness as she eagerly worked him over that liquid flowed down and coated her hand. She began to move faster.

The slipperier sensation had Gavin bumping his hips away from the table, into her face.

She liked this. No, she *loved* it. All of it. The intimacy. His trust. Her power. And those sexy, manly hisses and moans.

"Jesus. Don't stop. A little faster. Like that. Goddamn, Ree, what you're doing to me."

For a split second it seemed as if his cock lengthened. Then his hips snapped three times and he released a long groan.

Salty, wet heat splashed on her tongue and she held it in her mouth until Gavin's body stopped twitching. She slipped the head free from her mouth, trying to discreetly spit into the napkin. That seemed messier than just swallowing. Good thing to remember for next time.

When she glanced up, he was peering down at her, a goofy smile on his handsome face.

"What?"

"That didn't suck."

She laughed.

A moment passed and he cradled the side of her face in his hand. "You're beautiful."

Her immediate denial got stuck in her throat. The way he looked at her made her feel beautiful. Made her feel wanted. Made her feel so very feminine.

Gavin slowly ran his thumb over her lower lip. Her tongue darted out and licked the pad. His thumb slipped inside, closer to her teeth. Her tongue traced the contour of his thumb as he stroked the wet inner flesh, back and forth. Such a sexy, intense moment and she found herself nearly breathless, imagining what would happen next.

"Bed," he said hoarsely. "Now."

She rolled to her feet and began to pick up their clothing.

His hand on her arm stopped her and she looked at him.

"Leave it."

Then he clasped her fingers in his and led her to her bedroom. Gavin made love to her with the intensity she craved. Pushing her higher with each hard thrust. Seeming to know exactly what she needed.

And after they were spent, basking in the pleasure of skin on skin and lazy kisses, she understood what he gave her was so much more than hot sex.

While they'd been naked together, nothing else mattered.

But after they left the bedroom, the situation with Rory and Sierra put them at odds. The clock read twelve forty-five and the girls weren't home. Neither of them answered their cell phones.

Gavin muttered about car accidents, serial killers and rednecks.

While Rielle understood Gavin's concern, if he pushed her, she'd point out Rory was twenty-four. She didn't have a curfew. And if Gavin hadn't wanted Sierra tagging along with Rory, then he should've said something. Might be harsh—and she wasn't complaining at all about their alone sexy time—but he'd been more concerned about getting off than where his daughter was off to.

Part of her wanted to go to bed. Gavin's discussion with and discipline for his daughter were his business, not hers. But the mothering side worried for Rory and always would, demanding she wait up to see her daughter's face. And yeah, Rielle wanted to make sure Sierra was all right too.

At one-thirty, Gavin quit pacing and grabbed his coat from the coat tree.

"Where are you going?"

"To find them. To alleviate my worry that they're in a ditch somewhere or shitfaced and neither one is capable to drive."

"No one at the Golden Boot will serve Sierra." When Gavin opened his mouth to argue, she held her hand up. "Rory is a bartender in a college town, used to dealing with underage drinking. She won't buy drinks for herself and pass them to Sierra, nor will she let her drink. So I'm one hundred percent sure at least *your* daughter is sober."

"That's reassuring," he muttered.

"It should be."

"I'd be a lot more reassured if I could talk to her." He swore. "Why aren't they answering their goddamned phones?"

"Because they're both pissed off at us and that's what people do when they're mad, Gavin. Ignore the person who made them mad."

"You're not concerned about this at all?"

"Honestly? No. Rory is an adult. A responsible adult."

"Well, my daughter isn't."

Rielle held his gaze. "Then you shouldn't have let her go out with mine."

Gavin's mouth tightened, but he didn't say a word.

Headlights shone through the window.

She breathed a sigh of relief. Their conversation had been headed toward dangerous ground and she didn't have the mental energy to deal with it right now. She recognized the vehicle as Rory's truck since the engine continued to sputter after it'd been shut off. A truck door slammed. Just one, not two. The porch floorboards creaked. The handle on the door moved as if the person was testing to see if it was locked.

The door opened and Sierra stepped inside.

Sierra wasn't surprised to see her father glaring at her in the entryway. She removed her gloves and scarf, hung up her coat and kicked off her boots. She jammed her hands in the pockets of her jeans. "Sorry I'm late."

"Why didn't you answer your phone?" Gavin demanded.

"I left it in the car?"

"Bullshit. You're surgically attached to the damn thing. Try again."

"Fine. It was loud in there."

"You knew I called you. You could've texted me if it was too loud."

Sierra lifted her chin. "I didn't answer because I was having an awesome time. Talking to you would've ruined it. I already knew I'd be in trouble." Her eyes met Rielle's. "Rory told me to tell you she had too much liquid fun tonight. I dropped her off at her cabin and put a garbage can by her bed just in case she gets sick."

"Thank you, Sierra. I appreciate you looking out for her." Rielle looked at Gavin. "Good night."

She felt his angry and surprised gaze following her but she didn't turn around. He could deal with his daughter now; she'd deal with hers in the morning.

147

Rielle wasn't surprised to see Rory in the kitchen at seven a.m. making breakfast. Even as a small child, she'd been quick to anger, but she'd mend fences just as quickly. They'd never stayed mad at each other for longer than a day, but she had the niggling feeling this conversation would test that theory.

"Morning," Rory said. "Coffee's done."

"Thank you." Rielle poured a cup and sat at the breakfast bar. She eyed the bacon sizzling in the skillet and watched as her daughter expertly cracked four eggs. Then she dropped the bread into the toaster, flipped the hash browns and set out two plates.

"Want fruit too?"

"No. This is good." Rielle sipped her coffee. "How bad's the hangover?"

Rory shrugged. "Digesting grease and salt will give my body something to do rather than trying to expel the excess alcohol in my system."

She laughed. "Who'd you run into last night that made you get your drink on?"

"Dalton."

"How is he? I haven't seen him in a while."

"The man drives me insane. I almost got into a fistfight with him."

"What did he say that pissed you off?"

"What *didn't* he say."

"I thought you two were friends."

"We were. Until we weren't."

Cryptic.

Rory dished up the hash browns and bacon. The toast popped up, she buttered it and sliced it before adding the eggs to the plates.

"You would've been an awesome short order cook."

"Doesn't pay as much as bartending." She ripped off a piece of bacon. "Or a master's degree in Ag Management."

They dug in. Rory didn't chatter through the meal like normal.

Once the dishes were cleared and they'd refilled their coffee, Rory spoke. "So you're really with him."

"Yes."

"Why?"

Rielle squeezed Rory's forearm. "I love you. I'm here for you. I will talk to you about anything you want. Except for this."

"Why are you being so secretive?"

"Why are you being so nosy? I've never grilled you about the guys you've dated. So what gives you the right to do that to me?"

"Because this isn't like you, Mom. Because I'm worried about

148

you."

The frayed end of her patience began to unravel. "You know what? You should've been worried about me years ago. When as a young woman I never went on a date, never had a boyfriend—not one man passed through my door or your life during your growing-up years. I was one hundred percent devoted to being your mother. I did a damn good job raising you. But that part of my life—seeing myself as a mother first—is over. It has been for a while and I've needed to move on from that. Now I have."

Rory didn't look up from her coffee when she asked, "What does that mean?"

"It means my relationship with Gavin is not up for discussion with my daughter."

"Yeah, I get that having me at sixteen fucked up you having a normal life."

Rielle slammed her coffee cup on the counter. "For Christsake, Aurora, you think that's a fair thing to say to me?"

Her pale skin colored. "Probably not. But that's the way you make me feel sometimes."

"When?" Rielle demanded. "When have I *ever* acted like you were anything but the absolute joy and light of my life? Never. And don't let your jealousy that you might have to share my affections with someone else now distort the past."

"So you're saying tough shit, suck it up?"

"Pretty much. You are a twenty-four-year-old woman, Rory. Your reaction to your mother having a boyfriend is ridiculous."

Rory was completely taken aback.

"My relationship with Gavin won't ever affect my relationship with you. Unless *you* let it. Your choice." Rielle slid from the barstool and walked out.

An hour later, she'd reached the bottom of her pile of logs to split. Even though it was still snowing, she'd gotten so hot she'd ditched her jacket and only wore a thermal shirt.

If anyone asked, she'd blame her wet face on sweat. So what if a few frustrated tears leaked past her defenses while she was working out her aggravation.

"Ree?"

She let the blade fall before she looked at Gavin. "Yeah?"

"Is it safe to approach?"

"Why wouldn't it be?"

"Because you're in a bad mood and wielding an ax?"

She offered a sad smile. "Point taken."

Gavin moved in closer. "You and Rory had words."

"Did the little snot say something nasty to you?"

"No. But she shoveled the walkway. And swept a path to the garage and the barn." He gestured to the pile of chopped wood. "Like mother, like daughter. Literally working off a mad."

"More productive than drinking," she said lightly.

Gavin framed her face in his hands. "Do you want to talk?"

"That's the thing, Gavin. I don't want to talk about my kid or yours."

"Just what I was hoping to hear." He tugged her hat off and pushed his fingers through her damp hair.

"I probably smell like sweat."

"I don't care." His thumbs stroked her cheekbones. "I watched you out here. So strong and determined. You're beautiful and it's bizarre that seeing you whack the shit out of stuff turns me on."

Rielle laughed.

Gavin fastened his mouth to hers; the kiss was sweet and steady—like a first kiss. Maybe it was the first time he'd kissed her with such exquisite tenderness. He'd shown her passion. Playfulness. Lust. He'd flirted and teased. But this soft and slow meeting of tongues showed her another side to him and another side to herself. She accepted that he could comfort her, he could offer his support and it didn't make her weak or needy for wanting it.

Rory watched her mom from the upstairs window. Kissing Gavin. But it was more than that. Just by their body language she saw that her mom trusted him.

Before her mother had stormed off this morning, Rory had tried to get her to recognize that she was making the same mistake she had at age sixteen, falling for the first guy who paid attention to her.

Her mother's inexperience with men scared her. This wasn't a casual situation with Gavin. They lived in the same house. Of course the temptation would be there, but Gavin Daniels didn't seem like her mom's type.

Had she ever thought about the type of man her mother would be attracted to?

No. She'd spent her life seeing her mother as...sexless. Selfless. More an earth goddess than a sex goddess.

But the way Gavin had kissed her mom—*her mom!*—yesterday afternoon had caused her jaw to drop. Not only the passion between them, but the familiarity. Rory realized she didn't know that part of her mother at all.

And when she'd demanded an explanation, she hadn't gotten one.

Which again, wasn't how her mom usually acted. She couldn't believe her mother hadn't told her about one of the biggest changes in her life...well, ever.

Rory knew she was being a brat. Maybe it wasn't Gavin specifically that she had a problem with. Maybe she was bugged by the idea of her mom being with *any* guy—and that was stupid and childish and she didn't know what the fuck was wrong with her. She was just so...mad.

"I'm pretty sure the fiery looks of hatred you're sending my dad won't start his hair on fire from up here," Sierra said from behind her.

"You're a fucking laugh riot a minute."

"You're still pissed off about this?"

"Yep." Especially after Sierra told her she'd accidentally seen them making out weeks ago.

"Come on. Can't you at least admit they look happy?"

Rory didn't answer.

"Or don't you want your mom to be happy?"

"Of course I do."

"Doesn't seem like it."

"Why? Because I'm not teary-eyed that she's making out with your dad in the clearing while snow falls around them?"

Sierra snorted. "No. Because you picked a fight with her first thing this morning."

Rory turned around, startled that Sierra nearly looked her in the eye—few women were her height. "No, I tried to have a discussion with her. But she won't talk to me about this, when we talk about everything else."

"You talk about *everything* with her?" Sierra asked skeptically.

"Yes. Why?"

"Because I call bullshit on that." She crossed her arms over her chest. "In fact, I know it's bullshit."

"How?" Rory folded her arms over her chest, her posture equally argumentative.

"I was there last night, remember? Listening to your drunken rant."

Ah fuck. Goddamn Jaegermeister.

Sierra wore a smug look. "Rielle doesn't know what happened between you and Dalton, does she?"

Rory felt her cheeks heat up. "That's different."

"How? Did you tell your mom how many guys you've slept with in college? Or their names? Or whether you went into the date expecting it'd be the start of a relationship and not just a one-night stand?"

She opened her mouth. Closed it. How the hell was Sierra so freakin' observant? She was a spoiled sixteen-year-old kid.

"You can talk to your mom about a lot of things, Rory. But you draw a line with her."

"So?"

"So why are you so pissed off that she's doing the same thing with you? Do you really want explicit details about what sex is like between her and my dad?"

"Eww. No!"

"Then what is your fucking problem?"

"My fucking problem is him," she lied, embarrassed to tell her the real issue. "He's going to hurt her."

Sierra rolled her eyes. "Assume much? And don't give me that crap about him being a—" she made quotes in the air around the word, "—McKay."

"He is what he is."

"You'd think you were a West with the big chip you've got on your shoulder about the McKays."

Rory's eyes turned shrewd. "Maybe there's validity in the Wests' point of view. Seems the McKays screw everyone over."

"The point is, you assume that my dad will screw your mom over. But you know what? I've never thought for a single second that your mom might be a gold digger."

"Why would you even say that?"

"Because my dad has money. Your mom doesn't. Maybe *she* seduced him."

This girl was on some serious crack. "That's bullshit. My mom is *not* like that."

"Yeah? And my dad is not some asshole heartbreaker."

They stared at each other.

"So much for our agreement last night to stay out of it," Rory said.

"I tried to, but you won't let it go."

"Fine. I'm done. So is that why you're following me around this morning? To be all smug and shit?"

"Following you around?" Sierra snorted. "As if. I tracked you down to make sure you were still gonna bring up that thing before you left."

Rory played dumb. "What thing?"

"That thing we discussed last night where you tell my dad that he's retarding my social development in Sundance by not letting me drive? Remember?"

"Vaguely."

Sierra looked annoyed. "Don't be a dick, Rory."

"All right. But remember you told me I could say it however I wanted—"

"I never said that!"

"Yes, you did."

"Was that before or after you told Dalton—"

"What's going on?" Gavin asked sharply.

When had he snuck in?

Of course Gavin gave *Rory* the evil eye, not his precious Sierra.

"What's going on? We're about to demonstrate our favorite cage fighting techniques. Sierra was bragging about a couple of illegal moves and I called her on it."

"My money is on Sierra." He flashed his teeth. "I wanted to talk to you about—"

"Last night?" Rory supplied. "Fine. Sierra was my designated driver. And since I don't have a curfew, I wasn't ready to leave at midnight. Her lateness is my fault." But she wouldn't apologize for it. "However, during my chat with your daughter, I found out a few things that concerned me more than her missing curfew."

"Such as?"

"Such as why you're basically keeping her a prisoner out here. You've lived here almost three months? And you haven't taken her to the Golden Boot? Or to Ziggy's? Or to the Twin Pines? The only reason she went into Dewey's was to sell raffle tickets with Marin. Those are the hangout spots for everyone in this town, even teenagers."

Gavin studied Sierra but she was picking her fingernails.

"You don't know what high school is like in a small town. I do. Most kids in her class have been in the same class since kindergarten. They won't welcome her with open arms because she's new. But any time she brings it up—asking when she'll finally get to drive—you shut her down. I don't know if you're dangling her car as some sort of reward, or not letting her drive as some sort of punishment, but the truth is she's being ostracized...because of you.

"She goes to school and she comes home. That's it. She's been to three football games. She's not in any school clubs. You don't belong to a church. How are the kids supposed to get to know her when the only time they see her is at school? And you scheduled a family party on the one night of cheerleading tryouts so she couldn't even do that."

Gavin wasn't glaring at Rory; his sole focus was on Sierra. He crossed the room. "Sierra. Sweetheart? Can you look at me please?"

Sierra raised her head.

"Is what Rory's saying true?"

"Yes."

Gavin looked baffled. "Why didn't you say anything to me before now?"

"I did! Last week and *every* week. But you never listen to me. You think every time I bring it up it's only about me driving and it's not. Since we moved here we hardly ever do anything. We cook here. We watch movies and TV here. We don't go out to eat and we used to go out all the time in Arizona. We used to go out and do things. You don't even let me go grocery shopping with you anymore. You work from here. It's like you've become a hermit and you expect me to be one too. It's not fair."

"You're right. It's not. Get your coat. We'll go into town for a late breakfast and we'll talk about this."

"Now?"

"Right now."

"Can I drive?"

"Why is that always the first question out of your mouth?"

"See! This is exactly what I'm talking about."

They argued all the way down the stairs.

After they were gone, Rory returned downstairs and whistled for her dog. Jingle trotted over. She patted Jingle's head. "You ready to hit the road, mutt?"

Jingle barked.

Sadie loped over to see what the barking was about.

"So you're really leaving?" her mom asked.

"After all that's gone on, it's probably best." She looked up at her mother, leaning against the wall in the dining room. "This isn't me throwing a tantrum. Or punishing you. I have some stuff to work through."

"I get that. But why did you come home this weekend? Is there something else going on you wanted to talk to me about?"

She shrugged. "It'll keep."

"You sure?"

"Yes. I probably shouldn't have come anyway. If I get back in time, I can pick up a shift at the bar and I can always use the extra cash." She regretted the words right after they left her mouth.

"Sweetheart, if you need money—"

"I don't." Rory slipped her coat on and zipped it. She patted her pockets to make sure she had her gloves. "I'll text you when I get to Laramie."

Her mom hugged her tightly. "I love you."

Rory closed her eyes. Her mother was so tough and strong and proud. And yet fragile. Sometimes she came off brusque, but Rory knew it was only because every day of Rielle Wetzler's life had been filled with purpose. Work to accomplish. But beneath that life-toughened demeanor was a tender heart. She hid it well, masking that vulnerability with grit. Rory's gut clenched with fear that her mom would show those soft parts of herself to Gavin and he wouldn't appreciate them. Or worse, that he'd somehow destroy them and destroy part of her mom in the process. "I love you too."

"Drive safe."

"I will."

She pulled back and really scrutinized her mother. It sucked that little snot Sierra was right. Her mom did look happy. Very happy.

"What? Do I have woodchips on my face or something?"

"No." Rory fingered the short ends of her mom's hair and smiled. "So is Ainsley gloating?"

"About what?"

"She told you if you cut your hair, you'd hook yourself a man. It appears she was right."

Chapter Twenty-One

"No offense, but there's nothing in these boxes that I can use for my report," Sierra complained.

"You did call Vi and thank her, right?" Then a thought occurred to him. "You didn't tell her this information is worthless, did you?"

"God, Dad, way to think so highly of me. I'm not a completely thankless brat."

Speaking of brat... Gavin held his tongue and waited for his daughter to continue.

"When I called Vi to say thanks, after like the millionth time you reminded me, she asked if she could pick me up at the bus stop tomorrow and take me to Spearfish."

"Why?"

"Because Amelia's birthday is coming up and she wants me to help her shop for presents. She needs my advice, since she hasn't ever really shopped for girls."

Gavin wasn't surprised that Vi had asked, but that Sierra wanted to go. "You sure? She didn't pressure you into it?"

That comment earned him an eye roll. "Seriously? When have I *ever* turned down a chance to go shopping?"

"Point taken."

"Besides, I like Vi. She's super sweet and her texts are really funny."

"Wait. You text with Vi?"

"Uh, *yeah.* How else am I supposed to stay in touch with her? It's been two weeks since we had 'the talk' and I *still* don't get to drive anywhere."

Point out the weather has been shitty. But anything he said would increase her combative attitude today. "Fine. Go. Have fun."

"Cool. I'll call her."

When she left the dining room table, Gavin said, "Forgetting something?"

"God. I can't do *anything* right today." She backtracked and picked up her empty pie plate and stomped to the kitchen.

Gavin yelled, "Put it in the dishwasher, and don't leave it in the sink."

That earned him a cupboard door slam.

So naturally he yelled, "And clean up your damn room."

Rielle exited the swinging kitchen door, holding a plate. "Is it safe to come out?"

"Much safer now that the teen terror is headed to her dungeon." He eyed the plate. "What're you having?"

"A hot guy I know made this delicious peach pie. But I'm willing to share."

He scooted his chair back and patted his thighs. "Sit on my lap."

"Why?"

"Because I want a taste of you and the pie."

She straddled him. "You just want me to feed you."

His dick stirred the instant that delectable body was close to his. "Maybe. Take a bite."

Rielle sliced off a chunk, popped it into her mouth and chewed. "Not bad, tycoon. You are getting much better at this pie baking stuff. I liked the cherry better. Maybe we should go into business together." She cut another bite and held the fork to his mouth.

After Gavin swallowed, he took the plate from her. "I'll feed you. Open wide."

"You just like saying that."

"Yep. It's too bad you didn't add whipped cream. Because you know how much I like seeing white stuff on your lips."

She blushed. And smacked him on the shoulder. "Gavin Daniels, you have such a dirty mouth."

"Mmm-hmm. It goes well with my dirty mind." He latched onto her butt, pulling her pelvis closer. He traced her full bottom lip with his tongue, then he gently sucked the succulent flesh, tasting the tang of peaches and the sweetness of Rielle. "I want you," he whispered against her lips.

"I can tell." She rocked forward into his erection.

"Your room," he said huskily. "I'll eat the pie off you and then I'll eat you."

"You make me crazy when you put those images in my brain."

"Good. But I'm still not hearing yes." Gavin dragged openmouthed kisses down her neck.

"Omigod, seriously?" Sierra complained.

Gavin tried to discreetly remove his hands from Rielle's ass.

But Sierra wasn't done stating her opinion. "You guys have *two* rooms you could be doing that in, not here, where I have to eat."

"Watch your tone and think very carefully about the next thing that comes out of your mouth," he warned.

"How is this my fault? I just came back down to get my stupid notebook so I can finish my stupid homework and find you two like... What. Ever." She snatched her notebook and stomped off.

Rielle scooted back onto his knees. "Well, that was fun."

"You'd rather we were still sneaking around?"

"No." She traced the edges of his goatee. "We have to remember to restrict our displays to the bedroom when your daughter is home. But god, when you touch me the flame just ignites."

"Let's turn it down to simmer for now." He kissed her once more and helped her off his lap. "If you hadn't noticed, getting busted playing grab-ass made my dick deflate. I probably won't be able to get it up at all tonight."

"Poor baby. I can give you a hand with that. Later." Rielle pulled him to his feet. "Let's go upstairs and watch TV so Sierra doesn't think we're going at it in my bedroom."

"I think there's a college—"

"No sports."

"Why not?"

"Because that's all you watch. And you yell at the TV. Like you yelling at the players or the coaches or the referees will make a difference."

The woman had no concept of the responsibilities of a sports fan. Loud indignation about lousy calls and shitty plays were his right.

Hopefully she'd fall asleep, like she always did, during one of her blasted cooking shows and he could catch the day's highlights on ESPN.

He offered her a charming smile. "Whatever you want."

Sierra burst into the kitchen, shopping bags hanging from both arms. "Dad! You have to see all the totally awesome stuff I got today."

Vi trailed behind her, smiling.

"Hey, Vi. Looks like you guys had a productive day."

"We did."

"You have time for a drink?"

Vi appeared taken aback by Gavin's question. "What are you drinking?"

"Crown and water."

"I'll have one. Light on the Crown since I'm driving."

Rielle skirted the pile of shopping bags, intending to duck out of the kitchen, but he circled her wrist, stopping her. "Please stay."

"I don't want to intrude," she whispered.

"You're not. So stay."

"All right."

Gavin mixed Vi's drink and poured a soda for Sierra. "All right, sweetheart, tell me about your day and show me what you got."

"First, we went to the toy store. There were so many awesome fun toys it was hard to pick one. So I got Amelia a Gloworm because I remembered how much I loved mine."

That caused a pang. Didn't seem that long ago Sierra was dragging that dirty, well-loved Glo-worm everywhere.

"Then we went shopping for girl clothes at the western store. Omigod the stuff is so cute. You should see the tiny jean skirt with pink leggings and a button-up western shirt with lace edging. And she's getting matching pink cowgirl boots with rhinestones!"

Sierra was talking enthusiastically about all the things they'd bought...for someone else?

"Which leads me to this." Sierra flipped the lid off a shoebox, taking out a pair of pink cowgirl boots with rhinestones on the toes and dark pink leather decorating the shaft. "Aren't these the coolest boots you've ever seen? I wanted some so bad..." She squealed and leaned over to hug Vi. "Thank you so, so much, Grams, for buying them for me."

"You're welcome, dear."

Gavin went motionless. Since when did Sierra call Vi...Grams?

Since Vi started buying things for her.

"I cannot wait to wear these to school tomorrow. Marin will be so jealous."

"The bottoms have a slick finish so make sure you scuff them up first," Vi warned.

"Will do." Sierra hugged her boots. "It is insane how much I love these things already."

Vi laughed.

Sierra tossed the box on the floor and snagged another bag. "Then we went to this boutique called Sweet Repeats that sells the funkiest things. Jewelry, clothes, scarves, jackets." She grinned. "Check this out." She held up a black suede jacket with fringe on the underside of each sleeve. "Look at the metal studs on the lapels and down the front. It's bad-ass, but doesn't make me look like a thug."

"And you can wear black with anything," Vi pointed out.

"I will wear it with *everything*, I promise. Thank you."

Vi had bought her a fucking leather coat, too?

Sierra pulled out yet more things Vi had purchased for her.

A pair of jeans with rhinestones on the rear pockets and the front pockets.

A fur-lined vest.

A long-sleeved thermal shirt the same pink as the boots with *Cruel Girl* emblazoned across the front.

A bag overflowing with bangles and baubles.

"And last, but certainly not least..." Sierra unwrapped a cork bulletin board. She piled two stacks of fabric and two spools of satin ribbon on top of it. "A memory board for my room. We're gonna fancy it up next week, huh, Grams?"

"Absolutely. As long as it doesn't interfere with your school work."

Sierra jammed all her new items back in the bags and hugged Vi. "Thank you so much for today. I had a lot of fun."

Vi brushed the hair back from Sierra's face. "I did too. We'll do it again soon."

"I hope so. Gotta put my stuff away!" Sierra announced and raced from the room.

Gavin swallowed a gulp of his drink. "Well, that won't happen again."

"What?"

"You taking Sierra out and buying her everything she wants."

"Why is this a problem for you? Because I didn't ask your permission to buy my granddaughter a few things?" Vi held up a finger to stop his protest. "Yes, Sierra *is* my granddaughter. You may still have a problem with our family ties, but she doesn't. Don't expect her to have your issues with the situation, Gavin."

"So is it a coincidence, that she started calling you *Grams* after you bought all that shit for her?" he demanded.

"Sierra has been calling me Grams for months. Never in front of you, because she's been afraid of how you'd react. Now I see that her fear was justified."

Why hadn't Sierra come to him with this name change business? "And because she's accepting of the family tie, that gives you the right to try and buy her love or affection or attention or whatever it is you want from her?"

Vi skewered him with a hard look. "That gives me the right to spend my own damn money however I see fit. I bought gifts for my other granddaughter, so it's only fair I do the same for Sierra. And don't forget, you wouldn't let us buy her anything for her sixteenth birthday. Then today she sees me buying things for Amelia's birthday? How do you think that made her feel?" She jabbed her finger at him. "Exactly like you do. Like you aren't really part of the family. Like some family members matter more to me than others."

"Fuck."

"Why did you move here, Gavin, if you didn't want your daughter to be part of our family? You expect her to stand at arm's length like you do? She is not you. You are her father, but you shouldn't have the only say in whether we can build a relationship. Doesn't what she wants matter?"

"Oh, trust me; she'll be your BFF if you keep buying her things every time you're together."

"That's the only reason Sierra could possibly want to spend time with me? That's bullshit. You're making horrible assumptions about her. And about me. That girl is not shallow, and yet I suspect sometimes you treat her like her mother. So you shouldn't be surprised when she acts exactly how you treat her."

Gavin's jaw tightened.

"I'm not trying to buy her love. I'm not fostering a relationship with Sierra to get to you either, because if I thought I could buy your love? Son, I would've gladly paid the price the day you came looking for us. As far as today? I won't apologize. I won't let your paranoia and distrust ruin the wonderful afternoon that I got to spend with my granddaughter."

They stared at each other without speaking.

Gavin knew Vi had several legitimate points, but he was still pissy.

"I can't deal with this right now."

It wasn't until he went looking for Rielle that he realized she'd witnessed the whole scene...and he'd left her in the kitchen.

Rielle should've snuck out when she had the chance. Maybe she still could. But one look at Vi's miserable face and she knew she wouldn't. Especially after Vi drained her drink. "Want another?"

"I'd like to have the whole damn bottle."

"To drink? Or to smack Gavin upside the head?" Rielle asked lightly.

"Both." Vi studied the ice cubes in her glass. "I wasn't in the wrong."

A statement Rielle let lie.

"I keep hoping he'll come around."

"He will. However, it may take more time than you think it should."

"Being pushy, am I?"

"No. Gavin has his own way of thinking." Rielle didn't say more. She wouldn't violate the trust he'd placed in her.

"He's being ridiculous if he believes I was trying to buy Sierra's affection. When he lived in Arizona, I followed his parameters. But then he moves here, down the road from us, and I'm still supposed to wait for him to give the green light so I can get to know Sierra? Or she can get to know me? Gavin sure doesn't have a problem with Charlie spending time with Sierra, or that Charlie buys her food and little tokens every damn day. But he objects when I do essentially the same thing? That feels a lot like punishment and a little like manipulation."

Rielle agreed. "So you, or Charlie, or both of you haven't brought any of this up with Gavin?"

"No. We're aware of Gavin's boundaries. Before he moved here we kept contact casual because we were afraid if we pushed too hard, he'd cut off all contact with us." Vi's chin trembled, but she firmed it.

In that moment Rielle clearly saw the family resemblance between mother and son and her heart broke for both of them.

"Does he want me to apologize for giving him up for adoption?" Vi asked softly.

"Maybe this sounds simplistic, but have you sat him down and tried to explain to him what you went through? What it really meant to be pregnant at sixteen? How you felt during the pregnancy and after?"

"Not since he first came to us and I was in such a...state of shock that I don't think I explained myself very well. He hasn't brought it up since and I'm afraid to." Vi looked at her. "Have you talked to him about your life as a pregnant girl?"

"A little. But he doesn't understand. It's...vague to him. Like watching a forgettable TV movie of the week."

"We're different sides of the same coin, aren't we? You kept your baby; I gave mine up."

"Is that why you were so nice to me and Rory?"

"Out of guilt? Maybe. Nothing against your folks, Ree, but I got the feeling they saw Rory as a mistake. I admired you for doing what I couldn't. So part of me always wondered if I'd kept Gavin, if some woman would've taken the time to make sure I was okay."

From the moment they'd met Rielle had seen behind Vi's brusque nature to the sweet thoughtful woman beneath. It hadn't escaped her notice that a lot of people said the same thing about her being so prickly, which was probably why she and Vi had always gotten along so well. "I appreciated those random visits. Not because you brought over a bag of groceries, but because you spent time with me and listened to me."

"I only wish I could've done more. But I was happy that you broke free of your parents'...mold, for lack of a better word, and raised Rory how you wanted."

"Rory had as normal a childhood as I could give her."

"Is that the gist of this? Gavin doesn't know how thrilled I was to get to buy Sierra a pair of pink cowgirl boots? Every girl her age needs something frivolous. When I was her age I had the world on my shoulders and I'm happy that she doesn't."

Rielle reached for her hand, her heart hurting for Vi. "Gavin lashed out before he thought it through."

"Maybe I should consider it a good sign that he cared enough to get pissed off at me."

"There's a healthy way of looking at it."

"Can I ask...does he talk to you?"

"About his relationship with you and Charlie? No."

"But he does open up to you about other things?" Vi clarified, "I don't want specifics. I just want to know that he's finally got a woman in his life who cares about him like he deserves."

"I care about him. He knows that. He's just adrift in a lot of aspects of his life. And his ex-wife really did a number on him so he doesn't trust easily. Even with me."

"I'll admit I was happy when Sierra told me about you and Gavin. You two are good for each other. But between us, I won't tell him that, in case he gets it in his fool head to rebel against my approval and break it off with you."

"Deal. And I won't tell him he was acting like an ass."

"Oh, no, go right ahead and tell him that part."

After Vi left Rielle heated up a plate of leftovers. One thing that hadn't changed in their relationship was separate mealtimes. She'd done that intentionally—it'd be easy to get into the habit of cooking for him and Sierra and horn in on their family time.

Gavin was frustrated by Rielle's "separatist" attitude. But Sierra needed that alone time with her father. Just the two of them, cooking together and catching up on their days.

Rielle found Gavin upstairs, watching a game. She plopped down beside him. "You all right?"

"Nope. Still a little pissy if you want to know the truth."

"Should I trot my little self downstairs?"

"Funny. But if you expect me to be charming and witty? Probably."

"Mmm." She ran her hand over his short, bristly hair. "Sometimes I like a broody man. It's a different kind of sexy."

He expelled a disbelieving snort.

"You could drag me into your bedroom, using terse commands while having your wicked way with me. No talking. Just intense sex. Fast and demanding."

"You trying to get me hard, Ree? 'Cause it's working."

She angled her head to place a soft, sucking kiss on the skin below his ear. "I'm not busy now, Mr. Hot Brooding Man."

Sierra's music drifted down the hallway. Rielle shifted back so Sierra didn't see her mauling her father.

Seconds later, Sierra appeared. "I'm starved, Dad. What's for supper?"

"Hadn't thought about it. I could heat some soup. Or there's lunch meat for sandwiches."

"I was hoping for something like pork chops."

"We'll fix that tomorrow night." Gavin lifted a box off the floor.

"Must be your day to get presents. This came from your mom while you were shopping with *Grams*."

A snarky remark from Gavin? He was pissy.

"Yay!" Sierra grabbed a pocketknife from the bar. She carefully slid the tip of the knife along the airmail tape covering the box. As soon as she opened the flaps, a heavy perfume poured out.

Rielle sneezed.

Sierra offered an apologetic smile. "Sorry. Mom loves spritzing perfume on everything." She excitedly pulled out wrinkled sheets of white tissue paper dotted with black images of the Eiffel Tower. Then she stopped. A bewildered look settled on her face.

"Sweetheart, what's wrong?" Gavin asked.

Rielle watched the girl struggle to get control. Sierra tipped her head down but not fast enough; Rielle saw two tears plop onto the tissue paper.

Then she reached into the box and angrily threw a handful of material on the coffee table.

Upon seeing the contents, Rielle's stomach dropped and she shot Gavin a sideways glance.

He appeared calm, but the air around him vibrated with fury.

Sierra handled each piece of lingerie. A black peignoir, sheer except for the lace edging and the tiny, strategically placed pink bows. A pair of matching G-string panties. The next piece she held up was a short white bustier with what looked like padded cups. Another pair of panties to match.

No one said anything. Rielle expected Sierra to explode with the drama sixteen-year-olds were prone to. But she just shoved the lingerie back in the box.

"Sierra, sweetheart. Can you look at me, please?" Gavin said gently.

She glanced up. "Mom doesn't know me at all, does she? This is what she sends me from Paris? Not perfume or chocolates or even something tacky like a plastic Eiffel Tower, but something *she* likes?"

Gavin was on his feet, pulling Sierra to hers, hugging her. He murmured to her, comforting her as he led her downstairs.

As bad as she felt for Sierra, this was another reminder that Gavin had a higher priority than spending his free time with his live-in girlfriend. He needed to stay focused on raising his daughter. He also needed to deal with his hot and cold attitude toward Vi. That attitude didn't extend to Charlie, as far as she'd seen.

Rielle realized she'd been lax in keeping in contact with Rory since the incident a few weeks back. She returned to her room and called her, expecting to settle in for a chat, only to have that parental gut wrenching worry as her level-headed daughter sobbed hysterically.

School stressed her out. Her landlord was a prick. Her best friend in the Ag program was taking a job in Brazil. They'd overscheduled her at the bar. After Rielle calmed her down, she promised she'd spend the weekend in Laramie. She packed, made last minute phone calls and forced herself to sit at her spinning wheel and finish a few odd projects rather than pace and fret about her daughter.

A few hours later Gavin knocked on her door. She let him in only after she'd promised herself to resist the heated way he looked at her that always made her clothes fly off.

But there wasn't any sign of her insistent lover. He dropped into the chair next to the bed. "Sorry I bailed on you before."

"No worries. Sierra is your priority, as it should be. She had upheaval in her life today so it's natural she'd need her dad. I assume she's okay?"

"Yeah." He dry-washed his face. "I don't know what the fuck Ellen was thinking, giving a sixteen-year-old fuck-me lingerie. Jesus. How oblivious is she?"

Rielle didn't comment, just let him ramble and started winding loose yarn into skeins.

"Plus, there wasn't a note, or anything personal." He slumped back in the chair. "Sierra hasn't talked to her mom since that phone call, what...? Last month? I mean yeah, half the time I think Ellen is psychotic and she's manipulative and Sierra is better off. But Sierra misses her and it's cruel how Ellen just cut Sierra out of her life."

He wouldn't see the parallels to his relationship with Vi, so she kept her mouth shut.

"I told Sierra she didn't have to write her mother a thank you note for an inappropriate gift. But now I'm thinking if we let it slide, Ellen will see it as acceptable and send her more of the same—or worse."

She pulled more yarn.

"So I'll have Sierra call her tomorrow from my office so I can hear what she says." He paused. "Do you think that's a good idea?"

"Sierra is your kid, Gavin. You know what's best for her, not me."

"Are you pissed off at me too?" He released a deep sigh. "I'm sorry I left you with Vi."

"I like Vi. I always have."

"What'd she say?"

"Don't you think it'd be better if you asked her?"

"Jesus. You *are* mad. Are you so damn busy fussing with your knitting you can't even look at me?"

Rielle glanced up. "A, I'm not knitting. B, I'm not mad at you. How you handle your family business is your business, not mine."

"Meaning I fucked up with Vi today."

"No, meaning I don't want to get involved. I've been neighbors with

165

the McKays for years, and that hasn't always been easy, but I won't jeopardize that because I'll still be neighbors with them when I build my new place."

That reminder angered him. "So you have no opinion?"

"If I did I'd keep it to myself. Look, we're roommates and lovers. It's not my place to offer you advice or suggestions on how to deal with your family or to play referee when things don't go your way."

His mouth flattened. "Thanks for letting me know where I stand with you."

"Huh-uh. You *don't* get to get pissy with me. I like you. I like spending time with you, naked or not."

"But?"

"No buts. We agreed to continue to lead our separate lives. We agreed that if we each had free time, we'd try and spend it together."

Gavin stood and started unbuttoning his shirt. "Fine. I'm free right now. Let's fuck."

"Don't be a jackass."

"What's the problem? Didn't you just tell me this is all we are? Fuck buddies? So come on."

She'd never seen this side of him and she didn't like it. "Not interested. Now get out of my room."

His shirt fell open. "Oh, so you can proposition me, like you did upstairs three hours ago? But I can't proposition you?"

"*Let's fuck* is not a proposition. It's a demand, said in anger, just to be a dick." She tossed the yarn winder aside. "Know what? I don't have to put up with this shit. Get out."

"Why? This approach has worked for you in the past. No pretty words, no foreplay, just ripping our clothes off and fucking on the floor like animals. What's different now, Rielle?"

"You're different now. And fuck you for coming in here and taking out your shitty day on me. And double fuck you for taking something that's good between us and twisting it into something ugly."

The stark realization of how asinine he'd acted hit him. "God. Rielle. I'm sorry—"

When he moved toward her, she recoiled. "Get out."

"Can't we talk…?"

She vehemently shook her head. "It's best if we take a break. I'm leaving for Laramie tomorrow to see Rory anyway."

"You are? Since when?"

When she didn't respond, he sighed.

"All right. Please drive safe and I'll see you when you get home." He walked out and quietly shut the door.

After living in each other's pockets for the last couple months, a cooling off period would do them both good.

Chapter Twenty-Two

Gavin hung over the top of the wooden corral, watching Quinn drive cows into a semi-truck as Dalton and Tell pushed the cattle into the loading chute. Ben was on horseback culling from the corralled herd, while Brandt—also on horseback—chased down the runaways and drove them back to the penned area.

He'd been surprised when Charlie had called, inviting him to watch them loading cattle to take to auction. He'd been curious about how the auction process worked differently than sending cattle to a feedlot.

With temps in the low teens and the gray skies spitting snow, he bundled up, figuring this weather wouldn't faze hardcore ranchers like the McKays.

But Gavin also wondered if Charlie had issued the invite to chastise Gavin for the argument he'd had with Vi. An argument they hadn't resolved.

During a lull in the action, Quinn wandered over to the corral. The man was sweating despite the frigid air temp. "Dad, I might need a hand in a bit."

"No problem."

Quinn flashed Gavin one of his rare grins. "Ever ridden in a fully loaded cattle truck?"

"No. Why?"

"Because I need someone to ride with me. And since the old man is retired, he's no help, sitting at home with his feet propped on the coffee table having Mom wait on him."

"I done my share of cattle sale runs, boy."

"I'll be back from the sale barn tonight?"

"Yep, but it'll be late. And the weather and road conditions are flat out gonna suck." Quinn crossed his arms over his chest as if expecting Gavin to refuse. "You up for it?"

"Sure. Do I have to help unload cattle?"

"Nope. Ben and Tell will be in the truck behind us."

"Damn. I was hoping I'd get my own cattle prod."

"Somehow I knew you'd say that." Quinn wandered back to his post when Dalton yelled for him.

"So it looks like all the McKays help each other throughout the year?" Gavin asked Charlie.

"Carson has enough hands with his boys that he hasn't needed much help. Same with Cal's twins. None of them wanted to deal with Casper so he made his boys do everything on their own. Same with me'n Quinn and Ben and Chase if he was around. Brandt, Tell and Dalton increased the size of their herd and bought more land after Luke died so Quinn and Ben have been helping them and they help us." He shrugged. "It works out."

"Can I ask about the bad history between Casper and your brothers?"

Charlie remained quiet for so long Gavin suspected he was dodging the question. Then he scratched his chin with the back of his gloved hand. "I wish I could say there was some defining moment when it all fell apart, but it ain't that simple. As twins, Carson and Calvin have always been two peas in a pod—no one was surprised when they married sisters." A ghost of a smile appeared. "My dad wasn't happy they were West sisters but that's another story. Anyway, I think Casper had middle child syndrome. Dad had high expectations for his oldest boys and Mom doted on me as the youngest because I was a sickly kid. Casper got lost in the shuffle. He became a wild man and took hell raisin' to a new level. Hard to look at him now and see it, but Casper had the type of good looks and charm the ladies loved.

"We were all shocked when he married Joan Tellman. I'll admit I wasn't a supportive brother to Casper then, because that was right around the time Vi moved away. I moped for a few months. Then I thought; screw it, I'm the last single McKay and I'm gonna cut loose. I screwed any woman who'd have me, figuring that'd erase Vi from my mind, but it never did.

"Then my dad had a heart attack. He recovered but couldn't head up the ranch. He put my oldest brothers in charge, moved out of the ranch house, giving it to Carson and Carolyn—and we set him up in a trailer between Carson's and Calvin's place."

"Wait a second. Were you living in the house with your dad when he had the heart attack?"

Charlie nodded. "I was the one who found him out in the yard. At first he refused to go to the hospital. Swore he'd rather die on McKay land. I called Casper and we got Dad loaded up and hauled to town."

"He sounded like a tough old bird."

"Oh, Jed McKay was an asshole or an angel, depending on your point of view and the day. Anyway, we'd just bought this place, a couple thousand acres on the far south end of McKay land with two houses. Casper and Joan claimed one place and I took the other. Around that time, Casper had turned into a raging asshole. Everything changed in the family dynamic because I felt that Dad and my brothers were punishing me, making *me* live by Casper."

"Did Casper know you felt that way?"

"Probably. Another year passed and Dad had another heart attack. He couldn't live by himself. Logically he should've moved in with Casper and Joan. But Dad refused and insisted on living with Cal and Kimi. Casper took it as Dad would rather live with a West family enemy than live with him. Made him even more bitter and I didn't blame him. Meanwhile, we're all workin' the ranch and Carson is buying land up closer to where he lives. Ticked me and Casper off because we knew we'd never get to use those grazing areas and technically, the acreage belonged to us too. Then our neighbors the Burkes wanted out of Wyoming and didn't offer the land to us first. Not only is that an unwritten western tradition, but the Burkes sold it to a couple from out of state."

"The Wetzlers," Gavin inserted.

"Yep. They were an odd lot. So I gotta be honest, even though it's been a long time comin', I'm happy the biggest chunk of that land is finally in McKay hands." Charlie shot him a sideways glance. "So to speak."

As much as the McKays had wanted that section and the discord it'd caused when he'd bought it, no one had approached Gavin on utilizing it. And he was such a greenhorn he had no idea how to offer it.

"For a few years me'n Casper worked together. That's why I'm more tolerant with him than Carson or Cal. Then Vi returned to Wyoming. I hadn't seen her in four years and I knew the reason I hadn't found a woman to share my life with was because I was waiting for her to come back."

Gavin didn't know what to say. He wouldn't have believed Charlie was capable of telling him something so intensely personal.

"Most people think they know what kind of woman Vi is. She's bossy, nosy and opinionated. But that ain't what I see. That ain't who she is with me or to me. Back then or now." Charlie scratched his chin again. "Probably TMI as Sierra would say, huh?"

He laughed softly.

"I know you and Vi had words, Gavin. Alls I'm gonna say is you need to figure out a way to deal with it and her because I hate to see my wife hurtin'."

"Have you always been so protective of her?"

"Yep. Wasn't your..."

Gavin watched the rancher struggle to ask about the man who raised him.

"Wasn't Dan the same way?"

"My dad had a lot of great qualities. But being a protective

Lorelei James

husband wasn't one of them."

Charlie didn't respond. He just kept focused on Quinn and Ben's activities.

So Gavin kept talking. "He wasn't faithful to my mother. As a kid I didn't know. When I started working for him, I noticed he took long lunches. Wasn't smart, but I followed him. He'd gone to some woman's apartment. When I confronted him he told me all men cheat."

"Bullshit," Charlie spat. "I've been married to Vi thirty-eight years and not once, even when we hit rough patches, did I consider climbing into another woman's bed. A man loves a woman, he loves her. Period. He cares for her and he protects her. Not because that's his job but because he oughta want to."

"I agree. It was a point of contention for us up until the day he died. His excuse, or explanation, or whatever, was that as long as he provided for my mother, she didn't mind."

"Did you believe that?"

"No. I saw it hurt her, but she never told him to stop. Never threatened to leave him." Gavin poked at loose splinters on the wooden post. "When I found out my wife was cheating on me? I was more pissed off than hurt. I knew it wasn't my goddamn fault that *she* cheated. My mom was the most vocal person in encouraging me to divorce her. She said cheaters don't ever reform."

"You were close to Grace?"

It didn't escape his notice that Charlie didn't refer to Grace and Dan as Gavin's mom and dad. He obviously considered Gavin his son, not theirs, which was fucked up on a number of levels that neither of them had begun to address in the last two years. "Yes. Not to get off on a strange tangent, but my adoption was more her idea than his."

Charlie looked at him sharply. "Why's that?"

"My mom was forty and my dad was forty-eight when they adopted me. He was busy running his...affairs—" Charlie snorted, "—and having a baby gave her something to do. I never felt neglected or anything growing up—I had a great childhood—it's just an observation I made after I had a child of my own and was so much more involved in raising her. Like I said, my dad had a lot of great qualities, but he wasn't much of a family man."

"Then in my opinion, he wasn't much of a man," Charlie said.

"Dad," Quinn shouted, "I need that help now."

Charlie slipped through the gate without another word.

Gavin wasn't as bothered by the conversation as he feared he'd be. Charlie deserved to know what kind of father Dan Daniels had been to him. Not that Charlie could do anything about it and Gavin wasn't looking for reassurance that Charlie would've raised him differently. The best thing Gavin had learned from his father was that he never

170

wanted to be that type of father to his own child. And maybe some small part of Gavin wanted Charlie to know he was more like him.

He noticed when Charlie spoke to his sons and nephews, they listened. He remembered being so rapt with his father, hoarding his pearls of wisdom. Thinking the man could do no wrong. After learning his dad had continually cheated on his mother, Gavin wondered if he cheated in business too—which led Gavin to diversify the business after he'd inherited it.

Once the semi was loaded and closed up, Quinn parked it down the road and backed up the other semi-trailer to the loading chute. Took less time to load cattle into the second one than the first.

Quinn motioned him over. "You're riding shotgun. Ben and Tell are ready to roll."

Gavin looked over to see if Charlie wanted to speak to him before he left, but he was helping Dalton with the horses.

Maybe they'd said everything they needed to say.

Sierra stood at the kitchen island fixing a snack when she heard a series of thuds on the front porch. She slipped into the dining room and glanced at Sadie, curled up, snoring in her doggie bed. Did that mean she knew who was at the door at seven on a Saturday night, so she wasn't worried for Sierra's safety?

Or...Sadie was a lousy guard dog.

The heavy wooden door in the foyer didn't have a peep hole. As she weighed her options about checking out the noise, two raps sounded.

"S-s-sierra, it's B-b-boone."

She opened the door quickly. "Boone? Omigod! What are you...you're covered in snow." She grabbed the lapels of his coat and jerked him inside, and they nearly tumbled to the floor.

Boone righted himself. Then he was shaking really hard as he leaned against the door and it slammed shut. "Th-thanks. S-s-sorry if I interrupted s-s-something."

"What are you doing here?" Her gaze swept over him. He didn't move. His eyes blinking drowsily.

"Boone? Have you been drinking?"

"No. I...d-d-damn." His teeth chattered like crazy.

After all her dad's lectures about frostbite and the dangers of hypothermia, Sierra recognized the signs immediately. She didn't think; she just acted. She tugged off Boone's gloves. His hands were as hard and cold as icicles. Her gaze moved to his face. He wore an Elmer Fudd hat which covered his head and ears. It also had a pull-down face mask so only his eyes and lips were visible. "I wouldn't have opened the door if you'd had this over your face."

"S-s-smart ch-choice."

Sierra placed her hands on his cold cheeks and he made an odd noise, so she snatched them back. "Okay. I'll leave your hat on." She unzipped his coveralls. "You'll have to move if you want to get out of these clothes and warm up."

"K-k-kay." Boone leaned forward.

She stripped the coveralls off his arms and then pulled them to his ankles. "Kick them off."

He fell back against the door as he kicked the wide-legged coveralls aside.

"Don't move." She ran to the linen closet for bedding, grabbing a heavy wool blanket and a down comforter. She wrapped the blanket around his shoulders, gathering the edges in front of his chest. "Can you hold on to this?"

"I'll t-t-try."

Sierra dropped to her knees and brushed the snow off the laces of his work boots. It took several tries until the frozen leather would cooperate.

Boone shifted feet so she could pull the boot off.

She curled her hands around his foot. At least his socks weren't wet and his feet weren't blocks of ice. By the time she'd finished removing the second boot, he'd stopped shaking so hard. She stood and eyed him. "You warmed up enough to walk to the fireplace?"

He nodded.

"You sure? Because I can't carry you." She smirked. "Although, I could probably knock you over and drag you."

"I can walk."

He followed her into the living room. She dragged a chair directly in front of the fireplace and ordered, "Sit."

Boone sat.

She tucked the comforter around his front side. He watched her every move without speaking, his eyes locked on her face, and it made her nervous.

"How about if I make you hot tea." She practically ran to the kitchen. Her face was on fire, forcing her to rest her forehead on the cold marble to cool down. Okay. She'd acted like it was no big deal...while she'd *freakin' stripped Boone West.*

The water took forever to heat. She grabbed a teabag from Rielle's cupboard and squirted a bunch of honey into the hot water in case the tea tasted like crap.

Back in the living room, she noticed Sadie had parked herself in front of the fire, her happy little doggie mug resting on Boone's feet. His eyes were closed.

172

She nudged his shoulder. "Boone. You're not supposed to sleep if you've been chilled."

He mumbled, "Tired."

"Tough. Wake up."

No response.

She shoved him harder. "Boone. Wake up right now or I'll call your ambulance buddies here to haul your cold ass to the hospital and wouldn't that be embarrassing?"

"You've got a mean streak, McKay."

Good. He knew who she was. Sierra was peering directly into his face when those long lashes lifted. He gazed into her eyes so deeply her belly fluttered. Man. He had the prettiest eyes, even when they seemed slightly vacant.

"You want a hot drink?"

"No. Just water."

"Be right back."

Upon returning she saw Boone had stirred, removing his hat and lowering the comforter to free his arms. He stroked Sadie's fur.

"Here." She handed him the water.

He gulped a couple mouthfuls and wiped his lips with the back of his hand. His eyes were more alert. "How'd an Arizona girl recognize hypothermia symptoms and know treatment procedures?"

"My dad has been grilling me on this since the first week we moved here. He, ah, knows I'd probably walk out in the snow in flip-flops, without a coat, so he's been horrifying me with worst-case scenarios. I'd tell him that I remembered everything and helped you, but he'd gloat too much."

"Smart man, teaching you that stuff. Most people who move out here don't have a clue." He took another drink of water. "Is your dad around?"

"No, he went to an auction with my uncles and Rielle is in Laramie."

"I wondered if you'd be here. Didn't see any cars when I walked up."

"Walked up? Did you have car trouble or something?"

"I was riding my motorcycle home and the gas gauge must've broken or something because it said I had half a tank when I left town."

Her mouth dropped open. "You were riding your motorcycle in this weather? Why?"

He looked directly at her. "Because I don't have a car."

What? Didn't everyone have a car?

"The bike quit about a mile from here and I pushed it to your barn because I remembered seeing cans of gas."

"Wait. You pushed your motorcycle a mile, in the dark, in subzero temperatures?"

"Yeah. While I filled the tank outside the barn, exhaustion set in and I sort of..."

"Passed out?"

"Phased out," he corrected. "I don't know how long." Boone squinted at the clock. "It's seven-thirty? I left Sundance at four."

Sierra got right in his face. "You are lucky you aren't dead, Boone West."

"Probably. I was confused when I woke up but I remembered I had to tell you I'd borrowed some fuel. Didn't want anyone to think I stole it." He smiled and lightly bumped his forehead to hers. "I wouldn't want to add to the bad blood between the Wests and McKays."

"Thoughtful. Except can you imagine how much worse it'd be if you'd been found dead on McKay land?"

"I thought your name was Daniels," he teased.

She whapped him on the shoulder. "Smartass."

"Could I hang my coveralls over the chair so they dry out before I head home?"

Of course tough guy Boone would ride his motorcycle home after a close call with hypothermia. But she wouldn't have his stubbornness on her conscience. "Sure. But before you leave here, promise me you'll call your dad or your uncles or someone, and tell them exactly which way you're going, so if your bike breaks down again, they'll know where to look for you."

"Or we could skip all that shit and you could just give me a ride."

"I promised my dad I wouldn't go out of the house under any circumstances except for fire." God. Boone probably thought she was such a baby.

Warm fingers lifted her chin. "Hey. It's not a big deal."

As soon as he removed his hand, she blurted out, "Are you hungry?"

"You're always trying to feed me." He patted his stomach. "Do I look like I need fattening up?"

No, you look perfect. But maybe you should lift your shirt anyway so I can see your six-pack abs just to make sure.

"If you're not hungry you can come into the kitchen and watch me eat because I'm starved."

"Twist my arm. I'll put another log on the fire." He smiled. "You can cook me up some bacon and some beans."

"What?"

"You know...that's a line from that Tompall Glaser song?"

"Never heard of him. Is he local?"

Boone shook his head. "He was with the Outlaws. Your musical education is sorely lacking, McKay."

Sierra heated leftover angel hair pasta with basil cream sauce in the microwave. Boone watched as she diced a tomato and grated parmesan. She gestured to the cupboard with her knife. "You wanna grab plates?"

"Sure."

She divided the pasta in half, and sprinkled cheese and tomatoes on each pile. "Dig in."

Boone wound a good-sized bite around his fork and popped it in his mouth. "That is fantastic. Eating here is like dining at a fancy restaurant. You should be a chef."

"I don't know what I want to do after high school. How about you?"

"I've got a good idea."

He didn't elaborate.

Sierra wasn't as hungry as she'd thought and Boone ended up polishing off her plate of pasta too.

"Thanks for an outstanding meal. I feel like I oughta leave a tip."

"How about if you do the dishes?"

"Deal." He cleared the plates. When he opened the door to the dishwasher, she said, "Nope. Not that dishwasher. This one."

Boone frowned. "What's the difference?"

"That one is Rielle's; this one is ours. I know it's weird, but we had to divide the kitchen space and set boundaries after we moved in." She sighed. "It's sort of pointless now that my dad and Rielle are sleeping together."

"Really? How do you know? Did you catch them goin' at it?"

She rolled her eyes. "No. They're more discreet than that, except I catch them making out all the time. My dad has never had a girlfriend, which is weird when you think about it." She'd wondered if he was gay. And she'd tried several times to let her dad know she'd be fine with it if he preferred men.

"Never?"

"If he was seeing someone in Arizona he never brought her home when I was there." She rinsed the dishrag and hung it over the sink divider. "My dad's actually been a lot happier since we moved here. I wonder how much of that has to do with her." After Rory's little come-to-Jesus talk, he'd started doing more things with her outside the house. That'd taken some of the sting out of her feeling of isolation, but not all. She felt Boone staring at her and she looked up. "Sorry."

"Have you asked if he's practicing safe sex?"

Sierra laughed. "That'd go over well."

Boone wandered into the great room, inspecting Rielle's funky furnishings. "So if your dad didn't date, what about your mom? You said your parents divorced when you were five, right?"

He'd remembered that? "Uh-huh. My mom? She's a flake."

He whirled around and grinned. "Hey, so's mine."

"Really? Did your mom spontaneously bail to France with her twenty-eight-year-old boyfriend? And she's lying about her age, swearing she's just a *few years older*, when it's a decade."

"Have you met her boyfriend?"

Sierra shook her head. "Get this; she told him I'm her sister. If my dad knew that he'd lose his mind. Even when my dad annoys me, he's always acted like he *wants* to be around me, not because he *has* to take care of me." Not always the case with her mom. Her mom was fun and smiles when they were doing what she wanted, which was most of the time. So it made no sense why Sierra missed her so much, but she did. Especially after she'd called to confront her mom about the package of lingerie she'd sent as a gift. Her mom had cried and apologized and swore she'd make it up to her. And Sierra believed her—even when her dad made cracks about lowering her expectations.

"At least you had one good parent. Both mine sucked." Boone sat across from her. "My dad was always gone. When I was a kid and now."

"Have you always lived with him?"

"Nope. I lived with Mom until third grade."

"Did she get married or something?"

"No. Everything changed when my dad found out..." He clenched his hands into fists and he looked at the floor. "Fuck. Never mind. Forget I said anything."

Unnerved by his abrupt mood swing to anger, Sierra waited for him to explain, but he stayed quiet, almost closed off. "What did he find out?"

"Just drop it."

"Were you being abused?"

His head snapped up. "Believe it or not, I would've preferred that 'cause I could have fought back."

"Okay, now after that remark, you've got to tell me."

"I should've kept my mouth shut."

"Boone. Some part of you wants me to know if you mentioned it."

"I don't know why I did. It's just so fucking...embarrassing," he said softly. "I never talk about this shit. Why do I just spill my guts every freakin' time I see you?"

"Because we're friends." She scooted next to him. "Because everyone needs someone to talk to and you can trust me. I promise whatever you share with me will stay between us. So tell me. Please."

Another moment passed. Boone didn't look at her when he said, "My dad found out that I couldn't read."

Her heart squeezed hard at his confession.

"I was eight years old and I couldn't read a single word. My mom played dumb, but the truth was she was either drunk or high and she didn't give a shit, hell, she didn't know where I was half the time. Dad felt guilty, which made him mad, so he caused a big stink with the Moorcroft school board, railing against lazy teachers just passing me when I was illiterate. He had no idea I was a problem child and the teachers couldn't wait to get me the hell out of their classroom."

"How did he find out you couldn't read? Did your mom tell him? Or did you?"

"My Aunt Carolyn figured it out when we were at a West reunion. God. I wanted to die because I knew I was stupid and then everyone else would know it too."

"Did she single you out and embarrass you in front of your whole family?" she demanded.

He finally looked up at her and smiled. "Yep, you're definitely a McKay with how indignant you just got on my behalf. Aunt Caro did too. She read my dad the riot act. I've never heard her swear like that. She even threatened to petition the court for temporary custody of me."

"Did you end up living with her?"

"Just for the summer while my dad got his shit together. She and my Aunt Kimi and my cousin Keely worked with me. They were patient and understanding—everything my mom and dad weren't. I learned a lot, but not enough to make up for all I'd missed in first, second and third grade. So I repeated third grade in Sundance. Which is why I'm graduating at age nineteen instead of eighteen.

"My mom got herself cleaned up after she stopped getting child support payments. By the time I was in fifth grade I was bouncing back and forth between them. But even during those years when I lived with my dad, my grandparents or uncles ended up stuck with me since my dad wasn't around. Then my mom married, had another couple kids. I've more or less been on my own since I was fifteen."

Sierra put her arm around his shoulders, resting her cheek on his bicep. "Okay, West. You win the shitty parents contest."

He laughed.

"However...I saw your name on the honor roll for last quarter, Mr. Four Point Oh. You're not so dumb after all." She closed her eyes when she caught a whiff of his cologne. Tempting to rub her face against his soft flannel shirt and purr like a kitten.

What are you doing? Back off. Don't be stupid and act like you're making a move on him.

Sierra slowly sat up. "Thanks for telling me, Boone."

"There's something about you, McKay, that makes me trust you. Which is weird because I don't trust anyone."

177

"It's probably because I fed you that first time. You keep coming back like a stray dog."

He snorted. "But since I spilled an embarrassing secret, you gotta do the same."

"Why?"

"It's the rules."

"Says who?"

"Me. And my rules...rule."

"Do I have to?"

"Yep. Unless you're Little Miss Perfect Princess who's never done anything wrong."

She slapped his thigh. "Perfect. Princess. As if. I'll tell you if you promise not to tell anyone. Ever."

Those warm fingers were on her chin again, turning her to face him. Then she was looking into that handsome face of his and getting trapped in those gorgeous golden-brown eyes of his. "You can trust me, okay? It's not like I've got a bunch of guy friends I drink beer and bullshit with."

"What about girlfriends?" just slipped out.

"None of those either."

"I've seen girls all over you at school and the games."

"Yeah. I know."

"And you don't take any of them out?"

"Nope. It's because I'm...fuck, why are you so nosy, McKay?"

"You'd be disappointed if I wasn't. So what's the deal?" As soon as she said it, she hoped to God that beautiful, hot Boone West wasn't about to confess that he was gay.

His topaz-colored eyes searched hers. "The truth? I can't afford a girlfriend. I live with my dad, but he's never fucking there. He reminds me that I'm an adult and I have to pay for everything myself. Even working part-time means I'm full-time broke. I don't even have a goddamn car, so it's not like I can pick up a chick on my bike when it's twenty degrees below zero."

Sierra exhaled the breath she'd been holding.

"If anyone asks—and some girls just don't get the hint that I'm not interested—I tell them I'm seeing a woman who lives in Casper." He shrugged and dropped his hand from her face. "Not an original lie, but one that usually works." He gave her a light butt on the head. "Nice distraction, but you still owe me an embarrassing fact about you."

"I'm learning to knit and I really love it."

"That is *not* embarrassing. So quit hedging and lay the real dirt on me."

She blurted, "I was put in juvenile for shoplifting and had to go to teen court."

Boone whistled. "Wasn't expecting that. What happened?"

She told him. Her face flamed, as it always did, when she thought about how stupid she'd been.

"What'd you take?"

"A bottle of perfume."

He studied her. "Would your dad have bought it for you if you'd asked him?"

"Maybe. My mom definitely would've coughed up the cash. Of course, it would've been money she'd gotten from my dad."

"So why'd you do it?"

"A dare from my friends. They said I was too much of a goody-goody. Then they showed me the stuff they'd taken. So I tried to prove I was badass by stealing something. God. I was so fucking gullible and I got caught."

"Did you tell the cops your friends were ripping off stuff too?"

Sierra shook her head. "When the mall cops couldn't get a hold of my mom or my dad, they called the real cops who put me in juvenile detention. With all these kids who had serious problems." She shuddered. "A fifteen-year-old busted for prostitution, a twelve-year-old who'd passed out in the park after she'd nearly died from alcohol poisoning and a girl who assaulted a cop as a gang initiation."

"How long did they leave you in the holding cell?"

"Six hours before my dad showed up. It was horrible. And I said really awful things to him. I was just scared and took it out on him." She sighed. "He got the best shot in though, when he sprang the surprise move on me in front of the magistrate."

Boone grinned. "Bet that went over well with you."

"It was like he was purposely trying to ruin my life. My mom had ditched me. The people I'd tried to impress with my klepto ways? They lied; they *bought* all the stuff they'd supposedly stolen. Then those fuckers had the balls to tell me that they didn't want to be associated with a juvenile delinquent."

"Fuck, Sierra. That's harsh. So do you hate that your dad made you move to Wyoming?"

She shrugged. "Some days it's not so bad." *Like right now.* "But others...it sucks. It hasn't escaped your notice that I'm home on a Saturday night." For the third Saturday night in a row.

"I thought you were hanging out with Marin?"

"I was. Until she got a boyfriend. I mean, we still see each other at school, but she'd rather be with him on weekends. And I can only tag along out of pity so many times."

"Pity. Right. Haven't any of the guys in our school asked you out?" He paused and frowned. "That's a good thing. They're all boneheads. Or cowboys. You're better off at home." Boone stood. "Now that I know

all your secrets, I gotta head out so I can spread them far and wide."
He ducked when she swatted at him. "Kidding. But I do need to hit the
road."

"You're not leaving until you call your uncles."

"Maybe my cell phone is warmed up. The cold sucks the battery
life to nothin'." Boone reached into the pocket of his coveralls and
pulled out an older model cell phone with an antenna. "Just enough
juice to make a call."

"Use the house phone and save your battery life." She snagged the
portable receiver from the hallway.

He kept his eyes on hers as he waited for someone to pick up.
"Chet? Ha ha, asshole, no, I ain't in jail. Fuck you. I am having
problems with my bike though." Pause. "Yeah, I know. I'm on my way
home. Out Burner Road. I had to stop in at Rielle's place and warm up
after my bike crapped out. Okay. Yeah, I've got it with me but it shuts
down." Pause. "I will. God. I said I would. Bye." He hung up.

Then he started putting his clothes back on.

"Do I get your number? So I can check to see that you're home
safe?" That didn't sound skanky and desperate, did it?

"I don't know..." He tapped his finger on his lips as if giving the
matter great thought. "I don't usually give it out. But I *suppose* I could
make an exception to the person who saved my life." He rattled off the
number.

She added him to her contact list. "Why don't you give it out?"

"Because I'm not interested in dating, remember? But I'm pretty
sure you won't be calling me up to ask me out."

"How do you know?"

Boone's face turned somber. He reached out and tucked a strand
of hair behind her ear. "You don't want to date me, beautiful girl. Trust
me on that."

Sierra couldn't move. She couldn't speak. She barely breathed.

"Besides. We're friends. Now that we know each other's secrets,
maybe I'll swing by some Friday night and we can do each other's
hair."

She found her voice. "With the hat hair you're sporting? No way,
dude."

"You crack me up." He slipped on his hat and gloves.

"Promise you'll call me when you get home. Or text me. Something
that lets me know you're safe."

"I will. See ya around, McKay."

She wanted to stand on the porch and watch him take off, but
remained inside by the door, listening for the sound of a motorcycle
starting. She heard a high pitched whine and then the sound faded.

Chapter Twenty-Three

December...

The week after Thanksgiving Sierra entered Gavin's office, phone to her ear, stopping in front of his desk. "No, Mom. I don't get to decide that. It's between you and Dad. Hang on, he's right here." She handed him her phone. "You need to talk to her *now*."

Gavin's entire body tensed. "Fine. But stick around." Then he steeled himself for the conversation. "Hey, Ellen. What's up?"

"After speaking with our daughter? My blood pressure, *merci*."

Christ. Now she casually sprinkled French words into conversation? She was probably wearing a damn beret. "I don't know what's going on, so why don't you fill me in?"

"I asked Sierra to come to Paris for her Christmas break and she didn't seem very excited. That hurts because I haven't seen my only child since June. So have you spent the last few months turning my daughter against me, Gavin?"

Stay calm. "Not at all. You have to admit the *come to Paris for the holidays* invitation is a little out of left field."

"But not out of line," she retorted. "The court awarded you full custody, but I do have the legal right to request holidays."

"I realize that."

"Then you also realize you've had her for every holiday this year? And her birthday?"

"You've had her for Christmas the last five years! I only get her for one day on Thanksgiving, and then you pick her up at the crack of dawn to go shopping the next day. This is the first year I haven't had to share her on her birthday since she was five years old." He felt Sierra staring at him and his face heated. Dammit. He'd sworn he wouldn't do this in front of her.

"Fine. Whatever. But consider this my unofficial request. I want Sierra to spend Christmas with me. In Paris."

"You really expect me to put our sixteen-year-old daughter on a ten-hour flight to France...by herself?"

Sierra leapt up and leaned across the desk, her eyes beseeching. "No. Don't let her guilt you into it, Dad."

"She's not a baby. She's flown more times than most kids her age. Don't you remember she flew to New York by herself when she was twelve?"

"She wasn't by herself. That was a school-sponsored event with adult chaperones, so there's no correlation to this situation."

"I suppose we could take this issue to our attorneys." Ellen sighed. "Or we could save the legal fees and you could fly to Paris with her, and back to the U.S., since you're so concerned about her safety."

"Really? What would I do in Paris for a week?"

"It's the most romantic city in the world, I'm sure you could come up with something." She trilled that mean, annoying laugh. "Oh right, for a second I forgot who I was talking to. Gavin Daniels—the man without a romantic bone in his body."

Don't take the bait.

When he didn't respond, she blithely continued on, "Besides, it's not like you can't afford it."

"Not the point, Ellen."

"And Sierra's break is *two* weeks, not one week, so I'd expect her here for the entire time. Plus the travel days. I intend to show her more of Europe than just France."

"Ask her where her boyfriend will be," Sierra demanded. "And if he knows I'm her daughter and not her sister."

What the fuck? When had that happened? Why hadn't Sierra told him?

"What's Sierra saying?" Ellen demanded. "Has she changed her mind? Tell her we'll have a wonderful time together."

Ellen spoke so loudly Sierra had heard every word.

This back and forth bullshit hurt his ears and his head. Nothing would be resolved today anyway. "Look, Ellen, let me talk it over with Sierra and we'll figure something out. I'll get back to you as soon as I can, all right?"

A long pause. "All right. She's my daughter too, Gavin. And don't think for a second I don't miss her, because I do." She hung up.

Fuck. He wished he could just be pissed off at Ellen for being unreasonable, but she had a point. This was the longest she'd been away from Sierra. Granted, it'd been Ellen's choice, but he felt he should at least try to find a way for them to spend time together.

He handed Sierra's phone back.

"Please, Dad, don't make me go."

"Sierra, sweetheart—"

"I can't believe you're even considering this!"

I can't either.

"You won't let me drive into Sundance by myself but you'd send me halfway across the world by myself? That makes no sense."

"She's your mother. She has a right to see you." Gavin glanced up to see that *I'll argue this to death* stubborn set to his daughter's chin so he tried a different approach. "She misses you. And I know you miss her too. So think about that before you say or do something rash."

Sierra made an exasperated sound and stormed out.

He turned to the window and opened the shade. The sunshine reflecting off the snow made everything blindingly white. From this distance the pristine view looked like an old-fashioned scene from a vintage postcard.

Maybe it was silly and sentimental, but he'd been looking forward to their first Christmas in Wyoming. The snow covered pine trees and the chilly air made everything more festive. Add in all the upcoming McKay family parties and for once he wasn't dreading the holidays.

Sierra had spent the last five Christmases with Ellen, leaving him to face the day alone. After his mother died the pity invites for Christmas dinner tended to piss him off—to the point he morphed into Scrooge the week before to stave off said invites.

He'd never been that big on holidays anyway, not even when his parents were alive, save for the few times he had Sierra all to himself on Christmas morning. Seeing her eyes light up when she saw her gift from Santa and the piles of presents from him. The two of them lazing around all morning in their pajamas, playing with her new toys and eating Christmas candy for breakfast.

Eventually they'd get ready for Christmas dinner at his parents' house. Sierra dolled up in a fancy holiday dress—the more taffeta, lace and velvet the better, with matching shoes and hair ribbons.

Gavin remembered combing the tangles from her snarled hair and her explicit instructions on where to place the barrettes, headband or ponytail holder. Her instructions had amused him, because he'd been putting her hair in a ponytail or pigtails since she'd turned two.

Now she was sixteen. Sometimes he wondered how that'd happened so fast, her change from a sleepy-eyed toddler dragging her favorite Tigger blanket, to the eye-rolling teen with her hand out for the car keys.

Arms snaked around his waist. Body heat and his lover's sweet honeysuckle scent surrounded him. Rielle placed a kiss between his shoulder blades.

"You okay?" she asked. "I heard Sierra's door slam."

"Yeah. Just lost in thought."

"I know. I called your name but you didn't answer."

He turned around and held her face in his hands, kissing her deeply. When he eased back, she wore the secret smile that was an instant aphrodisiac. He seriously considered sweeping everything off his desk and taking her right there.

"I recognize that look in your eye, tycoon. But I'm afraid I'll have to take a raincheck, since there are four loaves of cranberry orange hazelnut bread and eggnog spiced pumpkin bread baking in the oven that will require my attention shortly."

"Mmm. Hot bread sounds almost as good as hot sex." He kissed her again, with a little more zeal, letting his hands wander to fondle her breasts. When Rielle emitted that sexy squeak, he grinned at her. "Sorry. Just a self-reminder that nothing compares to sex with you."

"You are tempting me to just let the damn bread burn."

He had a brilliant idea. "Ree. What are you doing for Christmas?"

Her eyes narrowed at the abrupt subject change. "Same thing we do every year. Put up a tree, bake and eat until my jeans are too tight and hang out by the fireplace with Rory, chugging hot chocolate or wine...depending on the day. Why?"

"How would you like to go to Paris with me for Christmas?"

Rielle's jaw dropped. "What? Paris? As in Paris, France?"

"I sure wasn't talking about dragging you to Paris, Texas," he said dryly.

"Are you serious?"

"Yes. Doesn't that sound romantic? You and me strolling along the Seine? Kissing on the Eiffel Tower? Checking out the handmade goods at the markets? Sipping wine by candlelight in a cozy café? Rolling around in a big bed in our hotel suite?"

A couple long seconds passed before she said, "Gavin. I'm...stunned."

"Good. Then say yes. We'll spend two weeks together, just the two of us. You'll be pampered like you deserve. You won't have to lift a finger or do anything but relax." He kissed her again. "You work too damn hard, honey. Let's take a break."

Rielle stepped back. "I can't afford a trip like that."

He tried to curb his offense, but his words came out clipped. "I don't expect you to pay your way. I was inviting you as my guest."

"As your guest?" The look in her eyes and her tone made the word guest sound like *whore*. "Then definitely not."

"I don't understand."

"Neither do I." She threw up her hands. "Who suggests a Christmas vacation in Paris? Who can just set aside two weeks and go play tourist? Maybe you can, but I sure as hell can't. I have responsibilities—"

"Here we go. You act like you're the only one in the world with a job, Ree. Like the entire state of Wyoming will fall into ruin if you're not around to do your part."

"That's not fair."

"You're damn right it's not. You work like a dog. Everybody takes time off once in a while. You never do. So excuse the hell out of me for wanting to give you something you've never had."

"That's it, isn't it? You want to show me all I've been missing by taking me to a place I'd never be able to afford to go to on my own. Well guess what? I don't care about any of that. I never have and I never will." She clenched her hands into fists. "Don't try and change me, Gavin. I am who I am."

"This has nothing to do with me trying to change you, or seeing it as an opportunity to rub it in your face that I have a bigger bank account than you."

"Yeah? Then how come you got so pissed off when you thought Vi was trying to buy Sierra's affection? How is offering to take me on an all-expenses-paid trip to France any fucking different?"

"It's a helluva lot different, but you're too busy..." Goddammit. *Take your own advice. Stop and think before you say something you can't take back.* "It'd be nice if you'd take that damn chip off your shoulder once in a while."

"I will. Just as soon as you take that silver spoon out of your mouth."

Fuck.

They were both angry. Breathing hard. Neither willing to back down.

The timer on her watch started to beep. She spun on her heel and left the room without a word.

He shouted, "Nice talking to you."

That was mature.

He paced. Then he slumped against the wall. Was he really such a bad guy for wanting to spend some alone time with the woman he loved? Not that he'd told her that.

Would he ask her to drop everything and go to Paris with him if he wasn't going for Sierra?

No.

Good thing that hadn't come up, because it did put his offer in a different light.

Trying to get any work done in this frame of mind would be pointless. He changed clothes and ran five miles on the treadmill. Then he beat the crap out of his heavy bag until he could hardly hold his arms up.

After a long shower, he felt calmer. In a better frame of mind to tackle the problem, because it wasn't going away, no matter how much he wished it would.

Paris.
What the hell was wrong with him?
Didn't Gavin know her at all?

When had she ever let anyone pay for anything she hadn't earned?

Never.

Being intimately involved with him shouldn't earn her a trip to France, for Christsake.

Rielle placed the loaf pans on the cooling racks and loaded the next batch of bread into the oven. She glanced at the time. Noon. Where had this day gone? She set her watch and tackled the stack of dirty dishes.

Paris.

Besides, she didn't have a passport. She angrily scrubbed the dishes. It was mortifying to admit that she'd never been on an airplane. She'd never been anywhere. She and Rory had taken a camping trip to Yellowstone once. She'd been to Denver a number of times. She'd driven into the Rockies. She'd visited the farm and range land in Nebraska. Same with the Black Hills and the prairie in western South Dakota.

So she couldn't see herself buying luggage and boarding a plane that'd fly over the ocean when she'd never actually seen the ocean.

That is not Gavin's fault.

Maybe she did have a chip on her shoulder.

Or worse, maybe she had the fear if Gavin took her someplace sophisticated, she'd embarrass him with her wide-eyed wonder. Maybe he'd realize that if she couldn't live in his world even temporarily, then he couldn't live in hers either.

Damned if she did; damned if she didn't.

Once the dishes were done, she updated her short to-do list. This was the slow time of year for her.

Gavin knew that. Was that why he'd suggested taking a trip now? Because he understood how hard she'd be working again in another few months?

Possibly. But she didn't believe it was a coincidence that Sierra's mother was living in Paris and all of a sudden he planned a trip there. Was he trying to prove something to his ex-wife by inviting Rielle along? Especially since Sierra had mentioned her mother's boyfriend?

Another three hours passed. She was thinking it odd she hadn't seen Sierra or Gavin in the kitchen looking for food, when Sierra walked in.

Rielle smiled. "I wondered if you were so engrossed in your homework you forgot to eat."

Sierra shook her head. "I'm not hungry."

That didn't sound good. "You feel sick?"

She looked away, but not before Rielle noticed she'd been crying.

"Hey, sweetheart, what's wrong?"

Then Sierra threw her arms around Rielle and sobbed.

Caught off guard, because this was unlike Sierra, she rubbed circles on the girl's back, trying to soothe her.

It must've worked because Sierra sighed. "Thanks for the hug, Ree. I'm just having a shitty day."

Welcome to the club. "You'd probably feel better if you ate. I made a loaf of pumpkin bread. Would you like some?"

"Sure."

Sierra watched from the breakfast bar as Rielle sliced two pieces and poured a cup of milk.

A small smile played on Sierra's lips.

"What?"

"It's like you're feeding me milk and cookies."

"Have you ever seen me bake cookies?"

Sierra's brow furrowed. "No. I guess I haven't."

"That's because I suck at cookies. I burn them. Or I undercook them. Or they're too big. Or too small. Or they're too squishy. Or too hard. So I'll stick to baking breads, rolls and muffins."

Sierra pinched off a corner of the bread and popped it in her mouth. "My dad used to eat a big blueberry muffin and a banana every day for breakfast. It drove me crazy because he never ate anything else. If he couldn't have that then he wouldn't eat."

"I remember. But I've yet to see him eat a single muffin since he's lived here."

"Not on his diet anymore. Now he eats cereal or yogurt. Or something else disgustingly healthy."

Rielle laughed.

Sierra broke off a couple more bites. Then she said, "I heard you guys fighting earlier."

She blew across her cup of tea. "Does your dad know you overheard?"

"No. He's been locked in his office." Sierra looked up. "My mom wants me to come to Paris for Christmas. He won't let me fly alone. So that means he'd be stuck in Paris for two weeks."

She made a noncommittal noise.

"My mom...she can be such a bitch to him. She basically said he'd be better off not going to Paris since he doesn't know the meaning of romance and wouldn't know what to do with himself."

Was that why Gavin had asked her? To prove his ex-wife wrong?

"I know he asked you to come with him. I know you said no. I don't understand why you'd say no. I mean, you're already with him and it wouldn't be like you'd be doing anything different there than you're doing here."

Insightful little thing.

"I think you have the wrong impression of him. I mean, since he's got money you'd think he'd be going cool places all the time. But he's always working and he's never taken a two-week vacation."

"Never?"

"He's never taken a vacation with anyone besides me either. So it'd be a big deal if he did go, especially if he went with you. And just so you know, if you don't go, he'll be there by himself. I'm not saying that to make you feel guilty, I'm telling you because I think he deserves to have fun. He should get to be in Paris with someone he cares about. So I'm just asking you to think about it."

"Sierra?" Gavin's voice echoed in the kitchen. He held his phone to his ear. "Your mom is on the line. Come up to my office so we can talk about a few things and get this finalized."

That's when Rielle knew it was too late. Her pride was keeping her from experiencing something amazing. Her pride was also making her question the motives of a man who meant more to her than she'd ever imagined and who needed her support, not her suspicion.

Rielle, you are a stubborn, arrogant fool for treating Gavin like you did. Buck up and apologize.

She heated another cup of tea and peeled a tangerine, arranging the crescents around a slice of pumpkin bread. She headed upstairs and waited in the family room as she sussed out what she intended to say.

Ten minutes later Gavin's office door opened. Footsteps faded down the hallway to Sierra's room and her door closed. She hadn't slammed it. That was a good sign.

Rielle took a deep breath and knocked. She expected to hear, "Come in," but Gavin answered the door.

He peered down the hallway almost as if he was disappointed to see her. "Ree? Hey. What's up?"

"I thought you might be hungry so I brought you a snack. And tea."

"Oh. Well. Sure. I could eat." He grabbed the tray from her, and slid it on his desk, but didn't invite her in.

She followed him anyway and shut the door behind her. Her heart hammered like crazy when he turned around, surprised to see her there. *No excuses. Just say it straight out.* She marched up to him. "I'm sorry for the way I acted earlier. It was wrong, I was wrong and I hope you'll forgive me."

Gavin rested his backside on the edge of his desk and crossed his arms over his chest in a *go on* posture.

"I don't want to explain because I'm afraid it'll come off sounding like an excuse. There isn't any excuse for the defensive way I acted and the accusations I made. I was shocked by the invite. Of course because it's me, I wasn't immediately thinking of all the fun and romantic things we could do together. I immediately thought, I don't have a passport. I've never been on a plane. You would be so cool and sophisticated and I'd stick out like a country bumpkin. During the panicked stage, I only thought of myself and how I'd feel. I shoved aside the thoughtfulness and sweetness of even being asked to spend two weeks with you in Paris."

He stared at her. "And?"

"And what?"

"And what about your comments about the differences in our financial situations?"

Rielle twisted her fingers together.

"What about that pride of yours that can fill an entire room?" Gavin stood up and stalked her. "What about the fact we're lovers, we've been lovers for several weeks and you still won't let me do things for you."

"I, umm, let you buy pizza the other night."

"Any other time, that would make me laugh. But the fact I have to explain to you just how ridiculous that statement is, is a big part of the problem."

"I'm used to splitting costs—"

"With your daughter. With your friends. Not with a lover. And as your lover, I've earned the right to do some things for you. Things that will make *me* happy."

Her back hit the door. How had that happened? "Like what?"

Gavin braced his hands beside her shoulders. "I want to take you out for dinner tomorrow night and you'll let me pay. For everything."

She started to shake her head but stopped when he made that growling noise. "Um. Okay."

"I want you to turn over the log splitting and wood hauling duties to me."

"Gavin. I can't do that."

"Why not?" He waited and then answered, "Because you've always done it by yourself, right? Well, guess what? No more. It will now fall under the realm of my household responsibilities. And the first time you ask me if I've filled the wood box? I will put you over my knee and paddle your ass."

Holy shit.

"We clear?"

"Yes."

"Good. Now there will be more things that occur to me, and we'll discuss them, just as long as you understand some of the *no thanks, I don't need your help* bullshit is gonna stop."

"Does it really mean that much to you?"

189

"Ree. It means everything to me. I'm tired of waiting for your permission to let me be the man you need. Accept that if we're together things are going to change."

Gavin was so close his body-heat-warmed cologne drifted into her nose until her entire being filled with his scent. She wanted him. No niceties. No foreplay. Just thinking about him yanking her jeans down and driving into her made her wet. Wet and achy. Wet and achy and wanting.

"Rielle."

He'd drawn out her name to three syllables. Her gaze snapped to his. "What."

Those blue eyes glittered. "Don't look at me like that."

"Like what? You said you wanted to do things for me."

His focus dropped to her mouth as she licked her lips.

"Prove it. There's something you can do for me right now."

"Name it."

She turned her head and sank her teeth into his bicep. Then she rubbed her face against that smooth, hard flesh. Her tongue traced the crease in the crook of his arm. "Fuck me."

That was all it took.

Gavin used one hand to lock the door and the other to pull her mouth to his in a ravenous kiss.

Her head spun and her blood coursed faster, pooling like liquid fire in her pussy and throbbing in her nipples. She thought he'd shove her against the door, but he brought them to the floor, his mouth hungry on hers as he tried to unzip her jeans. And his jeans. At the same time.

She broke the kiss. "You do yours, I'll do mine."

Then they were naked from the waist down and neither bothered with the top half.

Levering himself over her, he kneed apart her thighs. He rolled his pelvis, rubbing his shaft over her mound. Then he canted his hips and plunged inside her fully. He groaned, "Jesus you're wet," against her throat.

"I know. Get busy and fuck me."

"Repeat that last part again."

"Fuck me."

"I love to hear you say that." He held her hands above her head and rammed into her over and over. His eyes locked to hers. Leaning closer to bestow a kiss that made her thoughts sweetly muzzy, even as he pounded into her flesh like a pile driver.

The quietness between them heightened the intensity. Heat and breath and bodies in motion. Each thrust drove them closer to the top. Each kiss brought them closer to each other.

When Rielle couldn't take any more, when she felt the tingling zip in her tailbone and her vaginal muscles tightening around his cock, she arched, coming hard with a gasp she couldn't contain.

Then Gavin's lips were on hers, absorbing the sound. He pumped into her faster; his deep groan rumbled in her mouth as he followed her over the edge.

Sometime later—several minutes at least—sprawled on her body, he murmured, "I never want to move," and started kissing her neck in that distracting way.

"You have to so I can breathe. You are one solid man."

"And you're such a delicate flower." He pushed up and his perfect lips were curled into a very sexy, very satisfied male grin. "I'm starved."

"Good thing I brought you a snack. But I'll bet your tea is cold."

"Hot woman or hot tea. I'll take the hot woman every time."

Chapter Twenty-Four

Just to prove his point, Gavin made supper and didn't allow Rielle to help. He forced her to sit at the breakfast bar with a whiskey Coke, and the stack of catalogues she'd been stockpiling but hadn't made time to read.

After he'd thrown the sliced potatoes, kielbasa and onions in the pan, he poured himself a drink and sat beside her. She was idly flipping through a beekeeper's supply catalogue.

"See anything you can't live without?"

"Not so far. It's crazy how much the prices have increased since last year. Since there isn't a local supplier, I'm stuck paying premium prices and shipping."

"I admit, I find beekeeping a lot more fascinating than I used to."

Rielle batted her eyelashes. "Because I explained it so well or because I look so completely sexy covered up in the beekeeper suit holding a smoker?"

"Must be the latter." He snatched her hand and kissed her knuckles. "So honey, we need to talk."

She rotated on her barstool. "Is this about how hot it was when you threw me on the floor and fucked me senseless in your office?"

"No." He allowed a wolfish smile. "But it was fucking amazing."

"What's amazing to me is I finally know what heart-pounding passion feels like. It's a first. You say that I don't let you do things for me. Without sounding mushy, what you give me when we're alone together is something I've never had before." She kissed the back of his hand. "So thank you."

Maybe the booze had loosened her tongue, but he was grateful she was finally opening up to him. "You're welcome. You do know it's the same for me, right?" His eyes searched hers. "I've never had this with anyone else. I don't want to go too fast or push too hard because I'm used to getting things my way, on my timeframe."

"No," she said with sarcasm. "Really? I never noticed that about you, tycoon."

"Such a smart mouth. But I am serious, Ree. I don't want to screw this up."

"You won't. I won't let you. Because I'm right there with you in trying to figure this out."

"Good. Now onto the other thing we need to discuss. Christmas. Or more accurately Christmas vacation."

She didn't pull back.

Encouraged, he laid it all out there. "The Paris trip is off. For a number of reasons; the biggest one was that Sierra didn't want to go. There's no way I'll force my daughter into a situation she doesn't want to be in. But she also needed to understand her mother has every right to spend time with her. So we arrived at a compromise."

"Which is?"

"We'll spend Christmas here as planned. Then three days after Christmas, Sierra and I will fly to Arizona. Ellen will fly over from France and she and Sierra will spend two weeks together in Scottsdale."

"That's a great compromise, although I'd bet you're paying for Ellen's plane ticket."

Of course Rielle would pick up on that. "That's a much cheaper solution than us going to Paris."

"True." Rielle looked at him thoughtfully. "What else?"

"I want you to come to Arizona with me. Not for the full two weeks, but just a week. Rory will only be here for a few days over the holiday, so it's not like you'd have to sacrifice time with her to be with me."

"I want to point out that this is me listening to you, not immediately saying no."

"She can be taught." He grinned. "Ellen has made it clear that her time with Sierra does not include me. I need to go to Phoenix, not only to make sure Ellen actually shows up, but to handle year-end business. I own a piece of property we can stay in, meaning no hotel costs. I have a company car to use, meaning no rental car costs. So the only upfront, out-of-pocket expense is the airfare."

Rielle broke eye contact and sipped her drink.

"I'd prefer to pay your way, since this is my idea, but I know how...independent you are, so I'd agree to you buying your own plane ticket."

"If I let you pay for everything else."

"Yes. But what's left to pay for? Food? Gas? Sex toys?"

She laughed. "Such a naughty side to you."

Gavin curled his hands around her face, forcing her to look at him. "Please. Say yes. I want this time with you."

Indecision warred on her face. She closed her eyes and inhaled a long, deep slow breath. Then she opened her eyes. "Okay. Yes. I'll come to Arizona with you."

He kissed her, a little too enthusiastically because his dick immediately got onboard. But he couldn't help it. He was as excited as a kid on Christmas morning.

"I can't believe I'm actually getting on an airplane."

"I'll hold your hand the entire time. I promise." Gavin brushed his mouth over hers. "Thank you, Ree. You have no idea what this means to me."

"I'm starting to understand that," she murmured. Then she pulled on his wrists until he released her. "Do you smell something burning?"

Gavin bailed off the stool and checked the pan. The potato pieces on the bottom had built a dark crust, but it wasn't ruined, thank God, because he'd never hear the end of it.

Sierra wandered in and wrinkled her nose. "Dad, are you burning supper?"

"No."

Her gaze moved between him and Rielle. "So what's going on?"

"Ree and I were just discussing the Arizona trip."

"You're not yelling at each other so I assume everything is worked out?"

"Yes. Rielle is coming with us."

Sierra grinned. "That's awesome. Two whole weeks in the desert?"

He shook his head. "Just one week. You'll fly back the following week. No way to get around you missing a couple of days of school."

"Darn." She paused. "Wait. You're letting me fly back from Phoenix by myself?"

"It's a direct flight."

She pumped her fist. "Now I can put that fake ID to good use and get snockered on the plane."

Rielle laughed. "Snockered? Since when do teens use that term for being drunk?"

"Since my dad doesn't like the term *shitfaced*."

"What word would he prefer?" Rielle asked.

"Illegal   underage   drinking,"   he   and   Sierra   finished simultaneously.

Sierra snagged the barstool next to Rielle and sifted through the pile of catalogues. "Cool. Are you choosing things for your Christmas wish list?"

"I don't have a Christmas wish list."

Sierra gasped dramatically. "Seriously? Why not?"

Rielle shrugged. "It's only been Rory and me, except for when my parents were alive but they didn't celebrate Christmas, so there's been no need for a list. I knew what Rory wanted and I was happy with whatever she gave me."

"Well, it's different now, because we're here. I'm giving you a gift so I'll need ideas. And I know Dad will buy you something, so you'd better give him some guidelines or you'll find a new pickup or something in the driveway on Christmas morning."

Rielle aimed a laser-sharp gaze at him. "You wouldn't dare."

Gavin leaned across the counter and flashed his teeth at her. "Try me."

When her eyes widened he knew she'd remembered their earlier conversation.

Oh, Little Miss I-Make-My-Own-Way wanted to argue. She'd point out that Christmas wasn't about the presents, *blah blah blah.* Bull crap. This was the only time of year he could buy her anything he wanted and she'd have no choice but to suck it up and accept it with a smile.

"Stop smirking at me, Gavin Daniels. I'll make a damn list. But you get to pick *one* thing from it, understand?"

"Of course. Sierra, sweetheart, why don't you show Rielle how to make a wish list, since you're an expert."

"You know it."

As he watched Rielle and Sierra laughing together, oohing and aahing over the catalogues Sierra had dragged over, he had a sense of rightness that he was exactly where he needed to be.

Gavin finally understood why Christmas was referred to as the holiday season—parties, school and family events started at Thanksgiving and stretched through Christmas. Living in Arizona, with the temperatures in the seventies, wreaths, holiday decorations and twinkling lights hung from cacti, Santa sporting a pair of board shorts and fake Christmas trees, he'd never felt that holiday spirit for a day, let alone for an entire month.

But in Wyoming, things were a lot different. First of all, every household in the McKay family had some type of holiday get together at their place. He didn't feel like he'd missed out on longstanding family traditions when Quinn told him that most of these family holiday gatherings had just started in the last few years.

So far he and Sierra had spent time with every one of his cousins and their wives and children. Cider and cookies at Cord and AJ's, which was also a celebration of the birth of their daughter, Avery. All six of Cam and Domini's kids put on a holiday play at their house, followed by a feast of Ukrainian treats, most of which were eaten by their rowdy brood.

Since Carter and Macie lived out of town, they combined forces with Carolyn and Carson at their place for a cookie decorating party. Kade and Skylar opted to hold their shindig at the Sky Blue plant, along with Kane and Ginger, and Colt and India. While the adults gorged on appetizers, Keely spearheaded a Christmas ornament craft session for the kids. She'd enlisted Sierra's help, and Gavin was delighted to see his daughter having fun with glitter, glue and pinecones and the ten billion McKay offspring.

Brandt and Jessie, Tell and Georgia and Dalton hosted a Rocky Mountain oyster feed at the fire pit in Brandt and Jessie's backyard. At Colby and Channing's place, Colby hitched up the team of Morgans to a hay wagon. Carson, Cal and Charlie loaded up the kids for a redneck sleigh ride across snow covered pastures. Gavin wondered if Sierra would think it was lame and refuse to go, since she was the oldest kid by several years, but she'd surprised him once again. In fact, Charlie had told him that Sierra was the one who'd started the Christmas carol sing-along and handed out hot chocolate.

Vi and Charlie assisted Quinn and Libby with their annual fruitcake throwing contest. Which was such a weird tradition Gavin had to ask Ben about it. Evidently the first year Quinn and Libby had Adam, Libby had tried out a new fruitcake recipe that was so bad Quinn wouldn't eat it. They had a big fight and in a rare fit of anger, Libby had thrown the fruitcake at her husband. He'd taunted her, saying she had terrible aim, so she challenged him to see how far he could throw the dense fruitcake. The story spread through the McKay family and the following year everyone brought fruitcake and joined in the contest.

Ben and Ainsley had an adults only cocktail party. No one was surprised that Keely volunteered her babysitting services for all the McKay offspring that night. But everyone *was* shocked when Jack announced her pregnancy.

As much fun as Gavin had at the festivities the past few weeks, getting to know his family a little better, something was missing.

Rielle.

He'd invited her to the first McKay family event since everyone in the gossipy McKay family knew they were in a relationship. But Rielle had demurred. Her reasons were sound; she'd be an intrusion in Gavin and Sierra's family time. It made sense, but he still missed her.

Sometimes he felt theirs was a relationship borne out of their odd living arrangement. Rielle kept that dividing line in place, doing her own thing. She'd decorated her part of the house by herself. He and Sierra put up an enormous Christmas tree and added decorations from years past, plus new ones they'd found at the community bazaar.

But other times, when he and Rielle were alone, there was no her space or his space, just their space.

"Dad, come taste this," Sierra yelled from the kitchen.

Vi had come over to make candy with Sierra. His relationship with Vi had returned to how it'd been before their fight. But now Vi cleared every purchase and activity with him before she mentioned it to Sierra, which wasn't a snarky way to poke at him, but it gave Vi an excuse to call him up and chat whenever she wanted. Strange that he didn't mind.

Upon entering the kitchen, he saw globs of brown on wax paper, a pan of peanut brittle and chocolate balls topped with fancy red and green icing. "What am I trying?"

"Gram's caramels. They're the best thing ever." Sierra held a square up to his lips. "Try it."

He opened his mouth. Buttery vanilla goodness melted on his tongue. "Okay. Wow. Those *are* incredible." He shook his finger at Vi. "And you're taking them all home because I will sit down in front of the game and eat the entire batch."

"I'll save some for Christmas dinner." She wiped a section of the counter. "You're still planning on coming over?"

"Of course. I wish you'd let us bring something."

Vi looked him in the eye. "Having you both there with us and the rest of our family is more than enough."

Our family. She didn't push, but she clearly stated, at every opportunity, that they were family.

"You haven't said what you and Sierra are doing on Christmas Eve."

"We haven't decided. Although I'll bet Little Miss will try and convince me to open presents on Christmas Eve instead of Christmas morning."

Vi frowned. "You don't have a tradition?"

"No. Sierra's been with her mom the last five Christmases. She spends part of Christmas Eve with me. Then I drop her off at Ellen's that night."

"Dad, we're doing the same thing we always do. Drinking eggnog, cooking a batch of chili and watching *Santa Claus is Coming to Town*." Sierra grinned. "Then maybe we'll open up a present or ten."

"Don't you have plans with Rielle and Rory?" Vi asked.

Gavin shook his head.

She paused. "I'm sorry. I find that strange."

Me too.

"Speaking of Rielle...let's get this mess cleaned up so she won't have a fit that we destroyed her kitchen," Vi said.

That rubbed Gavin the wrong way. "Maybe it seems like Rielle's kitchen, but I do own this house. So technically it's *my* kitchen."

Silence.

"Well, I'm glad you cleared that up," Rory said walking past him, overloaded with grocery bags.

Shit. "Here, let me help you."

"I've got it. Just let me know when I can come back into *your* kitchen and put everything away," she retorted.

"Rory. That's uncalled for," Rielle said behind him. Then she too walked past with bags, and she too refused his help. "And Gavin is right. This is his place." She smiled at Vi and Sierra. "But I do appreciate having a clean spot to work in."

"We were just finishing up," Vi said.

"No rush. I'll put the stuff in the refrigerator. Rory and I planned to have a glass of wine first anyway."

Then they were gone.

Sierra mumbled, "Merry freakin' Christmas," and started to load the dishwasher, humming Christmas tunes.

Gavin leaned against the counter where Vi was dividing all the goodies into Christmas tins. "Like I said, Gavin, I find this situation strange."

"Yeah, well, it is what it is."

"You *are* in a serious relationship with Rielle?"

He nodded. Yes, they were taking things slow. Normally he'd be fine with that; after all, they had their own lives and interests. But Gavin had almost an obsessive need to define what was growing between them.

The hit and miss nights they spent in each other's beds caused some annoyance, even when he understood she had to be up at the crack of dawn three mornings a week.

Rielle got along well with Sierra. She didn't comment on his parenting practices and she never inserted herself into the time he spent with his daughter. Most men would consider it an ideal relationship: smoking hot sex whenever he wanted, a woman who made no demands of a commitment, and her complete disinterest in the fact he had money. But he wanted more.

"This is what she wants," he said softly.

Vi's eyes took on a defiant gleam. "What about what *you* want?"

Such a...defensive and motherly thing to say. "It's complicated. Rielle and I...we've both done our own thing. It's been her and Rory for so long neither of them knows any other way to be. It's sort of the same for Sierra and me."

"But you're adapting. You've embraced all the McKay craziness more than I ever thought you would."

She rubbed his arm in such a loving manner, he nearly hugged her. He missed the easy rapport he'd had with his mother. Her sweetness and generosity. Vi was nothing like her...and yet she was.

"What are you thinking about that's put such a melancholy look in your eyes?" Vi asked.

Gavin hedged. "How much I'm looking forward to having Christmas dinner with the crazy McKays."

That answer pleased her. "We'll eat around two. And open presents afterward."

His smile froze. "Presents?"

"A little untraditional, I know, but Quinn and Libby want to spend Christmas morning with their children. Chase and Ava are staying in Kane's trailer, and for the life of me I can't figure that one out. Ben and Ainsley are feeding cattle so Quinn can be home with his family. So we open our gifts to each other late."

He was so screwed. He'd bought a gift for Vi and Charlie, but no one else.

After he carried Vi's boxes out to the car, he returned to the kitchen just as Sierra started the dishwasher.

She looked up at him and smirked. "So, you forgot to buy presents for your brothers, huh?"

"Dammit. I didn't know there was a mandatory present thing."

"Dad. It's Christmas. Presents are always part of that. Which means you also need to buy gifts for their wives. Oh, and their kids." She flat out laughed at his panicked expression. "Don't worry. I'm a shopping expert, remember? We'll get you loaded up in no time."

"Do you have all of your shopping done?"

"Of course."

How? He hardly ever let her drive anywhere—even after she'd passed her driver's test two weeks ago. "I'll get my coat. And if we can really get this done in one night, I'll even let you drive."

Chapter Twenty-Five

Gavin and Sierra spent Christmas Eve stuffing themselves with chili, snacks and cookies. He even listened to the music on her iPod as they played her favorite board games. Including Candyland, which amused him, because she used the same strategy as she had at age six, which allowed him to win.

She'd been so excited to open gifts that he'd let her open them all. The number of presents under the tree from her surprised him. Fun, thoughtful, sweet items that proved she at least listened to him some of the time. His favorite was the hat she'd knitted for him in ASU colors. He'd had no clue that Rielle had taught her how to knit. It must've taken her hours. He immediately put it on and refused to take it off. Even when his head was sweating. Even after she called him a dork.

Her favorite gift was the set of Jeep keys he'd wrapped up with his promise that she could drive whenever she wanted—weather permitting—as soon as they returned from Arizona.

Afterward, she snuggled up to him on the couch and they watched Christmas movies. In a few years, this too would change between them. College. Boyfriends. Eventually a home and family of her own. It made him a little sad even as it reinforced his determination that he'd never let her get so far adrift from him again. As he looked at his bright, beautiful daughter he felt the bond between them had strengthened over the past few months, and he'd made the right decision moving them here.

Around eleven he kissed her forehead. "Better get in bed, girlie, or Santa won't come tonight."

"Dad. Santa? Really?"

"Yep. And he told me he was partial to those frosted cookies you made yesterday, so feel free to leave those out with a glass of milk."

She snickered. "Okay. But I might skip the carrots for the reindeer this year." She hugged him. "Night, Dad. Merry Christmas. I love you."

"Merry Christmas. Love you too, sweetheart."

"Outstanding meal, Mom. I think you'll have to roll me to the

Christmas tree," Chase said, suppressing a burp.

"We should all go for a walk."

Everyone groaned at the suggestion.

"I'm on dish detail," Ainsley announced.

"Me too," Ava chimed in.

"Me three." Libby looked at Quinn. "You wanna put the kids down for a short n-a-p?"

"Sure." He lifted Amelia from her high chair. "Come on, baby girl. Let's get you tucked in."

Thumb in her mouth, she nestled her head in the crook of her dad's neck.

Gavin remembered those sleepy toddler days with more fondness than they probably deserved. Sierra hadn't ever been an easy child.

Thump. Adam raced behind the dining room chairs and jumped in front of Quinn. "Daddy, where you goin'?"

"To a quiet, special place."

"Can I come?"

"Well, I don't know, sport. I'm thinkin' you forgot how to be quiet."

"I can be quiet," Adam insisted.

"Really?"

Adam nodded.

"Okay. But you have to tiptoe like this." Quinn demonstrated. Then he dropped his voice. "Can you whisper like this?"

Adam nodded again and tiptoed down the hallway after him.

Libby smiled. "That man can always get Adam to take a nap no matter how cranky or wild the kid is."

"Must be a McKay family thing. My dad had to trick me into taking naps too," Sierra said. "The one I remember best was the magical trip to la-la land. He made it sound like unicorns would prance around me and I could chase butterflies to my heart's content and the entire place was made of candy. I could hardly wait to fall asleep."

"It worked every time too."

Sierra dropped her arms over the back of his chair and leaned down to hug him. "I'd be happy to revisit la-la land now if it'll get me out of doing the dishes."

"Not a chance."

Everyone laughed.

The women headed to the kitchen while the men adjourned to the living room. Charlie passed out cups of eggnog.

Gavin listened while Charlie, Ben and Quinn talked about ranching stuff that he had no clue about.

Then Chase butted in. "No offense, guys, but that's enough talk about the damn cattle."

"What do you wanna talk about, Chase? Bull riding?" Ben asked.

"Nope. I wanna hear about Gavin's trip to Arizona in a few days. Anything interesting going on with your business?"

"I guarantee none of you want to hear me drone on about the real estate market. But yeah, I'm tying up some year-end loose ends."

"I don't see how you can run your business in Arizona from here," Quinn said. "Don't you gotta be there checking to make sure people get their shit done?"

"I did for a long time. It's a well-known fact that I'm generous with performance bonuses. Money is always an incentive to ensure the job gets done right. I still fly down every few months, for face-to-face time with my employees and a few key customers. But ninety percent of what I do can be done from anywhere as long as I have a computer and a phone."

"Huh. I heard Sierra mention she's meeting her mom there?" Chase asked. "I thought your ex ran off to France?"

"She did. But I gave Ellen two choices for Sierra's Christmas break: come to the U.S. to see her daughter or stay in Paris and not see her daughter." He sipped his drink. "So she'll be in Scottsdale."

Ben rested his forearms on his thighs, as if he intended to settle in for a long chat. "Ainsley said we're watching Sadie while you and Rielle are gone."

"Yep."

Silence. Then, "So you're still seeing Rielle?" Chase asked.

"Yep."

Quinn laughed softly. "Those responses sound like what I'd say. And Ben'd say. And Dad'd say. Chase on the other hand...he'll blab every thought that pops into his head."

"Screw you. I can keep a secret."

Ben coughed, "Bullshit," into his hand.

"Boys," Charlie warned. "You're getting off track. I believe Gavin was about to tell us what's going on between him and Rielle."

Gavin stared at Charlie. "Why you throwing me under the bus?"

"It's your turn. So start talkin'. And one word answers ain't gonna cut it," he warned. "Because I know you like to talk. That's where Sierra gets it."

"Not much to tell. We're living together, yet separately and she's got all these boundaries. The weird thing is sometimes I think those boundaries are smart, other times they drive me crazy. But I convinced her to take a break where there's no work, no—" he looked over his shoulder, "—kid. Nothing but us. So we'll see how it goes."

Charlie said, "Can I give you some advice?"

Gavin looked at him, surprised by the offer. "Sure."

"We've been neighbors of the Wetzlers for years. I don't know how else to put this, but her parents were off their damn rockers. Their ideas about agriculture and sustaining the land were archaic at best, unrealistic at worst. Damn child laborers, that's what they were—and yes, that's coming from me, who worked you boys hard. I always felt sorry for her, even as a child before she ended up pregnant as a young girl. Course, after Vi found out, she went out of her way to check on Rielle and Rory. Vi...she knew a little something about bein' pregnant at that age. Although, I never understood why she was so concerned about Rielle and that baby until she told me about you."

How was he supposed to respond to that?

"Even now, Rielle won't let up on herself because she doesn't know how. Anyway, my advice to you is to spoil the shit out of her while you're in Arizona. Not to flash your cash, but to show her that goofing off is the reward for hard work and everyone deserves a break. It ain't gonna be easy, but I believe she's worth the effort."

Ben, Quinn and Chase gaped at one another. Then Quinn said, "Ah, Dad? How much rum did you put in that eggnog? I've never heard you offer us advice on women."

Charlie shrugged. "That's because none of you ever needed it."

The ladies returned from the kitchen and paired off with their partners, leaving Gavin relieved he hadn't brought Rielle because Sierra would be the odd one out in her own family.

"Who wants wine?" Vi asked. Ainsley and Libby raised their hands. Vi looked at Ava. "Ava, sweetheart? What about you?"

Ava shook her head.

Chase blurted, "That's because she's pregnant!"

Amidst the congratulations, Ben leaned over and muttered, "I told you he can't keep a damn secret."

Gavin grinned.

"When are you due?" Vi asked.

"Six months." Ava stood and turned sideways, smoothing her hands over her perfectly flat belly. "See? I already look pregnant."

Libby choked on her wine.

Ainsley said, "Hate to break it to you, Ava darlin', but *I* look more pregnant than you do."

"Bite your tongue, wife," Ben half-snapped.

"And with that...Vi, don't you think it's time we open gifts?"

"Isn't it time for pie?" Sierra asked.

"Later."

"But it's pumpkin. That's my favorite."

"Hand out those presents, girlie," Charlie advised.

Then the kids were up and the dignified unwrapping ended.

Gavin got a huge kick out of Adam and Amelia. Such funny and friendly kids. Amelia even crawled right up into his lap.

When he caught Sierra's eye, she smiled. "She knows you're good with little girls."

Sometimes his daughter said the sweetest things.

Gavin noticed Vi's strange expression. She hadn't received a gift from him and was too polite to ask if anything remained under the tree. "Vi?" he said above the din.

Charlie whistled for quiet.

"My gift to you is in the garage," Gavin said to her.

"Really? Why?"

"Let's go find out," Charlie said.

They traipsed to the garage. He pointed to a blanket-covered box in the far corner. "Go ahead." He and Charlie exchanged a grin.

Vi pulled the blanket back and beneath it was an industrial oven like Rielle's. She gasped and whirled around. "This is mine?"

"I knew you wanted one, and Charlie said your oven was on its last legs. We all know he's too cheap to spring for that kind—" laughter, "—so I said I'd buy it for you if he'd put it in."

She just stared at him.

Crap. Maybe he had gone overboard.

But she marched right up to him and threw her arms around him. "Thank you, son. I love it."

"You're welcome."

Then she whapped him on the arm. "So sneaky, just like your father. Do you know one time he let me think he'd forgotten to buy me a birthday present? Then as I got ready for bed I found a wrapped box in my makeup drawer next to my cold cream."

"Grams, that's such a sweet, romantic story." Sierra put her arm around her shoulder. "Is it time for pie yet?"

"Sierra, is that all you can think about?" Gavin asked, exasperated. What was wrong with her? It wasn't like she hadn't just stuffed her face with an entire plate of homemade candies.

"It's fine. I remember teenagers' stomachs being bottomless pits. And that's what grandmas do best right? Fill you with sugary treats and send you home all hyped up on extra sugar." She patted Sierra's cheek. "I'll even put extra whipped cream on your pumpkin pie, punkin."

Sierra shot him a smug look. "Grandma makes the *best* homemade pie crust. You could learn a thing or two from her."

He caught Vi's eye and grinned. "You know what? I already have."

They didn't get home from Charlie and Vi's until nine o'clock. Sierra hauled her presents into her room, leaving Gavin at loose ends. He paced in front of the windows, too restless to even find a classic sports game on TV.

Then Rielle walked toward him, looking like a damn dream, holding a bottle of wine and two glasses. "Care to join me in a glass of Christmas cheer?"

"Mmm-hmm. But this first." Gavin kissed her. Hotly, sweetly, teasingly, pouring everything he'd been feeling into one long kiss before he eased back to stare into her eyes. "Merry Christmas, honey."

"That was a helluva Christmas kiss, tycoon."

"I missed you."

"Same here. Been a long two days."

"I'll say. I'm glad you tracked me down."

"Where's Sierra?" she asked.

"In bed, tuckered out from Christmas festivities." He nuzzled her temple, and her honeysuckle scent teased his nose. "Where's Rory?"

"At a movie. A Christmas night tradition with her friend Addie."

"So I can invite you to drink that wine in my bed?"

"Yep."

"Good. Because I have another present for you in my room."

Rielle looked him. "You already gave me a kick-ass gift."

"The extra-large electric honey separator wasn't too boring?"

"No. I've wanted one for so long. It's perfect. Thank you. I'm sorry; I probably should've waited to open it until you were there."

"No need to apologize. I loved the sweater by the way. It fits perfectly."

"I thought the color would bring out your eyes."

Gavin led her into his bedroom and locked the door behind her.

She settled against the headboard, setting the wine and glasses on the nightstand.

He tossed a package next to her on the bed. "Open it. And not with, *Gavin you shouldn't have*, or *Gavin I thought we agreed on one gift.*"

Rielle pulled the silver ribbon free from the green tissue paper and a red bikini rolled out. "A swimsuit?"

"I didn't know if you had one and the house we're staying in has a pool. To be completely blunt, this bikini is as much a present for me as it is for you. Because you will look fantastic in it lying on a chaise in the sunshine."

She laughed.

"The day after tomorrow I'll have you all to myself for two weeks. I cannot wait."

"Me either."

Gavin pressed a kiss in the hollow of her throat. Then on the side of her neck. Then on her jaw. He murmured, "Can we be done talking for now?"

"Yes."

Chapter Twenty-Six

As they deplaned in Phoenix, Rielle decided her first plane ride hadn't been that bad. The whiskey Coke had helped.

Sierra had been bouncing off the walls since dawn. She jabbered a mile a minute, reminding herself out loud of things she wanted to tell her mom. She could scarcely sit still and as they pulled into the circular driveway, Sierra leapt out of the car and raced up the cobblestone-paved sidewalk and barged right into the house through the gigantic front door.

Rielle didn't get a glimpse of Ellen, but then again she'd been too busy gawking at the house and landscaping.

The sprawling stucco structure was enclosed by a six-foot-high fence on all sides, save for the wrought iron gated entrance. The front area didn't have grass, but reddish-colored stones bordered by larger flat white rock. Bushes were spread out along the base of the house and disappeared around the side. Off to the left were half a dozen fruit trees, the bottom of the trunks painted white, which was weird. She didn't see cacti but groupings of different varieties and sizes of palm trees.

Mind boggling to consider that Gavin had lived here at one time and that he could afford to just give this ostentatious house to his ex-wife.

Gavin didn't stay inside long. His smile didn't quite reach his eyes when he returned and said, "Ready?"

"Is the place we're staying as upscale as this?"

He kissed her knuckles. "No. Ellen insisted on buying the house before Sierra was born. She kept it in the divorce settlement and we use her address since this area has a much better school district than where I moved. It's an enormous house for two people, but the property value quadrupled in the last sixteen years. Ellen isn't allowed to sell it until after Sierra graduates from high school and if she does, she's forced to use my real estate company as the listing agency. It's the only way I could ensure my daughter had some stability." He realized he hadn't answered the question. "The house we're staying in is pretty typical for Phoenix. Three bedrooms, three baths, two-car garage."

"Except it has a pool."

"Honey, all the houses down here have a pool. This one is heated, however. Not all are. Because heaters definitely aren't needed in the summer."

Houses and scenery scrolled by as she looked out the car window. "It's strange. Just a few hours ago we were brushing the snow off the car. Now the sun is blinding me and I'm actually hot."

"I'll say. I cannot wait to see you in that bikini."

"How much further?"

"Twenty minutes. Thirty if we hit traffic."

Shopping centers. Medical centers. Office buildings. More strip-malls. Every once in a while she'd see a grove of citrus trees—an oasis in the inner-city sprawl. She lost track of the number of golf courses. The huge swath of green among the dusty hues of the desert was a little surreal.

Gavin turned off the busy highway onto a residential street. With as many twists and turns as they'd taken, she'd never find her way out of this urban maze. He stopped at a gate and punched in a code.

A gated community? So much for his claim it was just a typical Phoenix house.

After more winding streets, he pulled into a driveway and parked in front of a garage. Most of the stucco-covered house was hidden behind a variety of trees.

"Ree?" He turned her face toward him. "You all right? You went from chatty to silent."

"Just trying to absorb all this, Gavin."

He kissed her softly. "Let's go in and get unpacked." He unloaded the suitcases and dragged them up the front steps.

A cool blast of air and the scent of lemon Pledge greeted her in the cavernous foyer. But the darkness made her claustrophobic, so she immediately crossed the room and opened the blinds and draperies.

The living room was connected to the kitchen through an arched doorway. The décor had southwest flavor, tiled floors, plain white walls, a Navajo influence in the rugs and the couches. The sliding glass door in the dining room opened to a brick-paved patio. Curious, she stepped outside.

Patio furniture was arranged around the large, kidney-shaped pool. Wide steps and a handrail accessed the shallow end. The deep end was marked at nine feet. The ledge surrounding the pool was trimmed with cerulean blue tiles. To her right, beneath a permanent awning, sat a picnic table and chairs. A firepit took up one corner of the yard; citrus trees lined the other side.

Gavin's arms came around her and he kissed her neck. "So? What do you think?"

"I think I might be dreaming. This is beautiful."

"Come and see the rest of the house."

Rielle didn't pay much attention to the spare bedrooms or bathrooms. The master bedroom was roughly the same size as her old room. The master bath was fancier, boasting a steam shower in addition to the glass-walled shower, a double vanity and built-in cabinetry in every nook and cranny.

She returned to the bedroom to see Gavin putting away his clothes. She still couldn't wrap her head around the fact they'd be here for a week. Alone. Just the two of them.

Gavin picked her up and threw her on the bed. Then he was on top of her. Kissing her with ferocity. Grinding his pelvis into hers, his cock already hard. His mouth moved to her ear. "Let me have you."

Usually she'd jump right on that idea, but not this time.

He sensed her hesitation and pushed up to look into her eyes. "What's wrong?"

"I don't know. The timing on this feels off. Like *hey, we're here alone, let's fuck first thing and get it out of the way.*"

"No pressure. This is supposed to be fun. Relaxing. I saw you bent over that suitcase and well, I'm a guy. I wanted to pull down your jeans and fuck you just like that." He grinned. "I thought I was being polite and gentlemanly by throwing you on the bed first."

Rielle laughed. "Tell you what. Can I take a raincheck on that for now?"

"Sure." He pressed his lips to hers and rolled off the bed. "On one condition." His very male, very possessive gaze started at her feet and ended at her chest. "You put on the bikini."

"Now?"

"Now."

"Fine. But I'd better see you in a Speedo too, bucko."

Gavin shuddered. "No Speedo for me ever. But I will put on my swimming trunks if it makes you happy."

"Very happy."

Then, like a complete chicken, Rielle undressed in the bathroom and didn't come out until she knew Gavin was gone. Since she'd forgotten a cover up, and had no intention of prancing around in a bikini all damn day—no matter what Gavin wanted—she snagged one of his button-up business shirts from the closet and slipped it on before she headed to the kitchen.

His drink stopped halfway to his mouth when he caught sight of her. "Are you fucking serious?"

"What?"

"I'm supposed to keep my hands to myself when you're looking that goddamn sexy in a bikini *and* wearing my shirt?" He groaned. "You're evil, Ree. Pure evil."

This man knew exactly what to say to her. She kissed him, using the distraction to swipe his drink and take a sip before she handed it back. "Mmm. Whiskey. So this place comes equipped with booze?"

"I sent my assistant a list. She brought everything over when she checked the house yesterday."

"How many minions do you have to do your bidding?"

"Employees," he corrected. "No minions. It's not like I demanded she prepare a gourmet feast for us. She just picked up a few things at the store for me. That's it."

"This is my first glimpse into your world, isn't it? A reminder that we live in two different worlds."

He hauled her against his chest. "We're in the same world, in the same place right now and that's all that matters to me."

Rielle let him kiss her, wanting the familiarity of his touch to shut down the doubts that'd begun to plague her.

"Would you like a whiskey Coke? Or a beer? Or a whiskey Coke minus the whiskey?"

"Whiskey on the rocks would be great."

"Are you hungry? There's chips and salsa or I could make you a salad."

Rielle put her hand on his arm. "Gavin. I don't expect you to wait on me."

"Tough. I plan to wait on you, cater to your every need, fulfill your every desire, so by the time we leave here, you're used to it."

She started to laugh until she realized the man was dead serious. What the hell?

They carried their drinks by the pool and settled into the chaise lounges. With the sun warming her body and whiskey buzz, she drifted into that happy place of marginal awareness. She heard Gavin chuckle beside her and she let herself go completely under.

A rough fingertip stroking her arm brought her out of her relaxation. She stretched and sighed. "How long was I out?"

"An hour, I guess. I dozed off myself. Would you like another drink?"

Rielle peered at him over the tops of her sunglasses. "You trying to get me drunk and take advantage of me, tycoon?"

"Yep."

"Okay. But add Coke to mine this time."

After Gavin returned to the kitchen, Rielle decided to take a dip in the pool. She floated on her back; the water muffled all noise except for the sound of her deep breathing. She stared up at the pale gray sky. Odd to think a sky that color in Wyoming meant snow. She dropped to her feet and noticed Gavin watching her avidly.

"I set your drink on the table. There's a towel there for you too."

Rielle smiled at him. "Don't want your shirt to get wet?"

His phone rang and he frowned at the number. "Sorry, I have to take this call." He abruptly disappeared into the house.

Was Sierra already having issues with her mother?

She snagged a chair by the picnic table. The air temp had cooled, and she let her head fall back, closing her eyes. This drinking and napping in the afternoon stuff was pretty cool.

A warm kiss landed on the center of her chest. Another one on the top of each breast. Gavin placed kisses along the triangles of her swimsuit top. Then nuzzling and sweet kisses weren't enough. He yanked the material aside. His hot, wet mouth encircled her cold nipple and he began to suck.

"Oh, God," she moaned and arched back. Then she remembered they were outside. Surrounded by neighbors. "Gavin. Stop. People might see us. Or hear us."

"So? Forget about everything but this." He flicked his tongue across her nipple.

She bit her lip to keep from crying out.

"Untie your top."

Not a request. She tugged the strings free and he flung the scrap of material away.

Gavin's mouth was everywhere. On her nipples, on her neck, on her belly. His fingers stroked her skin when his mouth was busy elsewhere.

She squirmed. If she tried to touch his head or his face, he made a growling noise that put her hands right back on the arms of her chair.

When his mouth opened over her mound and he sucked, her hips bucked. His hot breath teased the sensitive area between her hipbones. "Rielle. Look at me."

Opening her eyes, she noticed he'd slipped into the alpha male role. Gavin wasn't always like that, which made it so much more potent when he was. She watched as his fingers loosened the knots on her string bikini bottoms and they fell away.

He pressed the tip of his finger against her clit and rubbed circles around it before dragging his finger down her slit to the opening of her pussy. "Wet."

"Uh-huh."

"I can't tell if you're blushing or if you're sunburned."

Rielle didn't answer.

"Don't be embarrassed that you like the way I touch you."

"Then don't tease me about how I react. Especially when there are probably people around listening to us."

"So?"

"So, why are you doing this now? Out here in the open?"

"Because I can." Gavin chuckled confidently and kept stroking her pussy. "I'm going to put my mouth on you, Rielle."

She blinked.

"And I'm going to torture you. By the time I'm ready to let you come, you won't give a damn who hears you scream."

That comment made her wetter yet, but she said, "We'll see."

"So we shall. Hook your legs over the arms of that chair. I want to see every inch of your cunt."

Bossy man. Ooh, and dirty words too. She shifted into position, her heart speeding up.

"Play with your nipples. The only place I want to see those hands is on your tits. Understand?"

She nodded.

He held her drink to her lips. "Wet your mouth now, because your throat will be really dry after all the yelling you're about to do."

"You're pretty damn sure of yourself, tycoon."

For just an instant, Gavin's confidence faltered. Then he flashed her the most wolfish, most feral male grin she'd ever seen. "Yep. Drink up."

Rielle knocked back half the liquid in one swallow.

Gavin drained the remainder. Then he dropped to his knees and put his cold mouth on her belly button. Then keeping his eyes on hers, he fished a piece of ice out of her drink and popped it into his mouth.

"Oh no," she breathed.

His response was to clamp that half-moon shaped sliver of ice between his teeth and trace her slit. When he reached the opening to her pussy, he pushed the ice into her channel, holding it there.

Her hot tissues clamped down on the ice and his tongue. She gasped. Then his tongue was stroking inside her. Hot. Cold. Hot.

The ice started to melt. Gavin licked, lapped and slurped, while he emitted hungry noises.

She just about lost her mind.

No. Stay in control. Don't make a sound.

"Goddamn you taste so fucking good. Tart like honey and warm like sunshine. I could do this all day." He glanced up at her. "Tug on your nipples. I know how crazy that gets you."

"Gavin—"

"Do. It."

Rielle pinched hard enough she let out a whimper.

"That's it." He dragged his mouth between her hipbones, gifting her skin with sucking kisses. He nipped the inside of her thighs from her knee to the outer curve of her ass. Not soft nibbles, but with enough force she held her breath, waiting for, wanting the next sting. He licked the crease behind her knee.

She started to shake. Soon she might beg.

He just laughed. Pulling back the skin above her clit, he blew a stream of hot air across her swollen tissues, but his mouth never connected with her sex.

A frustrated noise escaped her.

"Feel like screaming yet?" he murmured against her lower belly. "Or do you intend to be stubborn?"

Rielle bit her lip and groaned.

Gavin kissed straight down her mound, stopping above her clit. He lifted his face and looked at her. Waiting.

Her head, her body yelled, *please please please! Give him what he wants,* but her vocal cords weren't cooperating.

"Your eyes are begging me. But not your mouth." He rapidly flicked the swollen nub with the tip of his tongue.

Her entire body broke out in chill bumps. She canted her pelvis and she moaned, hoping that was enough verbal encouragement.

He suckled her clit so thoroughly she felt the press of his teeth against her flesh. Then he stopped.

"Pinch your nipples. Imagine me using my teeth on them. Like this." He pulled her pussy lips into his mouth and bit down, releasing the sharp bite of pain that only increased her pleasure.

She felt more cream sliding from her pussy and a scream rising in her throat.

"Use those hands, Rielle."

She began pinching the tips with her thumb and forefinger, matching the rhythm of her blood pulsing in her throat. Her mouth was dry. She licked her lips but it didn't help.

Gavin tormented her. Licking and sucking. Fucking her pussy with one finger, then two, and finally with his tongue. Driving her to the edge of bliss and then yanking her back.

When she didn't make a sound, he started over from the top.

When his naughty tongue rimmed her anus, her face heated. The swirling, teasing wetness brought the sensitive tissues alive. She felt like a total pervert for liking it and she tried to scoot away.

He warned, "Don't. Move. Again."

Gavin's soft kisses on her pussy and rough caresses broke her last thread of control.

Rielle surrendered to him completely, wondering why she'd tried to retain any control, when his every touch, every lick, every kiss, everything he did to her...was exactly what she wanted. She let loose a long, deep moan.

His eyes were dark with triumph. Then his face was between her breasts and he captured a nipple, making more of those greedy male noises. "Wrap your arms around my neck and hold on." He lifted her out of the chair.

As soon as they were face to face, his mouth took possession of hers. The kiss was a war of wills until her spine met a solid surface and Gavin's upper body pressed hers flat.

His hands moved between them to grip his cock. Teasing her clit with the flared head until she writhed. Then he poised the tip against her opening.

The pause before that first thrust was excruciating, her body was strung so tight.

His breath was hot on her ear. "Ree."

"Please."

"Scream." His lips, brushing the shell of her ear, set a jolt of electricity zipping through her. "Scream. My. Fucking. Name." He slammed into her so hard the table rocked beneath her.

She screamed as the orgasm steamrolled her. Her nails dug into the back of his neck. Her legs locked around his flexing hips. The waves crashed into her, receded, and crashed into her again until she was adrift. Awash in pleasure.

Gavin's thrusts were relentless. He buried his shaft deep one last time, spilling his seed inside her, whispering her name against her throat with such ferocity, it was as powerful as a scream.

Later, as they were entwined together, lazing in bed, Gavin asked, "So what would you like to do tomorrow? We can stay here and do exactly what we did today. Except more lounging in the pool. And more sex."

"Gavin Daniels. We've had sex three times today." After he'd fucked her mindless by the pool, they'd ordered Chinese. He'd convinced her to let him check the scores on the bowl games. When she complained about being bored, she found her head in his lap with her mouth around his dick. He'd spun her around, burying his face in her pussy and...wow. Now she understood the appeal of sixty-nine. Then the man had dragged her to the shower and fucked her standing up, using the handheld shower massager in a whole new way. "What are my other options besides nonstop sex?"

"We could go into the desert. See all the touristy stuff. Have lunch at my favorite hole-in-the-wall Mexican restaurant. Or we could golf. Or we could visit a spa. Or we could go to an outlet mall or one of the billion places to shop in Phoenix."

That gave Rielle an idea. "You know I'm not one for shopping, but is there a farmer's market close by?"

"Yes, but you aren't supposed to be working."

"I hardly think me checking out the varieties of seasonal fruit and vegetables in Arizona could be considered working." She poked him in the chest. "Besides. You're working while we're here, right?"

"Only two days." His fingers pushed her hair out of her face. "What else are you burning to do?"

"This might sound weird, but I want to see the house you grew up in and where you went to school."

Confusion crossed his face. "Why?"

"You've seen where I grew up. It shaped me. And I'm betting where you grew up shaped you too."

"Okay. If that's what you want."

"Cool. I would like a desert tour tomorrow."

"Done."

Although they spent some nights sleeping in the same bed, would being together every night for the next two weeks change things?

"Honey. The gears grinding in your brain are keeping me awake. What are you thinking about?" Gavin asked sleepily.

He'd probably think she was neurotic if she told him the truth. She hedged. "Just wondering if it was hard for you to leave Sierra with her mom."

"Well that woke me up."

"Sorry. This day has been epically long and I realized I hadn't asked how that had gone."

"Ellen was as happy to see Sierra as Sierra was happy to see her. I wonder how long that joy of being reunited will last." He sighed. "It's different being here now than it was before. I was only a phone call away if Sierra needed me. In the last seven months since Ellen has been in France, I've dealt with all Sierra's major trauma and minor drama without Ellen's input or interference. I worry even if Sierra needs me, she won't call. Not knowing what she's doing for the week I'm not here will drive me crazy."

"You miss her."

"Like a limb. So much of my life, so much of who I am, is being a parent."

"I understand how that is, Gavin."

"I know you do, which is why you won't think it's strange that I keep looking over my shoulder thinking she'll barge in on us. Or expecting to hear her ransacking the kitchen at midnight for snacks. Or that she'll plop beside me on the couch to show me some bizarre video on YouTube." His hand tenderly brushed her spine. "But my selfish side is happy for the chance to be alone with you like this. No kid, no responsibilities. Just us."

"Mmm-hmm. I called Rory and told her I arrived safely."

"Rory still isn't happy we're involved."

"Only because, like she pointed out, I've pretty much lived like a nun the last twenty-four years, with the whole abstinence and poverty thing."

Gavin chuckled. "So her beef isn't because I've got McKay blood?"

"No. She claims she's worried I'll get my heart broken, but the bottom line is she's selfish. She doesn't want to share me with you. Sierra is more mature than Rory when it comes to that."

"Maybe because Sierra lives with us and sees us together every day. She did say she had a great time with Rory the night they went out."

"Rory's protective streak toward Sierra surprised me. Did you know they're texting?"

"Huh. I can only hope Rory has a positive influence on Sierra."

"Gavin. Sierra has been a model child, for the most part, since you moved to Wyoming."

"But see, she was away from her mother's influence. I'm a little fearful of how Sierra will act after two weeks with Ellen."

Rielle rolled until she was on top of him. "Worrying won't change anything. If I can take a break from work, you can take a break from parenting. So how about if I try and take your mind off it?"

Gavin sighed. "Well...you can *try*."

"So you'll be thinking about your ex-wife when I do...this?" Rielle reached down and jacked his shaft.

And no surprise Gavin lost the ability to think about anything by the time she finished with him.

Chapter Twenty-Seven

A week in Arizona with Rielle had been one of the best times of Gavin's life, ranking next to the Disney World trip he'd taken with Sierra the year she'd turned nine.

He gave Rielle props for embracing the vacation mindset. She let him choose their daily activities—where they went, what they did, where they ate. But she couldn't stop working completely. She cleaned the pool every morning before swimming laps.

After a few hours at the office had become more than half the damn day, he'd been a little tense walking in the door. Rielle noticed immediately, fixed him a drink and suggested he change into swimming trunks and come out to the pool.

He'd expected a fun, sexy swim. He hadn't convinced her to have sex outside on the deck or in the pool since the first night. But she'd spread out a puffy blanket poolside and offered him a massage.

The warmth of the day, the strong drink and the sensation of Rielle's oil-slicked hands on his arms, shoulders and back should've relaxed him. But his dick got so hard it dug into the concrete decking.

Then she turned him over and started on his front. Massaging every inch of his upper torso with coconut-scented oil. His jaw, his neck, his chest, his hands. Even his earlobes. When she'd told him to ditch the trunks, he'd happily obliged. She used that slick hand to jack his cock as she rubbed her mouth, teeth and her tits all over his chest. She sucked his nipples, bit his neck and stroked him until he squirted all over her hand and his belly.

When he'd found his mind, he'd opened his eyes to see her licking his come off her fingers. And then his stomach.

That was almost enough to make him hard again. She dove into the pool; he chased her. After hot and sexy water games, he'd carried her to the blanket, positioned her on hands and knees and fucked her from behind until she'd screamed.

Twice.

The next day Gavin drove her by the house he'd grown up in and the condo he'd lived in after the divorce. Then he'd shown her the schools he attended, the golf club where he and his dad played.

Rielle seemed melancholy after his trip down memory lane. He told her to dress up and he made reservations at the see-and-be-seen restaurant in Phoenix. They ran into a few of his colleagues, who invited them for a drink in the bar. Rielle attempted to retreat into her wallflower persona, but Gavin wouldn't allow it. She was beautiful, smart, funny and an interesting woman. She made him happy and he wanted her—and everyone else—to see it. And for her—and everyone else—to understand she was his.

He didn't take her on a tour of his office building until after his employees were gone for the day. Partially because he didn't relish getting stopped a million times about business issues. But he also wanted her to see the city lights from his office window. Wanted her to know how many nights he'd spent up here alone. Working. Wondering if he'd ever have a life beyond the walls of this room.

Gavin had an almost desperate need for her—needing to meld his past and his future. He'd taken her against the glass window, looking down on the urban sprawl, her feet straddling the floor air conditioner vent. Cool air blew over the hot tissues as his cock slowly tunneled in and out of her wet pussy. Rielle was always ready for him, always eager. She had no idea what a turn-on that was, so he told her. Showed her. Shared his life and thoughts with her in ways he hadn't known he was capable of.

She requested they stay in their last night, cooking together and dining outside. He'd scrounged up candles, placing them everywhere in the backyard, including floating some in the pool.

They hadn't made love, but it was still the most romantic night he could remember.

Early January...

"Gavin."

Come on, come on. "Dammit. It's not working. Try a different play. God. I cannot believe they called that one twice in a row."

"Gavin."

"Hang on. This is third down." The quarterback faked a handoff and then passed for six yards for first down. "Yes! That's what I'm talking about." He tossed a handful of popcorn in his mouth, eyes on the game. "What the fuck? Why are you putting him in? He can't block for shit."

"Gavin. Sierra's not here."

"I know. She comes home tomorrow." He watched the handoff and the running back bobbled the ball. It bounced downfield until someone took his head out of his ass and covered it. "Lucky save."

"Gavin."

"Yeah, honey, just a sec." It's a wonder they won *any* games with the lousy plays they'd been calling this season. They didn't have a running game, so it made zero sense why they'd tried that one—

"Gavin, I'm naked."

Okay. That got his attention. He turned around.

A naked Rielle leaned against the door to his bedroom.

Man, he loved her body. Small and compact, with sculpted arms and shoulders. Her muscular torso flowed into flared hips and strong thighs. And those tits. He couldn't get enough of those.

A whistle blew on the screen and he turned around to see what'd happened. The camera zoomed in on the ref. "Intentional grounding. Five yard penalty."

The calls in this game had been lousy.

The quarterback threw a long pass only to get picked off at the twenty-yard line. "Fuck." He took a long pull of his beer.

Rielle sauntered in front of the TV. Naked. "So. You wanna score with me?"

He glanced at the clock. Three minutes remained in the third quarter. If he could hold her off that long, then he could give her the kind of hard, fast fuck she liked. Tons of commercials and sportscaster bullshit played between quarters anyway so he wouldn't miss much of the fourth quarter.

"I saw that! For just a split second you were torn between staying on the couch and watching football or taking me to bed."

"Hey, I always want to take you to bed. Always. But Ree. Honey. It's the last game before playoffs."

"And your team is winning?"

"Ah, no. But there's a chance they can come back..." He angled his head, trying to see around her. What the hell was that penalty flag about? Jesus. Was it on the damn defense? Were they seeing the signals at all?

Rielle walked off. The door to his bedroom slammed.

No misinterpreting that signal.

Why the hell did she have to pick right *now* for a tumble? Couldn't she wait another seventeen minutes and twelve seconds until the game ended?

Really? A stupid football game is more important than hot and dirty sex with the woman you love? You're an asshole.

Fuck.

Gavin scrambled off the couch and paused in front of his bedroom door, opening it cautiously in case Rielle decided to throw some shit at him—which he deserved. But the bedroom was dark and quiet and he didn't see her. "Rielle?"

"Go away," came from beneath the covers.

He sat on the edge of the bed and reached for the blanket-covered lump, but he jerked his hand back at the last minute when he heard a muffled sound. He heard it again. Sounded like a...sob.

Shit. Was she crying?

Gavin pulled the covers back and she curled into a little ball, further away from him.

You're an asshole.

"Ree. I'm sorry."

"Go away."

"I'm here now." He put his hand on her butt and rubbed. "We could—"

"No! I will not be a quick fuck during a break in your stupid football game."

Tell her it's not the end of the quarter yet.

He should've earned some points for walking away from a game in progress, right?

You're an asshole.

"Please talk to me."

Rielle pushed up and glared at him. "I don't do this seduction stuff. And whenever I try, I feel like a total idiot because it doesn't have any effect on you and I'm never doing it again. So go away."

His gaze dipped to her chest. Damn. She'd already put on her nightgown.

"You've got to be kidding me. *Now* you're staring at my tits when they're covered up, but you couldn't be bothered when they were bouncing right in front of your face? Get. Out."

Man. He'd fucked this up. "Look. I'm sorry. I've spent a lot of years by myself, watching football games uninterrupted. And I didn't handle...you wanting my attention, in the best way."

"Ya think?"

Anything he said would likely piss her off, so he kept his stupid mouth shut.

"Do you know why I'm upset?"

Do not say because I didn't drop everything and fuck you.

Luckily, she jumped right in and answered. "You are so smooth. Seducing me with words. You've got all the hot sex moves and you know a hundred ways to turn me inside out. You intimidate me sometimes, Gavin."

That brought him up short. "I intimidate you...sexually?"

Rielle blushed but she didn't look away. "Yes. You know I don't have—didn't have—much experience before we got together."

"Why would you think I did?"

"Because you're amazing in bed!"

Gavin felt cocky even when he wanted to laugh. Time to come clean. From the bottom drawer of his armoire he took out the four books he'd hidden. "You have no idea how happy it makes me that you think I'm amazing in bed. Despite what you think, that's not because I have some type of...McKay sexual history."

"You don't?"

"No. I knew from the first time I kissed you we'd end up in bed. And I wanted to make it good for you, Ree. I wanted you to think I was amazing in bed and I might be the same kind of sex stud my brothers and cousins are rumored to be." Gavin tossed the four how-to sex books on the bed. "So I bought these. I read them cover to cover and hoped like hell I could remember anything when I finally got you naked with me."

Rielle stared at the books, frowned and looked at him. "I don't understand."

Gavin blushed. "I had to read up on how to be a good lover. Because before you? I didn't have a clue."

"Did these books help?"

"Some. But being with you...my instincts took over. Your body, your eyes, every sexy little moan you made taught me what I needed to do to be the lover you want. The lover you deserve. The lover I've always wanted to be, but I've only ever been with you."

Silence.

Way to throw it all out there, loser.

"Oh my God, Gavin Daniels, I love you."

He froze. "For real?"

She nodded.

"Because I wasn't some macho stud in bed before I met you?"

She nodded again.

That made no sense...and yet perfect sense because this was Rielle. "You are one weird-ass woman, but I'll take it." Grinning, he said, "So...you love me, huh?"

"Yes. Even though you are a pain in the ass sports fanatic. Who ignores a naked woman for football."

"I'm here now, aren't I?" He kissed her. "And just so we're clear. I'm in love with you too."

He stripped, ripped away the covers completely and crawled on top of her.

"Gavin. Don't you want to—"

"Nope." He smoothed his hands up the insides of her bare thighs. "Goddamn. I'm already hard. You—" his mouth meandered down her throat, "—have cast a spell on me."

"Same." She groaned. "Yes, put your mouth right there."

"You do like that," he murmured, teasing the spot with his teeth and tongue.

"I love that." Rielle moaned again. "It's another one of those hot spots I wasn't even aware I had."

Gavin mouthed the tip of her breast through the thin fabric of her nightgown.

Rielle hissed and arched back, thrusting more of her breast into his hot mouth.

He sucked her nipple through the sheer fabric. Then switched sides, lost in the way she clung to him and how much he loved having her nails digging into his back.

But he wanted her naked.

"Lift up so I can take this off."

She kissed him with sweet fire. Then she pushed him away with a smirk.

"What?"

"Go watch your game."

"What? *Now?*"

"Yes, now."

"But..." *I'm as hard as a fucking two by four.*

"I know you wanna watch it. And from now on, I won't seduce you on game day, at least until the game is over."

He grinned. "Rielle Wetzler, you are the perfect woman."

"You know it."

Gavin slipped on his sweat pants. "You really don't mind?"

"I'll be right here, waiting. I've got some good reading material. Who knows what new things I'll learn when I'm flipping through your sex books?"

Chapter Twenty-Eight

Late January...

Freedom could be spelled one way: C-A-R.

God. Her life had gotten so much better in the last month since she could drive.

No more begging rides.

No more sitting around doing nothing.

No more waiting for Marin to toss her a few scraps of friendship. She made her own fun and her own friends.

She'd met a lot of people at house parties the last four weekends, when she, a lowly sophomore, became the undisputed beer pong champion. She preened at the comments about living up to the McKay reputation.

Sierra Daniels had arrived.

Her transformation had started during Christmas break, when her mom had lifted her curfew, handed her the keys to her Escalade and told her to have fun. Wasn't it proof of how awesome she was that so many people from her old school wanted to hang out with her?

Amazing how many friends you have when you've got wheels and booze, isn't it?

She shoved that bullshit thought aside. People liked her. And she liked herself.

Her dad hadn't wanted her to go out tonight, but that was too bad. After all the times she'd sat at home by herself since they'd moved to Wyoming, it served him right to spend a night or two alone. Besides, if Rielle had been around this weekend, he wouldn't have even noticed she was gone.

"Sierra!" Kara yelled from across the room. "Come here, there's someone I want you to meet."

Sierra weaved through the crowd, saying hi to some people, hugging others. She'd heard the buzz around school after she'd started going to parties that she wasn't the stuck-up rich girl that people thought.

"This is the one I was telling you about," Kara said to the guy sitting next to her, who was probably five or six years older than her. "Sierra, Tyler. Tyler goes to Vo-Tech in Gillette."

A college guy. A cute college guy. Although he did appear a little rough around the edges. "Hey."

"You were right, Kara. She is hot." Tyler lifted a bottle and drank.

"Sierra just moved here from Arizona," Kara added.

"No shit. A buddy of mine is working construction down there."

"Really? Is that what you're going to school for?"

"Nope. I'm in auto mechanics." He cocked his head and his brown-eyed gaze flicked over her, from her boots to her eyes. "I like things that go fast."

Cheesy line, but he was obviously interested. She'd flirt. No harm in that.

Kara mouthed, "Later," and ditched her.

"So, ah, Tyler, how'd you hear about the party?"

"Around." He eyed her cup. "Whatcha drinkin'?"

"Beer. Why?"

He waggled a bottle of Jack Daniels. "I'm willing to share."

"Yeah? What's the catch?"

Tyler grinned. "Smart girl. Why don't you do a couple shots with me and we'll figure something out."

"Sure." Sierra drained her beer and tossed the cup aside. She snatched the bottle from him and drank. Somehow she withheld a shudder. Jesus. That stuff tasted like shit. The Crown XR her dad drank was way better.

He laughed and grabbed the bottle back. "Eager. I like that." He tipped the bottle, somehow keeping his gaze on her chest while he guzzled. "I haven't seen you here before."

"Really? I was here last weekend."

"I wasn't. I had to work."

"That sucks. It was a great party. Been a lot of great parties lately."

"And you've been to all of them?"

She grinned. "Yep."

"So you don't got a job?"

"No."

"Must be nice." He knocked back another slug. "So if you ain't workin', what do you do for fun?"

"I've been stuck at home for a few months without wheels, so it's been a long time since I've had *any* fun."

"Then you're in luck, 'cause I can think of a whole lotta ways we can have fun together tonight." He passed the bottle back to her. "Drink up."

Sierra held her breath and managed to swallow another mouthful. But she didn't stop the shudder this time.

"Gets better by about the fifth shot. After that, you won't know what you're swallowing."

Her warning bells went off. Especially when he wrapped his fingers in the necklace she wore and tugged. "I've been watching you all night."

Crap.

"Heard some things about you. You've got a nice ass, pretty face too." He kept putting pressure on her necklace chain, giving her no choice but to move closer to him.

Her brain warned her to tell him that he was choking her, even as she feared he was fully aware of what he was doing.

"Now. How about we talk about payment?"

Two shots in a row made her head spin.

Stupid, Sierra. What is wrong with you?

But she couldn't make her legs or arms work.

"Wanna hear your options?"

No. I want you to let me go. "I could just pay you."

"Nah. I'm wantin' something else. Your money is no good."

"But mine is. I figure she drank maybe five bucks worth of Jack." A hand waved a five dollar bill between her face and Tyler's. "So consider this payment in full."

Boone.

Oh God, Boone was here. She didn't know whether to be happy or embarrassed.

Tyler released her necklace. She sucked in a deep breath and snapped back against Boone's chest.

But Tyler didn't notice, he was too busy glaring at Boone. "What the fuck is your problem, West?"

"Don't have one, Ty. Just watching out for my girl." He tucked the folded bill in Tyler's shirt pocket. "We square?"

Sierra remained frozen.

"You're with her? Bullshit," Tyler spat. "Kara didn't say nothin' to me about that."

"That's 'cause Kara doesn't know. No one knows." Boone dropped his arm over Sierra's shoulder. "Our families would have a shit fit if they knew we were together." Then Boone's hot mouth teased the skin below her ear. "Right, sugar bear?"

He'd said the words loud enough for Tyler to hear. But her tongue seemed to be stuck to the roof of her mouth.

"Don't pull that silent treatment crap with me," Boone warned Sierra testily. "Tell you what. You don't get pissed off at me for bein' late and I won't get pissed off at you for drinking with another guy. 'Cause you know how jealous I get, baby."

Tyler's gaze moved between them. He looked ready to kill Boone. And maim her.

Boone twined his fingers in her hair and pulled her head back in a move that showed his displeasure she hadn't answered him. Then he put his mouth on her ear and whispered, "For Christsake, Sierra, act like we're together or Tyler will fuck me up, and then he'll fuck you."

That snapped her out of it. "Sorry, Boone. Don't be mad." Sierra turned her head and buried her face in his neck.

Boone sighed. "Look, I'm sorry. She's a big fuckin' cocktease when she's been drinking." He offered Tyler his hand. "No hard feelings?"

A beat passed before Tyler shook Boone's hand. "You're lucky you got here in time. Me'n her were about to have us a private party. You'd better keep a tighter leash on her. Most guys ain't as understanding as me."

"You got that right." Boone curled his hand around her hip and squeezed. "Any bedrooms open so Sierra and I can...talk?"

Tyler laughed. Then he yelled, "Jimbo. Clear out my bedroom so these two can fuck and make up."

His bedroom? Omigod. This was his house?

"Thanks, man." Boone dropped his free hand to her ass and kept his arm around her neck, almost in a headlock as he maneuvered her through the crowd.

Sierra felt everyone staring at them, but she kept her gaze on her feet. Even that didn't keep her from stumbling. She heard laughter and Boone's grip tightened.

He steered her into a bedroom and slammed the door behind them.

The shots hit her the same time as the reality of the situation. She tripped over something on the floor and Boone caught her before she fell.

He pushed her against the door, bracing her shoulders, and got right in her face. "What the fuck were you doing?"

"I don't know."

"That is goddamn obvious, Sierra."

She closed her eyes.

"Huh-uh. Look at me. Keep those eyes open because the room will start spinning and I don't wanna deal with you being sick as well as being stupid."

Stupid. She hated being called stupid. And it stung hearing it from him. "I'm not that drunk." Sierra put her hands on his chest and shoved him as hard as she could.

Boone wasn't expecting it and he stumbled back two steps.

"Leave me alone. I don't need you to fucking babysit me, Boone."

He clenched his hands into fists at his sides and stared at her. "What the hell do you think would've happened if I'd left you alone with Tyler Larkin?"

"I would've figured something out."

"Before or after he fed you more booze, dragged you into his bedroom and raped you?"

"What?"

"Rape. Sex without consent," he snarled. "Tyler doesn't fucking care if you're conscious."

She felt sick. "And how do you know that?"

"Because he did it to a friend of mine. They were drinking and then the next thing she remembered was waking up with him on top of her."

"Oh God."

Then Boone was face to face with her again. "I told you to stay away from Kara. And I heard you've been here, at her brother Tyler's house for the past two weekends."

"I didn't know it was his house." She swallowed hard. "I didn't know Tyler was her brother."

His eyes turned hard. "You just showed up at some random person's house and started drinking with strangers? Jesus. Sierra. You're smarter than that. Why would you do that?"

"Because I'm fucking sick and tired of sitting at home by myself all the time, okay? No one in this godforsaken town wants anything to do with me. So when Kara and Angie asked me to hang out, I said yes. I thought maybe I'd meet other people."

"You don't want to meet the people they hang out with," he snapped. "For Christssake, Tyler is twenty-three. He's been in jail. The only people who are around him are his loser jailbird buddies and his sister's high school friends who don't have any other place to drink."

"Then why are you here?" she demanded. "Are you one of his loser friends?"

"Fuck no. I showed up because I heard at school you were here last weekend."

"Bull. I haven't seen you in school for weeks, so I doubt you *heard* anything."

"I only need one credit to graduate so I'm only there for one class in the morning, so yeah, I heard."

"Why do you give a shit what I do anyway?"

"Because I also heard you're some kind of party girl now."

"*So?*"

"So you don't need to head down this road again, Sierra. Making bad choices like you did in Arizona."

Maybe he was right. But he had no idea how alone she felt. And it wasn't like he called to check up on her like he'd said he might. He had no business judging her anyway. They weren't anything to each other.

Closing her eyes, she slumped against the door. "You've done your good deed, protecting me from Tyler. Thank you. You've made it clear

I'm a fucking idiot. So go away."

"I'm just supposed to what? Leave you here?"

"I've got a car."

Boone's hands were on her arms. "You think you're gonna drive after you've been drinking? Bullshit. What the fuck is wrong with you?"

She twisted out of his hold. "I wasn't gonna leave right now, asshole. I'll be sober enough to drive in a couple of hours. I'll just hang out until then."

"Listen to yourself. Do you really think Tyler will let you *hang out*? Especially after I convinced him that we're together? What exactly do you think the people out there think we're doing in here? *Talking*?" he half-sneered.

She opened her mouth to deny it, but Boone was right. "Fine. You can stay in here with me. That oughta add to your stud reputation. That you banged me for two solid hours."

Boone blushed. Then he got pissed off. "Right. Because that's all I give a shit about. My reputation as some kind of stud. Even if we stay in here, that doesn't deal with the problem when we leave the bedroom."

"Which is what?"

"We'll have to act like we're together at least a little while, so Tyler doesn't track me down and beat the fuck out of me for pulling one over on him. That's the kind of guy he is. Making him look stupid turns him psycho." He ran his hand through his hair. "Dammit. This is the last thing I wanted."

Meaning, I'm the last one you wanted to be tied to—in reality or even pretend.

"You know what, Boone? Fuck off. You don't have to act so disgusted that people will think we're together."

Boone whirled around. "That's what you think? That being with you would be an embarrassment to me? God. You *are* drunk."

"Shut up."

"Think about it. If we're a couple at school the news will spread like wildfire through the McKay and West families."

"Then we will have a very loud and public breakup on Monday morning. Or better yet, let's have a big fight now. Want me to scream and storm out?"

"Jesus. I'm *not* doing this with you." He gave her a once over. "Where's your coat?"

"In the living room."

"Do you have snow boots?"

"No."

"Gloves?"

"Yes, I'm not a total idiot."

Boone scowled at her. "Did you even check the weather before you went out tonight?"

She blinked at him.

"I take that as a no. The road conditions were shitty an hour ago. They've gotta be worse by now."

"Did you ride your bike here?"

"No."

"How'd you expect to get home?"

"How'd *you* expect to get home?" he countered. "Or did you tell your dad you were spending the night someplace?"

"No. My curfew is midnight."

He glanced at his watch. "It's only nine thirty. Give me your keys."

"They're in my coat."

He blew out a frustrated breath. "When we get out there, go ahead and act like you're mad at me."

"Won't be an act," she flashed her teeth at him.

Boone jammed his hands into her hair and messed it up. He popped the button on his jeans. Then he pulled her shirt down her arm, exposing her bra strap. "There. At least it looks like we've been going at it."

Her head pounded and she just wanted to leave.

He held out his hand for hers and opened the door.

A few catcalls greeted them. She'd just slipped on her coat when Kara and Angie sidled up to her. "Omigod, Sierra. Why didn't you tell us you were with Boone West?"

She looked at him, too tired to come up with something clever. "Because our families will freak out. So don't tell anyone. Please."

"It's our secret. We promise." They exchanged a conspiring look.

Sierra allowed Boone to tuck her against his side as they left the party.

Fierce winds smacked her in the face, stealing her breath, and she jerked away from Boone. Immediately vertigo hit; she swayed and fell on her ass.

Boone picked her up without comment. He shoved her in the passenger seat and buckled her in.

The drive was tense and the visibility horrible, as Boone repeatedly pointed out. After a bit, he said, "Your car runs like crap. What's wrong with it?"

"I don't know. Been like that a few days."

"And yet you're still driving it?"

"Either that or sit at home."

Boone muttered.

As soon as they hit the cut-across to the paved county road, he drove faster. He probably couldn't wait to get rid of her. But given the weather and the fact he didn't have his bike, Boone would be stuck at her house. What would her Dad think?

He'll be pissed you've been drinking.

Snow swirled and blew over the windshield. It made her dizzy and she wanted to close her eyes. Why was it taking so long for the car to warm up?

A loud bang sounded and the car wobbled.

She glanced over at Boone to see both his hands clamped on the steering wheel. His feet intermittently pumped the brakes. She saw his horror when they picked up momentum and the road seemed to buckle and snap.

She was jerked forward as the front end connected with a solid object, throwing snow on the windshield before the world went dark.

Chapter Twenty-Nine

Gavin glanced at his cell phone when it rang at eleven-thirty. That'd better not be his daughter calling to say she'd be late coming home. Again.

The caller ID was a restricted number so he was tempted to ignore it, but he answered, "What?"

"Gavin? This is Cam."

Why the hell would Cam McKay be calling him this time of night? Then it hit him. Cam was with the sheriff's office. "What's happened?"

"Sierra's been in a car accident."

He sank into the closest chair. The words registered, yet not. "When?"

"Not sure. She's in the ER now. Look, the roads are nasty and there've been a lot of accidents. Do you have a four-wheel drive vehicle that'll get you into Sundance?"

He frowned at the phone. "What? I need a four-wheeler to get there?"

"No. Let's take this slow." Cam asked a question. Gavin answered. Cam asked another question. Gavin answered again. Cam asked, "Is Rielle there?"

"No. She's in Denver."

"You okay to drive?"

Gavin nodded.

Silence.

"Gavin, stay on the line."

Sierra. Ask him what's going on with Sierra before he hangs up.

"Cam?"

Dead air for what seemed like forever.

Then a click. "I called Ben. He'll be there in five minutes to get you."

That registered. Why hadn't he thought of calling his brother? It also registered he hadn't asked if his daughter was all right. "What can you tell me about Sierra?"

"Nothing. I'm sorry."

Fuck.

"Do you need me to stay on the line with you until Ben arrives?"

"No, Cam. Thanks. I'm...I'll...I need to get myself together."

"Understandable. See you in a few."

But he couldn't get himself together. He was absolutely numb. What if she was...? He squeezed his eyes shut. He couldn't think the word, let alone say it.

Every second felt like a day. He slipped on his cold weather gear. By the time he'd pulled on the hat Sierra had made him, a vehicle barreled up the driveway and he scooted out of the house and into Ben's big rig.

Ben whipped a U-turn in the drive. Then they were on the highway leading to Sundance. "Any word on her?"

"No. Just that she was in an accident."

Silence filled the cab as Gavin stared out the window into the black night. He finally said, "Cam said the roads are bad."

"Not here. But I flipped on the road condition report. Guess it's worse by Moorcroft. Was that where she was tonight?"

I have no idea.

Why didn't he know?

Because as soon as she'd gotten those keys she was gone. He'd been relieved the issue of her not driving wasn't an issue between them anymore, so he'd been lax asking her specifics on where she was going, what she was doing, and who she was doing it with.

Some parent. No idea where his kid had been, no idea how the fuck he'd deal with it if something bad had happened to her.

"Where is Rielle?" Ben asked.

"Trade show in Denver with Rory."

"Did you call her?"

"No. Not until I know..." He cleared his throat. "Same with Sierra's mom."

"Let's err on the side that everything will be all right."

"I'm trying. But if anything happened to her, I'd lose my fucking mind."

"I know. Don't think that way."

It was hard not to. "Sorry that Cam got you out of bed. I wasn't thinking straight when he called."

"That's fine. I wasn't in bed. I called Mom and Dad. They're a little slower on the draw, but they'll be there."

Wasn't long before they were in town. Gavin unbuckled his seatbelt the instant they turned into the hospital parking lot.

Ben pulled up to the front. "Go on. I'll see you inside."

He nearly fell on his ass when his boots connected with the slippery ground. He righted himself and headed through the ER doors. A woman not much older than Sierra managed the front desk.

"Sir? How may I help you?"

"Sierra Daniels. I'm her father. I need to see her."

"I'll let the staff know you're here. In the meantime, you'll need to fill out all the paperwork on this clipboard—"

But Gavin had already started down the hallway.

"Sir! You can't just go back there."

Watch me.

He stopped short of yelling her name as he passed by hospital rooms. He reached another desk and the woman behind it was no pushover. She got in his face. "You cannot barge back here."

He loomed over her. "My daughter was in a car accident and I've no idea if she's even okay. Please, just give me any kind of information—"

"They're doing a CT scan on her right now."

Gavin whirled around. "Who are you?"

"Alan. The EMT who brought her in." He raised his hand to forestall Gavin's question. "Before you badger me to tell you more, I can't."

"Who can?"

"I can."

He turned the other direction quickly.

A male in surgical scrubs moved toward him and Gavin's heart dropped.

"I'm Roger, the ER nurse. Before I can tell you anything you need to fill out the forms. There are a few questions we need answers to on Sierra's health history." He pointed to the small waiting room. "The sooner you get the bureaucratic portion done, the sooner we can treat your daughter and the sooner you can see her."

Gavin grabbed the clipboard and pen. His eyeballs pulsed with anger. This was bullshit. It'd be faster if they just asked him the fucking questions. He glanced at the clipboard. The words on the paper blurred into black blots.

Get control.

Five excruciating minutes later he handed in the paperwork. Then another five minutes before Nurse Roger appeared.

"I'll take you back to see Sierra. Two things you should know. Sierra admitted she's been drinking tonight."

Gavin's stomach dropped even as his blood pressure skyrocketed. Sierra had been drinking and driving?

"You can yell at her about poor choices another time. I need you to be focused on the positive side of this. Like she wasn't behind the wheel—"

"What? She wasn't driving?" As much as that relieved him, it also had him demanding, "Then who the hell was driving?"

Roger put his hand on Gavin's arm. "Calm down."

"I am calm. Who was driving?"

"Her boyfriend."

Since when did Sierra have a boyfriend? As he looked at Roger. "You said two positive things. What's the other one?"

"She wore her seatbelt. She only ended up with a broken collarbone and didn't go through the windshield."

White spots danced in front of Gavin's eyes and he swayed.

"Whoa, there. Let's sit down for a second."

"No. I'm fine. Just...no one's told me anything about what happened or how it happened or that she had..." *Broken body parts.* He managed a hoarse, "What else?"

"I'll let the doctor discuss that with you. You're ready to see her?"

"Yes."

Roger walked to a room at the end of the hallway.

With each footstep Gavin's heart beat faster. His mouth was so dry he couldn't swallow. His gut churned. His pulse pounded in his eyes, in his ears, in his throat. Hospital sounds morphed into brutal silence in his head, making him feel like he was underwater.

Then he was beside her and he almost wept at seeing the most precious thing in his life lying in a hospital bed attached to an IV. Her dark hair was pulled back, showing the paleness of her face against the white pillow. Bruises dotted her face, jaw and neck. Her lips were reddened, cracked and chapped. Her right arm was strapped in a sling and resting on her belly. She wore a hospital gown. The left side of her body from her shoulder down was covered with several blankets. He was as afraid to touch her as he was afraid not to touch her.

Roger said, "It's okay. You can get closer."

Gavin murmured, "Why's she covered up?"

"Hypothermia. She was really chilled when they brought her in."

"How long was she out in the elements?"

"Dad?"

His heart leapt at hearing her voice. "Sierra-bear. I'm here, sweetheart."

Her eyes opened. Tears immediately poured out. "I'm so sorry. I know I was stupid... I never meant—"

"Ssh." He held her face in his hands. She was so cold. "We can talk about all that other stuff later. I'm just happy you're mostly all right." He swiped away her tears with his thumbs and kissed her forehead. He let his lips linger, needing to reassure himself she was breathing.

"But I need to know if Boone is okay."

Gavin pulled back and looked into her pain-filled eyes. "Boone?"

"Boone West. He was driving."

Boone West. Why did that name sound familiar? Right. The punk-ass kid who'd worked on the garage with Chet and Remy West. If that little fucker was responsible for the accident it didn't matter if he was all right because Gavin was going to fucking kill him.

"Your boyfriend is okay," Roger said. "He's being checked out in another room."

"He's not my boyfriend," Sierra whispered.

"Even if he was, he wouldn't be after this," Gavin snapped.

"Don't be mad at him. He wouldn't let me drive because I'd been drinking. It's not his fault."

"Not his fault," Gavin repeated. "You're in the hospital after he wrecked your car. That puts him entirely at fault."

"Mr. Daniels," Roger warned.

Gavin clenched and unclenched his fists. He wanted to inflict pain on that kid for the pain Sierra was suffering through. Somehow, he got control. He touched Sierra's good shoulder, but she flinched anyway.

"Don't. That hurts." More tears slid down her face.

"I'm sorry, sweetheart." Gavin looked at Roger. "Have you given her anything for the pain?"

Alan shook his head. "She's a minor and we couldn't administer anything until you arrived. Plus, it's too risky with alcohol in her system. She's on an IV to clear it out faster. Meantime, we're putting an icepack on the injury every thirty minutes until it's safe to give her pain meds."

Dammit. He felt so helpless. He wanted her to stop hurting *now*.

A white-coat-wearing doctor came around the curtain. He said, "I'm Dr. Abernathy," to Gavin, but he focused on Sierra. "How are you feeling, young lady?"

She whispered, "Stupid."

He smiled. "I hear that a lot in here, trust me. Let's talk about your injury. You in pain?"

Sierra nodded.

"Scale of one to ten, ten being the highest."

"Nine."

The doctor jotted that down. "How about your head?"

"Hurts really bad. So does my neck."

"Your entire body will feel like that for several more days, sorry to say. But I'll point out that you're lucky. The accident could've been a lot worse." He gently patted her good shoulder. Then he faced Gavin. "You're her father?"

"Yes."

"I'll get right to it. The CT scan revealed a mild concussion, which is actually good news. I expected a little more head trauma since the airbag didn't deploy."

Jesus.

"Her clavicle sustained a fracture. A little worse than a hairline fracture, not as bad as a multiple fracture. Given her age, I'd say she'll heal completely in twelve weeks."

"Three months?"

"She won't have to wear the sling the entire time. She can probably remove it after three weeks and only wear it at night for the next four weeks. But any activity that requires her to put pressure on that part of the body? Minimum amount of rest is twelve weeks."

"What other treatment will she need?"

"We're keeping her overnight. Unless something unexpected shows up from the accident, I'll release her tomorrow. She'll need rest. I'll write a script for pain meds. She'll need to see her regular doctor in two weeks just to make sure everything is healing properly. She'll need physical therapy at some point."

His thoughts were racing as he tried to process it all. "What about school?"

"Your call. But since she is right handed, and she won't be able to use that hand or arm for the first two weeks, I suggest she remain at home. My other concern is an accidental fall. Sidewalks, parking lots and roads are dangerously icy this time of year. For her, even a minor fall could cause major damage."

"Understood. And thank you."

Dr. Abernathy motioned to Roger. "Start her on Demerol." They conversed in medical jargon.

Gavin kissed Sierra's forehead. "I love you. We'll get you fixed up, I promise."

"I have to stay here overnight?"

"They just want to make sure you don't have other injuries."

Her eyes filled with tears. "I'm scared."

"I know, sweetheart. But I'll be right here."

"You're staying with me?"

"Do you really think I'd leave you alone when you're hurting?"

"No. It's just...I thought you'd be mad. I'm so sorry."

"I know you are. Why don't you close your eyes? I know you're in a lot of pain."

She nodded.

Roger took him aside. "We're moving her into a regular room."

"A private room," Gavin insisted.

"Does your insurance cover that?"

"I'll cover it."

"Okay. I'll let them know. Once she's in her room we'll start the pain meds."

Gavin watched as they lifted Sierra from one bed to the next. He followed behind two nurses and one orderly as they wheeled the bed down the hallway and into a small room.

After hooking Sierra up to more machines, Roger injected the pain meds into her IV and spoke to her softly. He ditched the used surgical gloves and stopped in front of Gavin. "This stuff works pretty fast. But I'll be back in ten minutes to check on her."

Gavin hauled the chair beside the bed and held Sierra's hand between his, finally able to take a breath. Finally believing she'd be okay.

"Daddy?"

God, that made his heart hurt. She hadn't called him that in years. "Yes, sweetheart?"

"I love you."

Don't cry. "I love you too."

After a few minutes, she stopped stirring. Her breathing slowed.

Roger returned and discreetly checked on her, without disturbing her. "She's asleep. I know you're staying here tonight and that's fine. But there's a waiting room full of people asking for you. It's late and she can't have visitors, so could you please deal with them?"

Gavin sent Sierra an anxious look.

"She's out. I promise she won't know you're gone."

"Okay." He took a minute to compose himself before he left the room.

Charlie and Vi jumped up the instant they saw him. Ben was standing next to Cam, still in uniform. Quinn threw the magazine he was reading on the table and stood.

Vi rushed forward and put her hands on his face. "Are you all right?"

"No, not really." He inhaled and told them Sierra's diagnosis. "The pain meds just kicked in so she's asleep. I'm staying with her tonight."

"Anything we can do?" Quinn asked.

"I'll need someone to bring my car tomorrow."

"Or one of us could pick you up when you're ready," Charlie offered.

He didn't want to be beholden to anyone. Ben understood that. He said, "I can drop it by in the morning."

"Thanks."

The three people sitting in the back of the room approached the group. Gavin recognized Chet and Remy West. His gaze narrowed on the taller young guy standing between them with a blanket dangling from his shoulders.

That fucker Boone West.

He moved quickly, latching onto the kid's jacket and hauling him up until they were nose to nose. "You have a fuckload of nerve being here when you're the reason my daughter is in the fucking hospital."

"Let him go," Chet said sharply.

Gavin shook Boone. "Don't have anything to say?"

"Gavin," Ben said in that *listen to me* voice. "Let him go. It's not what you think."

"I think I want to kick his ass."

"Typical McKay macho bullshit," Remy snapped. "Let him go right fucking now or you're dealing with me."

"And me," Chet said.

He released him. But he didn't back off.

Neither did Boone. "How is Sierra?"

"How the hell do you think she is? She's got a broken collarbone, a concussion and she's in the hospital."

A petite redhead bulled her way between Gavin and Boone, her focus on Gavin. "Back off. Sit your ass down."

"Who are you?"

"Joely Monroe. I'm Boone's doctor. And if you shake him like that again, I'll have Cam arrest you for assault. He was also in the accident."

"But he's not in a goddamned hospital bed so it can't be that bad."

"Wrong. He doesn't have health insurance, which is why I'm here as a favor to his uncles. Checking to make sure he doesn't need to be hospitalized. He also had hypothermia and he refused to leave until he saw you and knew how Sierra was."

Gavin had no response for that.

"Thanks, Doc. I'll take it from here." Cam pointed at two chairs facing each other. "Gavin. Take a seat. Boone, you too."

Gavin didn't argue. Neither did Boone.

"Now, Boone, why don't you tell Gavin what you told us."

Boone aimed his face at the carpet.

Probably out of guilt that the kid couldn't even look him in the eye.

"No rush," Cam said.

Chet and Remy stood behind him; each had a hand on his shoulder. "The sooner you get this over with, the sooner we can get you to our place, get you warmed up and doped up so you can rest."

Boone nodded and winced slightly. "I showed up at a party and Sierra was there. She'd been drinking."

Gavin listened as the kid detailed what'd gone on. His stomach pitched when he heard the word *blowout*. "You were driving Sierra's car and you had a blowout?"

"That's how the accident happened, although her car was running like shit before that so it could've been a combination of factors. I was driving about forty-five when the right front tire blew. I stepped on the brake and the back end skidded out on the ice. I managed to get the car slowed down but we still hit the ditch at thirty miles per hour. My airbag deployed. Sierra's didn't. At the angle we hit, the passenger's door got wedged open."

A sick feeling took root. "It's twenty degrees below zero outside."

"Yeah. Once the powder from the airbag cleared out, I saw Sierra was unconscious and I knew we were in the middle of fucking nowhere..." Boone paused to take a breath. "I shoved my airbag aside and hoped like hell Sierra had stashed a cold weather emergency kit someplace. I crawled out and opened the rear hatch. I found the thermal blanket and tucked it around her as best as I could after I checked her vitals."

"Vitals?" Gavin repeated. "Why would you do that?"

"I'm an EMT. She came to when I was checking her and I suspected between the impact and seatbelt, she'd broken her collarbone. My cell phone was dead so I found hers and called the ambulance line directly. They were en route to the hospital from another accident. Given our location, I knew it'd be thirty minutes before the ambulance even reached us." That's when Boone looked Gavin in the eye. His eyes filled with guilt. "I'm sorry. The instant that tire blew I knew we were gonna crash. I tried to..."

This kid that he'd accused of hurting his daughter had actually saved her. *Saved her.* Saved her from drinking and driving. Saved her from hypothermia. Saved her by being an experienced driver. Because if Sierra had been behind the wheel? She probably wouldn't have known what to do during a blowout. It might've been hours before anyone found her...in subzero temperatures, alone, injured...she wouldn't have made it long.

The horror of the situation hit him anew and he started to lose it. His body shook. He couldn't breathe. He wanted to laugh, scream and cry all at the same time.

Then Vi was tugging him to his feet. Telling everyone he needed some air.

He clutched her hand, followed her blindly as she led him to another small waiting area. She placed her cold hands on his cheeks and got right in his face. "Gavin," she said softly. "It's okay. Let it out."

"I... What if... She..."

"She's okay."

"But... I can't..."

"It's just you and me here. Go on, son, and let it out. I've got you."

Gavin broke down, crying quietly, silently. His body trembling as he curled into her and let her hold him up. His thoughts bounced between being grateful that Sierra was all right and being paralyzed with fear about *what if* scenarios now that he knew the truth.

He began to regain control when his gratitude overtook his fear. He squeezed Vi before he released her. "Thank you." He could barely look her in the eye. "How did you know?"

"A tough front only lasts so long and then those tiny cracks start to appear. No one else saw it, if you're worried about that, but I recognized it." She fussed with his shirt collar.

"How?" Gavin expected her to say *because I'm your mother*, but her answer surprised him.

"Because I'm the same way. I never want anyone to see me as weak. Even when a few tears don't make you weak, they make you human."

"I'm really glad you're here. I..." *Just say it.* "Didn't think I needed anyone and apparently I do."

She smiled softly. "Along those lines...please let us help you when Sierra comes home. She won't be a happy camper bound up and homebound and the more people who show her they love her and want to entertain her, the better. Plus, it'll keep you two from being at each other's throats for the duration. I know the two of you butt heads frequently."

That was an understatement. "I'd appreciate that. Thank you."

"Good. Now I know you're chomping at the bit to check on her, so I'll send the people in the waiting room home." She kissed his cheek. "Not that I'm meddling or telling you what to do, but you owe that boy an apology."

Jesus. He acted like such a jackass. Assuming. Blustering. He owed Boone West more than he could ever repay him.

He'd deal with that another day. He had a long night ahead of him.

Chapter Thirty

Rielle couldn't get in touch with Gavin. After a couple of hours she tried Sierra's cell. No answer.

When another couple hours passed and still no word, she couldn't shake the bad feeling. She called Ben and Ainsley's house. Ben answered. "Rielle?"

"Hey Ben. I can't get a hold of Gavin or Sierra. Have you seen them since yesterday morning?"

Silence. Then, "Sierra was in a car accident last night."

Her breakfast threatened to come back up. "Is she okay?"

"Concussion, broken collarbone. She had to stay overnight in the hospital."

"Is Gavin all right?"

"He's..." Ben sighed. "He's really shaken up. He won't ask you to come home, Ree, and I ain't messing in your business, but he needs you here."

"I have to drop Rory off in Laramie and I'll be there late afternoon."

"They oughta be home by then."

"Thanks, Ben."

Rory came around the corner with four huge bundles of fleece. "Have you ever worked with Alpaca? This stuff is priced really low." She noticed the change in Rielle's face. "What's wrong?"

"Sierra was in a car accident last night."

"Holy crap. Is she okay?"

"She's in the hospital, but she's coming home today. So I need to get back to Sundance right away."

"Is everything you bought today packaged and ready to pick up?"

"I think so. Maybe tell Jim at Good Seed to step on it. I added to the order yesterday."

"Will do." Rory dropped the bundles on the counter. "I know you're worried, but you have to make sure you bought all the supplies to get you through spring planting before we leave."

"I know. I'm good. I wanted to comparison shop kit greenhouses, but that can wait."

"I'll get your seed order and meet you at the truck."

The Natural Age Trade show filled the gigantic convention center.

Some vendors had to take space off the main site. Navigating the aisles took time even when she wasn't looking for specific items. Since Jim's display was on the other side of the arena, she knew it'd be an hour before they'd get to leave. She paid for her fiber and picked up greenhouse brochures as she passed by on her way out the door.

Worried sick about Sierra, and Gavin, and facing a drive where she'd do nothing but worry more, Rielle knew this would be the longest day ever.

Rielle pulled into the driveway at dusk and saw Vi's car. Good. At least Gavin had some help and support.

Her purchases would be fine left in her truck overnight. She hunched into the collar of her coat as she climbed the stairs.

Sadie whined when she came inside. "Were you a good girl?" She gave her a thorough rubbing and petting.

Vi came around the corner. "I was hoping that was you."

"How is he?"

"Holding up. He's exhausted. I don't think he slept a wink last night at the hospital."

Rielle scratched behind Sadie's ears. "I'll make sure he gets some rest. How is Sierra?"

"Groggy. She's been out of it most the day."

"Is there anything I should know that he won't tell me?"

"No. I'm sure he'll tell you more than he told me." Vi reached for her coat. "There's a casserole in the oven. If you need anything, please call."

"I will."

"You'll probably be seeing a lot of me," Vi warned before she headed outside.

Shivering, Rielle closed the door behind her. It was much colder here than in Denver the last three days. She scaled the stairs two at a time. The TV was on, but the game wasn't as loud as usual. She crossed to the couch and saw Gavin stretched out. Poor guy looked tense even in sleep, but she was glad to see him resting and she didn't want to disturb him.

Turning to go, she heard a hoarse, "Ree?"

She backtracked and crouched beside him. "Hey. I heard it's been a rough day."

Gavin dry-washed his face. "Yeah. Hard to believe it hasn't even been twenty-four hours since I got the call."

"How's she doing?"

"She's in pain, so we're keeping her pretty doped up for a few days."

Rielle grabbed his hand and kissed his knuckles. "How are you holding up?"

"Better than I was."

She waited for him to say, *better now that you're here*, but he didn't. "Can I get you anything? You hungry? Vi cooked supper."

"I could eat." He sat up and put his feet on the floor. "Although, I'll probably bring it up here so I can listen for Sierra."

"Stay. I'll bring it to you."

"Thank you."

She returned a few minutes later with a plate piled with ham and potato casserole and a slice of seven-grain bread. He'd given her such a weird vibe she hadn't brought up a plate for herself.

"That looks great." He dug in immediately. One eye on the food; one eye on the game.

He's hungry and tired and stressed. Don't read anything into this.

Rielle started toward the stairs.

"Aren't you eating with me?"

She faced him. "You didn't ask and I didn't want to assume."

"Please assume that I'd like to eat with you whenever possible, okay?"

That mollified her. "Okay."

The meal was quiet. Afterward, Gavin pushed back his plate and sighed. "This has been a fucking nightmare."

"What happened?"

"You don't know?"

She shook her head.

Gavin relayed the events in a clipped tone and finished with, "I have to live with that."

"You're shouldering the blame for Sierra's mistake? She went to that party, knowing it was wrong."

"That's not the issue. I've been letting her drive wherever the fuck she wants, in this shitty weather, on these shitty roads, and I couldn't be bothered to do the maintenance on her vehicle in the last month when she's been driving all the time? Making sure her vehicle was safe? I should've just bought her a new goddamned car instead of a used one. That is totally on me." He closed his eyes. "What the hell has been so goddamned important in my life that I let that slide?"

Rielle had a pang of guilt. Since Sierra had become mobile, she and Gavin spent all their free time together. Did he blame her?

"Sorry. Wishing I would've been more attentive is Monday morning quarterbacking and totally fucking pointless." He opened his eyes. "Anyway, would you mind sticking around to listen for Sierra while I take a shower?"

"Sure. Do I just check on her?"

"She has a bell to ring when she wakes up."

Rielle's eyebrows rose. "A bell? Like a bell an English aristocrat uses to a ring for her servants at tea time?"

"No. A cowbell."

"You gave a sixteen-year-old a cowbell?"

"Quinn gave it to her," he grumbled. "I told him I'm buying Amelia bagpipes for her next birthday."

She smiled. "Go take your shower."

Gavin didn't try to steal a kiss or pat her ass—so unlike him.

After the shower kicked on, the sound of a cowbell drifted down the hallway.

Rielle knocked before pushing open the door. "Sierra?"

"Ree? Where's my dad?"

"He just jumped in the shower. Something you need?"

"A drink of water."

She grabbed the water bottle off the dresser. She couldn't help but smooth Sierra's dark hair back from her pale face. "How you feeling, sweetheart?"

"Sore. I can't move without it hurting." She struggled to sit up and Rielle adjusted her pillows. "Thanks. I thought you were gone until Monday?"

"I decided I was needed here. So make me feel needed. What can I do to help you?"

Sierra rested against the pillow. "Everything. I'm helpless. It's hard to even go to the bathroom. My right hand is useless. How can I wash my hair or even comb it with one hand?"

"Did you talk to your dad about this?"

She shook her head.

"Did he hire a home health aide to assist you?"

"I doubt it. He thinks it's his job to take care of me." She started to cry. "There's stuff I don't want him to help me with."

"Oh, sweetie, I don't blame you. Do you want me to talk to him?"

"Would you help me?" she asked in an unsure voice.

Rielle impulsively kissed Sierra's forehead and wiped her tears. "Of course. Anything you need, just ask." She rubbed a small section of Sierra's hair between her fingers. "It's been a while since I combed out a girl's hair. That said...payback will be sweet for the funky hairstyle you gave me."

That earned her a wan smile even through her tears. She winced. "I can tell it's time for a pain pill."

"I'll let your dad dispense that." She ran her hand up Sierra's good arm. "Need anything else right now? Food? Something else to drink? Another blanket?"

"What's going on?" Gavin said from the doorway.

Lorelei James

"Ree's volunteered to help me with some girl hygiene stuff."

Gavin stopped beside the bed and looked at Rielle with disbelief. "Really?"

Did he really think she'd just stand back and do nothing while Sierra struggled? While he struggled? Staying out of Gavin's parenting decisions with Sierra didn't mean she wanted to stay out of Sierra's life. Didn't he see the difference? Didn't he know how much she'd come to care for his daughter?

Cut him some slack. He's figuring out a way to deal with all this.

Rielle smiled. At Sierra. "Let me know when you need me. Have a good night." She brushed past Gavin without a word and returned downstairs.

In the two days since Rielle had returned from Denver, Gavin hadn't kissed her. Hadn't touched her. Hadn't explained why he wasn't doing any of those things. So Rielle let it ride.

But by the fourth day she wondered if Gavin's supposed distraction was actually dismissal. Of her. Of their relationship.

Ask him.

That would make her seem needy.

Then seduce him.

That would make her seem needier yet.

Still...that got her to thinking. Why should Gavin have to make the first move? Maybe he thought she wasn't interested in doing the mattress mambo since she hadn't made a move either.

So she'd seduce him tonight. Take his mind off his worry and make him mindless—if only for a little while.

Plan in place, Rielle helped Sierra until Vi shooed her away. She tackled her to-do list, but didn't accomplish much since various McKays traipsed in and out of the house all day.

By the time the clock struck ten, she ventured upstairs. Sierra's light was off. Gavin had stretched out on the couch to watch yet another sports game on TV.

Rielle straddled his lap and he smiled at her. "Hey."

"I missed you." She slid her hands under his T-shirt and leaned forward to kiss him.

Gavin emitted a deep, sexy rumble and kissed her back.

She touched him, teased him and felt his cock harden beneath her ass. "Come on. Let's go to bed."

"Okay."

In his bedroom, she stripped off his sweatpants, boxers and T-shirt. He sat on the edge of the bed, staring at her...expectantly? She peeled off her thermal T-shirt and stepped between his thighs, rubbing the upper swell of her breasts against his jawline and chin. He groaned and buried his face in her cleavage. She loved the feel of his rough whiskers on her tender skin. Still teasing him, she stepped back and her bra fell to the floor. She shimmied out of her jeans, hooked her fingers in her panties and eased them off slowly, then kicked off her socks.

Gavin wore a sexy, half-lidded, *keep going* look.

So she did. Rielle dropped to her knees and enclosed her mouth around his cock. Sucking and licking the hard shaft. Fondling his sac, then using her lips and teeth on just the wide head. She glanced up at him.

He'd closed his eyes, but he made soft growling noises.

Blowing him always got her hot, so she was wet and ready for the next stage of seduction. She chuckled at Gavin's sound of disapproval when she released his cock from her mouth. Pushing him flat on the mattress, she crawled over him. Her hands followed the contours of his muscled biceps and forearms. Then she pressed his arms above his head and warned, "Keep them there."

"Mmm."

Rielle rubbed her face over Gavin's upper body, inhaling his clean and musky scent. Nuzzling his neck and sliding her nipples against the hair on his chest. Rolling her hips and rocking her clit into the hard muscle of his lower abdomen.

She put her lips on his ear. "You can touch me now. I know how much you like to have your hands on my ass as I'm riding you."

He didn't answer. Didn't move at all. Then he made a noise. But not the noise she expected. She heard it again.

Wait. Was that a...*snore*?

"Gavin?"

No response.

Rielle placed her hands by his head, lifting up to look into his face. It was damn dark in here, but she couldn't believe what she was seeing.

Gavin. Asleep. And snoring softly.

Apparently his dick wasn't tired because it was still fully erect.

What the fuck?

Was her seduction technique so bad, he'd just conked out?

Tempting to slap him awake. But then...no. This was far too humiliating.

She got dressed and slunk out.

Gavin showed up in the kitchen early the next morning, whistling for Christsake. "Good morning, Rielle."

She slammed the cupboard door. When she turned around he wore the oddest expression.

"Did I do something to piss you off?"

Oh, I don't know, maybe, possibly, I'm just a teensy bit upset because you fucking fell asleep when I seduced you.

The oven timer went off. Slipping on her hot mitts, she pulled out the dinner rolls, setting the pan on the cooling racks. She lifted the towel on the next pan and slid it into the oven. When she turned around, she saw Mr. Narcoleptic had helped himself to a cup of coffee.

Too bad you didn't drink some coffee last night, buddy.

"So...I had the weirdest dream about you. I was watching TV upstairs and you showed up. We started going at it hot and heavy. Then you dragged me into my bedroom, where you stripped me and pushed me onto the bed. The way you sucked my cock..."

"Almost like it was real?" she supplied sweetly.

"Yes! I watched you perform a strip tease, then you were crawling all over me, rubbing on me, and..."

"And?"

"That's it. I woke up."

"Huh. Too bad it ended there." She headed out the swinging door, but Gavin caught her wrist and pushed her against the wall. "What the hell are you doing?"

He got right in her face. "No other comment on my dream? Like maybe...it wasn't a dream but a hazy memory from last night? A very hazy memory."

"Let me go."

"Why? Got cold feet?"

Why would he say that? "Have you been drinking?"

"No. But do you want to explain these?" He eased back, pulling a sock out of his right front pocket, then his left pocket. "I thought your feet might be cold since you forgot your socks in my room last night."

"Gimme those." Rielle snatched them and quickly ducked under his arm.

But he caught her, shoving her back in place. "Ah ah ah, not so fast. Tell me that I just had an incomplete dream and that I didn't conk out while you were—"

"Naked? Rubbing myself all over you like you were my personal stripper pole and then you started snoring? Yes, that did happen."

"Jesus, Rielle. I...I don't remember anything from last night after I checked on Sierra. I sat down to watch ESPN and I woke up this morning, naked in my bed."

She studied his eyes. Were they dark with guilt? Remorse? Disbelief?

"I'm not making an excuse, but this type of...thing has been happening to me."

"Oh really."

"Really. Two days ago I woke up in the middle of the afternoon on the toilet."

"You fell asleep on the toilet?" she asked skeptically.

"Evidently, for about thirty minutes." His cheeks colored and he looked embarrassed. "And that is the most mortifying thing I've ever had to admit."

"Why—"

"Let me finish. I haven't been sleeping. I figured as long as I was up, listening for Sierra, I might as well be working. I've been catching up on projects every night since Sierra came home from the hospital." He framed her face in his hands. "Do you really think I'd check out when you were having your wicked way with me if I wasn't suffering from sleep deprivation?"

"So you're not avoiding me?"

"God no. Why would you say that?"

"Because you haven't touched me, or kissed me, or talked to me much since I came home from Denver."

Gavin frowned. "Yes I have."

"No. You. Haven't." She poked his chest with each word.

"Then I'm sorry." He sealed his mouth to hers, kissing her in the deviously languid way that nearly melted her fillings. "How many days of missed kisses do I have to make up for, my love?" He brushed his lips across hers. "Six? Seven? Because I can't have you feeling neglected." Another soft smooch. "Unwanted." He rested his forehead to hers. "I love you. And I'm starting to think the reason I haven't been sleeping is because you haven't been in my bed."

"That comment earns you total forgiveness."

"Good. Now if you'll listen for Sierra, I might slip back into bed for a few hours to try and get my sleep schedule back on track. Because tonight?" He sucked on her lower lip. "You're mine. As many times as I want you, any way that I want you."

Chapter Thirty-One

Early February...

Boone appeared a week after Sierra's accident. Waltzing into her family room like it was no big deal, as she tried not to think about the fact she looked like hell, felt like hell and was embarrassed as hell.

Then he directed that breath-stealing smile at her the instant her dad was out of range. "McKay, you're looking a whole lot better than the last time I saw you."

She played it cool rather than breaking down in grateful tears the second she saw his face. "Oh, I don't know. I hear blue lips are the fashion color for spring."

He laughed. "I take it you're on the mend?"

"The pain isn't as bad. Sit down. Or aren't you staying?"

"I can stay." He settled next to her, draping his arm along the back of the couch and propping his feet on the coffee table. "Two weeks out of school, huh?"

"At least two. Probably three." She groaned. "I'm trying to keep up, but I'm so slow and I can't write anything with my left hand anyway."

"I'm left handed, so it wouldn't be a problem for me."

She stuck her tongue out at him. "So what's new with you? Saved anyone else from rape, drunk driving and a deadly car accident?"

"Sierra—"

"Please let me say this, okay?"

He nodded.

"Thank you for all you did for me that night. I vaguely remember you letting me squeeze your hand when the pain was too much as we waited for the ambulance. You made me talk to you and wouldn't let me fall asleep."

"You're welcome. But I figure we're even now in the life saving department."

"I heard my dad accused you of some stuff in the hospital and he got a little violent. I'm sorry you had to deal with it after..." She cleared her throat. "I know he's apologized to you and tried to make amends—"

"Hey. I don't want anything from either of you, understand?" His fingers traced the bruise on her cheek and the bigger one on her neck. "You have no idea what I..." He refocused on her eyes and stopped touching her. "Anyway, I'm glad you're all right."

"I'm getting there." Her cheeks grew hot. "Also...thanks for not telling my dad everything that happened before the accident. At the party. Especially that thing with Tyler...I can't believe I was so stupid."

"We all do stupid shit." A strange expression crossed his face and vanished. "Did you get in trouble for drinking?"

Sierra pleated the folds of the blanket. "Yes. I'm not supposed to drive for a while but it doesn't matter since my car is totaled. I'm back to where I was just before Christmas. Carless." Friendless. "So entertain me. Any good gossip at school?"

He frowned. "Hasn't Marin told you?"

"Marin hasn't come out to see me." And Sierra wasn't about to call her first. She hadn't heard from anyone, not even Angie and Kara. So much for all the great friends she'd made in the last month.

"Actually, you and I are in the hot seat of gossip."

"Really? Because of the accident?"

"Mostly. There are interesting rumors going around. Like...we've been secretly dating since school started. We had a fight while you were gone over Christmas break and you broke up with me. But we made up at Tyler's party with loud, raunchy sex. Everyone at the party heard us."

Sierra blushed.

"Then there's the rumor I purposely crashed your car so I could save you. But that backfired because your father forbid you from ever seeing me again. He took a swing at me and it became a West versus McKay brawl in the hospital waiting room."

"You are denying it all, right?"

Boone grinned. "Nope. I'm thinking of adding fuel to the fire by spending a few hours at India's Ink. Then the rumors will fly I got your name tattooed on my butt."

"Omigod. Boone West! You can't do that."

"Watch me. Anyway, there's another reason I'm here."

"I'm not fixing you lunch."

"Glad to see you haven't lost that bizarre sense of humor, McKay. I'm volunteering to be your study buddy." He poked her shoulder. "Your right hand man."

She groaned at his pun but immediately grew suspicious. "Hey, wait a minute. Did my dad hire you to do this?"

He raised an eyebrow. "Like I need payment to hang out with you? That hurts."

"Sorry. So tell me why you're volunteering."

"Because you're my girlfriend and you need me." He made loud kissing noises. "I live to serve you."

Sierra glared at him. "The truth, Boone."

"Fine. It's a selfish reason. I know you're working on a big project about McKay history. I thought if I helped you, I'd find out some West history. After all the bullshit and rumors going around, I got to thinking about the feud. Has anyone ever told you how it started?"

"No. Do you know?"

"No. But I'd like to."

"Well, you're in luck. When my Aunt Carolyn—"

"Our Aunt Carolyn," he corrected with a grin.

"When *our* Aunt Carolyn told me I could access the McKay archives, I asked if she'd let me scan all the old family documents. She claims there are letters and stuff from the late eighteen hundreds. Even she's not sure what's in there. As far as she knows, no one has looked at the old stuff in sixty or seventy years. She just keeps adding boxes of updated McKay history."

"What'd she say about you copying them?"

"No problem as long as I pass along an electronic copy of all the files in case something happened to the originals."

"Do you have a scanner?"

Her look said, *doesn't everyone?* "Yes."

"Do you know I don't even have a computer? I have to use the ones at the library."

She had a computer *and* a laptop, which had never made her feel spoiled until now. "If you're over here helping me with homework, you can use mine."

"Thanks."

"So are you busy today?"

"I work the graveyard shift tonight. Besides that, no."

"Good. Because my dad retrieved the archives."

Those beautiful brown eyes lit up. "Really? Where are they?"

Sierra pointed to the far wall.

He turned to look. "Holy shit. There's got to be thirty boxes there."

"Twenty-seven."

He groaned. "That'll take weeks to scan."

God, I hope so.

Boone faced her. "What did you say?"

"That we'd better get cracking."

When Marin called the following week, asking if she could come over, Sierra almost said no. Being in pain was a legitimate excuse for denying visitors, but Marin probably knew most of the McKay family had been by, so she said yes.

Rielle escorted Marin upstairs. Sierra sensed Ree wanted to hang around. During their knitting sessions before Christmas, Sierra had mentioned her frustration with Marin constantly ditching her for

Mitch.

Despite her closeness to her dad, he didn't understand *girl drama*. His advice was to ignore Marin, stop complaining about her and find new friends. God. That made her want to scream. So she should just walk up to a group of girls in her class and say, *hey, you wanna be my friend?* like she had in preschool? No one did that. She'd rather eat lunch by herself every day and have no friends than come off that weird and desperate.

Sierra tried to talk to her mom over Christmas break about her lack of friends problem, but she'd gone on a rant about how all women were bitches, they all started out mean little girls and never evolved. The trick, she'd told her, was to become the bigger bitch. *Don't care what people think of you. Tell them to kiss your size two butt if they don't like you.* Then her mother also warned her that women would always be gunning for her because she was pretty and rich. Sierra hadn't said much—she hadn't needed to; her mother had gone off on another tangent—but she'd secretly thought that'd be a cynical way to go through life.

But her mom had been nearly hysterical when she'd heard about Sierra's car accident. She swore she was leaving Paris and moving in with them until Sierra was healed up. As much as Sierra appreciated that her mom...well, was acting motherly, she knew having her here would put a huge strain on everyone. So they talked on the phone at least once a day. Her mom had sent her flowers and balloons, stuffed animals and candy. It seemed something came air mail every day. Fun things. Quirky things. Sweet things. Items that proved her mom had been listening to her.

How was it they'd gotten closer after her mom had moved across the globe? Sierra hadn't mentioned the positive change in her relationship with her mother to her dad, because he'd make some nasty comment about how it wouldn't last. She didn't believe it made her a sucker for hoping the change was permanent.

She glanced up and realized Rielle and Marin were staring at her, waiting for her to say something. "Sorry. The pain pills make me spacey."

"You'll be all right?" Rielle asked.

"Yeah."

"Okay. I'll check on you in a bit and see if you need snacks or something."

After Rielle left Marin said, "She's nice. Is it weird that she's acting like your mom?"

She couldn't point out that her mother and Rielle were nothing alike. "Ree is awesome. She's always there for me when I need her." Unlike you.

"She's still with your dad?"

Sierra nodded.

"Is that awkward?"

"Sometimes when I see them making out or if they both disappear and I know they're off doing it. But it's kinda nice, actually." Almost like she had a normal family.

Marin perched on the edge of the recliner. "Speaking of doing it...are you and Boone West really doing it?"

"Why? Is everyone at school saying we are?" she demanded.

"Well...you guys were at that party together before your accident. And Kara and Angie said you'd locked yourself in the bedroom together for a long time. So is it true?"

"Is that the only reason you're here, Marin? To verify gossip about me and Boone?"

"No!"

"Why *are* you here? Because it's not like you gave a crap about me since before Christmas. You're so all over Mitch all the time you don't have time for anyone else."

Marin stared at her. "That's what you think?"

"What else am I supposed to think? You never called me on the weekends or asked me to do anything. The only time I see you is at school."

"And every time I saw *you* before Christmas, all you did was bitch, bitch, bitch about how freakin' bored you are out here in this fancy house. How much of a jerk your dad was for not letting you drive. Do you know that's *all* you talked about for months? How you couldn't wait to drive. Oh, and you bitched about how much it sucks here and how much you'd rather be in Arizona. Yeah, Sierra, you were some fun friend to talk to. Can you blame me for not begging you to hang out?"

Sierra's jaw dropped. That wasn't true! That's what Marin thought about her? She hadn't been like that at all.

Had she?

"Then you came back from Christmas break and started partying with Angie and Kara. Did you ever think of asking me to go out with you? No. How do you think that made me feel?"

Like crap. A guilty feeling started to creep in and overtake her indignation. She closed her eyes and thought about their conversations at school. So maybe she did complain sometimes. But that wasn't a reason to completely ditch her like Marin had. "Fine, I can see where you might take it that way. But every time you started talking about Mitch—"

"Mitch and I broke up during Christmas break."

"What? Why didn't you tell me?"

Marin rolled her eyes. "Because you were so busy bragging about how hard you partied in Arizona and how much you rock at beer pong. I knew you wouldn't care so I didn't bother. Besides, it was all over the school. Everybody knew." *Except you* went unsaid.

Sierra's chin dropped to her chest. She'd fucked up again on the friend front, and she'd hurt Marin, who'd never been anything but nice to her. She squeezed her eyes shut but that didn't stop her tears from falling.

Then Marin sat beside her. "Hey. I'm sorry. I didn't mean to make you cry."

"I can't help it. I'm such a jerk." Sierra sniffled.

"Maybe. It's just...I've been so mad at you and I'm not good at saying stuff like that. I had no idea how to tell you that you pissed me off and hurt my feelings."

"You did pretty good today."

"Guess I'm kind of a jerk too for letting it slide." Marin leaned her head against Sierra's shoulder. "I'm sorry you were in a car accident. I bet it really hurts, huh?"

"Yeah." Sierra cleared her throat. "Marin, I'm sorry for being such a total bitch to you. I know I haven't been nice since I got back from Arizona, and I thought you deserved it for basically blowing me off before that. I mean, we hardly did anything together. Now I see I should've invited you over...I shouldn't have expected you to make all the effort."

"Part of the reason you didn't see me wasn't only because of Mitch. I had to get a job after Halloween and I was too embarrassed to tell anyone. Especially you, since you're, well...you know..."

Rich. "Does that make it hard to be friends with me?"

"It's not like you flaunt it. But I know it's there. It was really hard for me *not* to be resentful when you complained about being bored out of your mind and I'm cleaning bed pans at the nursing home in Hulett every weekend."

"So it sucks?"

"It sucks *ass*."

Sierra snickered.

"But my mom and dad had a bad year on the ranch and my mom had to get a job too. You're so lucky that you don't have to work."

Her guilt increased. Boone wasn't the only one struggling. "Are you helping support your family?"

"No. I have to pay for my own gas and earn my own spending money and I wanted to make sure I could get my little brothers something decent for Christmas."

"You are such a good person, Marin."

"I'm glad you're finally figuring that out, Arizona." She elbowed her. "Enough about that. What's really going on with you and Boone?"

"Huh-uh. Tell me what happened with you and Mitch first."

"He was so sweet. He's such a great kisser and we just kept taking it a step farther each time until I had sex with him." Marin sat up and sighed. "I almost did a really dumb thing and got pregnant."

Shocked, Sierra said, "Are you serious?"

"We had sex a few times, like maybe five times, and we didn't use birth control, which was stupid. So I was a week late and freaking out and Mitch was all, *I ain't marryin' you if you were dumb enough to get knocked up.* That pissed me off. So after I got my period, I broke up with him. Asshole."

"God. That is scary. I can't even imagine you pregnant right now."

"Me neither. This really sweet and shy girl who you'd never think was messing around? She dropped out last year because she got pregnant. Now she's workin' at the Pizza Barn in Moorcroft and living with her parents. Her baby daddy was another one of them scum-sucking cowboys like Mitch."

Sierra grinned. She'd missed Marin so much.

"So..." Marin poked her in the shoulder. "You and the hottie known as Boone West. I'll warn you I'm gonna be pissed as hell if the rumors are true and you've been sneaking around with him since school started and you didn't tell me."

"I'm friends with him, but nothing else, I swear. I did a dumb thing too." Sierra told her what had happened at the party and how Boone had rescued her. "So we decided we had to pretend to be together for a little while, but I'm not sure if we're still doing that. I'll have to ask him when he comes over tomorrow."

"Your dad lets him in the house? I heard he punched Boone in the face and knocked him out cold at the hospital."

"Puh-lease. I love my dad, but Boone? He's like don't-fuck-with-me tough. Know what I mean?"

Marin sighed. "Yes. And that is so totally hot in a guy."

"No lie."

"So you and Boone didn't even...?"

"Kiss? Nope. But I have to ask..." Sierra fought a blush. "What was it really like? With you and Mitch?"

"It hurt the first time. Then the next time it didn't hurt, but it didn't feel that great either. I kept hoping it would get better, but honestly, I don't get what the big deal is." She grinned. "But I bet it would be awesome with Boone."

"Marin!"

"Oh, don't tell me you haven't thought about it."

Her dad walked into the room and she was happy for the interruption.

"How are you feeling?" he asked.

Sierra looked at Marin. "Much better now."

"Glad to hear it. Good to see you again, Marin."

"You too, Mr. Daniels."

"Please, call me Gavin. You girls need anything? Drinks? Snacks?"

"Can you stay a little longer?" Sierra asked Marin.

"Sure. It's not like I'd rather be doing homework."

"Thanks, Dad, pizza rolls would be good."

"I'm on it." He cut to the back staircase.

"You know, Arizona, your dad is kinda hot."

"Eww!"

A beat passed. "Know who else is hot?"

"Who?"

"Boone West."

Sierra sighed. "I'm never gonna live this down, am I?"

"Nope." Marin smiled. "Because you'll have me around every day to remind you."

"Awesome."

"Admit it. You missed me."

"I really did."

Chapter Thirty-Two

Late February...

Gavin scanned the crowd at Ziggy's. With more than half the damn men wearing black cowboy hats, he wandered through the entire bar before he saw Dalton, sitting at a table in the corner, far from the action. He took the chair opposite him. "Hey, Dalton."

"Gavin. Glad you could make it."

"I was surprised by the invite."

"Well, we haven't had a chance to catch up..." Dalton sent him a sheepish smile. "I'm fresh outta drinking buddies, now that Tell and Georgia got hitched, so since you ain't hitched either, you were selected."

Gavin grinned. No bullshit. He liked that. He ordered Crown and water from the cocktail waitress after she finished flirting shamelessly with Dalton. "Vi told me Tell and Georgia flew to Vegas. Did you go?"

"I stood up for Tell. I never turn down a chance to go to Vegas. That said, I wouldn't get married in Sin City on Valentine's Day, but that's what they wanted. From there they flew to Acapulco. I hung around a couple days after, played some cards."

"Did you win?"

"I won big enough one night they upgraded my room at the Hard Rock to the high roller's suite. Immediately all sorts of lovely ladies volunteered to help me celebrate."

Gavin laughed. Dalton, like the rest of the McKays, had the rugged good looks women seemed to go for. He was a strapping guy, easily several inches taller than either of his brothers. Broader too. That baby-face was deceiving, according to Vi. Dalton McKay liked to fight. And he liked to win.

Once the drinks were on the table, Dalton lifted his glass for a toast. "To the last two single McKays standing."

After Gavin drank, he felt the need to point out, "Since Rielle and I are in a relationship, technically I'm not single."

"Technically you're not a McKay either." Dalton laughed. "Sorry. Couldn't resist. So it's serious with you and Rielle?"

"Wasn't something either of us expected, but it's..." He wanted to say *she's the best thing that's ever happened to me,* but that sounded sappy, so he said, "Good. We're taking it day by day."

"Sierra is cool with it?"

"She seems to be. Sierra's been a bit of a humble Tigger since the accident, if you know what I mean."

"I've been there, as you well know."

He looked Dalton in the eye. "I don't hold that intervention with Ben against you, Dalton. You did what you thought was right. You were looking out for someone you cared about."

Dalton turned his lowball glass on the cocktail napkin. "It sure opened my eyes about a lot of things."

"Mine too, to be honest. Anyway, Sierra and Rielle get along well. They like each other and spend time together, but I don't force the issue. Might sound obvious, but I'm Sierra's parent, Ree is not. It'd be easy to put expectations on her since we're living together and because she's a woman who's been a single parent. We're still figuring out boundaries."

"How did Rory react to Rielle being in a relationship with you?"

"Not so well. Why?"

Dalton shrugged. "I ain't surprised. Bein' an only child, she's always been spoiled by havin' all her mom's attention. She ain't gonna be happy sharing it, even when she's old enough to know better."

That just reminded Gavin of how big a step it'd been for Rielle to keep her daughter out of the intimate relationship in her life.

"Plus, it's gotta piss Rory off that Rielle is involved with a McKay."

"Why's that?"

"Oh, I suspect the McKays offering to buy the Wetzler's land over the years had some to do with it." Dalton sipped his drink. "I suspect I had a lot more to do with it."

"Yeah? What makes you say that?"

"It's...complicated. I've always considered Rory a friend. But after that night in Laramie, she'd rather punch me—and she usually does—than look at me." He paused. "Me'n Rory got into it the night she was at the Golden Boot with Sierra."

"Sierra didn't mention it."

Dalton laughed. "That surprises me since your girl had to put Rory in a headlock to keep her from goin' after me."

Gavin decided he'd be better off not knowing what else had gone down that night. "So you really called me up because you're looking for a drinking buddy?"

"Partially. Feelin' sorry for myself. The other part is to ask if you've got any plans for the land you own that abuts your brother's section?"

"I'll be honest, Dalton, after what happened before, I suspect it's in my best interest to keep the family peace, to change the subject now, before you ask me something or tell me something I don't want to know."

"How about if I share what's on my mind but we'll keep this discussion between us for the time being. That way, both our asses are covered."

"Deal." Gavin leaned back in his chair. "So what's going on?"

"This fall we agreed to lease Charlene Fox's place for two years, and at the end of those two years, we have first purchase option. Do you know what piece of land I'm talking about?"

"Does it make me a greenhorn if I say no?"

Dalton offered a wide smile. "Nope. The land is adjacent to your creek access."

Gavin frowned. "My creek frontage is only about thirty yards. Rielle's section has most the creek frontage."

"Yeah, I know. But she's—or rather Rory has—made it plain she doesn't want cattle close by. But with your section adjoining Ben's, there's a chance Ben and Quinn will address leasing grazing rights from you."

"Leasing?"

"Yes. Ben and Quinn are your brothers, and they wouldn't expect to get the rights for free—but bein's you are a greenhorn, their brother and rich in your own right, they'd try to get a deal and tie up the lease rights for years. The chunk you own isn't the ideal piece of dirt, and it's undeveloped, which means it'd be a lot of work on their part to get it cleared. So I'm wondering if that work load is beyond your brothers' capabilities, since it's just the two of them running things and they don't have extra time or hands."

"But it's not beyond your capabilities?"

Dalton leaned forward. "No. We've got two extra set of working hands in Jessie and Georgia. Libby don't help Quinn out as much as she used to on the ranch after their kids were born, and Ainsley ain't the type to devote a month to clearing brush.

"What I'm asking is to keep in mind we're interested in leasing that land. We're willing to do improvements on it—on our dime. We're not at that point yet where we can consider signin' a lease with you. But we will be in the next year. So it'd be a serious blow to us if you'd already signed a long term lease with Ben and Quinn. Me, Tell and Brandt will pay the highest going rate. I know your brothers won't offer you that, so I'm pointing out ahead of time that doin' business with us will be the better deal for you. And since it appears you're in Wyoming for the long haul, we wanted to state our...offer—for lack of a better term—up front."

He allowed a moment to digest the information. But he had to admit Dalton impressed the hell out of him. Not playing on any type of family connection, laying out the facts. Appealing to Gavin's practical side. "Out of the original 140 acres Rielle owned, she has forty. One hundred acres is a piss-ant amount in the scheme of McKay Ranches."

"Maybe, but the right hundred acres, adjacent to our four thousand acres, with creek frontage ain't nothin' to sneeze at."

"How many people underestimate you?"

Dalton grinned. "A lot. Especially when I'm playin' cards. They see my baby-face and assume...well, not many of them assume I'm a rookie anymore."

"Is that how you funded your land purchases? Through gambling?"

Dalton hung his head. "Yes sir."

"Don't even try to pull off contrite, Dalton."

He laughed. "Sorry. So as long as we're swapping stories about how we made our millions—ha ha—I gotta know if all of yours was inherited."

Strange to think his brothers hadn't asked him this question. But since Dalton had been honest with him, he owed his cousin the same courtesy. "My dad started a real estate development company in the 1960s. He did very well in the 70s, 80s and lost more than half when the credit market collapsed. He recovered, but never like during the heyday. He died when I was twenty-eight and I was already VP of the company, so I took over." Gavin sipped his drink. "My father was a great guy, but I found out a few things he'd done that were shady and I worried his mistakes would come back and bite me in the ass.

"So a few years after his death, I started buying cheap properties. Rentals in decent areas that didn't require more than basic updates. Two properties turned into four, four turned into eight...and so on. Around that time, I'd had enough of my cheating wife and filed for divorce. Instead of letting that bitterness eat away at me more than it already had, I became more hands on, buying government foreclosures, houses auctioned by banks, any little gem I could turn fast. I'd go in and gut the place. There's nothing more cathartic than beating the fuck out of stuff with a sledgehammer."

"Are you kiddin' me?"

"No. I worked out my aggression toward my ex-wife and started flipping houses at exactly the right time in the market. I made a killing. I reinvested it in rental properties. Daniels Development Group is still in business, I'm still a figurehead CEO, but with the spectacular crash of the housing market, the bulk of my business focus is Daniels Property Management. Since I'm not hands-on, ripping places apart, I can work from anywhere. Made it easy to move here."

"I had no idea. I gotta say. That's impressive." Dalton gave him a self-satisfied smile. "Everyone else in the family sees you as a suit, making real estate deals. From this point on, I'll see you busting shit up with a chainsaw."

Gavin laughed.

"So we have a deal?"

"All right."

"This stays between us," Dalton cautioned. "If anything changes on your end or my end, we'll agree to meet to discuss it before making a decision?"

"Sounds good."

Without missing a beat, Dalton said, "Now that that's out of the way, you wanna play pool?"

Gavin studied the too-innocent face. Pool shark as well as card shark? Probably. But Gavin still had a few tricks he could teach this pup. "Sure. But we're not playing for money, right?"

"How about if we play a few games and see how it goes?"

"Sounds fair."

Two hours later Gavin went home three hundred dollars richer.

He doubted Dalton would underestimate him again.

Chapter Thirty-Three

March...

Rielle stormed into Gavin's bedroom. "Do you know who I just got off the phone with?"

"*Publishers Clearing House?*"

"Not even remotely funny, Gavin Daniels. A trucking company based out of Denver just called, asking me when I'd be home to accept shipment for a greenhouse. Not a greenhouse kit, but a fully finished greenhouse."

He had a hard time containing his smile.

Her gaze pierced him. "You wouldn't happen to know anything about that, would you?"

"Could you describe this greenhouse?"

Rielle threw up her hands. "It's a greenhouse! You know very well what a greenhouse looks like."

"Oh, right. Then that's probably the greenhouse *I* bought you."

"Did I just hear you say you bought me a greenhouse?"

"Is there an echo in here? Yes, I bought you a greenhouse. And I'm disappointed because they were supposed to deliver it last week."

"Oh. My. God. Are you serious?"

"Completely."

"Who buys someone a fucking greenhouse?" she demanded.

"I didn't buy *someone* a fucking greenhouse, I bought *you* a fucking greenhouse," he shot back. "Big difference."

"How did you even know I was pricing them?"

Gavin cocked his head. "Rory told me."

"What? When the hell did you talk to my daughter?"

"Last week she called to check on Sierra, when Sierra was sleeping, so I chatted with her. She apologized for being a jerk when she found out we were together. I confessed I'd been difficult to live with in the weeks after Sierra's accident and I wanted to make it up to you."

"That's your way of apologizing? You buy me a greenhouse?"

"Yep."

"Jesus, Gavin. Why didn't you just buy me flowers?"

"In a way, I did. You can grow your own flowers in your new fucking greenhouse." He grinned.

"You are impossible. I can't accept this from you."

Gavin scooped her up, threw her on the bed, and loomed over her. "You don't have a choice. I custom ordered it. It's on the way and it's nonrefundable." He studied her face. She had that determined set to her jaw, which meant arguing was pointless. So he kissed her.

"No fair," she panted after he slid his mouth between her breasts.

"Say, *thank you, Gavin, for such a thoughtful gift.*"

"I will pay you for it."

"Now you are starting to piss me off, Ree. I didn't buy it out of guilt. I bought it because you needed it and because I could. I wanted to do something nice for you."

"This goes way beyond nice."

"I know. What I feel for you can hardly be described as nice. I love you."

That's when she softened. When her pride took a serious smackdown from her heart. "I love you too. It's just weird to have you buy me things. I don't know if I'll ever get used to it."

"Get used to it. And practice that saying *thank you* thing, because I had them toss in a new tractor with a trailer attachment."

Her mouth dropped open. "Did you really?"

"Yes. But it's just a little tractor, so a little thank you will be fine."

She laughed. "You are so ridiculous. That's probably why I'm ridiculously in love with you." She lifted up and kissed him. "Thank you, Gavin, for such a thoughtful gift."

"My pleasure."

"This greenhouse is enormous," Ainsley said.

"Tell me about it. It's twice the size of the one I'd been saving for."

"And Gavin just bought it for you three weeks ago? Out of the blue? Was it a lucky guess?"

Rielle unhooked a hose coupling. "No. He talked to Rory and she told him. I suspect she exaggerated just a bit about what I wanted."

Ainsley laughed. "How is Rory?"

"Busy. We only get to catch up about once a week."

"So has she come around as far as you and Gavin being in a relationship?"

"Actually, yes. She apologized to me and to Gavin, although he didn't go into detail about what she said to him."

Ainsley's eyebrows rose. "That's progress."

"I thought so. I'll admit I suspected Rory was trying to pull one over on me. Claiming she had accepted the relationship in the hopes I would confide the intimate details to her. She's sneaky that way."

"Has she been hinting around she'd like to know more?"

"No."

"Uh-oh. I recognize that contemplative look. What's up?"

Rielle twisted on the spray nozzle until it loosened and fell off. "What I don't understand is even when everything is going so great between Gavin and me, why do I still feel like I'm waiting for the other shoe to drop?"

"Ree. That's natural. It's completely normal that you're afraid now you've found this incredible happiness, you'll lose it or something will screw it up."

"Exactly! If it's so natural and normal did you talk to Ben about this stuff at this stage in your relationship?"

Ainsley squirmed and Rielle wished she could retract the question. Although Ainsley alluded to it, she never came out and said her intimate relationship with Ben was...more intense.

"Not until Ben and I decided we wanted the same thing. We didn't have the added pressure of kids meddling or trying to manipulate our emotions. So is Sierra completely accepting of your relationship with Gavin?"

"Most days. She's sixteen, though. One day she's on top of the world, the next day she's in the pit of despair. Everything is a crisis in her life. A bad hair day. A B minus on a test. If a friend ignored her in the hallway. Or she's elated because her favorite song came on the radio. Or if she's having a good hair day."

"Was Rory that way?"

"Worse. I think most girls are like that. I'd forgotten how small things are such huge angst inducing incidents in teen girls' lives. Things we dismiss as irrelevant are life changing events in their world. It boggles my mind, what event constitutes a major breakdown and then is easily shrugged off the next day."

"Now that you mention it, I remember being exactly like that," Ainsley said with a groan.

"Gavin handles it really well. He's a great father. And I know this will sound weird, but his nurturing, unconditional love and fluid discipline style he shows as Sierra's father is one of the reasons I was so attracted to him."

"You and Gavin are so perfect for each other. The hippie chick and the businessman? Who'da thunk, right? But it works." Ainsley squealed and hugged her. "I am so thrilled for you—for both of you. Just think, when you and Gavin get married? We'll be sister-in-laws!"

Rielle's belly tumbled. "Married? That's jumping the gun, isn't it?"

"Neither of you went into this relationship thinking it would be casual."

"How do you know that?" she demanded.

"Because I know you."

A division of space and time still continued in the house and their relationship. It frustrated her at times; sometimes she welcomed the separation of selves. Despite their declaration of love, neither had spoken of changing their agreed-upon living arrangement.

Ainsley wandered to the far end of the greenhouse, poking her finger in random peat pots. "I do have another reason for showing up besides to gossip about your love life."

Rielle grinned like a loon. She did have a love life. She had a fantastic love life. "And what's that?"

"This is a nosy question, so go ahead and get your back up."

She snorted. "A nosy question from you? Really?"

"Yes." Ainsley set her hands on her hips, in confrontation mode. "So straight up, Ree. Are you planning to cultivate twice as many plants this year since you have twice the growing space?"

"And this concerns you...how?"

"Because you already work hard enough for two people. If you double the size of your operation, you'll be doing the work of four people and as your friend, that really concerns me."

Had anyone else stuck their nose in her business like that Rielle would've bristled. But Ainsley based her observation on logic, not emotion. "Truth? I feel guilty that half of this top of the line, state of the art, brand spanking new greenhouse isn't being utilized. I went so far as to scour my seed supplier's online catalogue. But I realized I can't do that and have any kind of life outside the gardens. I've decided to curtail what I plant, as far as the yield to work ration."

"Thank heavens. I know how much of this"—Ainsley gestured to the space around her—"defines who you are. But you need to tend your relationship with Gavin with as much care as you tend your plants." Her nose wrinkled. "That sounded a lot less hokey in my head."

"I get what you mean. And I really appreciate your concern. But I have to ask what prompted this?"

"Joely. Her patient load is too much for one doctor. So my nagging must've worked because she is bringing another doctor into her practice."

"Good for her. I've hardly seen her in the last four months."

"You and me both. A celebration is in order."

"I'm in."

"I'll get the ball rolling." Ainsley frowned and pulled her cell phone out of her pocket. "My darlin' husband is mighty impatient today, so I gotta get. Take care, Ree."

"You too."

After bending and lifting and being covered in dirt, Rielle indulged in a long, hot shower—in Gavin's bathroom. The scent of his body wash sent her thoughts back to how thoroughly Gavin had rocked her world in this shower. He'd defined relentless, making her come three times before allowing his own shuddering release. As much as she loved his commanding side, it didn't leave her many opportunities to lead the charge in the bedroom.

That's an excuse. You want him, show him.

For the next hour, their previous sexcapades ran on a continual loop. So by the time she heard the front door open, her anticipation for him had reached fever pitch.

When he strolled into the kitchen, so hip and hot in a sexy-ass black suit, Rielle had to grip the edge of the counter to keep from pouncing on him.

His eyes registered surprise. "Hey. I thought you'd be in the greenhouse."

"I'm done for the day. How was the meeting with Jack and the guys from Lodestone?"

"Went better than I expected. I've always considered myself a tough negotiator, but I'm an amateur compared to Jack Donohue. Jesus. He hammered them on several points, which forced them to shave off a considerable amount of their asking price." His teeth gleamed in a shark-like smile. "It's a done deal. Be interesting to see what Jack does with a historic hotel in Whitewood, South Dakota."

"He didn't tell you his plans?"

"No. I'm just the money man."

Her eyes were glued to Gavin's nimble fingers as he unknotted his tie. When the ends hung beside the lapels, he flicked open the top two buttons on his pristine white dress shirt.

She said, "Stop."

"Stop what?"

"Stop undressing. I'll do that." Rielle ambled toward him. Wrapping the ends of his tie around her fingers, she drew his mouth to hers for a teasing kiss. Licking at his parted lips. Keeping her mouth a whisper away, she began to leisurely unbutton his shirt. "I've been thinking about you all afternoon. How hot and sexy you are. How every time you touch me I lose myself in you."

"And that's a bad thing?" he asked softly.

"Yes, when I'm content letting you have your wicked way with me and I forget turnabout is fair play." Rielle's hands were greedy on his bared chest. "I want you. Just like this. Looking professional and a little tight-assed in this snappy suit. But I want you my way. Do you have a problem with that?"

"Ah. No."

She placed a kiss on his sternum. "Put your hands on the counter behind you and don't move." She tugged the tie from around his neck, watching it slither free. Holding the body-warmed silk up to her nose, she inhaled. "I love your scent. Cologne and man."

Gavin's eyes were a stormy blue as she snapped the tie between her hands.

She reached up and draped the silky fabric across his eyes and fashioned a knot at the back of his head. Wouldn't be light tight, but it'd work for her purposes.

"Ree. What are you—"

"This is my show, remember?"

"How can I see the show with my damn eyes covered?"

Laughing, she kissed his pouting lips. "Poor baby. You'll just have to focus on your other four senses, won't you? Stay put. I'll be right back."

His mouth opened. Then he closed it without a word.

She couldn't stop the smug smile as she heated the squeeze jar in the microwave and tested the temp. Using a feather-light touch, she traced the bottom edge of the tie stretched across his eyes. Then her finger moved to outline his lips. "I love this mouth. The things it can do to me..."

Gavin didn't lodge a protest as she unbuckled his belt, unzipped his suit pants and dragged them and his boxers to his ankles.

"Oh, I forgot to mention I'll pay for dry cleaning."

"Dry cleaning?" he repeated hoarsely.

"Yep. This is gonna get a little messy." Rielle squeezed the bottle, releasing two thick rivulets of warm honey on his chest.

He hissed.

She dug her nails into his hard pectorals as her tongue lapped from the bottom of his ribcage up. She used her teeth to scrape up every bit of sticky goodness on the second stream of honey. Once she'd licked him clean, she reached for the bottle and squirted a dollop above his left nipple, watching as it slowly slid down and coated the dark disk. She attacked, sucking, rubbing the tip of her tongue over the hardened nub. Over and over.

"Goddamn."

Rielle directed the next river of honey down the center of his body. She didn't begin lapping until the stream teased the top of his belly button.

Gavin arched into her with a deep groan.

Drizzling honey all over him had become more than a sexy game. She gloried in eating every amber-colored drop, sometimes ferociously, sometimes delicately, his masculine textures a feast for her senses. While her tongue happily zigzagged here and there, looking for spots of forgotten honey, her hands became stickier. But she couldn't stop from touching his sides, his ribs, his hips, his abdomen.

And Gavin made these fucking hot little noises, deep, almost growling whimpers.

Then Rielle dropped to her knees.

"Oh, fuck no."

"Oh, fuck yes," she said before her mouth engulfed every inch of his rigid cock. She withdrew slowly and blew a stream of air across the wetness.

Gavin's whole body jerked.

She chuckled and dropped a glob of honey on the sweet spot where his shaft flared into the wide head of his cock. Sucking the sweetness until the only flavor that remained was his.

Her hands were too sticky to use on his cock, so after drawing a line of honey on the underside of his shaft from tip to root, she fluttered her tongue down to his balls. And back up. She brought that long, hard honey stick into her mouth and opened her throat. Gripping his thighs, she shuttled his cock in and out of her mouth exactly how he liked it.

Gavin's legs started to shake and he pumped his pelvis into her face.

Rielle closed her eyes. Blowing him always made her body throb with want and her pussy slick with readiness. Even her skin seemed stretched too tight.

"Ree."

She kept on plunging his dick in and out.

"Stop. Please."

No way. This was her show. Her prize.

"Rielle, stop. It feels so goddamned good but I don't want to come in your mouth."

We'll see about that. She wanted a full taste of him mixed with the honey sliding down her throat.

Then his hands were on her face, stopping the movement of her head and pulling his dick free from her mouth. She looked up and saw he'd ditched the blindfold too. "Not happy that you're trying to steal my moment, tycoon."

Gavin answering smile was decidedly...animalistic. "Your moment is over. Now it's my turn."

If he put his hands on her anywhere she'd come undone. She couldn't make this easy on him.

"You want your turn?" Rielle rolled to her feet. "You'll have to take it." She ran out the swinging door.

She was feeling pretty smug, because she'd basically hobbled him with his pants and underwear, when two steel bands clamped around her upper body, immobilizing her. She screamed. Her heart slammed into her throat.

"Don't dare me," he breathed in her ear, "because I always take it. And I always win." His mouth latched onto the curve of her throat in that knee-weakening spot and her traitorous legs buckled.

He laughed.

Then he spun her around and ripped her blouse open, jerking it down her arms and to the floor. "I'll pay the sewing bill." He peeled off her camisole and he pressed his sticky chest to hers, ravishing her with a kiss packed with raw passion, completely erasing her will to do anything but surrender.

Using his mind-controlling kiss, he herded her backward until her butt connected with the couch.

Gavin tore his mouth away and bit that same spot on her neck and she fell into him with a startled gasp. "I'm going to bend you over the couch and fuck you, Ree." He nipped the skin again. "Fuck you hard."

She shuddered.

"Stay right here. But those jeans better be down around your ankles when I get back."

Talk about bossy. His sexy, terse commands did it for her in a bad way, yet she had the urge to push his buttons a little. See if she could get that control panel to short out completely. She pulled her jeans down, but left her panties on.

Gavin strolled into view. That's when she realized he still wore his suit coat, and his shirt, but he was naked from the waist down—except for his socks. He should've looked ridiculous, but damn he looked like sex on legs.

His eyes blazed, seeing her underwear still on. "Didn't I tell you—"

"To lower my jeans? Yes. But you didn't say anything about my panties."

That devilish gleam appeared and she understood she was seriously fucked.

"Leave them. Just like the first time I fucked you, remember? You said you came so hard you forgot to breathe, so let's see if we can't up the ante some."

So so so fucked.

Gavin held up his hand and a skein of yarn dangled from his fingers. "Bend over the couch and put your hands behind your back."

"What the hell are you doing with my yarn?"

"Using it to bind you since I'm fresh out of rope." When she continued to stare at him, he snapped, "Move it."

She whirled around and leaned over the couch.

"Hands."

"Impatient much?"

Gavin laughed. A little meanly. "You have no idea."

Her anticipation skyrocketed as he wound the soft fiber around her wrists.

"Lift your chest up."

As soon as she obeyed, Gavin slid the buffalo robe underneath her. When he pushed her chest down, the incredibly soft hair rubbed her nipples.

Then his mouth was on her ear again. "There's one other thing before we get started." Two sharp smacks landed on her ass cheeks and she yelped. "That's for leaving your panties on."

Gavin kicked her legs out and adjusted her underwear so the elastic stretched directly over her clit. His big hands angled and spread her lower half to his liking.

Then he plunged into her.

Rielle arched up. "God."

Then he curled his hands over her shoulders, using her body for leverage as he hammered into her. Bottoming out with every thrust, pulling out completely and surging into her pussy again and again.

The buffalo hair constantly caressed her nipples like soft tongues. Add in the continual friction against her clit and she knew it wouldn't take long.

Her ass stung, she couldn't move her arms, she was utterly at Gavin's mercy. And she loved every second of it.

He pressed a kiss at the top of her spine. "You blow my fucking mind, Ree, every time."

Gavin owned her. Heart. Soul. Mind. Body. His every primitive groan and animalistic thrust drove that point home.

"Please—"

"What will it take to get you there?"

Mouth dry, brain scrambled, she could barely speak. "You know."

"Will it take...this?" He sucked on the side of her throat and it was over.

The warning flutter in her lower belly lasted a nanosecond before she climaxed. A gasping, shuddering, shattering orgasm. The sensations coalesced. Then her body and mind splintered—her mind cried *uncle*, the sensations overwhelmed her as her body pulsed and throbbed, screaming *more more more*.

Gavin roared, his hips furiously pounding into her pussy with such force the couch slid forward.

His body shook.

And shook.

He layered his chest over her back and panted in her ear. "You destroy me."

Something about that sweet masculine bewilderment settled the emotions raging inside her.

Turning her head, she breathed him in and tenderly kissed his strong jaw.

"I love you. Jesus, Rielle. I love you so much."

"I know. I love you too."

"We're a sticky mess. Let's get cleaned up."

"Okay. But no water games. I have a feeling I'll be a little sore."

"Shit. I'm—"

"Don't say it. It's a good sore, okay?"

"Okay. But I will point out it still makes you a sore loser."

She heard the smirk in his tone. Such a crazy competitive man. But she loved that about him too.

Chapter Thirty-Four

Late March...

Gavin listened to Rielle's slow breathing as she started to drift off. They were both exhausted but they'd managed to sneak in some alone time for the first time in over a week. She was gearing up for spring planting and he'd been drafted to help with calving.

Quinn and Ben had a great time teasing him about his missing rancher gene, but Gavin hadn't minded. He looked forward to spending time with his brothers—even in the dead of night in the miserable cold and snow. Nothing built a brotherly bond faster than having your arms up a cow's birth canal together. Chase had shown up for a week, claiming to need a break from his pregnancy-hormone-crazed wife, but the truth was he hadn't wanted to be left out. It was weird having brothers...and yet, not.

Sierra had made a full recovery after her accident and was at the physical therapy stage. He drove her to Moorcroft for sessions with Keely. He hadn't replaced her car and so far, Sierra hadn't asked for a new one, which weighed heavily on his decision to buy her one. If his daughter wasn't with her best friend, she was hanging out with Boone West. Sierra swore they were just friends and Gavin believed her—he'd never caught them even holding hands. Sierra also spent time with Charlie and Vi, who absolutely doted on her. The entire McKay family had rallied around her after the accident and she fit in with them like she'd always been part of the rowdy clan.

Which led him to the issue he and Rielle needed to address.

He idly stroked the side of her breast. "Ree? You awake?"

"Barely. You wore me out, tycoon. Man. You can do that thing with your tongue anytime."

Gavin laughed.

She yawned. "So now that I'm awake...why am I awake?"

"We need to talk."

Her body stiffened slightly. "Okay. About?"

"This living arrangement."

She rolled over. "What about it?"

"I don't want you to build your own place. I want you to stay here, living with me."

"Like we've been?"

"No. I want to end the division of your space and my space, and make it all our space. Our home. I want to end the division of our time, too. I want you doing family things with us." Gavin ran his hand down her arm and threaded his fingers through hers. "This isn't a fling for me. It hasn't been from the start. I love you, Ree. I want to spend my life with you. Every part of it."

"You're not just saying that in the wake of smoking-hot sex?"

He frowned. "Can you be serious—"

She smothered his protest with a laughing kiss. "You accuse me of being too serious." She propped her chin on his chest. "The honest truth? I don't want to build that house. I want to live here with you. I adore Sierra and I know she's part of the package. That said, I've always been so independent and in a short amount of time I find myself depending on you more and more. What if..."

"What if I leave, and you've come to depend on me and I'm no longer there? Honey. That's not going to happen."

"I know you love me. You know I love you. But things can change so fast."

"Not this." He kissed her knuckles. "Years down the road, I want to look at you and remind you of this moment and do a little I-told-you-so dance."

She laughed softly. "Now, that is something I can't wait to see. Do we tell Sierra about the change?"

"I like that you said *we.*" He liked it a lot. "I don't know that it requires a sit-down discussion. The melding of our lives has been a gradual shift over the last few months, and she's accepted those changes. If she asks, then we'll address it."

"All right."

"There is one thing I want to do to prove that I'm serious about permanently tying our lives together."

"What?"

"Putting your name on the title to this house. Before you automatically say, *no, no way, I'm not taking that gift from you,* I'll point out it's not a gift. You'll have to pay half the property taxes. And I'll want you to start kicking in more money for utilities because those ovens of yours are a serious electrical suck."

Tears filled her eyes.

"Shit. Ree, honey, I was kidding about the utilities."

"I know that, dumbass." She sniffled. "It's just more than I ever expected. You...this...everything."

God, he loved this woman.

"For me too."

April...

"Boone. Check this out."

Sierra aligned photocopies from the *Crook County Monitor* newspaper on the coffee table.

"What did you find?"

"This newspaper went out of business in the early decade of the nineteen hundreds but here's mention of a land transfer from Ezekiel West to Silas McKay in 1898." She squinted at the blurred text. "I can't tell how much land, but I bet that's the land the McKays supposedly 'stole' from the Wests."

"Huh. Did it say anything in Dinah McKay's journal about it?"

"Not that I've come across, but she detailed just about everything else, so I'll look closer. Although, she didn't start chronicling her life as a ranch wife until she married Jonas McKay in 1901."

"Wait. Who is Silas McKay?"

"Jonas's twin brother. And you're not the only one who hasn't heard of him." Sierra slumped back into the couch, her eyes aching from trying to read old, faded text.

"Something wrong?" Boone asked, concern on his face. "Where does it hurt?"

"Just a twinge. I'm fine." Boone constantly fussed over her, but she liked it so sometimes she let him soothe her pains—phantom or not. After her car accident and all the hours he'd helped her with homework and her research project, they'd become even better friends. She liked him, liked spending time with him. They both had an offbeat way of looking at things and they shared the same strange sense of humor. If friends were all they ever were, she was good with that. But she'd be lying if she didn't admit part of her would always hope for more.

"Earth to Sierra."

"Sorry. What was I saying?"

"Something about Jonas and Silas McKay."

"Right. How can the McKays be so proud of their family name and lineage and not know their basic history? I talked to my Aunt Kimi—"

"*Our* Aunt Kimi," he corrected with a quick smile.

She stuck her tongue out at him as she always did when he reminded her of their shared family connection. "Our Aunt Kimi told me in the years she knew Jed McKay, he refused to speak of his father's twin brother. He said they'd paid good money to ensure the past was left buried in the past."

"Cryptic. Did Kimi ever ask *her* father about it?"

"I guess he expressed his displeasure that two of his daughters married into a family of thieves and murderers." Sierra absentmindedly tapped her pen. "Kimi said not even the gossip about her and Carolyn marrying into the McKay family revived the old scandal, whatever it might've been. How can it be such a big secret?"

He wore a reflective look. "The Wests and the McKays have been settled in Crook and Weston counties longer than any other existing families. With coal mining, railroads, oil production and agriculture, people constantly moving in and out of the area, not only in the last fifty years, but the last hundred years...things that happened, even scandalous things, *would* get lost in the shuffle, Sierra."

"I get that. Our families have forgotten the actual event that caused the feud in the first place, but they've kept the hatred for generations? I don't buy that. There's a cover up on one side or both sides."

"I agree." Boone pushed his hair out of his face. "I can't believe that neither Aunt Kimi nor Aunt Caro knows the West family history besides that all the Wests have always hated all the McKays and always will. Caro and Kimi are the most gossipy, in-the-know women in the area."

"Exactly what I said! So I'll admit I was a little...pushy with Kimi, especially since Jed McKay lived with her and Uncle Cal and I think she was dodging my questions. But I'm interested in the real story, dammit."

"Maybe you oughta be a reporter. Or a private eye." Boone nudged her. "So how *did* Aunt Kimi react to a pushy non-McKay acting like a pushy McKay?"

She nudged him back. "She asked me when I was officially changing my last name to McKay so it accurately reflected my overbearing genes."

"Is that a possibility? Your dad changing your last name to McKay?"

"He's never mentioned it. But that's how everyone introduces him—Gavin Daniels, Charlie and Vi McKay's oldest boy." Sierra shuffled the papers in front of her. "I wouldn't have an issue if he did want the change. *Some* people—" she knocked her knee into his, "—already call me McKay, so it wouldn't be such a big shift for me. But it would be a big deal for my dad. Anyway, I'm just frustrated with the lack of information."

Boone covered her restless hand with his. "You've done your report. Why are you still combing through these old papers?"

His touch—even casual—caused a hot jolt of awareness. She stared at his rough-skinned knuckles and the smattering of dark hair across the back of his hand. She wanted to run her fingertips across the rugged texture and memorize every inch.

"Sierra?"

"What?"

"Why does this matter?"

"Maybe to show my dad that I *am* invested in my family. I know it probably sounds weird, but I've never had this type of connection. I don't know anything about my mom's side of my family, except that she cut off all contact with her dad after he left her mother for another woman. Then her mom died when she was in college. I've never had cousins, or aunts and uncles and now I've got so many I can't keep them all straight.

"I'm also interested because Dinah went to all the trouble to keep records for future generations of McKays. These archives haven't been touched in years and someone needs to care, to bring it to life, so it might as well be me." She sighed. "My Grandpa Charlie said after his mom died his father boxed up all her things, shoved them in the attic and warned his sons if he ever caught them messing up there, he'd tan their hides."

He whistled and sank back into the sofa, breaking their handhold. "Yeah, I wouldn't take the chance and go poking around either."

"But I want to know what the damn scandal was. It had to be big. It had to be documented some place in these papers."

"I'll remind you half the papers jammed in the boxes were worthless."

"But there's got to be more information somewhere that we don't have." She had a thought. "Small town newspapers—especially back then—detailed the lives of people in the community by calling local gossip *news*. So and so went for supper at so and so's house. So and so won the pie-eating contest at the church social. Ellie Mae was seen dancing with Tom, Dick and Harry at the street dance."

Boone laughed. "Ellie Mae? Is that name from what I think it's from?"

"Yes, I watched every episode of *The Beverly Hillbillies* on classic TV at least three times." Sierra poked his arm. "What old TV show was your guilty pleasure?"

"Guess."

She groaned. "You know I hate guessing games."

"Yep, but if you guess, I'll help you scour these pages and we'll dissect the library archives piece by piece until we break the news of the hundred-year-old scandal."

That perked her up. Boone's appearance today had shocked her since she'd finished the history project last week. And if he promised his help, she'd still get to hang out with him. "Even if I guess wrong?"

"Yep."

"*The Love Boat.*"

Boone laughed. Hard. "God, McKay, you are so freakin' hilarious sometimes."

She buffed her nails on her chest. "But I guessed right, didn't I?"

"No. Guess again."

"*The Adventures of Daniel Boone.*"

"Seriously?"

She blinked innocently. "What? Am I wrong?"

"Do ya think?" he half-snarled. "I was saddled with this ridiculous name because of that man. And my ditzy mother named her other son Crockett, after Davy Crocket."

"No lie?"

"No lie. She named her daughter Oakley. After Annie Oakley. Who does that to a kid?"

"You're off topic." She jabbed his chest with her index finger. "Tell. Me. Your. Favorite. Old. Show."

"*The Dukes of Hazzard.*"

"Funny."

"I'm serious. And for me it was all about Daisy Duke and those short shorts. Man. She was something."

Seeing the dreamy look on Boone's face...now she knew exactly what pieces to add to her summer wardrobe. Speaking of summer...she'd wondered how to bring this up. "So can you believe there's only a month left of school?"

"Can't say as I'll be unhappy to see the ass-end of high school."

"Is the West family throwing a graduation party for you?"

"I told them *no way* and if they did I wouldn't show up. I don't even want to walk with my class. I can't fucking wait to walk *away* from my class."

"Are your parents coming to the ceremony?"

Boone closed his eyes and leaned his head back into the couch. "Gives me a headache thinking about it. In fact, I've had a low-grade headache all day."

Almost without thought Sierra reached out, and her fingers brushed away the thick hank of hair that perpetually fell in his eyes. She flattened her palm on his forehead. He didn't flinch, or ask why she was touching him; he made a low groan.

"Your hand is cold, but it feels good."

She seized the chance to study his beautiful face up close. Starting with the wide span of his jaw and the dark razor stubble that reached the hollow of his cheeks. He'd said his nose had been broken twice, but it looked straight to her. Her focus drifted to his mouth. She'd spent hours imagining the fullness and softness of his lips on hers.

Boone's long lashes slowly lifted.

Her belly jumped. But she didn't back away. This close she could discern the various shades of brown that swirled together to create his striking eye color. His eyes were so expressive. But she had no idea what he was thinking right now.

He's thinking you're a pervert and you need to get your hand off him.

She casually brushed his silky hair back and retreated.

"Thanks. It actually feels better."

"Any time." *Seriously. I can put my hands on your face any time you need it.*

"You know something?"

"What?"

"This is the first time I've been here and you haven't offered to feed me."

So much for a personal moment. She smiled. "Let's scrounge up food so you're not sorting through piles and piles of papers on an empty stomach."

He leveled that bad boy grin at her. "You are a taskmaster, McKay. But a promise is a promise, right?"

"Right. And I hold everyone to their promises."

Chapter Thirty-Five

Gavin and Rielle hammered out details on the housing situation. She agreed to her name being put on the title to the house, but they'd opted to keep their original land split. Rielle retained her forty acres; Gavin kept his one hundred acres.

He'd been prepared to deal with backlash from her when he mentioned leaving the land unimproved seemed like a waste of resources. But she'd confessed part of the reason it'd remained fallow under her ownership was she hadn't the time, money or drive to make improvements. Since he now owned it, she didn't much care what he did with it as long as his plans didn't encroach on her growing space.

During the spring he'd been so busy he hadn't revisited his conversation with Dalton about future land usage possibilities. Thinking back, Gavin hadn't gotten the impression Dalton was scheming to undercut potential lease and land expansion for his closest McKay relatives. Now that he'd received the green light from Rielle, he needed to broach the subject with his brothers.

Ben had offered to tour the area with him, but Gavin found himself calling Quinn instead. Quinn showed up with the two horses. They saddled up and began to explore, picking their way through overgrown scrub cedar, weaving around scraggly pine trees and dodging the multitude of rock outcroppings. The piece of land was small, but it took them over two hours to forge a path to the creek.

Quinn dismounted and held the reins as he led his horse through the mud to the water. "I gotta say, you're doin' much better on horseback, Gavin."

"Riding at least," Gavin said. "Saddling shouldn't be the hardest part."

"Neither one would be hard if you rode every day."

Gavin followed Quinn, and Duchess didn't fight him as much as she used to. He just hoped she didn't try to bolt when he released the reins to let her drink. He squinted at the stream flowing in front of them. It ran higher in the spring, so it'd be harder to cross now, but not impossible. He couldn't tell where the land Dalton, Tell and Brandt had leased started on the opposite bank.

"I figured you'd have a horse of your own by now," Quinn commented.

"Why would I do that when all's I have to do is call you and you bring the horses and the tack right to me?"

Quinn laughed. "True. I'm makin' it too easy on ya. Sometimes because of your greenhorn status I have to remind myself you're my older brother, not younger."

"Does it bother you that people are calling me Charlie and Vi's oldest son?"

"No. Why would it? You *are* their oldest son."

Matter of fact—that was Quinn.

"Besides, I've never put much belief in them rules about birth order determining anything. Bunch of mumbo-jumbo if you ask me. We've already broken them rules by not bein' raised together. Would we be different people if we had? Yep. But we weren't."

"You never had any qualms about me just showing up? What I might want? What I might do? The problems my existence caused?"

"I wasn't worried you'd insist on havin' a piece of the ranch as your birthright. I'm a good judge of character and yours has always been sound. I'll admit some...concern when we first found out about you, what level of involvement you'd have with us—but that was more concern for our folks. I didn't want Mom or Dad feelin' less than, if that makes sense." He shrugged. "You're here now. You're part of the family. We're all glad for it."

"I am too." Gavin watched Quinn urge his horse back from the creek. "Now that you've seen this piece of dirt, what do you think?"

Quinn pushed up his hat. Then he smirked. "Honestly? I think you probably overpaid for it. By a lot."

Gavin laughed, but he withheld additional comment, wondering if Quinn had as good a poker face as Dalton.

"Look, I know the initial purchase of this place caused a rift between you and Ben, and I'm glad you two got it sorted out. I didn't take sides, mostly because I never understood the big push for havin' access to this section anyway. Probably just a McKay pride thing, since it wasn't in McKay hands, or a competition thing between Dad and Uncle Casper. If I brought Dad out here now, he'd shake his head and consider us better off for not payin' taxes on land we can't use for nothin'."

A harsh assessment. "So this section doesn't have any redeeming value?"

"I didn't say that," Quinn said evenly. "It just doesn't have value for us." He gestured to the overgrown trees along the creek bed. "It'd take one helluva lot of work to get it remotely useable. Since it's just me'n Ben runnin' our ranch since Dad retired, I don't see takin' that workload on as any kind of long term benefit."

"You think Ben would feel the same way?"

"Probably now he would. The time of the failed land deal he was in a whole other mindset. He's got a different life these days and his extra time is spent with Ainsley or on his furniture business. Ben won't wanna spend months clearing brush when we've already got enough goin' on to keep both of us busy fulltime. And I'd rather be with my darlin' wife and kids than wasting time tryin' to improve something that ain't gonna give us much in return." Quinn's eyes narrowed on him. "What's up with all the questions?"

Gavin shrugged. "Like you said, this piece of land has been a point of contention. I thought I'd gauge your interest in it now that you've seen it up close."

"Fair enough. I'd put it at zero."

"I appreciate your honesty. Between us, Dalton and Tell have some interest so I might hear them out."

"Be interestin' to hear what they come up with."

And that was that. He could discuss partnership possibilities with Dalton, Tell and Brandt without guilt.

Hanging out with Quinn was very low-key. Almost peaceful. He didn't fill the silence with meaningless chatter. Quinn was so different from Ben—yet, in some ways they were exactly alike, and strangely enough, Gavin had many of the same characteristics of his brothers. Gavin was starting to believe he had a place in this family besides being an object of curiosity and regret.

They mounted up and skirted the inner section in favor of following the fence line that ran on flatter land.

Once they returned to Gavin's place and dealt with the horses, he handed Quinn a beer and sat next to him on the tailgate of Quinn's truck.

"So I have to ask you something a little random."

"That's a scary start to a conversation, but go ahead."

"The first time I showed up here and we had the meeting? Vi got upset telling her story and Charlie told her to calm down because of her high blood pressure."

After lowering his beer bottle, Quinn looked at him curiously. "That is a random thing to remember. What're you askin'?"

"How bad *is* Vi's blood pressure?"

"Better than it was. Mom ain't the type to talk about it. She don't wanna be seen as anything less than Teflon-coated."

That did fit with Gavin's impression of Vi.

"Me'n Ben did get Dad to tell us that the doc had put her on high blood pressure meds and ordered a change in diet. But after a year, she lost weight, they switched meds and her health is a lot better." He raised his bottle again and drank. "Why?"

Gavin swung his feet. "I was diagnosed with high blood pressure a few months after that meeting."

"No shit?"

"Surprised me too. I was a little overweight, but not bad. So I wondered if high blood pressure is hereditary, and on which side. The McKays or the Bennetts."

"It comes from the Bennett side. Mine has been steadily climbin' in the last five years." Quinn swiveled his head to look at him. "I take it you haven't said anything to Mom?"

"No reason to. It's under control. I just wondered if that health issue might be a double whammy from both sides."

"Dad is healthy as an ox." Quinn snorted. "Course, when Ma went on a diet, Dad did too, whether he wanted to or not. He ended up losing weight and that improved his overall health. I ain't gonna claim all the McKays are a hale and hearty bunch—Grandpop had a heart attack, but it wasn't early on. And the uncles seem to be fine. Aging well, if you ask me." He frowned. "But there is one other thing."

"What?"

"No one in the family talks much about it." Quinn sent him a look. "Sierra didn't find any mention of it in the family archives?"

"No. What are you talking about?"

"A...physical thing."

"What kind of physical thing?"

"A physical anomaly."

"What the hell? Like a heart murmur or something?"

He shook his head.

"Do you have this anomaly?"

Quinn's gaze dropped. "Not yet. This condition shows up at a specific age."

"What age?"

"Forty-four."

Now Gavin was getting spooked. "What is it?"

"I don't know if it's my place to say. Maybe you oughta ask Dad."

"Ask him what?"

"If you can see it."

"See what?"

"His third nipple."

Gavin turned toward Quinn and repeated, "He has a third nipple."

Quinn didn't say anything.

"Are you serious?"

A pause, then, "Nope. Just pullin' your leg."

"Really fucking funny."

"It was." Quinn grinned. "I'da given anything to see the look on Dad's face when you demanded to see his extra nipple."

"Fuck off, Quinn."

He laughed. "I almost said we McKays grew a third testicle. And since Dad is the McKay castration king, he'd just whack off your extra ball during branding."

"Like I said. Fuck. Off." Gavin groaned. "Jesus. I'm not that green. Am I?"

"Yep. But we're workin' on ya."

Marin's Blazer ripped up the driveway, music blasting out the windows.

Quinn muttered, "Amelia's teen years are gonna kill me, huh?"

"If Adam's don't do you in first. I hear boys are worse than girls."

"Thanks for the sympathy, bro," he said dryly.

Sierra hopped out of the car, holding her backpack on her left side.

Marin backed up and yelled, "Bye, McKay, don't forget to call me later!" out the car window before she sped off.

McKay? That was new. Wasn't it?

Sierra stopped a few feet from the tailgate. "Hey, Q."

Quinn smiled widely at her. "So, McKay, huh?"

Sierra shot Gavin a quick glance before looking at Quinn. "Yeah. That's what the kids at school call me."

Why hadn't Sierra mentioned this?

Because it'd gone over so well when you found out she called Vi Grams.

"I guess that's a better nickname than Trouble," Quinn said. "Though to hear most folks around here talk, McKay and trouble mean the same thing."

Sierra grinned. "I've heard some of the stories about the wild McKay boys."

"All lies," Quinn said with a straight face.

"That's what Grandpa Charlie says too."

"Find any proof of those wild ways as you're doin' your family research project?"

"A few. I found out a lot of stuff about the McKays and Wests and I can't wait to talk about it at the branding." She made a face. "Grandpa Charlie and Grams are making me give an oral report to the entire McKay family."

Gavin could see Sierra's excitement and pride, even when she tried to pass it off as a chore.

"But most of the recent McKay dirt I've heard has come from Kyler or Keely."

"Speaking of Keely..." Gavin said. "Grab a snack and we'll hit the road in about ten minutes for your physical therapy session."

She sighed. "Do I have to? My collarbone feels completely healed." She rotated her arm forward and back. "See? It's fine. The sessions are a waste of my time and Keely's time and your money."

"Not according to Doc Monroe."

Sierra shifted her stance, acting as if she needed to talk but wasn't comfortable doing so in front of Quinn.

Quinn caught the vibe and slid off the tailgate. "I best be goin'."

"Thanks for bringing the horses over today."

"Not a problem. Just holler anytime you wanna ride." Quinn tugged on Sierra's hair. "You can ride any time you want *after* you get the doctor's official all clear on your physical therapy."

"You're gonna be so surprised when I just show up, demanding riding lessons, Q."

"I look forward to it." Quinn drove off.

Sierra dropped her backpack on the ground and moved in to hug him. "Hey Dad."

He wrapped his arms around her and kissed the top of her head, enjoying this sweet spontaneous hug. She held onto him for the longest time. Finally, his curiosity got the better of him. "You okay?"

"I just had a bad day. Nothing specific happened, I'm just feeling kind of sad. I miss my mom."

"I know you do, sweetheart."

"I feel like I haven't seen you in forever. I'm low on Dad hugs and need some Dad time."

Gavin held her a little tighter. "So we should do something after your physical therapy appointment."

"Just you and me?"

"Sure. It's been a while, hasn't it?"

She nodded against his chest and sighed.

Moments like these were worth suffering through every slamming door and petty fight. "I'll run in, grab my wallet and leave a note for Rielle."

"I hope it won't hurt her feelings that we're doing something without her."

That Sierra even mentioned it was a sign she'd accepted Rielle as a permanent part of their life—he refused to look at it any other way.

May...

"You know, I think it's sucky that Boone isn't taking you to prom this weekend."

Me too. "Prom is *so* not his type of thing."

"How would he know if he's never been to one?"

"You do have a point." She couldn't tell Marin that Boone couldn't afford to take anyone to prom. What girl would ride on the back of his bike in a fancy dress?

You would. In a freakin' heartbeat.

Marin sighed heavily. "I just don't get you, McKay."

"What did I do now?"

"You turned down Paxton Green's invite to prom, which is just stupid because *hello*, he's hot, sweet and...did I mention hot?"

"Several times."

"So you should've said yes. We should be in Rapid right now trying on slutty prom dresses."

Sierra laughed. "You really think my dad would let me wear a slutty prom dress out of the house?"

"Hell no." Marin grinned. "I didn't say we were gonna *buy* them, just try them on."

"I suppose I'd be wearing fuck me heels too, with this imaginary slutty prom gown?"

"Naturally. And carrying a sparkly rhinestone purse big enough to fit a flask, condoms and a small handgun."

"You are so crazy-wrong."

"What is crazy-wrong is that you're not goin' to prom with pretty Paxton the bulldoggin' stud, because you're mooning over boring Boone."

"Mooning. As if. We're friends. That's it. Besides, prom wouldn't be any fun if you weren't there, Marin, so that's really why I'm not going."

"Bull. But next year we're double dating no matter what." A few minutes passed and Marin complained, "Why are we sitting out here? I can feel my white skin frying like bacon and more freckles popping up on my face."

Sierra knocked her foot into Marin's. "It's a gorgeous day. Warm air, blue skies. No snow. One thing I miss about Arizona is soaking up the sun. So suck it up, cupcake, and sit here with me until Rielle picks me up. I do all sorts of stuff with you that I don't want to."

"Like what?" Marin challenged.

"Like listening to country music."

She snorted. "I'll admit that there are worse things we could be doin' than watching the guys on the track team running around in shorts and tank tops."

"Have you ever thought about going out for track?"

"Not until right this minute...omigod." Marin peered over the tops of her sunglasses. "Who is that guy in the black shorts and white wife beater running sprints by the fence?"

Sierra didn't even hesitate to say, "Boone," with a sigh.

"Really? I didn't recognize him without his thug hat and coat on. Is that why you made me come here? So we could drool over him from afar?"

Yes. "No. I'm waiting for a ride, remember?"

"Sierra—"

"Fine. I want to talk to him, okay? I've texted him a couple times and I haven't heard back. And I don't wanna come across as"—desperate—"a pest, so I hoped I'd see him."

"What do you want to talk to him about?"

"Whether he's coming to the branding. I'm supposed to share my McKay family history report—the stuff that didn't make it in the actual school report—and since he helped me so much, I hope he wants to be there."

"How's he supposed to see you if you're crouched down in the grass?"

Sierra's gaze slowly tracked over Boone's body—obviously amazing even at this distance. His skin gleaming, his muscles straining as he performed a pivot and run body conditioning exercise. The last time she'd spoken to him, he'd talked about a new strength and stamina training regimen. She'd asked tons of questions until he'd offered to demonstrate his new moves, which made her feel a little pervy, but a victorious pervy.

"Sierra?"

She said, "What?" offhandedly, keeping her eyes on Boone as he bent forward. Nice buns. But she preferred them in jeans.

"I said how is Boone supposed to notice you if you're halfway across the damn football field?"

"He knows I'm here."

"He does? How?" Marin demanded.

It'd sound like a lie, or at least wishful thinking, if she told Marin she knew Boone had watched her walk the entire way from the gym exit. "He, ah, waved to me."

"Huh. I didn't see that." Marin stood and brushed the grass from her rear. "You sure you don't need a ride? I could drop you off on my way home."

"Rielle is in town so she offered to pick me up. I'll be fine hanging out here."

"Okay. Call me later."

Within three minutes of Marin leaving, Boone strolled over.

Her belly did that flip, swoop, roll thing even when she acted bored.

Boone flopped beside her, stretching out on his back and groaning, "Man, I'm so fucking whupped."

"No, *Hi, Sierra, how are you today?* No, *I've been ditching your calls because I pulled a muscle in my phone dialing finger?* Just, *I'm so fucking whupped?*"

"Touchy today, aren't we?" He showered her with a handful of grass.

"Hey! That's it. I'm leaving." Sierra started to stand but Boone grabbed her around the waist and rolled her beside him in the grass, ignoring her yelps.

He kept his hand on her stomach, holding her in place. "Hey. If it isn't sexy Sierra McKay. You're looking damn fine today. Is that a new shirt? It does amazing things for your...eyes." He aimed a quick grin her direction. "Did you do something different with your hair? The chocolate-colored tresses are so silky and shiny in the sunlight."

"You're a dickhead. And I'm still mad at you."

"No, you're not."

"Yes, I am."

"Then how come you're still here?"

Sierra pointedly looked at his palm that seemed to be burning a hole through her shirt, right to her skin.

Boone removed his hand. Those striking brown eyes met hers and he lifted his eyebrow in challenge.

She didn't move. She stayed right there, gazing into his handsome face, understanding what Marin had meant by mooning over him—wanting what she couldn't have. Somehow she forced herself to sit up. "You suck at returning text messages, West."

"I've been studying for finals and covering Alan's shift since he's on vacation. Or I've been working out."

"I can tell. You've got some beefy biceps going on."

Boone flexed. "Check 'em out."

Yes please. She bumped him with her shoulder. "No. It might compromise your virtue if people saw me feeling you up."

"Might be worth it." His intense focus traveled from her eyes to her hair. "Sorry for throwing grass at you." He leaned close enough she could see his pulse pounding in his throat. "I'll get it."

"Boone—"

"Relax."

She stayed frozen as his fingers started at her scalp and drifted down the strands of her hair with such deliberation she'd swear he was dragging it out.

You know better.

"So what did you need to talk to me about?" he asked.

Sierra's gaze roved over his face. From his dark eyes, so intent on his task, to his full mouth, his lips parted to release shallow breaths, to his angular jaw. Such a beautiful man. She could just look at him all day.

"Sierra?" he murmured.

"Oh. Right. I wanted to see if you were coming to the branding next Saturday. You don't have to help with the actual work part, just come to the after party."

"Why the invite? The McKays need a West whipping boy? Or are your dad, psycho uncles and cousins gonna castrate me?"

She turned her head and sank her teeth into his wrist. Hard.

"Jesus, McKay! Let go."

She slid her mouth free and licked her lips. "Yep. As salty as I expected."

"What'd you do that for?"

"Because you're being a dick."

"Remind me not to really piss you off," he muttered.

"Too late. I'm already mad at you. Anyway, I'm filling in the blanks on the McKay/West feud for the entire McKay family. I wondered if you wanted to be there since you helped with the research."

He tucked her hair behind her ear. "I can't. I'm working a twelve that day."

Disappointment flooded her.

"But I heard there's a pre-graduation party at Phil Nickels' parents' cabin at the lake that night."

"Are you going?"

"I wouldn't have told you to come if I wasn't."

Close enough to an invite for her. "I'll show up. Think Angie, Kara and Tyler will be there?"

His eyes turned cold. "I'll flatten that fucker Tyler if he comes anywhere near you."

"So we'll have to pretend we're together again?" *Stop acting like that's what you want.* "You have to be tired of that."

"Never." Boone gave her a light head butt that shouldn't have been sweet, but was. "I gotta get back on track."

Sierra groaned.

"See you around, McKay."

Chapter Thirty-Six

Rielle stayed in the greenhouse long past dark. She'd finished her work hours ago, but she couldn't force herself to be in the house with happy Gavin and his equally happy sidekick Sierra.

She was in a mood. This type of surly, sulking mood was rare, but once she became infected with it, look out. Which was why she'd hidden herself away from the people she cared about.

Gavin wouldn't track her down. He understood the demands of her business. So with any luck, and with the help of isolation and booze, she'd shake this mood and return to normal tomorrow.

For the next hour she accomplished exactly nothing except pacing and fretting. Running calculations in her head caused a headache and she threw in the towel. She slipped on her jacket and shut the lights off, her trusty pal Sadie trotting alongside her on the road to the house. On the porch she crouched and hugged her dog. "You're a good girl, Sadie. Sorry I've been lousy company."

The house was quiet but she saw the glow from the TV upstairs which meant Gavin was glued to some sporting event. Addicted to sports was better than being addicted to porn, she supposed, but she'd never understand the man's undying love of the games. Rielle found it ironic the sport Gavin's brother competed in on a professional level held zero interest for him. He'd watch Chase ride, but he turned the channel the instant Chase was done.

A long shower removed the dirt but not the black cloud hanging above her. She stared out the window for a while, until she realized if she'd be up all damn night without a sleep aid. She wandered to the kitchen and grabbed a six-pack of Mike's Hard Lemonade. During her unproductive navel-gazing in her room, she'd already downed half the second bottle when a knock sounded on her door.

"It's open."

"I heard you in the kitchen. I thought you were still working." Gavin's arms encircled her waist and he pressed a kiss on her neck. "Why didn't you come upstairs?"

Rielle pointed to the six pack. "I'm lousy company."

"I doubt that."

"Trust me, it's true." She drained the bottle and set it on the windowsill.

"Would you like to talk about it?"

"Gavin, I appreciate your concern, but I'm bitchy right now and I'd rather you didn't see this side of me."

His mouth brushed her ear. "Am I to take that as you've never been bitchy with me before?"

"Funny."

"Or you think I can't handle you being less than my Ree of sunshine?" He paused. "Ray of sunshine. Get it?"

She smiled, in spite of herself. "Yes, I got it."

"Were you really going to sleep down here?"

"Yes."

"Well, that sucks. Not only because I looked forward to having my wicked way with you—which I was—but because that means you've shut me out. And you know what? I don't like being shut out."

Rielle didn't detect hurt in his tone, just concern. "I'm sorry. This...*sharing your bad day* stuff is still new to me."

"To me too. But we both know every day won't be perfect and I want you to be able to tell me what's eating at you."

She always handled stuff on her own. "It's not a personal thing between us, but a business thing for me."

"Oh. Well, that's different. Fuck this talking about your business shit; if it doesn't have anything to do with me and you, I'm going to bed."

She froze.

Gavin's arms tightened around her. "See how crazy that sounds? Ree. I'm in your life. All aspects of it. I'm a pushy dick who won't leave this—or you—alone until you talk to me."

How had she ever gotten so lucky to have this man in her life? She leaned back into him. "I lost the Twin Pines bread account today. Which means I also lost the Creekside B&B account since they're owned by the same people." There. She'd said it without choking on it or letting loose a string of profanities.

"Did they indicate why they were terminating the contract?"

"They're bringing the baked goods in-house."

"No wonder you're upset," he murmured.

Now that she'd opened her mouth, everything just spilled out. "The Twin Pines is the first place that contracted me for baked goods before the bakery closed. So it feels like I'm losing a cornerstone of my business, even when their orders had dropped off in the last year."

"I understand that. But the upside of this situation is that it isn't the quality of your product that caused their decision. So there's nothing you could've done to prevent it."

Gavin wasn't just being the sweet supportive boyfriend, but he looked at this from the business side and she appreciated that.

"Are you worried other restaurants and businesses will follow suit and take the baking in-house?"

"That's part of it. But I know a big plus to the restaurants I supply is my products are unique to each place. The only restaurant you can get the savory and honey seven-grain rolls is at Fields. Same with the other five restaurants I supply."

"Which is smart. You don't need me to tell you that." Gavin gently turned her around to face him. "What else has put that wrinkle in your brow and the clouds in your eyes?"

"After I left the Twin Pines today, I didn't immediately start researching other restaurants I could sell to, to fill the gap."

"You've always done that in the past?"

She nodded. "I've always needed to replace the income right away. Over the last few hours as I've dissected this reaction every possible way, I realized I don't want to seek out replacement restaurants." She hated talking about money with Gavin, but her mindset in this case went beyond money and it involved him. "So I have to ask myself: Have I gotten lazy?"

Gavin burst out laughing.

"Gavin. I'm serious."

"Ree. Honey, rest assured you're not a slacker. I'm pretty sure losing the Twin Pines and Creekside B&B business will only be a blip in your daily routine. If the income loss isn't substantial enough to worry you at all, then you're exactly right in questioning the immediate need to find replacement income."

She kissed his smirking mouth. "You're so...I hesitate to say right because you'll get a swelled head, but you are. Even if you are pushy."

"Only so I won't have to push you again and you'll come to me on your own next time."

"I will. I promise. Thank you."

"What else?"

"I also had to question whether the reason I didn't want to add more business was because of you." She hadn't choked on admitting that either.

His brow furrowed. "Personally or professionally?"

"Both."

"Because filling that gap is no longer a financial necessity? Since you now have me as a fall back guy?"

She blushed. "Does that make any sense?"

"Whacked out Ree sense, yes, but that's why I love you." His eyes grew serious. "You're permanently involved with me, a guy who has no financial worries. If you lost all your businesses now it wouldn't affect your standard of living because I'm there to pick up the financial slack—even when I know you'd never ask me for a dime. You've never

had that long-term stability before and it scares you." His voice
dropped to a husky whisper. "You know I'd like to make your life
easier.

"Don't let that be an issue between us. I love your independence
and that you are a self-made woman. I still think you work too hard,
but that's a huge part of who you are and what formed you. I love the
whole of you, Ree. But I'd be remiss if I didn't point out that counting
on me—physically, emotionally, financially—doesn't make you soft or
lazy."

"Gavin. I..." She forced the words past the lump in her throat. "I
don't want you to make my life easier. But you already make it better.
That's all I want from you."

He rested his forehead to hers. "I know. Just don't shut me out
anymore, okay?"

"Okay."

An odd sort of acceptance shifted between them in the silence.

"Can I make love to you now?"

"Yes. Please."

"Close your eyes," he murmured and kissed her eyelids to ensure
she did.

Gavin's hands cradled her face and he kissed her so softly, so
sweetly, she felt tears welling again. Then his hands moved down her
neck and beneath the collar of her robe. He said, "Untie the sash." As
soon as the tie fell free, he slid her satin robe off her shoulders until it
pooled on the floor, leaving her naked.

"So beautiful, every inch of you," he breathed against her skin.

His mouth cruised to all the hot spots he'd discovered. The arch of
her neck. The side of her right breast. He feasted on her nipples until
she became dizzy and wet with want. The entire time his sucking
mouth and flickering tongue drove her out of her mind, his hands were
on her. Caressing. Squeezing. Soft at times, rough at others, but every
sweep and brush of his fingers and mouth told her of his possession.

Rielle gave herself over to him completely, understanding that's
what he wanted—her total surrender.

Gavin worshiped her. With his hands. With his words. "You're so
strong here," he said, his voice soft against her throat as his fingertips
mapped the muscles in her arms. Then the slope of her shoulders.

Normally she'd urge him to hurry, push her on the bed and
mount her like a rutting beast. But she'd given him control and it
appeared he intended to take his own sweet time in exercising it fully.

Not that she was complaining.

He stood behind her. Scattering openmouthed kisses down her
nape and spine until she shook from the eroticism of it. His breath, his
lips, the play of his hands all swirled together into an overwhelming

maelstrom of sensation. Yet she felt every press of his fingertips, every kiss, every stuttered puff of air across her skin. And he left no section untouched. Unloved.

Then Gavin turned her around again. He lowered to his knees.

The muscles in her abdomen rippled as he pressed kisses from her belly button to the rise of her mound.

"You're so sweet. My own personal honey pot. I love this hot, sticky honey your body makes just for me." The tip of his tongue followed the slit down to her opening. After wiggling his tongue inside and softly sucking, he flattened his tongue and dragged it back up.

Rielle couldn't keep her legs from wobbling.

Using his thumbs, he opened the folds of skin hiding her clit. He murmured something and settled his mouth on her sex.

He'd wound her so tight that thirty seconds after his wicked mouth began to suck, she unraveled. The short, intense orgasm had just primed her for more. She eagerly waited for him to command her to get on the bed.

But Gavin didn't budge. His tongue traced the lines of muscles in her quads. His teeth nipped the inside of her thighs. When he fucked two fingers in and out of her swollen pussy, her legs became Jell-O again. That tingling tease of release hovered close to the surface.

"Come for me."

"I..." She groaned when he slid his thumb over the seam of her sex.

Between the pressures of his thumb pushing her clit up so his tongue could torture her with wet swirls and the constant rubbing of his fingers on her inner vaginal wall, she hit that detonation point. The throbbing heat licked through her body. She felt the waves in her nipples. In her throat. In her lips. Gavin held on and held her up through every pulse. Then he nuzzled and petted her as she floated down from that foggy bank of pleasure.

As soon as he was on his feet, she tried to remove his clothes, but he stayed her hands. He kissed her fingertips. The center of her palms. The insides of her wrists. Planting his mouth on hers, he kissed her deeply, with sweetness, with finesse. Sharing her taste and giving her a taste of his need.

He kept touching her as he ditched his sweatpants and T-shirt. His hands were in her hair as they landed on the mattress, warm skin meeting warm skin.

His seduction was all consuming. Powerful in a quiet fever of desire. It seemed he'd shown her in a hundred different small ways that he loved her. But this was different. This was action speaking louder than words. This cemented their connection completely. Physically. Emotionally. Permanently.

Watching her eyes, he entered her, stopping when they were fully joined. Letting her see in his eyes everything she brought to him, everything she gave to him when their bodies became one.

Rielle wrapped her legs around his hips. She lifted her arms to circle his neck but he made a growling noise and pinned her right arm above her head. That brought their bodies even closer.

Then he started to move. Showing her that passion didn't have a set speed. Gavin's need for her was there in every measured undulation of his hips. In every drawn out glide of his chest against hers.

Sinking into the slow sizzle and burn of his kisses. Breathless in anticipation for the long thrusts of his body linking to hers. This was acceptance. This was love. This was perfection.

And this man was all hers.

By the time he'd taken them to that pinnacle of pleasure, sweat coated their skin. Their hearts thundered. Need clawed with tiny teeth.

He ground his pelvis into hers and her orgasm unfurled. Unending, glorious. And with her inner walls rhythmically clamping around his shaft, Gavin let himself go.

There was no need for words. Rielle wasn't sure if there were words for what'd just happened between them.

They curled into each other and drifted into peaceful sleep.

Branding day dawned misty and warm. Gavin had no idea what to expect, so he asked his brothers. Ben and Quinn had looked at the sky, looked at the ground and said, "Mud."

Dalton, Tell and Brandt arrived early to help round up cattle. Ben, Quinn and Brandt were on horseback, the rest of them were on ATVs. An hour and a half later the herd milled around the corrals. The calves inside; the mamas outside. Mamas did not like to be separated from their babies. Babies didn't like being away from mamas. The noise was deafening. They all had to shout over the din.

Other McKay cousins arrived and Charlie told him it took four days of branding to get all the McKay cattle branded. One day at their place. Kade and Kane's, and Brandt, Tell and Dalton's calves were branded on the same day. And two solid days to mark the calves that Cord, Colby and Colt raised.

Gavin watched as the guys worked in teams of two. They grabbed a calf from the pen, pinned it on its side. One held the head; one held the rear. Quinn and Ben did the branding with the irons. Libby and Ainsley handled vaccinating the calves. Gavin never imagined the suit and high-heel-wearing bank president down in the muck, but she got right in there.

Cal used the small round iron for de-horning if needed, and Charlie was tasked with castration. One of Colby's boys was in charge of the "nut bucket" and followed Charlie as he cut off the testicles, turning potential bulls into steers. Gavin peered into the big dump bucket. There looked to be a whole lot of Rocky Mountain oysters.

As the day wore on they were all grateful for the cloud cover. Charlie had warned him to be prepared for anything because the month of May could be as hot as eighty or cold enough for heavy snow.

At first Gavin had been self-conscious about jumping into the fray, but his curiosity won out over pride. It was a challenge, holding the head of an animal as its flesh got seared, its balls got whacked off and its horns were burned away. Down in the trenches the air was thick with the stench of burning hide. By the time he took a breather, his coveralls were covered in mud, manure and hair.

His cousins teased him. "We'll make a rancher out of you yet."

After they finished branding, everyone showed up at Quinn and Libby's. Kids and dogs ran wild. Beneath two canopies tables were piled with enough food to feed an army.

Gavin looked around for Sierra. She waved to him and continued her conversation with Colt's wife India. Hopefully she wasn't discussing future tattoo options.

When he saw Rielle, laughing with Ainsley and Libby, he had a feeling of rightness. Of contentment.

Rielle strolled over. "Hey, cowboy. So after a day of branding are you ditching your loafers for spurs to wrassle cattle?"

"No." Gavin snuck in a kiss or three. "I'd rather wrassle you. You don't put up nearly the fight."

She smiled, then shot a look at Sierra before she leaned closer. "What do you know about Sierra's presentation? Because she's nervous."

"Did you talk to her?"

"I tried. But she's a little high-strung, like someone else I know."

He raised his eyebrows. "Me?"

"Nope. Me." She pecked him on the mouth. "Gotta run. Save me a seat at the table."

Even with so many people the chow line moved fast. Gavin sat across from Keely and Jack. Sierra scooted over when Rielle showed up and didn't say much.

"Keely, how are you feeling?" Rielle asked.

"Good, for the most part. I'm tired. I could sleep all damn day. This kid kicks all the time."

"Do you know if it's a boy or a girl?"

Keely shook her head. "There are so few surprises in life, we want this to be one of them."

"Any weird cravings?"

"Tomatoes and Hershey bars," Jack answered. "And yes, she eats them at the same time."

That sounded nasty.

"But I'm not hungry at all today," Keely said. She turned sideways on the bench seat and leaned into Jack.

Jack stretched his hands across Keely's rounded belly and murmured to her.

Then Gavin was drawn into conversation with Carson and when he turned back to talk to Sierra, she'd vanished.

After everyone had eaten, and they were milling about under the big tent, Vi clapped her hands for attention. "Sierra has something she'd like to share. A piece of McKay history." Vi gently patted Sierra on the shoulder as she shoved her front and center.

Gavin grinned. Vi had her own way of doing things.

Sierra looked nervous being in front of the entire McKay clan. Her gaze scanned the crowd until she found him. He smiled, elated his daughter still looked to him for support. He gave her two thumbs up, which would earn the, *Dad, you're such a dork* remark later.

Sierra clutched a sheaf of papers and began. "Most of you know I did a paper on the McKay family for history class. I started out with an old family tree, branched out, and wow, there are a lot of McKays running around these days. It took me forever to do that part." That earned her laughter. "Anyway, when I finished, I was still confused about a few things. For one, the lack of information about Jonas McKay's twin brother Silas, who was unofficially marked as deceased. He isn't buried in the McKay cemetery and there is no official record of his death."

A wave of conversation broke out and then Dalton whistled for quiet.

"Aunt Carolyn lent me the McKay archives and I scanned all the information in twenty-seven boxes, including Dinah Thompson McKay's journals. The other reason I kept going on my search, is because I've heard about the West-McKay feud, but no one—in the McKay family or the West family—knew what'd happened. And I mean no one. Not even my Grandpa Charlie and he's old." More laughter and Sierra blew Charlie a kiss when he tipped his hat to her.

"Because I didn't want to be accused of skewing any information I might uncover as favorable to the McKays, I enlisted Boone West to help me search for facts. Boone had no idea what the original source of friction between the Wests and McKays might be either." She paused and thrust her arm in the air and waved the paper. "And guess what? We found it!"

Excited chatter erupted.

Gavin watched as Sierra waited for the crowd to quiet down, a smug smile on her face.

Keely whistled to cut the chatter. "Pipe down. I wanna hear what she has to say. Go ahead, tell us everything."

"Thanks, Keely." Sierra took a deep breath. "Silas and Jonas McKay were identical twins who wound up in Wyoming in 1896. Jonas worked as a deputy. Silas worked as a ranch hand. In 1897 Silas bought a tract of land, which is still part of the McKay ranch today. Then in 1898, during a poker game at a bar in Moorcroft, which was likely a whor—" she shot a look at the little kids sitting in front and amended, "—a house of ill repute, Silas McKay won a chunk of land from Ezekiel West.

"Ezekiel's brother Zachariah disputed the validity of the game, but the sheriff vouched for Silas. Since Jonas worked for the sheriff, the Wests accused the sheriff of corruption. In the meantime, whenever Ezekiel and Silas crossed paths the following year, they'd end up in a fight. According to Dinah's journal, Ezekiel broke Silas's arm one night when Zachariah joined in and they beat Silas to a pulp."

"See, this is already playing in favor of the McKays," Cam shouted from the back.

"Hush, you," Carolyn scolded. "You got just as much West in you as McKay."

A chorus of "Oohs," broke out.

"This is where Dinah Thompson enters the picture. She was the school teacher and she boarded with the town's doctor and his wife. Dinah was also expected to help the doctor out on weekends. Silas wasn't much of a fighter; he ended up at the doctor's office frequently after his tussles with Ezekiel. Silas became smitten with Dinah and wooed her." She wrinkled her nose at the term. "Taking her to church socials and community events. They fell in love. Since school teachers couldn't continue teaching after marriage, she asked Silas for a long engagement, so she could keep earning money to put toward building a new house on the ranch.

"But Ezekiel also had his eye on Dinah. He wasn't the gentlemanly type that Silas was—Dinah's words, not mine—and Ezekiel became a stalker of sorts. Dinah wasn't wearing Silas' ring, so that made her fair game." Sierra scowled. "This next part is a little hazy, but near as I could tell, Ezekiel got Dinah alone and hurt her. When she told Silas, he went after Ezekiel. They got into another fight, Ezekiel pulled a gun on Silas, but Silas ended up shooting him."

Everyone stayed quiet.

"With Ezekiel dead, Jonas had no choice but to arrest his brother, even though it was clearly self-defense. But Zachariah West swore the murder was premeditated and he'd see Silas hang for killing his brother."

"That's what happened to him?" Kyler demanded. "That's why no one talks about Silas, because he was hanged?"

"No. But Silas believed he was headed for the gallows. One night he attacked Jonas inside his cell and escaped from jail. Silas disappeared, never to be seen around here again. Several people swore they saw Silas get killed during a train robbery in Montana, but it was never confirmed. Others said Silas lived with the Crow Indians on the Montana border, but again, nothing was ever confirmed.

"Dinah wrote that Jonas knew his brother would be unjustly hanged so he made it possible for Silas to escape. Then Jonas resigned as a deputy and took over Silas's ranch. We discovered Zachariah West ended up with a small section of land in Campbell County that's still in the West family today. Dinah's last entry alluded to that land being paid for with blood money. What that means is up for debate and probably always will be. Some secrets really do go to the grave. Anyway, Jonas and Dinah fell in love and got married." Sierra looked up. "And they are the reason we are all here today."

Applause and wolf whistles rang out.

Charlie sidled up and put his arm around Sierra. "How about my smart and determined granddaughter? Getting to the bottom of all this family stuff and putting rumors to rest with facts?" He kissed the top of her head. "I'm so damn proud of you for taking an interest in our heritage."

She ducked her head and Charlie hugged her.

Then she was surrounded by curious McKays.

"Quite the girl you have there, proud daddy," Rielle said.

"She is something. She really fits in with the McKays, doesn't she?"

"Yes, but so do you. Did you have any idea that Sierra had done so much research?"

"I knew she was working her butt off on it. She mentioned she'd found something to Quinn and Charlie and Vi, but she wouldn't tell me what it was." He put his mouth on her ear. "To be honest, I thought she and Boone were using *just doing research* as an excuse to hang out together these last few months."

Rielle laughed.

Sierra fairly bounced over after being waylaid by questions. "Dad, can I go now?"

"Where are you going?"

"Where is the only place I ever go?" she said with exasperation. "To meet Marin."

"So can I?"

"Where are you and Marin going?"

"To a graduation party at the lake. And no, we won't be drinking, smoking weed or having sex."

"No swimming at night either," he warned.

"I know. And Boone will be there."

That didn't exactly alleviate his worry. "You haven't had any issues with your new car?" Maybe he had gone a little overboard, buying her a Mercedes M Class SUV, but he couldn't put a price on her safety. A little peace of mind was worth a lot.

She rolled her eyes. "Dad. We studied the manual together. You read the manual to me when I was driving. I read the manual to you when you were driving. I've studied the manual more than I have for my English final. So can I go?"

"Okay. But drive careful."

"I will." She kissed his cheek. "I love you. I know my curfew's at midnight. There. I saved you from saying it." She gave Rielle a half-hug. "See you later." She practically skipped across the gravel driveway.

"So...she's gone for a few hours," Rielle said.

"What do you say we head home? School will be out in two weeks, ending our mid-morning quickies."

"And our afternoon delight." Rielle threaded her fingers through his. "Since we have two vehicles, and I know how competitive you are, let's have a race."

"What's the prize?"

"Winner's choice."

"Hot damn." He whispered, "Your ass is mine tonight, honey."

"Don't bet on it."

But Gavin beat her home by a full two minutes.

He was feeling pretty cocky after a spectacular bout of raunchy sex, until Rielle whispered, "So, for the record, I let you win."

Chapter Thirty-Seven

The bright moon glow sent silvery light across the clearing. Sierra bumped over the cattle guard and saw him shielding his eyes from the glare of her headlights. Seemed a little strange, Boone calling her out of the blue and asking her to meet him. She hoped it meant something more than he was bored.

Sierra ignored Marin's snarky voice in her head, asking why she went running every time Boone crooked his little finger at her. But she hadn't seen him since his graduation and he'd slipped back into the not-returning-texts zone. School had ended two days ago, and her summer plans were still up in the air.

She put her car in park and killed the ignition. Butterflies danced in her belly. Where had her nervousness come from? She was out here with Boone. Mr. Trustworthy. Mr. Oblivious.

His butt rested against his motorcycle seat. His booted feet crossed at the ankle. His arms folded over his chest. He wore a super tight T-shirt which displayed the ripped muscles in his arms and the ridges in his lower abdomen. She'd seen that shirt on him a dozen times, and every time she whispered a little thank you to the T-shirt gods.

Stop gawking at him.

Nothing wrong with being attracted to her best guy buddy.

Was there?

No. Especially when he still didn't have a clue how she felt. She walked up to him, her hands jammed into the back pockets of her jeans. "You summoned me?"

Boone frowned at her attire. "Wasn't tonight the dance?"

"No. It was last night."

"Oh. Was it fun?"

"I don't know. I skipped it."

"But...you said that night at the lake you wanted to go."

She shrugged. "Marin is at her grandma's for a week so she wasn't going. Besides, they probably only played country music."

"You should've gone."

But I knew you wouldn't be there.

"You asked me here to chew my ass about a dance I didn't go to?"

"No."

"What are you doing out here, anyway? Did your bike break down again?"

"Funny. It was a great night for a ride. I lost track of time. When I pulled over, I realized I wasn't far from your place."

"So you called me." Instead of just showing up at her house. That made no sense. Especially if Boone thought she was at the dance. What was going on with him? He acted...jumpy.

"You got any decent tunes in that piece of crap car you're driving these days?" he asked.

The Mercedes was hardly a piece of crap and he knew it. Boone also knew that the only reason her dad had bought it was for the safety features, including an excess of air bags. "I'll play music as long as you don't bitch about what it is."

"Deal."

She rolled down the windows and plugged her iPod into the stereo system. She mimicked his pose against the car, standing opposite him.

Boone grinned when the music started. "Foo Fighters. Cool."

"Don't get used to it. The next song might be by Flogging Molly."

"I don't even know what the hell that is, McKay. You're more *urbane* than me."

"Right. Seriously, West, what's up? It's not like you to text me, demanding I meet you out in the middle of nowhere. Especially this late."

He lifted an eyebrow. "Since when is ten late?"

"Since my dad grills me about where I'm going at ten at night and who I'm going with."

"Did you tell him you were meeting me?"

"Yeah." She smirked. "He said not to let you drive my car."

"Smartass." Boone paused and tipped his head toward the sky. "As much as I love how bright the moon is, I miss seeing the stars on nights like this."

"Me too."

Neither said anything for several minutes.

"But this moon-gazing shit is killing my neck." He moved to lean next to her. "Much better. So, what are your plans for this summer?"

"I've thought about becoming a carny."

"Yeah? What's the appeal? Getting hooked on meth? Hooked on pot? Hooked on fried food? Or is it getting to rip off little kids every day? Maybe you'll grow a mustache and get a bad tattoo."

She laughed. "You've weighed the pros and cons way more than I have. I was just in it for the unlimited cotton candy."

"What's option two for your summer?"

He was more persistent than usual, so she hedged, in case he had a specific reason for asking her plans—like he wanted to spend the summer with her. "I don't know. It depends."

"On?"

"How much my mom and dad argue over me and where I should be. My mom's boyfriend bought a place in Paris with an extra bedroom, so she wants me to stay at least half the summer with her." She shot him a sideways glance. "I haven't mentioned this to my dad yet."

"Why not?"

"I just found out yesterday. He'll ask me what I want to do, and like I said, I'm not sure."

"But he gives you a vote in your options?"

"Yes. What about you? Now that you've graduated, what are your plans?"

"Well, that's the reason I asked you to meet me."

Her stomach performed a hopeful summersault.

But as usual, he didn't elaborate. He just kept looking skyward.

"Boone? I'm lousy at guessing games, remember? So just tell me."

"I won't be here this summer because I joined the army."

Sierra gave him a ten-second pause and hip-checked him. "You have a bizarre sense of humor sometimes."

He faced her. "I'm not joking. I joined the army."

A sick feeling took root as she realized he was serious. Then she exploded. "Why would you just up and do that?"

"It wasn't an impulsive decision. I've been thinking about it for a while."

"How long?"

"Almost three years. Since my youth forestry counselor suggested it when I was sixteen."

And this was the first time he'd mentioned it? After all the time they'd spent together? "But we're at war! The military sends the newest recruits over there." Another horrible thought occurred to her. "You've got medical training, which means they'll put you on the first cargo plane and drop you right in the middle of a combat zone."

"Sierra. That's what I want."

"To get yourself killed?" she demanded.

"No, to help keep others from dying."

"But you do that every day as an EMT."

"It's not the same. I can't make a living as an EMT in rural Wyoming. I'm tired of being broke and there are a lot of things I'd like to do with my life that I can't do if I'm stuck here."

"Then go to college like normal people do."

Boone scowled at her. "If I don't have money for a car do you really think I've got money to go to college? Or that anyone will lend me the money?"

"Then we'll ask my dad. He'll float you a loan. Heck, he'd probably just give you the money since you saved my life."

He pushed off the car. "I don't want your money or your charity."

"What? I'm only trying to help. You took that the wrong way."

"Did I? What part of making it on my own is confusing to you? I have to do this. I *want* to do this."

"So there's no talking you out of it."

Boone shook his head. "It's a done deal."

She wanted to scream at him, throw herself at his feet and beg him not to go, but that was the epitome of childish. Instead, she tossed off a breezy, "Fine. Whatever. Go be a hero. Get yourself killed. Later." She sidestepped him and ducked around the front of the car, hoping to make it inside before her tears were obvious.

But he latched onto her upper arms and forced her to look at him. "You don't mean that."

"Yes, I do."

His gaze roamed over her face. "Then why are you crying?" he demanded softly.

"Because I hate that you're doing this stupid thing. And I hate you." The last word came out as a sob.

"No, baby, you don't."

"Don't call me that!"

"Sierra. Come here."

"No! Don't touch me."

"You don't mean that either." Boone crushed her to his chest.

Sierra fought him for a few seconds, swinging punches that didn't land, yelling and thrashing, but he just held on. She gave up fighting the pull of him and clung to him as she cried.

How many times had she imagined Boone holding her, stroking her hair and murmuring sweet things to her? Hundreds. But never like this.

Her voice was muffled against his chest when she finally spoke. "When do you go?"

"Tomorrow morning."

She froze. Then she squirmed away. "You're just telling me *now*? When did you sign up?"

Boone looked away.

"Tell me."

"Three days after your accident."

Sierra felt all the air leave her lungs. The blood drained from her face and she was drowning. Her lips formed the word *why*.

"Because that night at Tyler's party when I told him we were together? I wanted it to be real."

"You think I would've shot you down, Boone?"

"No." His eyes were locked on hers. "I know you would've said yes."

Her cheeks burned with mortification; he'd known how she felt all along.

"You understand my history. Since I was twelve years old I've been counting off the damn days until I can get the hell out of Wyoming. Last fall, the start of my senior year, I was taking the prep classes I needed and I was getting a year of practical experience as an EMT and moving on was finally within my grasp. And then you showed up.

"From the moment we met on the bus, you sucked me in. You were so gorgeous, feisty, funny and sweet—and so easy to talk to. I tried to stay away from you, but something about you, Sierra, just kept pulling me back."

She stared at him, absolutely speechless.

"That night at the party I wanted to kill Tyler for thinking he had the right to put his hands on you. After the accident, I about lost my fucking mind because you were hurt... That's when I knew you could keep me here. If I got involved with you, like I wanted to, I wouldn't leave. And I *have* to leave. I had to have a solid plan to go so I enlisted."

"No." Sierra found her voice and said it louder. "No." Then she was screaming at him. "No, no, no, no, no! You don't get to do this to me, Boone. You don't get to treat me like a friend, and then tell me you've always felt more for me...the night before you *fucking* leave! You don't get to make me feel guilty for you joining the army because I have some kind of magical hold over you. That's total bullshit and it's not fair!" God. This could not be happening.

"Not fair? You think this has been easy for me? Especially the last four months? When we've been together all the damn time because I couldn't stay the hell away from you? And I had to act like it's not fucking *killing* me when you look at me like your world would be perfect if I just kissed you."

She slapped her hands on his chest and shoved him. "The only thing you can kiss, Boone West, is my ass." She spun around and considered kicking over his stupid bike as she skirted the back end of her car. Jerk. Asshole. Jerkoff. Asshat. He wanted to leave her? Fine. He could leave her. She'd be better off.

Such a fucking liar you are, Sierra.

"So that's it?" Boone shouted. "That's how you're gonna say goodbye to me?"

Sierra whipped a U-turn and marched back up to him. "How did you expect I'd say goodbye? Strip my clothes off and let you take my virginity in a field of wildflowers under a full moon? Screw that. I'm saving my virginity for someone who deserves it. And. That. Is. Not.

You." She punctuated each word with a poke on his hard chest.

Boone said, "You do that," in a throaty rasp she'd never heard from him. "In the meantime, I'm taking this." He wrapped one hand around the back of her neck and clamped the other on her butt, pulling her in for a kiss.

She should've shoved him away. But his kiss was like a drug. Intense, determined, amazingly seductive—as if he was trying to convince her that his passion for her was real. That he'd been imagining this kiss for as long as she had. That he'd wanted it as much. Mouths and tongues clashed and she slipped her arms around his waist, her hands clutching his shirt.

The kiss was beyond anything she'd ever experienced. Rough and sexy, bringing alive things inside her she'd heard about but had never felt.

Then Boone slowed it down. The kiss became soft. An unhurried tease, as if they had all the time in the world to explore. To learn each other.

But they didn't. By this time tomorrow, he'd be gone.

Sierra kept kissing him even as her tears fell.

Then Boone's hands were on her face, trying to wipe away the moisture but her tears ran over his fingers.

He moved his mouth back; she felt his lips against hers and his breath in her mouth as he whispered, "Sierra. Baby, please don't cry." He planted tender smooches on her lips. His mouth wandered down her neck and her entire body erupted in goose flesh. He nuzzled the sweep of her shoulder and stopped, breathing against her skin.

She had to bite her lip to keep from sobbing when he strung soft kisses along her collarbone, right where the injury had hurt the most. But that pain was nothing compared to the pain she felt now.

Boone's fingers entwined in her hair and he tipped her head back. His beautiful eyes were dark with remorse and something else, something that made her pulse quicken. "I knew it'd be like this between us."

"But it's still not enough."

He didn't answer. He just consumed her mouth again.

While kissing him was better than she'd dreamed, she still felt like someone was stabbing her in the gut with a rusty knife as Boone took the kiss deeper until she feared she'd never get out.

She broke away, resting her forehead to his.

"Sierra—"

"Don't say anything."

They stayed like that for a long time. Not looking at each other, clinging to each other, so close but so far apart.

She whispered, "I have to go."

"Not like this."

"There's no other way. This was your choice."

He placed one last soft kiss on her lips.

Sierra pulled away from him. "Goodbye, Boone."

"See you around, McKay." His hands fell away.

Sierra didn't look at him. Not even in her rearview mirror as she bumped over the cattle guard and drove away.

Chapter Thirty-Eight

Ben and Quinn had enlisted Gavin's help moving cow/calf pairs from one pasture to another. Helping wasn't entirely accurate—he'd been designated the gate opener. But it'd been a great morning. Cruising around on four wheelers and watching his brothers work cattle. Listening to Charlie tell stories.

He climbed out of his Lexus, in desperate need to ditch his dirty clothes and hit the shower, when Rielle yelled at him from the closest garden. He met her halfway down the road and stole a kiss. "Hey, sexy lady. What's up?"

"Have you talked to Sierra today? She swore she wanted to help me and I haven't seen her."

"No. But it's summer vacation. She mentioned it was her right to sleep in until noon, at least the first week." He couldn't believe how early the school year ended in Wyoming. In Arizona, Sierra would be in school at least another month. "I'll check on her."

After brushing off the ever-present dust, he scaled the stairs and knocked on Sierra's door. "Sweetheart? Are you up?" He heard a thump. But no answer. Then another thump. He turned the handle and opened the door.

Boxes were stacked beside her bed. Everything had been stripped off the walls. She stood by the closet, dumping winter clothes into a box.

"I told you not to come in without knocking first," she snapped.

"I knocked. You didn't answer." His gaze moved over the organized destruction. "Are you planning to redecorate?"

"No. Just getting ready to leave."

"Leave?"

Sierra whirled around. "Yes, leave. I'm done with the living-in-Wyoming experiment."

Gavin stepped in the room, avoiding a pile of papers. "Whoa. You want to rewind and tell me what's going on?"

She crossed her arms. Her face distorted into the sneer that indicated he'd just entered the battle zone. "Whoa? Enough with the fake-cowboy shtick, Dad. It's embarrassing."

He ignored the verbal jab. "What are you talking about, going home?"

"I promised you I'd stick it out an entire school year. School ended. You promised me if I hated it we could go home. I freakin' hate it here and I cannot wait to get back where I belong."

"Now wait just a damn minute. Nothing was set in stone. We were going to discuss it."

"Nothing to discuss. I held up my end of the deal, it's time for you to hold up yours."

"What the hell happened? You didn't hate Wyoming two damn days ago. I don't get where this is coming from, so will you please explain it to me?"

"No. My mind is made up."

"You change your mind about everything, Sierra. So you have to give me more than, *I hate Wyoming I want to go home.*"

She glared at him.

"Really? I'm just supposed to drop everything and move back to Arizona because you want to?"

"You made me drop everything to move to Wyoming. How is this any different?"

"It's a helluva lot different." *Do not remind her you're the adult and you make the decisions. Take a different tack.* "You want to tell me what happened to you in the last day? Because this change of heart or mind, or whatever, came completely out of left field."

She vehemently shook her head. "If you think this is sudden then you haven't been paying attention. But that's not a surprise since most your time is spent with Rielle."

"You're really going there, Sierra? Making Rielle the root cause of your problem?"

Her cheeks colored with guilt. But that didn't keep her from snapping back, "Rielle *is* the cause of this problem—your problem—you don't want to leave Wyoming because of her, which is not *my* problem."

His daughter had him there.

"Anyway I thought she was building a new house so she didn't have to live with us."

"Plans change. She's living with us permanently."

"And you didn't even think to tell me about that? Great. Well, it doesn't matter because I won't stay here and you can't make me."

"What are you going to do? Drive to Scottsdale by yourself? You certainly can't live there by yourself."

"You're forgetting Scottsdale isn't my only option."

His stomach pitched.

"Mom has been asking what my plan is for the summer."

"Why is this the first I've heard of it?"

"Maybe because you only hear what you wanna hear," she shot

back.

Hadn't Rielle accused him of the same thing? "I would've remembered that. What did your mother—"

"Are you going to move us back to Arizona or not?" she interrupted.

"I have to decide right now? Then fine. No. This is ridiculous, Sierra. Let's just take a step back and discuss this rationally."

"No. I haven't seen my mom in almost six months. I miss her. I want to be with my mom. You don't care about that at all. You hate her and you're trying to keep me away from her." She started to cry. "I don't want to be here anymore. I hate it here."

"Sierra. Don't."

"I can't help it! If you don't move us back to Arizona, I'm moving to France. And not just for the summer."

His heart nearly stopped. "What? How did this go from you spending the summer in France to you living there for the entire school year?"

"Mom's boyfriend is staying there two more years and he bought a house."

"Your mom will be living in Paris two more years?"

Sierra nodded. "Do you think it's fair that I'll hardly get to see my mom at all in the next two years?"

"Moving was her choice," Gavin pointed out.

"For a year. I know the custody agreement gets reviewed after my birthday. So if I tell Mom I want to live with her, you know she'll fight to make that happen."

And Ellen would win for all the reasons Sierra had just given him.

A profound sense of grief choked him. He managed to eke out, "Why are you doing this to me? To hurt me?" He swallowed. "Guess what, it's working."

"Dad, it doesn't have to be like that. Let's just go back to Arizona. Please."

Gavin stared at his child; she was nearly unrecognizable in this state. Beyond stubborn. Almost wild with the need to get her own way. And she always did. He could see everything that he'd ever done for her wasn't enough. It'd never be enough. In that instant he saw her resemblance to Ellen and it made him nauseous. But how much was his responsibility for letting her become this way?

"This discussion is far from over. And don't think for a second you get to make this decision. I do. Don't call your mother. I mean it. And I suggest you steer clear of me until I've had time to think this through."

"But Dad—"

"I mean it, Sierra. You need to back off and leave me the hell alone."

Thirty minutes in the shower did nothing to clear his head.

It wasn't yet noon and he needed a stiff drink.

So he poured himself one.

How had he ever thought he'd escape this issue? If someone held a gun to his head and made him answer if Sierra was miserable here, his answer would be no. Living around his family had changed his life. All he'd had in Arizona was his business and his daughter. Looking ahead, in two years Sierra would be in college and he'd be alone. The daily parenting part of his life would be over. That thought had always scared him.

Now when he looked ahead to the future, he didn't see emptiness. He saw Rielle.

He knew Rielle loved him. But how would that change if he walked away? If only for Sierra's sake, if only for two years?

Rielle would feel like his second choice. That no matter what, he'd always put his daughter before her. She deserved better than that.

But how could he, in good conscience, send Sierra off to France? Two weeks with her mother in Arizona had put her right back on the edge of that destructive path. Sierra had taken full advantage of her mother's need to prove that she was young, hip and cool.

If he returned to Arizona, he could monitor his daughter for the next two years. Make sure she was being responsible in all aspects of her life. Sierra could choose the college that best suited her, rather than having limited choices because she pissed away two years in another country.

Did he let his daughter go and let her make her own mistakes?

Vi popped into his head. Although she avoided calling his birth a mistake, it was. A mistake that changed the course of her young life.

Would he really have to choose between the stability of his daughter's life and his life with Rielle?

Rielle's arms came around him and he jumped.

"Sorry. I thought you heard me come in."

"No." He sipped his drink.

"You never came back outside."

"Ran into a little problem with Sierra." He grunted. "Scratch that. A huge fucking problem."

"What's going on?"

"When we moved here last year, in a moment of guilt, much like promising her a car, I told Sierra if she hated it, we'd return to Arizona."

Rielle stiffened behind him. "You told her that?"

"Promised her that, actually."

Her hold tightened on him. "Oh, Gavin."

The words weren't meant to chastise him, but somehow they did. "School is out. Sierra has decided she's had enough of Wyoming and is holding me to my promise...by way of a threat. If I refuse to move back to Arizona, she'll go to France and live with her mother. We revisit the custody agreement this month after Sierra turns seventeen. I know the judge will favor reverting custody to Ellen, given the lack of contact between her and Sierra in the last year. Sierra has a voice in the decision and she will side with her mother."

Rielle was quiet. Too quiet. Then she said, "What are you going to do?"

He drained his whiskey and set aside the empty glass. "No idea."

She stepped in front of him. "Gavin. Think about this. You're giving Sierra all the power here. She's a sixteen-year-old girl. Can you imagine how difficult she'll be from here on out if you give in to her threat? You're her parent. Not her puppet. She's a child and she's got way too much control."

"She's had control of me since the minute she was born."

"No. She's had your love and support since the minute she was born. There's a big difference."

"I will lose any influence I have over her if I let her move to France. I'll lose her." That caused an acute ache. "I can't imagine her not being in my life every day."

"Then you have made your decision," she stated softly.

"No." He pulled her to him. "I love you. We have a life here. A life I'm happy with. I don't want to lose you either."

"But you will."

That startled him. "I will what? Lose you?"

"Yes. I love you. I'm grateful that you're in my life. But if you decide to go back to Arizona...then this won't work. You can assure me it's only for two years until she graduates from high school, but you're hoping Sierra goes to ASU. Can you really see yourself leaving Phoenix if she's still living there? What if she picks a college in California? Will you stay in Phoenix the next four years because it's so much closer than Wyoming? If Sierra needs you, you can hop on a plane and be at her side in an hour."

"You really think I'd drop everything to be at her beck and call?"

"Don't you now?"

"That's not fair. You know you're the same way with Rory."

Rielle shook her head.

"You didn't drop everything when she called you last fall, so stressed out about school?"

"That was different. Rory is an adult. She needs me when she has the occasional breakdown, not every day like Sierra still needs you."

"Okay then. Move to Arizona with me. If you love me and you don't need to be in Wyoming because Rory is here. We'll find a place with gardens and you can grow exotic chili peppers. After Sierra graduates, we can return here."

"Move to Arizona? Really, Gavin? How am I supposed to make a living there? You expect me to just walk away from the business I've built the last fifteen years? It's taken me a long time to get to the point that I'm not starving."

"You wouldn't have to work, Ree. You could take a couple of years off. Do things because they interest you, not because you have to."

"I love the way I live my life and how I make my living. You accepted that about me. I wouldn't work this hard if I didn't love it and I know I'd miss it."

"Would you miss me if I wasn't here?"

"Yes."

Gavin touched her cheek. "Can't we start there and find a way to make us work?"

"I don't see how. This is a lose-lose situation for both of us. I won't go to Arizona. And if you don't go, you'll resent me for making you choose."

"So what you're telling me is if I'm willing to compromise for us to be together, that's fine. But when I ask you to compromise, well, no way."

"That's an oversimplified statement," she argued. "Because the move to Arizona wouldn't be based on mutual compromise. The move would be because your daughter threatened you into a decision you didn't want to make."

Was that really how she saw the situation? Sierra throwing a fit and him just giving in?

Wasn't that what was happening?

Rielle retreated. "I love you. I never thought a man like you would ever love me. We've had similar parenting styles with our only children. But I'm telling you...please don't make my mistake. I didn't see myself as anything but a parent to Rory until I met you. You gave me love and worth as a woman—as your woman. It was hard to tell my daughter, who, yes, had me at her beck and call even as an adult, that I deserved a life outside of being her mother. I've embraced it and she didn't like the change but she's accepted it. I didn't have the guts to do that until you came into my life and changed it completely for the better. So don't wait until Sierra is twenty-four to come to the same realization."

Gavin was too stunned to say anything as she walked out and quietly closed the door.

Chapter Thirty-Nine

Rory knew the instant she'd talked to her mom yesterday that something was wrong. Like horribly wrong.

She assumed that fucking McKay bastard had done exactly what she feared—ripped her mom's heart out and run over it with his goddamned Lexus. So she'd been shocked to hear the McKay male wasn't causing the problem, but his precious spawn.

At first her stubborn mother stayed true to her decision to exclude Rory from issues in her relationship with Gavin. But she wasn't deterred. She adopted her mother's soothing style of extracting information and her mom finally broke down.

And Rory had broken down too, silently, on the other end of the phone because she grasped her mom's dilemma. If the situations had been reversed and Rory had made those demands? Her mom would've sided with her—seen to her child's needs above her own without question. Even right now when her mom was miserable, she wouldn't fault Gavin if he chose his daughter over her. But hearing her mother cry...Rory wanted to hop in her truck and kick some serious McKay ass—starting with Sierra's.

But she'd promised to cover her co-worker's bar shift last night and she hadn't left for Sundance until early this morning.

Upon arriving home, Rory parked her truck at her cabin and skulked through the trees, avoiding her mom as she made a beeline for the house.

Gavin wasn't around. Good. That might've been awkward, him asking what she was doing there and her answering...*I'm here to bust Sierra's balls.*

Rory knocked on Sierra's door, but didn't allow the girl a chance to deny her entrance so she barged right in.

Sierra sat on her bed, earbuds jammed in her ears and the music cranked so loud Rory heard it by the door. Sierra's head was back, her eyes closed. A notebook sat on her lap with words scrawled across the page.

Rory recognized heartbreak when she saw it. Grabbing the footboard, she jostled the bed.

Sierra's eyes flew open. She scrambled out of her slouch, wiped her eyes and pulled out her earbuds. "Rory? What are you doing here?"

"Came to see my mom. She's busy making hay while the sun shines, so I thought I'd grab you and we'd go get ice cream or French fries or something equally junky."

"I'm not really hungry."

"I am. Let's go. You can keep me company while I eat."

"Rory. I'm not dressed, I'm in a shitty mood and I just wanna be left alone."

"Tough shit and toughen up, little sister." She jostled the bed frame again. "Move it."

Sierra tossed her iPod aside. "What is your problem?"

"You are, Little Miss Mopey Face. You're hunched up in your bed, acting like your pet hamster died and I'm PMS-ing for chocolate and grease. I've never ridden in your fancy-ass new ride, and since I know how much you *love* to drive, I'm telling you to get up and chauffer me around, be-yotch."

"You are such a pain in the ass."

"Yeah? What's your point?"

"Fine. Give me a fucking minute."

Rory chattered about bullshit on the way to town. College and bartending and guys that'd been sniffing around. Sierra was occupied with driving so she was only half-listening anyway and didn't suspect a thing.

At Dairy Queen, Rory went inside to order since Sierra refused to go through the drive-thru. An extra-large fry and two gigantic mocha Moo-lattes later, Rory directed Sierra to drive to Flat Top. If she thought it weird two girls were headed to the local make-out spot, she didn't mention it.

They sat on the bench overlooking the deep, red-rock rimmed canyon, with prairie on one side and Devil's Tower on the other. Once they demolished the order of fries—so much for Sierra not being hungry—Rory broached the subject.

"So. I guess you won't be round much longer, huh?"

Sierra glanced at her sharply and then suspiciously. "Did your mom put you up to this?"

"Put me up to what? Gorging ourselves on junk food? My mom is the prophet of healthy eating, remember?"

"No, did she ask you to take me aside and talk me out of it?"

"Talk you out of what? Holding a knife to your dad's throat and insisting he do what you want?"

"My dad said something to you," Sierra accused.

"I'll admit to shock when I called my mom yesterday and she was sobbing so hard I couldn't understand her."

All the blood drained from Sierra's face. "What? Rielle was crying?"

"No, sobbing. Like her heart was breaking and she couldn't get enough air. There's a difference between sobbing and merely crying. I'm sure you know that."

Sierra squirmed. "Did she tell you why?"

"Some. That your dad was probably leaving her and here for good."

"He doesn't have to," Sierra protested. "He can stay here with Rielle if he wants."

"But if he does, you'll punish him by moving to France with your mother," Rory pointed out.

"He promised me if I didn't like it here we could go home."

What a little shit. So self-righteous and involved in her stupid teenage dramas that she couldn't see the aftershocks of stamping her foot and demanding her way. Rory had been that girl too. But she'd be damned if she'd stand by and watch it happen. Her mother had put aside her own life for years to make sure Rory's life was happy. It was time to pay it back.

Rory got right in her face. "You are such a fucking brat, Sierra, I can't even believe it."

Sierra reared back, completely floored.

"Your dad has done *everything* for you, sacrificed any kind of personal life, selflessly put up with his ex-wife because he wouldn't deny you a relationship with your mother. And now, when he's finally found happiness, when he's found a woman he loves and who loves him back, when he's building relationships with the family he didn't know he had...you're gonna pull the fucking rug out from under him? You're essentially saying, *Daddy, your life is solely devoted to seeing that my needs are being fully met, one hundred percent of the time and I don't give a shit about anything else but getting my own way.*"

"That's not true!"

"That is *so* fucking true it makes me sick. You wouldn't think twice about ruining his relationship with my mom. You'd do it, devastating two people, and then it'd be out of sight, out of mind as you flit off and get your damn nails done."

Sierra leapt to her feet. "Where the fuck do you get off saying that shit to me? You were a total brat to your mom when you found out about her and my dad. You threw a little baby tantrum and stormed off, remember?"

"Yes, I was upset, but not because our parents were together. It was something entirely personal on my part and I had to do a shit ton of soul searching to figure out why I felt that way. And I did. Then I mended the rift in my relationship with my mom. I apologized to her. I asked for her forgiveness. I told her I wanted her to be happy because she deserved it. And I meant it. Oh, and I also apologized to your dad."

"So I'm just supposed to suck it up and be miserable for the next two fucking years until I can escape this godforsaken place and go to college?"

"Stop blaming the way you feel because you're hating on Wyoming. I know you were just as miserable in Arizona, no matter how you try to paint the desert with rainbows and butterflies."

"How do you know?"

"Sierra. You told me."

"When?"

"You called me late one night in January. Crying about not fitting in anywhere. You said it didn't matter where you lived, it was always the same."

Sierra looked away. "I'd been drinking."

"Probably. But it doesn't make the things you told me any less true," she said gently. "And I don't think moving to France will change anything. Except you'll be stuck in a foreign country where you don't speak the language, with no escape. You will have to live with your impulsive, spiteful decision. And I ain't gonna lie. Part of me hopes you make that choice. A dose of reality would do you good because you don't understand how good you have it right now."

Sierra paced, acting as if she was contemplating Rory's words. "You really think my dad will decide to stay here?"

"I hope so. For my mom's sake and for his." Rory watched Sierra, so torn; she knew something else was at play. "What happened in the last couple of days that made you so eager to leave Sundance immediately?"

She bit her lip and studied the ground.

"Were you bullied by girls at school? Verbally harassed or physically assaulted or threatened?"

She shook her head.

An awful thought occurred to her and it wouldn't go away. "Did a guy touch you in a way you didn't want to be touched? Or force you? Because if that happened, we can get you help—"

"I wasn't raped or anything like that."

"Thank God." Rory exhaled. "I didn't want to push you, but I know you're holding something back and I was really scared that's what it was."

"Why?"

"Because, like you reminded me a few months back, there is some stuff we can't talk about with our parents, no matter how much we should. I suspect you don't have many people you can talk to if you're calling me."

Rory waited for Sierra to speak. When several minutes passed and she stayed mum, she pushed her. "Sierra. What's really going on?

What couldn't you tell your dad?"

Sierra had closed herself off, wrapping her arms around her upper body. "I have—had—two people I can talk to. Marin. But she's staying at her grandma's. The other person I could talk to? He left yesterday morning."

Sierra had only ever mentioned one guy. "Boone?"

She nodded.

Well that explained a lot. "What happened?"

"He joined the army. We've hung out so many times and he never..." She cleared her throat. "Then after he told me he was leaving, he said all these things to me...how he felt about me—which I didn't know—and he kissed me."

"And?"

"And he left and it hurts! It pisses me off and I can't stop crying. I want to leave. I want to put him behind me, put this whole year behind me and start over."

"But you wouldn't be starting over if you went back to Arizona," Rory pointed out. "Do you think you could start over in France?"

She sniffled. "I don't know. I don't know anything. I'm so confused."

Rory let her settle before she spoke. "Can I give you some advice, little sister?"

"I guess."

"Change yourself, not your location."

Sierra looked up. "What?"

"You *let* things happen to you instead of making them happen for you."

"How do you know?"

"Because I'm the same way. Or I was. You didn't confront your dad about the stuff that was bugging you last fall. You made me do it. I went through this too, learning to be assertive without changing who you are inside, so listen to me." Rory tucked a strand of hair behind Sierra's ear. "You're a fun, smart, funny and sweet girl—when you're not being a total brat."

Sierra gave her a watery smile.

"For some reason, you hide that. Don't. Be proud of who you are." Then Rory laughed.

"What?"

"I just realized I'm telling you to act like a McKay."

Tears shimmered in Sierra's eyes again.

What was up with that?

"You don't need a pack of friends, okay? If you have one good friend, one you can talk to, one who can talk to you, one you have fun with...then count yourself blessed. There are a lot of lonely people in the world who don't even have that, to say nothing of all the people you have in your life who love you. The McKays may annoy me to no freakin' end, but if you called any of them and told them you were having troubles, they'd all be there for you in a heartbeat. I think you know that."

A full minute passed before Sierra spoke. "So if you were me, Rory, what would you do?"

"I know what I *wouldn't* do."

"What?"

"Let Boone West or the memory of Boone West fuck up my life any more than he already has. Move on. Use his leaving as a chance to make yourself stronger, not let it weaken you further."

"You sound just like your mom."

"And that is the best compliment you could ever give me."

Sierra paced in her room after her conversation with Rory. She hadn't seen her dad since the blowup yesterday morning and she missed him.

You'll miss him a lot more if you move to France.

As soon as he'd walked out, telling her that he didn't want to deal with her, Sierra knew she'd screwed up bad. Like usual, she'd said the first shitty thing that popped into her head. Lashing out because *she* hurt. Knowing exactly what to say to her dad to make *him* hurt. Twisting the circumstances—not telling her dad the real reason she wanted to leave because he wouldn't understand.

After what'd happened with Boone, she'd spent the whole night cursing him, cursing herself, cursing this stupid town. She'd called her mom and cried for over an hour, telling her about Boone—things she'd never told anyone. And her mom had been so sweet, not offering some snarky advice but really listening to her. Then her mom urged her to visit her in France, not in her usual manipulative way, but because she missed her daughter and then Sierra couldn't see anything beyond just getting the hell out of Wyoming.

Her mom had no idea she'd given her dad an ultimatum. Now she'd dug herself into a hole. She couldn't march into her dad's office and say, "Just kidding! I don't want to go back to Arizona... By the way, what's for supper?"

This time she'd gone beyond crying to get her way. This time her rash response was having life changing repercussions because hers wasn't the only life that would be affected.

She flopped on the bed and stared at the ceiling.

Every sickening thing Rory had thrown at her was true. But Rory was mistaken if she believed Sierra hadn't already recognized those nasty truths about her childish behavior. But she was stuck. She couldn't talk to her dad. And she was so embarrassed by what she'd said and done that she just wanted to hide in her room and hope all this shit blew over.

It'd serve her right if her dad called her bluff and shipped her off to France.

Her mom would be happy. She'd sent Sierra three emails in the last day, begging her to come and stay in Paris. One thing she hadn't lied about during the big blow up was that she missed her mom. Yes, sometimes her mom acted ridiculously self-centered—now Sierra understood where that trait came from in her own knee-jerk responses—but other times, her mom was thoughtful, honest and helpful and she understood her in ways that her dad never would.

Divorce sucked. It'd turned her dad completely against her mom. He always pointed out her mother's worst qualities and didn't see her good side. He claimed she didn't *have* a good side but it was there. Maybe Sierra wished it were there more often, but it was there.

Her stomach growled. She hadn't eaten anything except French fries and a bag of chips she'd found during her packing frenzy. But she was too much of a chickenshit to go into the kitchen in case she ran into Rielle. What could she possibly say to her after what she'd done? Thinking about it made her sick to her stomach all over again.

Her cell phone buzzed on her desk and she rolled to her feet. Why was Marin was calling her? "Hello?"

"What the fuck, Sierra? I get a text from you that says you're moving? What's that bullshit about?"

"What? I didn't send you a text!"

"Uh, *yeah* you did. Two hours ago. It says, and I quote, *please try and talk me out of moving away forever.*"

Rory. That sneaky bitch. She'd asked to see Sierra's iPhone under the pretext of buying one and used it to send Marin a text.

"So tell me what's going on."

"It's a big mess, Marin. It's my fault and I don't know where to start. I don't know if I can fix it." She started to cry again. "I just…"

"Stop crying. Get in your car and meet me at the football field."

Sierra sniffled. "What? I thought you were at your grandma's?"

"Do you really think I could stay there after my best friend texted me that she's moving away? I oughta bitch slap you for even thinking I wouldn't care."

That brought tears to her eyes. "I'm sorry."

"I still may bitch slap you. And you cannot move away. We have plans for junior year, remember?"

"What? Uh. No. I think you made plans."

"Which always includes *you,* duh. Anyway, get to the football field." The line cut out but Marin's next words were loud and clear. "Friends help each other out. They listen to each other. They're there for each other. Whatever happened...we'll find a way to fix it."

Sierra didn't get her hopes up about that, but she snuck out of the house and drove into town anyway.

Chapter Forty

Gavin needed someone to talk to.

He wasn't quite sure why Vi was the first person who'd come to mind. Maybe because her kids were grown and she'd lived through the turbulent teen years. Maybe because she'd listen and offer her unvarnished advice.

Or maybe because she's your mother.

She met him on the porch. She wore a straw hat, her *World's Greatest Grandma* sweatshirt from Sierra and jeans—which shocked him. He'd never seen Vi in jeans.

She inspected him head to toe. "At least you're wearing decent shoes. I thought we could walk a bit."

"Where we going?"

"To my favorite thinking spot." She laughed when Gavin wrinkled his nose. "Cow shit will wash right off those loafers."

"Good to know."

She sobered quickly. "Gavin. Sweetheart. You look like hell."

"Feel like it too."

She handed him a bottle of water. "Follow me."

They cut through the first pasture and followed the fence line up a steep incline. Gavin found himself studying the ground, seeing the variances in grass and the occasional wildflower. Gray rocks popped up and sagebrush abounded. But the only scent carried on the wind was manure and a hint of Vi's perfume.

They stopped at the apex of the rise. The land spread out in a carpet of green, which he knew would only last a few more weeks if it didn't rain soon. The view wasn't a breathtaking vista. No steep canyons. Just a view of rangeland. Simple. Timeless.

Two chunks of rock, embedded in the earth about six feet apart rose up like stone pillars. The heights were nearly identical and someone had placed a foot wide piece of wood across the top.

"So, you come here often?"

Vi snorted. "Often enough. Something about this place helps me sort stuff out." She uncapped her water bottle and drank. "I figured it might work for you too. So, son, you wanna tell me what's going on?"

Gavin intended to give her the basics. But for some reason, everything just poured out. Everything he was thinking, feeling and he didn't bother to filter any of it.

She mulled over his words for a good long while before she said, "Well, that's a bit of a shocker."

"To say it's knocked me on my ass is putting it mildly."

"I assume you're talking to me about this because you want my...insight?"

"Yeah."

"Okay. Sierra has overstepped her bounds. But she won't see it that way."

"Why not?"

"Because she's used to getting her way. Is she forcing this on you maliciously? No. She is a sweet girl. I wouldn't be surprised if she didn't know she'd done anything wrong. Teens are notoriously self-absorbed. Her rationalization is that this behavior has always gotten her what she wants in the past and she doesn't know any other way to be at sixteen. However, she is using manipulation and you cannot give in to it."

Gavin faced her to argue.

"Hear me out completely before you jump in. You're a good father. But that is not all you are. You are a good man who deserves what you've found with Rielle." She smiled a little devilishly. "Between us? For a few years I thought Ben and Rielle would get together. Until I realized she'd never let him boss her around the way he likes to."

He choked on his water.

Vi patted him on the back. "You and Rielle complement each other. You're both stubborn enough and set enough in your ways that you won't settle for the first warm body that walks through your door. I've known Rielle a lot of years. She was content. But when I see her with you? She's happy in a way I haven't seen. You, my dear boy, are the same way with her. Why on earth would you give that up?"

"I don't want to."

"Then it's simple. Don't. Tell Sierra you're sorry she's so miserable here and you only want her happiness. So if that means her skipping off to France, then *bon voyage.*"

Somehow he kept his jaw from dropping. "You think it's that easy?"

"Heavens no. But she's the one who put you in this position. Remember she's not making it easy on you. She'll make mistakes whether she's here, Arizona, France or Timbuktu. Some you'll even know about. You can't protect her from everything. And she'll never learn to protect herself if you're always there to do it for her." Vi took a long pull from her water bottle. "Does that sound harsh? Who would ship a sixteen-year-old off to handle things by herself?"

Light bulb moment. "Your father did."

"That wasn't a parallel I was trying to make, believe it or not. Your biggest worry is that Sierra will go off the rails in France if you're not there to stop the train. Don't look at it that way. Look at it as you're telling her that yes, if she really wants to go to France, then you're trusting her to make the right choices once she gets there."

In that moment, a huge weight fell off his shoulders.

"You'll miss her. That's part of the guilt. The other part is that you're consciously choosing to do something that'll be good for you at the expense of what might be best for your child. I'm pretty sure that's a brand new feeling for you."

"I don't know if I can live with either decision."

"Oh, I know how that feels, trust me."

Gavin took a breath to ask the question Vi had been expecting for a long time. "Do you regret your decision to give me up for adoption?"

"Every single day of my life. Would I do things differently?" Vi looked right into his eyes. "No."

That answer didn't sting as much as he thought it would. "Why?"

"Because I would've been a terrible mother at that time in my life. As much as I ached that you were gone, I would've resented you if you'd been there." Vi reached for his hand. "Can you imagine Sierra with a baby right now?"

He'd tried to look at it from that angle and the image never jelled. He shook his head.

"As irresponsible as you think Sierra acts sometimes? Multiply that by ten and you'll get me—Violet Louise Bennett—at that age. A naïve rebel. Sneaking out at night, gloating I was oh-so-mature having sex with an older guy like Charlie McKay. Then the next morning after my secret rendezvous? My mother had my breakfast on the table. My lunch packed for school. She'd probably ironed my clothes. I was a *child.* I had no idea how to be a mother because I didn't *see* my mother. She was there to do things for me. So I'll admit, it was selfish of me to give you up. But at that time in my life? I didn't know any other way to be."

An almost thoughtful silence lingered between them.

"So you don't blame your father?" Gavin asked.

"There is that...side of the issue. Yes, my father made the decision to send me to the unwed mother's home. He knew once I was living with other girls in my condition, I'd follow the herd mentality. And I did. But that just strengthens my point. I didn't have a backbone to stand up for myself, let alone stand up for a child I'd be responsible for, for the next eighteen or so years."

Gavin blew out a breath. "I'll admit I thought of you the day Sierra was born. Not in a good way. I wondered what type of woman could look at a baby and say, *take it away, I don't want it.*"

"I don't know what to say to that. I don't know if I can ever explain my mindset at that time to your satisfaction, Gavin. Adopted kids, no matter how happy their childhoods with their adoptive parents, are resentful on some level. I talked to a counselor about that when I needed an unbiased opinion on how to handle you either being in our lives or not being in our lives."

"You saw a counselor?"

"Yes. This hasn't been easy on me, or on your father. Let me ask you a hypothetical question. If you would've tracked me down and discovered I'd married another man, and had children with him, would you feel differently? Instead of knowing I went back to your father and had three other sons with him?"

"Probably. Because I'm odd man out in any family situation."

"Maybe it feels like that to you, but it doesn't to the rest of us. Especially not to me. I finally feel like my family is complete."

Gavin processed that. His family had accepted him with open arms and hearts. He liked them and his life was better for all of them being part of it. He didn't want to give that up either.

"I know you're wondering how this situation with Sierra popped up from out of nowhere. I think I can shed some light on that."

"Really? Did she call you?"

"No, I talked to Carolyn today and she mentioned that Boone West just up and joined the army. He left for basic training yesterday."

"Shit." Gavin briefly closed his eyes. "Now it makes sense. She met Boone the night before last. The next morning she was packed and ready to go."

"Boone must've told her that night he was leaving."

"But why would she throw her life into upheaval over some boy?" *Why wouldn't she tell me?*

Vi patted his leg. "Gavin. Sweetie. You aren't that clueless. Think about what you just said."

He frowned. "But she and Boone weren't even dating."

"That doesn't mean Sierra didn't feel something for him. Something big. Something that crushed her entire world when he took it away."

"Like...love? For Christsake. She's sixteen years old! How can she possibly know what real and lasting love is at that age?"

Vi remained quiet and a little stoic.

Gavin knew he'd stepped in it. "I'm sorry. I don't get it. I never had that feeling until Rielle."

"You didn't feel that way about Ellen when you first met her?"

"I don't remember. What happened after we got married tainted any good memories I had of her or us." Gavin let out a slow breath. "Can you please explain this to me?"

"No, sweetie, I can't. Because no matter how well I explain it, you've never experienced it so you won't understand. I knew Charlie was the one for me at that same age. Charlie knew I was the one for him. Same with Quinn and Libby. To some extent, it's the same with Tell and Georgia. The gut feeling that you've met the person who is the one for you is powerful and it's very real.

"So it's more than Sierra throwing her life and everyone else's into upheaval over *some boy*. She's devastated in a way you can't understand. Not only has she lost him, she's lost the potential of anything ever happening between them. It's not trivial to her. So please, whatever you decide to do, don't discount how serious this is to her. If you do, it will change your relationship with her—not in a good way. Especially since she hasn't felt comfortable telling you the real reason for wanting to leave."

"What am I supposed to do?"

"Love her. But be ready to let her go. She'll come back to you."

Gavin impulsively gave her a hug. "Thanks. You have no idea how much it means...how much I..." *Just tell her.* "You've been there for me every time I've needed you in the last year and you didn't have to be."

Vi smiled. "I am a little persistent."

"I'm sorry I've been an ass to you. And I appreciate that you don't let my shitty behavior slide. Christ, I'm a grown man who's supposed to know better. Then I hear my mom's voice in my head telling me to knock it off. I think the reason I'm so reserved with you is I'm constantly reminding myself that I can't like you because it feels disloyal to my mother."

"I know you were close to her, Gavin, and I'm not looking to replace her. That's never been my intent. She raised you to be a good man. That was all her doing. I'm grateful to her, because she loved you enough to send you back to us."

That choked him up a little.

She sighed. "So where does this leave us now that we've had this overdue discussion?"

"We can move on. The truth is I like you, Vi. A lot. I'm glad you're in my life. Charlie too. So I'm, ah...working on the loving you part, okay?"

"Okay. In the meantime I'll love you enough for both of us." She patted his cheek. "Let's stop with this mushy stuff. Let's go back to the house. I baked a pie in my new oven."

"Homemade crust?"

She peered over the tops of her glasses. "Not on your life."

Gavin tracked Rielle to the garden. But she wasn't on her hands and knees in the dirt. She rested her forearms across the top of the fence and stared at the recently planted alfalfa field across the road.

He took a moment just to watch her, the beautiful, amazing woman he'd fallen in love with. He'd made his decision after talking to Vi, but being here, seeing her, just cemented it.

Rielle finally noticed him. She smiled uncertainly. "Hey."

"Hey." He walked to the fence. "I missed you."

"I've missed you too."

"Have you immersed yourself in dirt therapy?"

"I've been trying to...but even that isn't working. I've been wandering. Aimlessly."

"Is that why you seem lost in thought?"

"Maybe I'm just feeling a little lost."

"Ree. Honey. I've always been a little lost...and then I found you."

Her gaze bored into his. "You've made a decision."

Gavin didn't see a reason to drag it out. "Yes. I'm staying in Wyoming."

"Did you tell Sierra?"

He shook his head. "I wanted you to know first. So you understand you're my first choice. Not out of guilt or manipulation, but out of love. We have something I never thought I'd find and I'm not walking away from it. I'm not walking away from you."

She slapped her dusty gloves on his cheeks. "You're serious? I..." She took a breath. "You should know I was out there wrestling with whether I could leave the only place I've ever known and move to Arizona. And the answer was yes." She pressed her mouth to his so decisively he had to grin. "I would've gone to be with you. This chunk of dirt has mattered to me for so long, but it's nothing compared to how much you matter to me."

"God, woman, you undo me." He touched her dirt-smudged cheek. "However, since we're agreed this is forever, you *will* marry me. You don't have to take my name, you don't have to be on my bank accounts, but I want you to be my wife. *Mine.* As soon as possible."

"Gavin." She looked at him. "That was the shittiest proposal I've ever heard."

"Well, yeah, I'm not exactly Mr. Romance." He looked at her shrewdly. "Is that what you want? Me on bended knee? Because I can—"

"Stop. I'm good with that."

"Yeah?"

"Oh yeah. And I have a demand as well." She cocked her head. "I want my damn bedroom back. We can keep your big bed, but the rest of that ugly bachelor shit has got to go, since your bachelor days will be behind you."

"Consider it done." He leaned closer to nuzzle her neck. "How about if we go inside and seal this marriage deal on that big bed." He kissed behind her ear. "I missed you last night."

"Same here. As I laid alone in my room I kept thinking this would be my life if you weren't in it. I never want that feeling again."

"Will you please put me out of my misery and leap over that fence so I can touch you?"

Rielle climbed up the rails and threw her leg over.

Gavin braced himself to catch her, but when she scaled over the top, she knocked him off balance and they both crashed to the ground with Rielle on top.

She grinned at him and waggled her eyebrows. "Well, well, this is an interesting possibility."

"Wrong." Gavin rolled, putting her beneath him. Just as he'd settled into a loving kiss, pounding footsteps came down the walkway.

"Omigod. Seriously? You guys are doing it out here in the dirt practically on the front yard where anyone can drive by and see?"

And...there was a verbal equivalent of a cold shower.

He pushed up and helped Rielle to her feet.

They faced Sierra together.

Sierra's eyes darted to Rielle and then back to him. "Dad, I know you said you didn't want to talk to me and I should stay away from you until you made your decision, but can we ah...talk about some stuff? Alone?"

"No. Whatever you want to talk about will affect Rielle."

"Okay." Sierra shoved her hands in the front pockets of her shorts. "Sorry I've been a jerk."

He waited because that pseudo-apology wouldn't fly and she knew it.

"I was a total dick, okay? I said a bunch of horrible shit I didn't mean. God, I'm so sorry and I don't know why I keep doing that."

Because you're sixteen.

"I was hurt and mad and I took it out on you."

I keep hoping one of these days you'll figure out that lashing out and hurting those you love doesn't make you feel better. He'd done this over her teen years, not answering her questions out loud but in his head; it allowed him to speak his mind without saying a word.

"I...some stuff happened that I didn't know how to handle and I couldn't think of anything besides I wanted to go home." She kicked a rock. "I wanted my mom."

Gavin wondered why Sierra had such a hard time admitting it.

Because sometimes you don't curb your dislike of her mother and she picks up on that.

She looked at Rielle. "I like you a lot, Ree. In fact, I love you more than a little. You've never tried to be my mom, but you've always been there for me. Even before you and my dad started being...whatever. So when I was hiding in my room, I wished I could talk to you, because you listen until I figure stuff out on my own. Then I realized how much I'd hurt you and that I wouldn't blame you if you never wanted to talk to me again." She sucked in a deep breath. "I'm sorry. Really, really sorry. I didn't mean to make you cry."

"I know, sweetie."

Sierra was back to staring at the ground.

"Sierra? Can you look at me please?"

She shook her head.

"Why not?"

"Because I'm embarrassed," came out softly.

He wanted to go to her, and Rielle even relaxed her hold on him so he could, but he forced himself to let his daughter struggle a little. "Why?"

"I was awful to you. Making demands. Being mouthy, hurting your feelings, not caring about anyone but myself. I'm sorry. So, so, sorry and I don't know how I'll ever..."

When Sierra broke down completely, that's when Gavin went to her. That's when he pulled her into his arms and let her cry it out, holding her tightly. Listening to her babbling about acting stupid again.

She calmed down but her arms were squeezed around him. "I love you, Dad. I'm sorry I was such a selfish, bratty kid."

He kissed the top of her head. "I love you too. Yes, you're bratty and selfish sometimes, but not all the time, so I'll keep you." He felt Rielle's hand on his arm, silently offering her support. He glanced at her, standing beside him, where she belonged.

Sierra stepped back and wiped her face. "So, I've had time to think, and I still want to go to France."

Gavin's heart broke, just a little. "All right. If that's your choice, you should know—"

"But just for part of the summer," she said quickly. "Maybe six weeks. I do want to spend time with Mom."

"That's a great idea. She'll be thrilled to see you."

"But when I get back? Before school starts? I'd like to talk to you about some changes. See, Marin and I were talking about this stuff today after Rory chewed my butt—"

"When did you talk to Rory?" Rielle asked.

"This morning. We went to DQ and then up to Flat Top."

"Rory is *here*?"

"Yeah. She's in the kitchen. You didn't know that?"

Rielle shook her head. "What did she say?"

"Basically she told me I was a whiny-ass spoiled baby and to knock it off and think of someone besides myself for a change."

Somehow Gavin kept his jaw from hitting the dirt.

"When I talked to Marin she said the same thing; quit acting so childish and selfish." Sierra snorted. "Which is kinda funny because she begged me not to move and that was selfish of her, but whatever."

Gavin had agonized over the decision for a solid day. He hadn't slept or eaten...and all it'd taken to change Sierra's mind were Rory and Marin telling her...to grow up and not act spoiled?

Unbelievable.

That was parenting—he could talk until he was blue in the face and then one of her friends would make the same suggestion he had and suddenly...wow, that was the best idea in the history of the world.

But he sure as hell wouldn't complain that his daughter had come to the right decision, regardless of how it'd come about.

"Dad? Are you listening?"

"Sure. Can you give me an idea on what you want to talk about when you get back?"

"Like...I want to try out for the cheerleading team. That'll mean practices after school and cheering at games on the weekends and stuff."

"That sounds doable, as long as Doc Monroe gives you the okay and you keep your grades up." He could tell she wanted to roll her eyes—bonus points for her for resisting.

"Also, I want to get a job. Either one that pays me or doing volunteer work. Marin pointed out that I sounded so entitled whenever I complained I was bored. So we're gonna try and get jobs at Dairy Queen because that's where everyone goes."

Sounded like Marin had put the screws to his headstrong daughter and he reminded himself peer pressure was sometimes a good thing. "I'd agree to that, but the same rule about—"

"My grades applies, yeah, I get it, okay?"

"That's plenty to keep you from being bored first semester."

"There is something else I'd like to do and it's a pretty big thing." Sierra jammed her hands further into her pockets. "I want to legally change my last name to McKay. When I was doing research on the McKays...it just clicked that it was my heritage. No offense, but I didn't know your dad, so his last name means nothing to me, especially since you were adopted. But I do know what Grandpa Charlie means to me. The McKay name means something around here. That's who I'm part of. And I want everyone to know it. Besides, most the people in my school already call me McKay anyway."

Shocked, but oddly pleased, he hugged her. "Sweetheart. If that's really what you want..."

"It is. I want to make it Grandpa's birthday present. So I'll tell him first, if that's okay."

"That's perfect." He brushed her hair from her cheek. "Is there anything else?"

"Yep. I want a pony."

Gavin snorted. "Nice try, but no."

Sierra grinned. "I thought I'd give it a shot." Then she paused. "So, are we okay?"

Gavin looked at Rielle. "Are we?"

"As far as I'm concerned, yes. But your dad and I have something else to discuss with you later."

"Cool. Oh, the other reason I came outside, besides Rory nagging me to freakin' *death* about marching down here and facing the music, was to tell you that your martini is done. She said to hurry up because she didn't like drinking alone. But I told her it might be a while because I had groveling to do. A lot of groveling to do."

"What kind did she make?"

"I volunteered to taste test it, but she turned me down. Then she snapped me in the butt with a towel and told me to get my ass moving. She's so bossy. I'll tell her you're both on your way." Sierra jogged up the driveway. Sadie and Jingle came from out of nowhere and ran alongside her.

"They're already fighting like sisters," Rielle said with amusement.

"Does that make you happy?" he asked.

"Very. But there's gonna be some fireworks when they start advising me about my wedding dress."

"Can't we just sneak off to Vegas and get married?"

Rielle shook her head. "They'd never forgive us if they didn't get to be part of the wedding. Heck, they'll plan the whole damn thing, most likely."

He kissed her. "I don't care what kind of wedding we have, just as long as our daughters aren't part of the honeymoon planning."

"Really? So the tycoon won't mind if it's an old-fashioned country wedding—held in the barn, with hay bales for pews, followed by a hoe-down?"

"Nope. I'll even wear a bolo tie, a Stetson, Wranglers and shitkickers if you want."

She laughed. "I like you a little country, but that sexy citified vibe does it for me in a bad way, so I definitely want you in a black tuxedo."

"Done." Gavin kissed her again. "Let's go back to the honeymoon. I want to take you someplace exotic. For at least two weeks."

"I assume you'll insist on paying for it entirely?"

He growled, "That is not even up for discussion. And trust me, it's going to be spectacular. I won't spare any expense when it comes to you."

"Speaking of..." Rielle poked him in the chest. "You'd better not buy me some big tacky diamond."

"Tacky? Never. I have great taste. Big? Absolutely. I'm thinking it'll be at least seven carats."

A pause.

"That's a whole lot of carrots," they said in unison, and laughed in unison.

"We're such punny dorks."

"Yep." Gavin pulled her into his arms and rested his forehead to hers. "I love everything about you, Ree. You know that, right?"

"Yes, I do. I love everything about you too."

Grinning, Gavin plucked her up and swung her in a circle until she shrieked at him to let her down. He whispered, "Never," and carried her home.

About the Author

Lorelei James is the *New York Times* and *USA TODAY* bestselling author of contemporary erotic western romances set in the modern day Wild West and also contemporary erotic romances. Lorelei's books have been nominated for and won the Romantic Times Reviewer's Choice Award as well as the CAPA Award. Lorelei lives in western South Dakota with her family...and a whole closet full of cowgirl boots.

Connect with Lorelei James:

on Facebook: www.facebook.com/LoreleiJamesAuthor

on Twitter: @loreleijames

email: lorelei@loreleijames.com

website: www.loreleijames.com

She's got the rhythm, but he's got all the right moves.

Ballroom Blitz
© *2012 Lorelei James*
A Two to Tango *story.*

After years on the road, rock drummer Jon White Feather is home from tour to reassess his music career. When his shy niece begs him to take a ballroom dancing class, Jon agrees, aware he's not Fred Astaire material. Still, it stings when his sexy-hot instructor—who makes his heart do the cha-cha—deals his ego a low blow: he has no rhythm.

Maggie Buchanan is doing everything to make ends meet since her IT career fizzled, including teaching couples dancing at the community center. She's prepared for anything—except her immediate attraction to the bad boy rocker who doesn't know his right foot from his left.

As Jon sets out to prove he can rock his body—and hers—their sexual chemistry burns a path across the dance floor, straight to the bedroom. And Maggie wasn't expecting a man with limited dance skills would know exactly how to sweep her off her feet.

Warning: Sweet and hot...this couple knows how to bump and grind.

Available now in ebook from Samhain Publishing.

Enjoy the following excerpt for Ballroom Blitz:

But the second night was more of the same torture. Jon was hapless and Raven tried not to act annoyed or mortified about the extra attention they received from the instructors because of his screw ups.

However, Jon certainly didn't mind having Maggie's soft curves pressed against him as she walked him through the dance steps. The woman was an enigma; confidently giving instructions to the entire class and yet blushing so prettily when they were pressed body to body. He was actually sorry when class ended.

After the rest of the students took off, Jon noticed Raven wasn't racing out the door, but in deep conversation with Seth. He wandered over to where Maggie sat on the bench, changing shoes.

"So it is true," he said, sitting sideways on the bleachers beside her.

Maggie glanced up. "What is true?"

"There is such a thing as putting on your dancing shoes." *Lame,*

Jon.

"Different types of dancing shoes for different dances. Probably like you use different drums for different parts of a song?"

"You'd be correct." He angled forward. "So while I've got you alone...give it to me straight. Am I failing class?"

The corners of her lips curled into a smile even as she remained focused on buckling her shoe. "This isn't a pass-fail situation. I'm giving you an A for extra effort." Maggie's eyes met his briefly before her attention drifted to his arms. Her gaze started at his wrist and moved up to his bicep. "I'll admit I've been admiring your cool tattoos during class."

"Do you have any tats?"

"No. Never had much chance to see artwork designs up close to see what my options are."

He held his arms out. "Go ahead and take a closer look if you want. See if there's anything you like." *Feel free to touch as much as you want.*

Her eyes clearly broadcast *I want,* even if her alluring mouth stayed closed.

The first tentative touch on his forearm was potent as an electric charge. He held himself still, willing that charge not to travel straight to his dick.

Her cheeks were flushed. Her blue eyes bright. Tendrils of reddish-blond hair had escaped from her tight bun, tempting Jon to loosen it completely and crush the soft stands in his hands. Or smooth the strands back into place just to touch that creamy-looking skin. Maggie unsettled him. She was wholesome looking and a little shy—not his usual type. So his immediate attraction to her was baffling. Not unwelcome, just confusing. Question was, did she feel the same pull?

Yes, if he went by the way her hand trembled when she touched him.

When her soft fingertip drifted over the crease of his arm, he bit back a growl. Oblivious to his response, she continued the northerly progression, one hand clamped around his wrist, the other hand driving him out of his mind with a mix of innocent curiosity and overt sensuality.

"Are these marks tribal symbols?" she asked, continually caressing the same section of black swirls and scrolls.

"I told a buddy of mine who's an artist I wanted markings with a tribal feel, but more artistic. So they don't mean anything specific."

"So it's wearable art that's unique to you." Her thumb swept across the stylized barbed wire motif on his bicep. "Even if the design was used on another person it wouldn't look the same. Your skin coloring gives it a different dimension. As does your musculature." She ran a fingernail on the underside of his arm. "Your biceps and triceps are amazing."

"I can't take credit for that."

"I'm pretty sure you weren't born with all these muscles." Maggie looked at him, as if startled by what she'd said.

When she attempted to remove her hand, Jon placed his palm over hers. "Thank you. Most of the time I get grief for the tats. I'm happy to hear a beautiful woman appreciates them."

"I do." She wet her lips and her gaze dropped to his mouth.

Sweet Jesus. She was killing him. Everything about her embodied soft and sweet—her hands, her mouth, her eyes, her tender touch. Which ironically enough, made him hard as a fucking drumstick.

"Maggie?" Seth called out.

They both jerked back.

"Yes, Seth?" she said a little breathlessly.

"Can you show Raven a couple of steps?"

Maggie said, "Sure," and stood. She faced him. "Truly magnificent, Jon."

"Glad you like them."

"I wasn't talking about the tattoos." Then she spun, leaving him staring after her.

Whoa. That comment had dripped with sexual sizzle.

Hmm. Maybe Maggie Buchanan wasn't as soft and sweet as he first believed.

www.samhainpublishing.com

Green for the planet.
Great for your wallet.

It's all about the story...

Romance

HORROR

www.samhainpublishing.com

CPSIA information can be obtained at www.ICGtesting.com
Printed in the USA
LVOW08s1941200714

395188LV00001B/307/P

9 781619 215009